A friend of the family

Also by Marcia Willett

A Week in Winter

A Summer in the Country

The Children's Hour

The Birdcage

First Friends

Echoes of the Dance

A friend of the family

Marcia Willett

Thomas Dunne Books

St. Martin's Griffin ≈ New York

THOMAS DUNNE BOOKS.

An imprint of St. Martin's Press.

A FRIEND OF THE FAMILY. Copyright © 1995 by Marcia Willett.
All rights reserved. Printed in the United States of America. No part
of this book may be used or reproduced in any manner whatsoever
without written permission except in the case of brief quotations
embodied in critical articles or reviews. For information, address
St. Martin's Press, 175 Fifth Avenue, New York, N.Y. 10010.

www.thomasdunnebooks.com

www.stmartins.com

Library of Congress Cataloging-in-Publication Data

Willett, Marcia.
    [Thea's parrot]
    A friend of the family / Marcia Willett.—1st U.S. ed.
       p. cm.
    Originally published under title: Thea's parrot.
    ISBN-13: 978-0-312-30664-9 (trade pbk.)
    ISBN-10: 0-312-30664-4 (trade pbk.)
    1. Widows—Fiction. 2. Man-woman relationships—
Fiction. 3. England—Fiction. 4. Friendship—Fiction. I. Title

PR6073.I4235T47 2006
823'.914—dc22   2006044693

First published in Great Britain by Headline Book Publishing,
a division of Hodder Headline PLC, as *Thea's Parrot*

First U.S. Edition: October 2006

10 9 8 7 6 5 4 3 2 1

To Bridget and Baron

A friend of the family

One

1985

FELICITY MAINWARING SAT BEFORE her dressing-table staring at herself critically in the looking-glass. She was forty-five years old and looked fifty. Her scrupulous dieting and rigorous exercise routines ensured that there was not a single extra ounce of weight on her body but where once she had been merely thin she now looked scrawny. Exercise may keep the muscles firm but it doesn't prevent lines from forming or preserve the youth and elasticity of the skin. After the shock of her husband's death from cancer a year ago, she had begun to look her age and dyeing her hair to hide the threads of grey merely served to make her look harder than ever. Unsparing though she was of herself, Felicity couldn't see that the matt black hair aged her and that it was no longer in keeping with her skin tone. She rather liked it and, turning her head slightly, she approved the severe geometric cut that she had stuck to since Mary Quant first made it famous in the sixties. Mark had always admired it; that and the fact that she had never become flabby and careless of her appearance as her friends had. Her success here was partly to do with their decision to remain childless which meant that there was plenty of time and money to be spent on her appearance. Even when Mark's cancer had been diagnosed and he had died shortly afterwards, she had never regretted that decision. It was possible that children might have been a comfort but it was more likely that they would have required consolation themselves and Felicity preferred to look after number one.

It had been a cataclysmic shock. Mark had hardly ever been ill. And he was doing so well in his career. Ever since he had passed out from

Britannia Royal Naval College, he had gone from strength to strength within the submarine service. Great things were promised him: he was, in naval parlance, 'a flyer'. He had shot ahead of all his oppos such as Tom Wivenhoe, George Lampeter and Mark Webster, and his eyes were firmly fixed on Flag Officer rank and more. So were Felicity's. She could see herself as Lady Mainwaring and had imagined, with enormous pleasure, rubbing Cass Wivenhoe's nose in the dirt. And now it was all over.

Felicity raised her chin, narrowed her eyes and examined her neck. It was there that ageing showed quickest. Turning this way and that, rather like a sharp-eyed bird sizing up its lunch, Felicity studied herself. She'd taken to wearing high-necked jerseys and was delighted with the piecrust-collared shirts that Princess Diana had made the vogue. She found them very flattering. After all, there was no point in letting herself go because her husband had died. Mark would have approved her determination to keep the flag flying. Perhaps it was a little easier for a woman whose husband had been away so much. She was used to being alone and had long since equipped herself with a circle of friends and amusements with which to ward off loneliness and boredom and, if she were to be brutally honest, Mark had become a little dull towards the end, his mind and will so firmly bent on his career. It went without saying that she'd been all for it. Nevertheless, promotion-chasing is a full-time occupation and Mark had become preoccupied and less companionable. She missed him. Of course she did. They had been well matched: shrewd, ruthless, self-seeking. Because they had been so alike there had been no need to dissemble and they had, therefore, found the other's company restful.

Well, it was no good going over and over things. Felicity added a few last touches to her skilfully applied *maquillage* and sat back satisfied. At least she still had George. It was odd that George, who had never married and who had saved Felicity from loneliness on many occasions throughout her married life, had become much less available since the funeral. He had given her to understand that it wasn't quite the thing, under the circumstances, to advertise their relationship and that they should wait a while before making anything public. Felicity could see the point. George was still in the Navy and it might not do his career any good to be seen stepping quite so hastily into the dead man's shoes. Not that he hadn't tried them on many times in the past. Still, it was sensible not to take any chances. George, who was soon to be finishing his command of a nuclear submarine, would probably be appointed to a desk job at the Ministry of Defence or to HMS *Warrior* at Northwood and, if so, would be looking for a flat. That would be perfect. London was so big and anonymous, unlike the small moorland village a few miles outside Tavistock where Felicity lived in her old Devon longhouse, and where, in the surrounding area, naval families abounded.

Felicity stood up. She would be very much happier when George was settled somewhere and—a very welcome change—on the end of a telephone. Meanwhile, life must go on. She glanced at herself approvingly in the long looking-glass, picked up her bag from the bed and sallied forth.

COMMANDER GEORGE LAMPETER FINISHED his breakfast, pushed back his chair and, nodding to one or two of his fellow officers, went up to his cabin, collecting his post on the way. He glanced at the envelopes as he shut the door behind him. One was from Felicity and one was from his mother. He sighed and opened Felicity's letter first. There were various items of gossip, a reproof for the fact that he hadn't been in touch and a reminder that she was off to stay with a girlfriend in Exeter for a week. George put the letter on his bed and slit the second envelope. His mother was hoping that he might get down to see her when the submarine was in. Neither woman knew that this was already the case. George maintained his freedom by playing his cards very close to his chest and, since he hated scenes and disliked feeling guilty, he tended to avoid close relationships.

It seemed that his mother was anxious to see him. She told him that she had quite decided she could no longer cope in the Old Station House which was much too big for her now that she was all alone. Nor could she manage the garden with its half-mile of grassed-over track. If George didn't wish to take the house on, then he must arrange to sell it for her. She had made up her mind to move into sheltered accommodation and she would very much like to talk it over with him. George sighed again and rubbed a well-cared-for hand over his smooth, razor-polished jaw. He ought to go to see her. His father had died some years back and George was the only child. His reluctance was explained by the simple fact that she lived nearer to Felicity than George found safe at present.

He'd been rather taken aback by his emotions when Mark Mainwaring had died. He'd been shocked, of course. After all, Mark was only the same age as himself, not much over forty, and it had made George think about how transitory life was and other unsettling and unpleasant thoughts. But hardly had poor old Mark been planted than Felicity was making suggestive noises and George was very glad to have the excuse of going back to sea. She'd concurred, rather reluctantly under the circumstances he felt, with his suggestion that it would be in poor taste for them suddenly to make public their relationship—although most of their acquaintance must know about it by now—and had agreed to proceed discreetly for the time being. But what then? There was no doubt that Felicity would have marriage in mind and not without reason. George had been one of Mark's closest friends and had been deceiving him with his wife on and off for the last twenty years. Hardly surprising then that Felicity should imagine he would now want to legalise the situation. George was rather shocked to realise that he was not at all sure that he wanted her on a full-time basis. Under the right circumstances Felicity could be a wonderful companion. She had a witty, corrosive tongue and was very athletic in bed but would that be enough in a more permanent relationship? George liked a peaceable, ordered existence—which was another reason why he had never married—and he knew perfectly well that Felicity could be a harridan. But what could he do? He could hardly tell her that she was fun as a mistress but that she wasn't what he wanted as a wife. To be fair, there had been several occasions over the years when he had tried to call a halt but, one way or another—often because she made him feel such a heel—he had gone back to her.

He looked again at his mother's letter, remembered that Felicity would be in Exeter for a few days and made a decision. He would go down to Devon to see his mother and try to get things sorted out for her. After all, he had been wondering what to do with his leave and it was only right and proper to put her mind at rest. He might pop in on Felicity afterwards: he'd play it by ear. He glanced at his watch. The trip from the submarine base at Faslane to Tavistock was a long one but he could be there in time for supper. His mind made up, George went to find a telephone.

MRS LAMPETER REPLACED THE telephone receiver and went straight to the kitchen. Even now, with George at forty-three years old and her in her seventies, she was still inclined to look upon him as the schoolboy who had come home for half-terms and holidays and made directly for the larder. But although her first instinct was to feed him up she did not regard him as a child. She looked at him clearly, even ruthlessly, and saw him with a gaze that was unclouded by mother love. She knew his weaknesses. She knew him to be a kindly, vacillating man whose instinct to keep himself out of trouble caused him to take the easy way out. His modus vivendi was to keep his head down in the hope that problems would go away. Just like his father there, of course. Mrs Lampeter, bustling in and out of the larder, clicked her tongue. Old-fashioned enough to imagine that the right wife was the answer, she had almost resigned herself to the fact that she would never be a grandmother: almost but not quite. She knew all about Felicity. She'd met her once and the two women had dis-liked each other on sight. When she'd heard of Mark's death she had lived in terror of George bringing Felicity home as his wife but a year had passed and Mrs Lampeter had breathed again. She knew quite well that George was vacillating and had decided that he needed a good sharp kick in the seat of his well-cut flannels with her size four-and-a-half shoe. She suspected that Felicity was merely biding her time until a respectable period of mourning had passed and Mrs Lampeter hoped to get in first.

Having made her preparations for supper, she returned to the telephone and, after peering short-sightedly at her address book, she lifted the receiver and dialled. A young, clear voice answered its ring.

'Thea, my dear. This is Esme Lampeter . . . Yes, very well indeed, thank you. Could you give a message to your great-aunt for me, dear? . . . That's right. It's exactly that. Could you tell her that I should love to come to luncheon on Wednesday but there's one small problem. George will be home . . . Yes. My son. You've never met but of course he knows Hermione . . . Do you think so? Would you like to ask her? I see him so seldom, you see, that I wouldn't really like to leave him here alone for the day . . . How sweet of you. If you're sure then. He can drive me over. I'm a little nervous on the roads these days . . . And I'm sure that he will love to meet you, too, my dear. Bless you. Wednesday, then. Love to Hermione.'

Mrs Lampeter smiled to herself as she went back to the kitchen. She would never interfere, of course. That was not her way. But a helping hand in the right direction was something else again, something, even, that might be looked upon as a duty.

THEA CROUCHED ON THE club fender and stared into the fire. The Lampeters had gone and after an early supper she and Hermione Barrable had retired to the library. The April evening was cold and the log fire was necessary. Broadhayes was an old granite house built on the edge of Dartmoor not far from Moretonhampstead and none of its inhabitants had ever had the courage to lift its flagged floors or drill through the thick walls to install central heating. Hermione Barrable was used to it. She had lived there for nearly sixty of her eighty-two years and was impervious to the chill. She dressed herself in layers of clothes, winter and summer alike, and looked like nothing so much as an ageing Siberian peasant. Her husband was long since dead, as was her dearly beloved elder brother who had been Thea's grandfather.

Thea, whose father had the care of a parish in the Shropshire hills, had been brought up in a large, draughty rectory and was as impervious to the cold as her great-aunt. She sat on the fender because that is where she liked to sit. With her red-gold colouring, she glowed in the shadowy room almost as much as the roaring log fire. She was a tall girl, big-boned, long-limbed. Her bright hair was caught back into a thick plait and her amber-brown eyes gazed unseeingly at the leaping flames.

'I liked George, G.A.,' she said at last and smiled a little to herself.

'Mmm?' murmured Hermione. Her long-fingered old hand was poised over her patience cards as she sat at her small table. She did not raise her eyes but the murmur had been an encouraging one.

'I liked the way he was with his mother,' said Thea unexpectedly. 'He didn't patronise her and pretend that she was some sort of tiresome child. So many people do that to the elderly, don't they? It's as if they think that because they've passed a certain age they've become children again and are uninformed and incapable. It's insulting.'

Hermione made her decision and the cards went down, flick, flick, flick. She knew that Thea was more at ease with older people than with those of her own generation, which was probably because her mother had been well into her forties when Thea, her only child, was born, and her upbringing had been a very sheltered one. It was not surprising, thought Hermione, turning a card, that she should be taken with George. He probably seemed like quite a young man to Thea.

'I think it is possible,' said Hermione with admirable restraint, for she usually liked the truth as plain and unvarnished as possible, 'that he may be a little pompous.'

'He was a bit, wasn't he?' Thea chuckled. 'When he was telling us about the Falklands War, he was definitely the Man in the Know. I thought it was rather sweet.'

Hermione raised her brows as though making a mental note of something and then frowned at an undesirable court card.

'Of course, he's a very distinguished-looking man,' she offered generously.

Thea looked thoughtful. 'Makes him sound a bit middle-aged,' she said at last.

'My darling girl, he is! Must be forty. Probably more.'

'He didn't seem middle-aged to me.' Thea sounded rather wistful.

Hermione gave a tiny sigh. She felt it was only right that Thea should see George clearly but at the same time she knew that Thea would never settle down with a young man of her own age. Her experiences had moved her beyond them. She had gone away to a carefully selected girls' boarding school at thirteen and had left at seventeen to go home to nurse her mother, who had suffered a stroke and was partially paralysed. Thea had taken on these duties with a courage far beyond her years and, when her mother had died three years later, she was too mature to be able to back-pedal and enjoy the lighthearted fun of her peers. She had continued to look after her elderly father and to manage the Rectory and her visits to the elderly Hermione were still the great treats that they had been when she was a child and she had come to stay with her cousin Tim, Hermione's grandson.

'I wonder why he's never married?' mused Thea, leaning sideways to reach for another log. 'His mother would like him to settle down. She's moving into sheltered accommodation and would like George to keep the house and live in it.'

Hermione thought that dear Esme had been a shade too obvious here. She had displayed George's attractions before Thea as a peacock might spread its tail but it seemed that the girl was oblivious to what might lie behind these tactics and had taken it all quite seriously. She considered what answers she might offer Thea and tried to decide whether she should be encouraging her in her interest. After all, the girl should have her own home and family. She shouldn't be spending her young life ministering to her father and his parish in the vastness of the Welsh marches. But was George Lampeter quite the right man for her? He had certainly been very taken with her. And what chance had she of meeting desirable and available men who would be attracted by her rather unusual qualities?

'I expect that Esme would like to be a grandmother,' said Hermione lightly. Thea might choose to walk into the trap but she, Hermione, would make quite certain that she saw all its workings quite clearly first. She must go of her own free will and with her eyes open. 'As for why he never married, he may simply have been pursuing his career, although I believe there's been a married woman he's been involved with.'

'I see.'

Thea looked thoughtful and Hermione wondered if she should have introduced the subject of Felicity. Esme had poured it all out one day when she had been terrified that George might marry her. The fact that, a year after her husband's death, he had not done so said something significant; nevertheless, it was only right that Thea should be forewarned. Hermione decided that the whole truth should be told.

'Apparently she's been free for a year now so the fact that George is still single must tell us something.'

Thea's brow cleared a little. Flick, flick, flick went the cards and the logs rustled and creaked a little, sending hissing flames dancing up the wide chimney.

'He's invited me over to lunch tomorrow.' She was smiling again. 'He offered to drive over to fetch me. Wasn't that sweet of him?'

'Very. Did you tell him that you're perfectly capable of driving yourself?'

'Well, I didn't.' The smile widened. 'It gives us longer together, you see. And then he'll have to bring me back.'

Hermione began to laugh, realising that all her warnings would be so much hot air if Thea had made up her mind.

'Then I hope you enjoy yourself, my darling. These damned cards won't come out.' She gathered them up with a great sweeping movement and began to shuffle them.

'Night cap then?' Thea stood up, stretched herself and wandered over to the big cage that stood on a round mahogany table in the corner. 'Percy's very quiet.'

She stared in at the big African Grey parrot who was hunched sleepily on his perch.

'He was very good today.' Hermione pushed back her chair a little. 'No biblical quotations. Just as well. Poor Esme gets very upset. She doesn't mind Shakespeare but she can't quite come to terms with a parrot who quotes from the Bible. Your Great-Uncle Edward was mainly to blame for that, of course. He taught Percy great passages from the Bible as well as other things. Esme, poor soul, thinks it isn't quite suitable. Heaven knows why. Percy is a very talented parrot and we didn't see why he should be restricted in his education. I hope that George isn't as sensitive as his mother.'

'How d'you mean?' Thea turned to look at her.

'It's always been agreed that you would have Percy when I die.' Hermione gave her a glinting, mischievous smile. 'I wouldn't like to think of a parrot coming between a man and his wife!'

Two

GEORGE PACED THE 'PLATFORM' behind the Old Station House. The old seats still remained, placed at intervals and interspersed with half-barrels which would soon be overflowing with flowers. From what had been the ticket office and waiting room and was now a comfortable sitting room, Esme Lampeter watched him anxiously.

George lit another cigarette and paused to gaze down on the grassy track below him. If only he could make up his mind. Thea's unaffected charm, openness and warmth had completely bowled him over. Her sensible clear-eyed approach to the practicalities of life was so charmingly emphasised by an old-world and unmaterialistic view that he was fascinated by it and her. He had never met anyone like her. Her tall, muscular frame, the glowing hair and warm brown eyes were a complete contrast to Felicity's black, diamond-bright, bird-like looks. Thea seemed to overflow with superabundant health and generosity. You felt that you could almost warm your hands at her and George was deeply attracted. Above all, there was her youth. She couldn't be much more than twenty-two or -three.

Twenty years younger than Felicity, he thought. Felicity. Ay, there's the rub. But after all, he argued with himself, there's never been any actual talk of marriage. There was certainly no question of it when Mark was alive. It's only because she's all alone now that she wants me. She's afraid of being old and lonely. And she's too old to have children, never wanted them anyway.

He saw himself coming back to Thea, to a warm happy house in which his sons—naturally he would have sons—were growing up and where he was cherished and cared for, and his heart expanded. He thought of Felicity's tongue-lashings, her tendency to treat him as a small boy to be granted favours or to be punished if he transgressed, and drew another thoughtful lungful of smoke. He had never said that he would marry her. A tiny thought suggesting that it might have been implicit in the continued relationship nagged at the back of his mind. He deliberately conjured up the idea of Thea and the sheer magnificence of it crushed the unwelcome intruder.

George turned back to pace the way he'd come. Of course, he'd be damned lucky if she accepted his offer of marriage—after all he was no youngster—but there were unmistakable signs that Thea was very fond of his company. She was not one to dissemble nor was there anything of the flirt about her. He would have been frightened off by a modern, trendy girl but in some ways Thea seemed more his age than her own. He thought of all his oppos, imagining their faces if he strolled into the Mess with Thea by his side. They'd be green with envy. And, after all, if he presented Felicity with a fait accompli, what could she do about it?

Nevertheless, it was a big step, a huge step. He was used to living in the Mess, being perfectly free to come and go as he chose and, as a 'spare man', always much in demand although, as far as that went, it was not as much fun as it had been once. He often felt out of things these days with all his oppos married and with growing children. The 'spare' women that he was invited to pair off with were, often as not, disillusioned divorcées, some of whom greeted him with a predatory delight which quite terrified him. Young women and girls found his old-world charm rather passé and Mark's death combined with his meeting Thea made him now look carefully at the future. Thea. Her image rose up before him: warm, glowing, kind. He thought of the way she looked at him and the way she received his cautious, very cautious, advances. His heart bumped erratically and he swore softly to himself. Dear God! He'd be mad to let her slip away. If only he could be sure that he could make her happy, that he wasn't too old.

Well, he must chance his arm. She was so unusual, so different from other girls that it might well work. As for Felicity . . . He pushed the thought of Felicity to the back of his mind. He'd deal with it later.

George took a deep breath, straightened his shoulders and pitched his cigarette butt on to the track. His mind was made up.

His mother, who knew by some instinct or possibly from his body language that he had taken the decision, hurried out to him.

He smiled down at her affectionately and slipped an arm about her. She looked up at him questioningly and he nodded.

'I've made up my mind,' he said. 'I'm going to ask Thea to marry me. I know it's quick but there's no point in wasting time. What d'you think? Is it too quick? Will she have me?'

'Oh, darling.' Esme Lampeter looked up at her tall handsome son and was overcome with a variety of feelings: a sense of relief, delight at getting her own way so painlessly and a fierce pleasure at the thought of Felicity being put in her place. All these sensations over-whelmed her and she burst into tears.

George patted her. He felt strong and happy, confident that he was doing the right thing. Nevertheless, as he followed his mother inside he couldn't help wishing that the Old Station House was rather far-ther away from Felicity's cottage and that he was going back to a nice, safe three months at sea.

IF THEA THOUGHT THAT George was behaving oddly during the second week of his leave she made no remark. His proposal of mar-riage and her acceptance of it had filled her with a serenity, a deep-down joy that nothing could ruffle. She had known almost from the beginning that she and George were right for each other and it seemed a natural progression that they should become quietly en-gaged and—as quietly—married. That George had come to the point so quickly rather surprised her since she felt that, after all these years as a bachelor, he might have needed quite a lot of encouragement to get him past the matrimonial starting post. However, now that he had made up his mind it seemed that nothing was going to stop him and he simply couldn't wait to get started. Thea wandered in the grounds at Broadhayes and thought long and carefully. She had fallen quite irrevocably in love with George and could see no point in postponing the time when they would be together. Here she was egged on by Esme, who was anxious that George shouldn't get cold feet or that Felicity should discover what was going on and try to sabotage it. Esme longed to see George and Thea move into the Old Station House and herself settled in the cosy little bungalow in Tavistock near her bridge-playing cronies. For Thea herself, after the years of nursing her mother and being a housekeeper to her father, the thought of having her own home and a devoted handsome husband was almost overwhelming. She was well aware that the young men of her own age found her quaint and old-fashioned and she had begun to fear that she might never find anyone to love and understand her and here, suddenly, was George, who had come riding up the drive at Broadhayes almost like the prince in the fairytale.

At this point Thea laughed a little at herself. Nevertheless, it was quite dreamlike enough for her to want to grasp it with both hands before it dissolved or—and this was much more real and frightening—before the mistress of whom Hermione had spoken reappeared and claimed George for herself. After all, what was there to wait for? Hermione approved and her father would want what was best for her happiness. She had already spoken to him at length on the telephone, not knowing that Hermione had already had her say, and he was looking forward to meeting George. Thea's heart told her that she and George were meant for each other and that nothing could come between them. Her head warned her to get a move on before George lost his nerve and began to weigh his freedom in the balance. He had proposed an autumn wedding in six months' time and there seemed to be no good reason to delay. Thea turned back to the house, her mind made up.

As for George, he gave thanks to all the gods at once that Thea was a simple, unspoilt girl who wanted to be married from her own home with as little fuss as possible. He was living in terror that

Hermione should demand a formal announcement of the engagement be sent to *The Times* but when no mention of it was made he began to wonder if he might not be able to get through the whole business from first to last without Felicity hearing about it. Knowing that she would be back from her visit to Exeter, he spent almost all of the second week at Broadhayes, driving over early and returning late by as many back roads as possible, his eyes peeled for the sight of Felicity's little red hatchback. He was fairly certain that she would have telephoned the base by now, discovered that the submarine was in and been told that George had gone on leave. He now wished that he'd written to her telling her that he'd been invited to visit someone whom it was impossible to refuse or that he was having to start at the MOD at once.

He was obliged to warn his mother that it was just possible that Felicity might telephone her to ask for news of his whereabouts and Esme took immediate action.

'You must write to her at once,' she said, 'telling her that you've to go away on an assignment which is top secret. Tell her that you can't give her any information about it. As a naval wife she'll understand that.'

George looked at his mother with a certain amount of respect. 'Won't she wonder why I didn't telephone?' he ventured. 'It would be more natural, wouldn't it?'

'You tried to telephone,' said Esme at once, 'but receiving no reply you came to the conclusion that she must be away and you decided to write.'

George stared at her, respect now bordering on awe. 'That's pretty good, Mother,' he said. 'She'll think I tried to get in touch while she was in Exeter.'

Esme beamed upon him, delighted at both his quick-wittedness and his obvious willingness to cheat and lie as much as was necessary to untangle himself from Felicity's clutches. She had feared that he might prove intractable, insisting that Felicity should be informed and everything kept aboveboard. She realised now that she should have known him better and that his passion for a quiet life meant that he was prepared to connive at almost anything to keep Felicity off his back.

'There's no point in asking for trouble,' said Esme. 'The last thing we want is Felicity rushing over or confronting Thea.'

George felt his blood run cold. He imagined Felicity, poised like a bird of prey, beak and talons outstretched, above the unsuspecting, innocent Thea and the thought made him tremble. His mother was watching him.

'Once you're married there will be nothing she can do,' she said comfortingly if naïvely. 'We must just get through the next few months. After all, she doesn't know Thea or Hermione and you must say nothing to anyone who would tell her.'

'But we'll have to send out invitations,' protested George. 'I shall want some of my friends at my wedding. I'd like old Tom to be best man. Not that he and Cass have any love for Felicity. She hates Cass like poison.'

Esme was silent, thinking. She realised that the naval grapevine would spread the news faster than bush-fire. She imagined Felicity turning up at the wedding and making a scene. She knew very well that when it came to being a woman scorned Felicity would play it by the book.

'You must make a list of those you wish to ask and then we must decide how many of them can be sworn to secrecy. I know it sounds melodramatic but we must get through it without giving her the chance to destroy Thea's faith in you. Have you told her about Felicity?'

'Certainly not!' George looked alarmed. 'I couldn't possibly. Honestly, Mother. Have a heart!'

'Oh, well.' Esme gave a grim little laugh. 'I shouldn't worry too much. If you haven't you can be pretty certain that Hermione has!'

THEA WASN'T WORRYING ABOUT Felicity. For all her youth, she had a surprising grip on the realities of human frailties and she would have been surprised, and even worried, if George had reached the age he was without having a few adventures. She could imagine that it might be easier for one of his temperament to have a mistress than to tie himself down to the responsibilities of marriage and she was merely thankful that he felt that, with her, he could take the plunge.

Hermione had already pointed out that marriage to a bachelor in his forties and a naval officer to boot might have its difficult moments but she was forced to agree with Thea's reasonable reply that most marriages were liable to difficult moments. So Thea spent the days with George, not particularly surprised that he wanted to go no farther afield than the house and grounds for the April days were cold, and when she returned to Shropshire it was with his promise that he should follow her as soon as possible so as to meet her father and obtain his formal permission—not that Thea needed it but they both felt it was a courteous gesture—for his daughter's hand.

First, though, he must return to Faslane to sort out his immediate future. He had been gone only hours when the telephone rang. Esme hurried in from the garden to answer it.

'Mrs Lampeter? It's Felicity Mainwaring. Is George there?'

Esme gave silent thanks that she didn't have to lie. 'I'm afraid not, Mrs Mainwaring.'

'I've just had the most extraordinary letter from him. Do you know where he is?'

'I understood from him that, wherever he is, he's incommunicado.' Esme's voice was cool.

'He's been with you, though? I see the postmark is a local one?'

Silently Esme cursed her own short-sightedness and Felicity's perspicacity alike. 'He came down for a few days to collect some things. I understand that he tried to telephone you but got no reply.'

Felicity gave a vexed sigh. 'I've been away for a few days. How annoying. So you can't tell me where he is or when you expect to hear from him?'

'I'm afraid not,' said Esme with perfect truth. 'And now if you'll forgive me, I have visitors.'

She put the receiver down and stood thinking. There was no doubt that Felicity's voice had the confidence of a woman who had expectations. Whilst Mark was still alive she would never have telephoned George's mother, let alone demand information regarding him. Esme returned to her gardening with an anxious heart.

FELICITY SLAMMED THE RECEIVER back on its rest and went into the kitchen. There had been something odd about George's letter and she couldn't decide quite what it was. Of course, she hadn't expected much change from George's mother. It was unlikely that she would want to be of any assistance to Felicity. On the few occasions that they had met, Mrs Lampeter had made it plain that she disliked her and that she held her responsible for George's part in their relationship. No doubt she would prefer him to marry and start producing children. She was exactly the sort of woman who would delight in being a grandmother. Felicity's lip curled in disdain. She glanced at the kitchen clock and decided to have a stiff gin and tonic before her lunch. As she went to the cupboard she found that odd phrases from George's letter were passing through her mind: '. . . all terribly hush-hush . . . no idea when I shall see you again . . . unlikely that I'll be in touch . . .' It was all too Le Carré for words. Felicity simply couldn't imagine George in the role of secret agent and had telephoned the base at Faslane only to be told that Commander Lampeter was away. She took her drink to the table and sat down, drumming her fingers irritably as she wondered whom she could pump to find out where he was and what he was doing. She hadn't liked the tone of his letter, apart from all the secrecy and silence nonsense. It sounded as if he couldn't give two hoots how long it might be before they were together again and there was no hint of regret or apology. He might have been writing to a casual friend and Felicity was annoyed. She knew that he was supposed to be starting at the MOD any time and found herself idly wondering which of her friends had husbands there at the moment. Tom Wivenhoe was there, of course, but she'd rather die of curiosity than telephone the Wivenhoes for information about George. It would be bad enough asking her friends. It would all have to be done very casually. 'Of course, George is at the MOD now. Has John seen him yet?' and so on. But why did she think that he would be at the MOD when his letter implied he would be doing something different? Felicity thought about this for some while as she sipped slowly at her drink. After a while she realised that it was because she simply didn't believe a word of it. Not a single phrase of the letter rang true. And it had been posted locally after she had returned from Exeter. He had been down but hadn't tried to get in touch with her, even knowing that he was going away and wouldn't be seeing her for a long time.

Felicity shook her head and got up to prepare her lunch. Even as she mentally worked out the amount of calories in her cream cheese, adjusting the size to counteract the gin and tonic, she was deciding how she could discover what George was up to and catch him out at it. She was already suspecting that it might be another woman although she would have thought he had already learned his lesson on that score. Felicity chopped chives with a vicious hand that boded ill for George and mentally reviewed her possible sources of information. No stone would be left unturned, no avenue left unexplored. She ate her lunch without tasting a single bite and rose girded for battle. Some infallible instinct told her that George had either cheated—or was about to cheat—on her and the scent of blood was in her narrow, haughty nostrils.

Three

CASSANDRA WIVENHOE BACKED HER car out of the open-fronted barn that served as a garage and set off down the drive past the Georgian rectory that she and her husband Tom had bought eleven years before. She turned left into the lane and headed towards Plymouth. She quite enjoyed these drives to the station on Friday evenings to collect Tom from the London train although she knew it would not be so pleasant when the winter arrived and she would have to cross the moor in the dark, accompanied by driving rain or perhaps in a thick fog, not to mention the occasional blizzard.

She drove slowly, enjoying the new growth and unfurling of tender green leaves. Although the high moors were still gripped in the iron hand of winter, here in the deep sheltered lanes the banks were studded with primroses and violets, the hedges above them white with hawthorn blossom, and, now that the cold winds of April had backed to the warmer southwesterlies of early May, it seemed that summer might be on its way at last.

It was more than three years since their eldest daughter Charlotte had died in a riding accident. Accident? Or had it been suicide? Cass would never know. For months afterwards she had thought of her daughter, not quite sixteen, taking her pony out and riding off in the wild storm of that dreadful day, up to the quarry which she knew to be a dangerous area even in good conditions. Was she running away from the terrible car smash, that she, in her innocence, had caused? Or was that simply the last straw in a series of emotional upsets? The problem with the highly strung and sensitive Charlotte was that it was impossible to judge her actions.

Cass drove through Clearbrook and on to the open moor. Slowly, very slowly, she had come to terms with it. She had always lived on the principle of 'live now, pay later,' enjoying lighthearted flirtations and affairs while Tom was at sea, suspecting that he was also taking his pleasure where he found it. She had taken risks and chances which had added spice to life, and then payday had arrived. Her lifelong friend Kate Webster, another naval wife whose marriage had finally ended in divorce, had always warned her that it would. It was Cass who had first dubbed it 'playing Russian roulette' and Kate who had told her that one day she would get the bullet. But it was Charlotte who had got the bullet: serious, quiet little Charlotte who had adored her father and loved her smaller brothers and sister and who had been terrified that Cass's infidelities might lead to trouble and break up the family. She had got the bullet meant for Cass.

For both Cass and Tom it was not just the death of their daughter that they had to come to terms with but their own guilt. During the appalling days and weeks after the funeral they had attempted to comfort each other whilst remorse and shame hammered away at the back of their minds. If Tom hadn't been with Harriet, if Cass hadn't been with Nick, would things have been different?

For Tom, the Falklands War had come at exactly the right moment and he had become deeply involved in strategic planning, relieved to have something else to distract his mind. Cass was thankful, too. Occasionally, overwhelmed by guilt and misery, Tom had tried to push the weight of it on to her. Cass held her own but, understanding his pain and what drove him to try to blame her, she also held her peace and did not question him in turn. She knew very well that he had been with Harriet but could see no future in their tearing each other to shreds. And, after all, it was she who had pushed him into Harriet's ready arms, hoping to hide her own affair with Nick. The blame was hers and she took it to herself and attempted to deal with it. She spent as much time as she could with her other three children and, by the end of the war, time had played its part in healing all of them to the extent that they could start again.

There were still anguished moments, agonised feelings of loss, but at least now, more than three years on, they were able to cope with that loss and with each other and they had once again picked up the threads of their lives together. Life went on.

Cass drove into the station and looked for Tom. He was waiting outside the plate-glass doors and he raised his hand as he saw her approach. Cass pulled in and watched him hurry across the road to her. It was still a little odd to see him in his London suit instead of naval uniform. The last few years had added lines to his face and grey to his brown hair, which was as thick as ever, but today there was something different about his demeanour, the way he walked and the expression on his face, and Cass looked at him expectantly as he got into the passenger's seat. He leaned across to give her the customary peck on the cheek and they exchanged the usual greetings.

'Good week?'

'Not too bad. You?'

'Fine. Train's on time for a change.'

Cass headed for Tavistock and waited.

'I've got some amazing news. You'll never guess what it is.'

'What?' Cass negotiated the lights and crossings of Mutley Plain with care.

Tom waited until she was through the worst before he spoke.

'George is getting married.'

'Good God! So she's got him at last. Well, it's not all that amazing, darling. It was only a question of time once Mark died. I'm only surprised that they waited this long.'

'Aha! But that's the whole point. He's not marrying Felicity.'

'What?'

'Careful! You nearly had that cyclist. You'll never believe it. It seems that he went on leave to see his old mum and met this girl at some friend's house. He's fallen for her, hook, line and sinker.'

Cass drove for some moments, grappling with this information while Tom observed the effect of his news with immense satisfaction.

'Incredible, isn't it?'

Cass shook her head. 'Felicity will never let him,' she said at last. 'She'll kill him first. Don't tell me she knows about it?'

'No, she doesn't. And poor old George is like a cat on a hot tin roof.' Tom chuckled. 'Poor old boy. I couldn't help feeling sorry for him. He's absolutely shit-scared that she's going to find out. He's sworn me to secrecy.'

'How stupid. Of course she'll find out. What an idiot he is. Why did he tell you if he's so scared?'

'He wants me to be best man,' explained Tom. 'So I had to know. Which means you have to know. But he trusts us both not to breathe a word to another soul. He's asking one or two others to the wedding and swearing them to secrecy, too.'

Cass burst out laughing. 'Oh, honestly, Tom. What a farce! Only George could imagine that he'll get away with it. What's he going to do? Carry on with Felicity as if nothing's happened until the eve of the wedding and then send her a little note thanking her for her kind hospitality which will no longer be required?'

'He's not seeing her at all. He's told her that he's been sent away on some top-secret stuff and hopes to keep a low profile until the wedding's over. He thinks that it will be too late then for her to put a spoke in the wheel.'

Cass laughed then in earnest. She laughed so much that Tom found himself laughing with her between his admonishments to watch her driving.

'Top secret!' she said, when finally she could speak and they were driving through Roborough. 'I've heard it all now. If he thinks that Felicity will believe that then he's even more of a twit than I realised.

She'll hunt him down in no time. And the girl. Who is she? Do we know her?'

Tom shook his head. 'She's not local. Her name's Thea and she's only twenty-three, apparently. Old George is like a dog with two tails.'

'Dear God! If Felicity finds her she'll eat her alive. It's too bad of George. God knows, I can't stand Felicity, but I think he should have told her the truth. I think she deserves that after twenty-odd years.'

Tom looked uncomfortable. Manlike, he felt that if Felicity had been prepared to deceive her husband all those years, she deserved what was coming to her at the end of it. He felt that George had a perfect right to marry whom he wished and if a charming and attractive girl twenty years his junior was prepared to take him on then good luck to him. He had sympathised openly with George and encouraged him. He shifted a little in his seat and Cass glanced at him.

'I suppose you urged him on,' she said, accurately assessing his discomfort. 'Well, I can't really say that I blame you. I simply think that it will be worse for George when Felicity finds out he's lying and deceiving her than if he'd told her the truth. But either way he hasn't got a hope. Poor George. And poor Thea. Oh well, can't be helped. So come on. Spit it all out. You haven't told me half of it yet.'

KATE WEBSTER WAS RATHER surprised when Cass telephoned her on Monday morning as soon as she had dropped Tom at the station and got back home. Her news was too riveting to wait, she said, and no, it couldn't be told over the telephone.

'I want to see your face when I tell you,' said Cass.

'Honestly, Cass . . .'

'No, I won't hear any excuses. I don't care about your old dogs and anyway I haven't seen you for ages. Shall I come to you or will you come here?'

'Well, I was just dashing into Tavistock to do some shopping . . .'

'Even better. I'll meet you in the Bedford for coffee. Half an hour?' And without waiting for a reply she'd hung up.

Now, sitting in a corner of the hotel lounge, Kate smiled to herself. No one can be the same after the death of a beloved child but even with the traumas of the past years Cass hadn't really changed. She'd kept her strikingly beautiful blonde beauty and underneath she was still the same lighthearted, fun-loving girl that Kate had met at boarding school twenty-eight years before.

It was to Kate that Cass had poured out her innermost feelings. They had, by then, been through so much together, marrying so young and having to deal with naval life. Cass had supported Kate through the unhappy years of her marriage with Mark Webster and Kate had watched anxiously as Cass juggled with her lovers and with Tom. They had brought up their families, moving them from one base to another, with their husbands away at sea, and had comforted each other when first Kate's mother died and then Cass's father, the General, who had been such a tower of strength to them both. Cass had been on hand when Kate's affair with Alex Gillespie had foundered on the rock of her twin boys' antipathy and Kate had been there when Cass had fallen in love with Nick Farley and everything had crashed round her ears when he had rejected her only days before Charlotte died. The tragedy had the effect of making Cass and Tom turn back to each other, to see the foolishness—and danger—of their playing around and to resume the close, loving relationship that had always been there underneath. They had learned their lesson the hard way and they were taking no more risks.

Kate poured herself some coffee. She looked all of her forty years. She had pulled a hasty comb through the rough short curls that were well dusted with grey but had made no effort to change out of her old navy-blue cords or the rugby shirt which had once been Guy's—or was it Giles's?—and was in their old school colours of black and red. Both Cass's sons were now at Blundell's, the twins' old school: Oliver was working for his A levels and Saul was in his second year. The twins were away at university and Kate, who was always short of cash, was working her way slowly through their cast-off school clothes.

She glanced up as someone came in and saw not Cass but Felicity. Although all their three husbands had been good friends these three women had never hit it off and Kate was surprised when Felicity came over to her table rather than giving her the usual frosty nod.

'Hello, Kate,' she said in her rather abrupt way. 'Waiting for someone?' Her eyes ranged over Kate's somewhat unkempt appearance and Kate smiled a little.

'For Cass, actually,' she replied. She was sure that this would frighten Felicity away quicker than anything else and was very surprised, therefore, when she sat down in one of the other chairs at the table.

'That's rather lucky,' she said. 'You don't mind if I sit for a moment? I'd like a word with Cass.'

Knowing that it was probably three years since Cass and Felicity had exchanged speech, Kate could only nod and was even more taken aback when Cass, arriving moments later and seeing Felicity, assumed an expression of undisguised horror far greater than the situation warranted. Almost instantly she controlled herself and by the time she arrived at the table Kate was aware that she was suppressing some overwhelming emotion.

'Well, well, Felicity,' she said, looking down at her. 'It's ages since I saw you. How are you?'

'I'm well, thanks. And you?'

'I'm fine.' Cass embraced Kate. 'Oh, good. You've ordered the coffee. Oh, dear, only two cups.'

'Don't worry about me,' said Felicity. 'I'm meeting a friend. I just thought that I'd say hello.'

She hesitated and Cass raised her eyebrows. 'Very civil of you,' she said. She sat down in the remaining chair and leaned forward to pour herself some coffee. She sent Kate a tiny wink and settled back in her chair. 'So how are things with you? I was sorry to hear about Mark.'

'Not too bad,' said Felicity. 'Life goes on, as we both know. How's Tom?'

'Fine.' Cass sipped her coffee and Kate felt more than ever that something was going on that she didn't understand.

'He's at the MOD now, isn't he?'

'Mmm. That's right. Weekending. He's sharing a flat with Tony Whelan.' Cass chuckled a little and Kate smiled, too. Tony was one of Cass's ex-lovers.

'I expect there's quite a few of the old gang there at the moment.' Felicity was watching Cass closely. 'It's the age for it, isn't it?' She named one or two of their mutual submariner friends. 'And George, of course.'

'George?' Cass looked surprised. 'Is George at the MOD? I must get Tom to look out for him. He always enjoys a session with old George.' She made a naughty face. 'So do I!'

Kate looked at Felicity, waiting for the usual expression of outrage that she could never control when Cass alluded to the fact that George had always had a soft spot for her. Today it was missing. Felicity was still watching Cass, her black eyes narrowed, as if she were waiting for something.

'Tom hasn't seen him then?'

'Who? George?' Cass shook her head. 'I would have known if he had. George always sends his love to me. Anyway, he said he was going to share with Tom and Tony if he got sent to London. They've got a spare bedroom and they need the extra money. The rent is positively terrifying. Has the rotten devil got his own place after all?'

Felicity looked discomfited. 'Oh,' she began and then got up quickly. 'Here's Pat,' she said. 'Must go. See you around.'

They watched her trim figure, clad in tight black trousers and a cerise pink jacket, thread its way over to the far corner where another woman was putting down her belongings. Kate turned to Cass.

'So what's all that about?'

Cass blew out her lips in an expression of relief and then began to chuckle. 'Talk about coincidence,' she said. 'You'll never guess. Not in a million years. Pour me some more coffee, there's a duck, and then I'll tell you all.'

four

FOR GEORGE THE SUMMER seemed endless. He refused
Tom and Tony's offer to share their flat on the grounds that he and
Thea would prefer to be on their own when she stayed with him in
London and, having taken up his post at the MOD and found a little
place to rent, he spent every weekend with Thea in Shropshire. He
refused to look further than the wedding ceremony. Because it was
what he wished to believe, he deluded himself that once he and Thea
were firmly married Felicity's teeth would be drawn and he would be
out of danger. At some point he would make a clean breast of it all to
Thea and she would understand and forgive and he could be happy.
He was managing to hold at bay all feelings of guilt regarding his relationship with Felicity. He mainly achieved this by concentrating determinedly on Thea: her youth and simplicity, her happy disposition
that looked at life without cynicism or gloom yet had its roots in a balanced acceptance of good and evil. For Thea the words 'it isn't fair'
would never have any point. Life wasn't fair, had never said that it was
going to be fair, promised nothing. Accepting this, she would be
looking for the good, the happy, the positive; George instinctively
recognised this and wanted it for his own. He wanted to hitch his rat-
tly old wagon to this bright particular star and nothing and no one was
going to prevent him.

Thea, meanwhile, was busy providing for her father's future. Here
luck was on the lovers' side even if it were in the form of a personal
tragedy to somebody else. A local widow had lost her only son in a
motorcycle accident and was no longer able to support herself prop-

erly without him. Since she was a faithful member of the congrega-
tion Thea, after careful consideration and consultation with her father, approached the woman and asked if, in return for a home, she
might be prepared to accept the position of housekeeper.

It seemed to be a sensible and even a happy resolution to several
problems and Thea was grateful. It is always difficult to enjoy happiness at the expense of those we love and Thea, sensible enough to
know that she couldn't stay with her father for ever and that he would
not have wished it, felt that she had done all that was possible and
could look to her own future with a clear conscience.

George began to receive occasional letters from Felicity, re-
addressed from Faslane, and wondered how long it would be before his
cover was blown. Slowly, with dragging feet, the summer passed and
the day of the wedding drew nearer until one warm September afternoon George cleared his desk, left London and headed for Shropshire.

'SO HE'S MADE IT.' Kate leaned across Cass's kitchen table for the
sugar. 'I have to say that I'm amazed. I can't believe that no one's
spilled the beans.'

'It's just sheer luck that none of Felicity's cronies are in London.
Mind you, only about eight of his friends know. It's the world's best-
kept secret.' Cass sat down and Kate pushed the bowl towards her.
'I'm glad. Thea's perfectly sweet and quite in love with dear old
George and he's totally besotted. It would have been too tragic for
words if Felicity had managed to break it up.'

'She's going to find out one day and when she does she's going to
come down on them like Genghis Khan and his boys.'

'Dear Kate.' Cass stirred her coffee and smiled to herself. 'I always
did say that it was you who should have been named Cassandra.'

Kate shrugged. 'I haven't met Thea yet but do you honestly think
that she'll be a match for Felicity? George never was. My God, Cass!
Imagine how angry she's going to be when she finds out what he's
done. And for once in my life I can't say I blame her. After all those
years. It's a bit thick, you've got to admit.'

'I do admit it. I said so to Tom but at the same time I have a sneaking sympathy for George. It's one hell of a situation. I think he had visions of her tearing Thea limb from limb or putting arsenic in the champagne. I wish you were coming to the wedding.'

'I hate weddings,' said Kate. 'All those innocent young things making solemn vows without having a clue what might be going to leap out of the woodwork at them to prevent them from keeping them.'

'I wouldn't call George an innocent young thing.'

'Perhaps not. But Thea sounds it. Twenty-three.' Kate shook her head and began to laugh. 'How on earth did George manage it?'

'To be honest, I don't think he knows himself. Tom says he goes about in a haze of gratified amazement.'

'Well, I wish him luck. I'm not saying that he should have married Felicity but I do think he should have had the guts to tell her the truth.'

'Oh, come on! You know George. He can't stand scenes and confrontations. And he was always scared stiff of Felicity. Oh, Kate! What wouldn't I give to see her face when she finds out!'

They looked at one another and began to laugh.

'Let's hope that she hasn't already or she'll be lying in wait at the church tomorrow. Perhaps I wish I was coming after all.'

'I shall tell you all when I get back. And when we've finished our coffee I shall show you my hat.'

FELICITY'S SEARCH FOR TRUTH had been impeded by the deterioration in health and subsequent death of her mother. This elderly if indomitable old lady had been in a nursing home for some years and had finally chosen this moment to breathe her last. Felicity chafed over the lack of consideration exercised by her aged parent and fumed silently about the hours spent at her bedside and in consultation with the doctor and matron. Felicity and her mother had fought and argued all their lives. Like her daughter, Felicity's mother preferred the male of the species, and blamed Felicity for not being the son she had always wanted. After a series of miscarriages she sank into a tyrannical invalid's existence, expecting Felicity and her father to be at her beck and call, and her disappointment in her daughter increased tenfold when she discovered that Felicity had no intention of supplying her with grandsons. When her husband died, she felt that Felicity should move back and take his place, fetching and carrying for her, and that Mark should commute from wherever he happened to be based if he wished to see his wife. When they made it clear that they intended to do no such thing the relationship deteriorated further and when she and Felicity were together they spent their time arguing and recriminating, a state of affairs that continued until the old lady went into a coma.

Thereafter, Felicity found her mind more often occupied with George's unusual behaviour than with anxiety for her mother's physical or spiritual welfare. If her state of mind could have been summed up as she left the crematorium in Plymouth it would probably be fairly accurate to say that she was thinking, Thank goodness I can get on!

She had received no answers from her letters to George and no joy from his mother, who persisted in the ridiculous fiction that he was engaged in some mysterious exercise and was still incommunicado. By the time she was back on the trail it was rather cold and the truth finally arrived in the form of a letter from George himself, now safely married, telling her that during his sojourn—the whereabouts of which he was not at liberty to disclose—he had met a young woman to whom he had become very attached and who had consented to become his wife.

He realised, he wrote with masterly understatement, that this would come as a great shock to her as, indeed, it had to himself but he hoped that she would not grudge him this chance for happiness and would wish him well.

Anyone knowing Felicity would have regarded this as a very vain hope and far from wishing him anything of the sort she prayed that all the plagues of Egypt—plus a few more of her own invention that were a great deal more fiendish than anything the Almighty had dreamed up—would visit George and his unknown bride. Rage, hurt and jealousy rose in a huge black tide that positively foamed and lapped at the back of her eyes and for several days she was prey to one of the blinding migraines that had dogged her life. Presently, however, though rage still knotted her stomach, she was able to present an outward show of calm. Her seething brain stilled and grew thoughtful and she made one or two enquiries which were met with a certain measure of success.

One January day she drove across the sodden moor lying dank and dark beneath the swollen, weeping sky and made her way to the Old Station House. The five-bar gate was shut and Felicity, leaving her car outside, opened it and made her way across the tarmac forecourt. She noticed that George's Rover was parked in the garage and that there was no sign of his mother's little hatchback and guessed that her information was correct. She rang the bell and waited. After a few minutes she heard movements within and the door was opened by a tall girl with vivid colouring and an open smiling countenance.

Confronted by this vision of almost aggressive youthfulness, Felicity was visited by yet another violent stab of unadulterated jealousy.

'Good morning,' she said, summoning a smile with an almost visible effort. 'Is Mrs Lampeter in?'

The girl smiled at her. 'I am Mrs Lampeter,' she said in a tone which invited congratulation. 'Can I help you?'

'You must be George's new wife,' said Felicity, controlling with difficulty the urge to leap upon Thea and rend her with her bare hands. 'The Mrs Lampeter I know is rather older.'

'She's not here, I'm afraid. Will I do?'

'Oh, yes,' said Felicity softly. 'I'm sure you'll do very nicely indeed. My name's Felicity Mainwaring.' She watched closely for any signs of reaction but Thea's expression remained friendly and enquiring. 'I'm a friend of the family. I heard that George was married and I came to offer my congratulations to his mother. My own mother has just died and I've been rather out of the swim of things.'

'I'm so sorry.' Thea looked concerned. 'Won't you come in?

George's mother has got a little bungalow in Tavistock now. This all
got too much for her. I'll give you her address. What a pity that you
missed the wedding.'

'Wasn't it?' said Felicity and hastened to lighten her grim tone as
she followed Thea into the house. 'I'm hoping that you'll tell me all
about it. And about George.'

'I should love to,' said Thea, leading the way into the kitchen.
'Perhaps you'd like to see the photographs? I'll make some coffee.'

'That would be lovely. And I want to hear every little detail. How
you met and so on. It must have been so romantic. It's just what I
need after these rather sad months with my mother.'

'You poor thing,' cried Thea sympathetically. 'I'll put the kettle on
and get the photographs and we'll have a good chat. It's sweet of you
to be so interested.'

'I promise you,' said Felicity as Thea disappeared to find the photographs, 'nobody could be more interested than I am.'

AFTER FELICITY HAD GONE, Thea continued to brood over the
photographs. Her father had conducted the ceremony and his closest
friend, Thea's godfather, had given her away. She looked affectionately at the smiling faces, at her and George standing beneath the arch
of swords with his brother officers very smart in their uniforms. She
moved the photographs about reflectively. Felicity, she recollected,
had looked rather strange when Thea had asked her if she knew the
best man and his wife. Felicity had stared fixedly at the picture of
Tom beaming into the camera with Cass looking elegant in a wonderful hat. After a moment she said that she did indeed know them and
told Thea that her own husband had been a naval officer and had only
recently died of cancer. Thea was shocked, imagining that Felicity's
slightly odd behaviour was due to the fact that these pictures must be
calling up old and painful memories, but when she tried to sweep
them away and talk of other things Felicity had quite firmly insisted
on looking at them all. It naturally did not occur to Thea that she was

mentally compiling a hit list of her enemies: those people who had known all about George's defection and had aided and abetted him in it.

Thea put the photographs back in the envelope and glanced round her new home with satisfaction. She was very happy. She had started off in London at the flat with George but she found the city noisy and smelly and the pavements hard beneath feet that were used to springy turf. The rented flat was small and the furniture indifferent and, having toured the usual 'sights', Thea began to find the days long and boring. By the time they got back to the Old Station House on Friday evenings of the long winter months, they were tired and the house was cold and unwelcoming. It was just getting warm and cosy and feeling like home when they had to pack up again and leave. George had Christmas leave and at the end of two wonderful weeks when the Old Station House was full of warmth and redolent of the smells of delicious food and log fires, they decided that Thea should stay behind when George went back to London. They would try a compromise. George would come down at weekends and Thea would go up midweek, arriving in London on Tuesday afternoons and catching the train back on Wednesdays. It was working quite well although George would have preferred to have his bride waiting for him every evening and Thea wished that they could have settled down together in their new home. Well, *her* new home. It had been George's home for the last twenty years. Thea had been perfectly content to take it over lock, stock and barrel when Esme had departed for her little bungalow, taking with her only a few of her very favourite possessions and delighted that the rest of her belongings would stay in the family to be cherished by Thea. Thea much preferred to take over the well-loved pieces than to start anew, feeling a sense of continuity in caring for things that had been loved and tended by other hands for so many years. So much nicer, she felt, than rushing out to buy new things or even old things whose history was unknown. Here she felt among friends. Esme had taken her round introducing her, as it were, to the companions of her married life and, before that, her childhood: her mother's old bureau, the Georgian breakfast table that had been Esme's grandmother's, a bow-fronted chest that had graced the bedroom of George's paternal grandmother and lovely old rugs that an uncle had brought back from India. The Rectory was filled with such treasures that would one day belong to Thea; meanwhile she was delighted to become the custodian of these and Esme yielded them to her with confidence and gratitude.

Thea took the photographs upstairs to the little room that had been Esme's sewing room and was now Thea's study. Here she had set out some of her own personal possessions and one of these was a large deal table set beneath the window that looked out across the grassed-over railway track and away towards Dartmoor. The table was covered with the paraphernalia of the artist, for Thea loved to sketch and paint and the results were scattered about, some pinned to a fibre-board panel attached to the wall. There were pen and ink drawings and tiny watercolours of flowers and birds and animals and babies, all charmingly done. A closer look showed that what redeemed these works from the clinical or merely twee was an almost cartoon quality about them that lifted them right out of the commonplace and made the observer want to look again and again. One of the subjects, and obviously a favourite, was Hermione's African Grey parrot, Percy. On a shelf some notebooks were stacked. These contained children's stories that Thea loved to write and illustrate and which she hoped one day to read to her own children. Having tucked the photographs away in a drawer, Thea wandered over to the table and looked at her work. Presently she picked up a piece of charcoal and moments later was lost to the world.

FELICITY DROVE HOME THOUGHTFULLY. Thea had very nearly overwhelmed her and she felt weakened, almost helpless. She had not expected someone like Thea. When she had read George's letter and the red mist of rage had finally receded from her eyes, she had pictured this woman by whom George had so obviously been taken in. She had imagined a woman in her thirties who had, perhaps, missed the matrimonial boat and saw George as an easy meal ticket. After all, an unmarried naval commander was quite a catch if you wanted a secure middle age and retirement: no ex-wives and children littering the landscape and eating into the substantial salary or, later, the generous pension. Or perhaps this harpy was a widow like herself, frightened of facing the future alone and seeing in George an easy-going generous companion. It would be simple enough to captivate George. He'd always had a weakness for a charming pretty woman and was easy prey to flattery. Felicity's lip had curled but the little warning bells were telling her that she could have been nicer, more loving, less ready to point out his weaknesses. If she had . . . But it was no use repining. She had never wasted time in regrets and might-have-beens. It was much more sensible to use her energies more positively. Accordingly, she had plotted and planned, preparing to come face to face with an equal, a woman like herself who would be perfectly happy to fight it out. But Thea . . . Felicity saw again the youth, the warmth, the generosity and felt again the sensation which was almost fear. It was nonsense, of course. She should be able to take a child like Thea and crush her with one hand. So what was making her feel that she should withdraw and summon all her abilities before she made an attack?

She brought her mind to bear on it, remembering her feelings and sensations. It was as if there were something behind Thea, some strength or power that she couldn't define. Felicity shook her head as if trying to clear her sight. She was imagining things. Much more likely that the shock of seeing so young and vital a girl had thrown her off-balance. And, naturally, the sight of George beaming so complacently and foolishly out of the photographs was not likely to make her feel better. And Cass and Tom . . . She felt a wave of fury rising and deliberately willed it back, clenching the steering wheel and setting her jaw. She would not lose control. She simply must not think of them laughing and plotting; that way madness lay. She had seen the opposition and must lay her plans more carefully. Nothing crude or unpremeditated must happen in this campaign, no matter how long it took. Felicity parked her car and let herself into her house. Never in all her life had she been more in need of a stiff drink.

'OH, BY THE WAY. A friend of yours called in this week. Felicity something. Mainwaring, was it? Yes, that's it. Felicity Mainwaring.'

George, who was sitting at the kitchen table watching Thea make the custard to go with his apple pie, gave a tiny start and was silent. He swallowed once or twice and tried to control the irregular behaviour of his heart. After a moment she glanced over her shoulder at him and then turned back to her stirring.

'She said that her mother had just died and that she'd only just heard the news. About us, I mean. She wanted to see the photographs.'

'And did she?' George asked after a moment. He cleared his throat. 'Did she see them?'

'Oh, yes.' Thea was pouring the thickened custard into a jug. 'Yes. She knew some of the people. Well, obviously. She said that you and her husband were old friends before he died.'

Tell her, said a voice in George's head. Tell her now and get it over with. Now is the moment.

He stared at Thea, at her supple movements and long legs, and thought of the open loving way she took him to her heart and the way she treated him with caring and even gratitude. He swallowed again and his heart raced.

Do it now, said the voice, before someone else does. Felicity perhaps?

His heart turned to jelly, quivering in the cavity of his chest and making him tremble. He had so much to lose and, after all, if Felicity hadn't mentioned it . . .

Thea approached the table, her clear gaze untroubled and warm. 'Just between you and me,' she said confidentially, 'I felt that she was capable of being a bit of an old bat.'

She smiled at him with an intent look, almost as if she were waiting for something. George looked back at her, willing himself to meet her eyes.

'Yes,' he mumbled at last. 'She does have that reputation.'

Thea sat down in her place looking rather thoughtful and started to cut the pie. George shifted a little and watched her hands. It seemed, after all, as if the moment had passed.

Five

HERMIONE SHUFFLED HER PATIENCE cards and, turning a thin wrist, peered at the tiny gold watch whose face she could barely see. As she reached for the spectacles that hung on a chain round her neck, the door opened and Thea came in.

'Thank goodness you've arrived,' said Hermione, receiving Thea's kiss. 'What a dreadful day. I nearly telephoned to tell you not to come. It must be thick across the moor.'

'Terrible,' said Thea cheerfully. 'It makes you think of the Hound of the Baskervilles leaping out of the mist with slavering jaws. Or homicidal maniacs escaping from the prison.'

'I was thinking more of car accidents,' said the prosaic Hermione. 'And now that you're here, have you told Mrs Gilchrist?'

'I have indeed. She's bringing coffee.' Thea looked round appreciatively at the familiar scene: Hermione at her card table, the lamp lit against the dreary February day; the log fire, its flames licking and the wood settling gently into ash; the parrot in his cage on the table in the corner. She went across to him and looked in. 'Hello, Percy. How's tricks?'

The parrot was manipulating a grape which he held dexterously in one claw. 'A trick that everyone abhors in little girls is slamming doors,' he quoted and dug his beak into the grape.

Thea laughed and went to sit on the fender. 'Tim and I taught him that one,' she said. 'It was that summer we discovered Hilaire Belloc. We'd take it in turns to recite it to Percy. It was the only sort of poetry Tim liked. It was a very wet summer and I used to read him *The*

Hobbit while he made those endless model planes. His bedroom was like a continual Battle of Britain.'

She stood up again as Mrs Gilchrist, Hermione's housekeeper, came in with the coffee tray and various pleasantries passed whilst it was placed on a low table and Thea's bunch of violets, which Mrs Gilchrist had put into a miniature vase, were admired. When she had gone, Thea lifted the elegant silver Georgian coffee pot and poured hot black coffee into fragile cups. The delicious aroma filled the library and Thea sniffed luxuriously as she placed Hermione's cup and saucer on her table and took her own back to the fender.

'And how is George?'

'George is . . . well.' Thea seemed to hesitate and then make up her mind. 'George is very well.'

Hermione dealt the cards and waited.

'George is very fit.' Thea seemed anxious to establish the fact of George's physical well-being. 'But he's been rather quiet lately. Everything's fine between us. No problems. It's just that I sense something. And he's . . . Well, he's quiet.'

'Quiet.' Hermione repeated the word, not as a question but rather as though she were brooding over it. 'And have you drawn any conclusion that might explain it?'

Thea sipped some coffee and then turned a little and stared into the fire. 'There's this woman who keeps popping in to see me.'

Hermione sat so still that only the flashing and glittering of the stones in her magnificent brooch, pinned casually to an ancient jersey, showed that she was still breathing.

'It seems that her husband was one of George's best friends. He's dead now but the odd thing is that George shows no interest. He doesn't want to know how she is or how she's coping. It seems so odd.'

Hermione took a deep breath and the cards went down, flick, flick, flick.

'G.A.?' Thea had turned back again. 'Do you remember telling me that George had been involved with a married woman?'

Hermione hesitated. 'I think Esme did mention something in passing,' she said lightly at last.

'Can you remember what her name was?'

Hermione stared at her cards. Her thoughts doubled and twisted, raced and turned. She knew only too well how doubt and jealousy could corrode a relationship, how fear and guilt could destroy. It was plain that George wanted his past affair wiped out, forgotten. Was it possible? Of course, he should have told Thea everything at the beginning. It is so much easier to forgive in the first flush of passion and it could be argued that what happened before she met him was none of Thea's business. On the other hand, if Felicity had taken to popping in, George would have been wise to tell Thea at once about their affair before Felicity did or, indeed, any one of their acquaintance. What would happen if, at this late date, she, Hermione, were to let the cat out of the bag? Might Thea go back and confront George? Would there be arguments and recriminations? And might not that be just the chink that Felicity was waiting for, hoping for? How could she take that responsibility to herself? Hermione became aware of Thea, watching her from across the room.

'D'you know, I don't think it was ever mentioned.' For the first time in their relationship Hermione lied and as she turned a card her hand shook.

'Oh, well, I'm probably imagining things.' Thea stood up. 'More coffee?'

She went to the table and glanced at Hermione. She was struck by the stillness of the old lady's posture. Her face looked drawn and brittle, the bones pronounced, the eye sockets arched and cavernous, and Thea glimpsed the fact of her mortality. She went to her and knelt beside her and Hermione looked into the eyes now level with her own and suffered herself to be hugged. She was not an emotional or tactile woman but she understood the needs of others and knew that she owed Thea this reaffirmation of her love.

'Don't worry. I have no idea of dying yet,' she said with remarkable acumen as Thea scrambled up. Her smile dismissed the emotion and sent Thea's fears back to the shadows. 'Certainly not before I've had that cup of coffee.'

Flick, flick, flick went the cards: a five on a six, a two on a three, a jack on a queen.

'I think I'm going to get this one out,' said Hermione.

Thea laughed and carried her cup back to the tray. Perhaps, after all, that foreshadowing of death had merely been a trick of the firelight.

FELICITY WAGED HER WAR with patience and finesse. She felt quite sure that her visits to the Old Station House must be causing George all sorts of anxieties. She knew that Thea told George that she popped in and the fact that Thea continued to treat her with openness and growing friendliness indicated quite plainly that George was keeping quiet. But what was he thinking? Felicity hugged herself when she imagined George's thought processes. He must surely be waiting for her to strike and yet he did nothing. Was it possible that he assumed that she had forgiven him and accepted the present situation to the point of befriending Thea? Felicity smiled incredulously and shook her head. After twenty years George must know her better than to imagine that to be the case. She remembered the hard time she'd given him after he'd strayed with Cass and knew that he couldn't possibly be hoping for any such thing. Much more likely that George was living by his favourite maxim: let sleeping dogs lie. He was keeping his head down and praying that something would prevent the blow from falling.

Meanwhile, she and Thea were becoming quite friendly. It was almost bizarre. Felicity knew that Thea was the innocent party and some days she felt almost sorry that she would suffer as much as George, who deserved everything that was coming to him. Unfortunately, the innocent had always suffered with the guilty and this would be no exception but, just occasionally, Felicity wished that Thea could be spared. Sometimes, when she sat at Thea's kitchen table, drinking Thea's coffee and listening to her stories of village life in the Shropshire hills, she had the feeling that she'd like to throw the whole thing up and make a real friend of this unusual girl who seemed to own something, some inner peace, some strength, that she, Felicity, did not.

Back in her own home, alone and lonely, the feeling faded and she fed upon her ideas for revenge and knew that the time was very near now to advance the second part of her plan.

ON A BLOWY DAY in early May, Thea drove across the moor on her way to have lunch with Cass at the Old Rectory.

'It's a girls' get-together,' she'd told Thea on the telephone. 'I think you know most of them now. Come early, in time for a drink.'

Thea had taken a very firm liking to Cass and, since she had moved to the Old Station House, had seen a great deal of her. Cass had introduced her into her circle of friends and had made her feel at home at once. She'd met Kate, Cass's oldest friend, who was divorced, had twin boys and bred dogs; Abby Hope-Latymer, who lived up at the Manor with her husband William and three children. There was Harriet Barrett-Thompson, whose husband Michael was an estate agent in Tavistock, and Liz Whelan, who was an accountant and whose husband was sharing a flat with Tom in London. These and a few others Thea had met at the Rectory but she had never seen Felicity there. When she'd mentioned to the group at large that Felicity had come to introduce herself, she was aware of a slight frisson that passed over the assembled company. Asked if they knew her, there had been a momentary silence before everyone had started to talk at once and somehow it was implied that they knew her but that she wasn't popular or part of their group. Well, that was reasonable enough. Even her short acquaintance with Felicity had made Thea realise that she and Cass were probably incompatible. Nevertheless, there'd been a little something, a constraint, a reluctance to elaborate, that had puzzled Thea. She had mentioned it to George, who said at once that Felicity and Cass were old enemies but, when Thea asked why, George had become inarticulate and confused and she had let the matter drop.

Thea slowed the car so that she might have a moment to gaze out over the moor, which was becoming as important to her as the Welsh mountains had been, and watched the cloud shadows hurrying across the short turf and the stony-sided tors. The glossy, golden gorse glowed in the intermittent bursts of sunshine and the bracken sprang up, green and bright, from tightly balled brown fists. Thea made a tiny prayer of thankfulness and drove on.

She was the last to arrive and was pleased to see the usual little group with the addition of a friend of Harriet's, who was staying with her for a few days: Polly Wickam. She and Thea shook hands and liked the look of each other. Polly was younger than the others, more Thea's age, and her husband, Paul, was a research scientist at Exeter University, where Polly had met him when she was taking her degree. She had married him on graduating and had lived a rather solitary life ever since, Paul being deeply attached to his microscopes. Polly was rather amusing about it and by the end of the lunch the two girls were well on the way to friendship. Thea suggested that Harriet should bring Polly to lunch before she went back and Polly accepted with pleasure.

As usual, Kate remained after all the guests had gone and she and Cass wandered back into the kitchen and sat down at the table. Cass took an apricot from the bowl and dug her teeth into the furry skin whilst Kate poured the remains of the coffee into her cup.

'So when is someone going to tell her?' Kate tasted the coffee, made a face and pushed the cup away.

'Tell who what?' Cass got up to fill the kettle.

'Thea. About Felicity.'

'Oh, that. Bit late now, don't you think? We've all had the chance and missed it. Felicity obviously isn't going to do it. George certainly won't.'

'Soon it'll be too late.'

Cass came back to the table and sat down again. 'Who do you suggest? Why don't you do it yourself if you think it's the right thing to do? The question is: is it? I think it's already too late. I must admit that I'm amazed at Felicity, though. Popping in and out, all jolly chums together. I'd never have believed it.'

'I still don't believe it.' Kate frowned. 'It simply isn't Felicity. I have a horrid suspicion that she's simply biding her time.'

'And then what?'

Kate shook her head. 'I don't know. But I have this awful feeling that it's all going to end in tears.'

GEORGE MADE HIS WAY back to the flat wishing that Thea had stayed up for an extra night. He had wanted terribly to persuade her, to beg her, even, to stay. He'd had no idea that he could come to need anyone as he needed Thea. He loved her and longed for her and yet he had been unable to ask her to stay on in London. Felicity's shadow had slid between them and he could no longer be open and honest with her. He felt that he had no right to ask for favours whilst he was deceiving her. And he *was* deceiving her. All the time that he let her receive and entertain Felicity in her home without knowing what he and Felicity had been, she was being deceived. He longed to tell her, longed to unburden himself and pour it all out. What, after all, should prevent him? It had all happened before he and Thea met. Was it because Felicity had been married and he had been abusing his friendship with Mark? Or was it merely the fact of Felicity herself, who seemed so second-rate beside his new young love? George knew that this was an unworthy thought. If Felicity had been good enough for him then, he should not despise her now. The trouble was, he knew quite well that he should have told Thea right at the beginning. By putting it off he had made it seem bigger, more important than it was, and with each day that passed it became more and more difficult. Each weekend he geared himself up to tell her. Each time she said, 'Oh, Felicity popped in again,' he tried to bring himself to the point. He tried to frame the words and couldn't even begin, despite his rehearsals in the silence of the flat. He imagined her look of shock or, worse, disappointment. He saw that look of love fading and his heart failed. Even supposing she took it well, then what? He would have to forbid Felicity the house. He imagined Felicity's reaction, and despair washed over him. What a fool he was, allowing this wonderful, golden experience to be tarnished because he was a coward.

This weekend, he vowed as he let himself into the flat. Come what may, this weekend I shall tell her.

He had just changed into cords and a jersey when the doorbell rang and for one glorious moment his heart leaped up. Could Thea possibly have come back unexpectedly? He hurried out into the tiny hall and flung open the door.

'Hello, George,' said Felicity. 'How nice to see you again. May I come in?'

She stepped past him, across the hall and into the living room, gave a swift glance round and turned to him with a smile.

'Felicity . . .' George, recovering from the overwhelming shock, gestured awkwardly, shrugged helplessly and then shook his head.

'Sorry to take you by surprise.' She was still smiling at him. 'I missed the four-thirty-five train and the next one is always so crowded that I decided to catch a later one. And it occurred to me that it would be nice to see you. It's been a year, George. Do you realise that?' She laughed at his expression. 'I see that I've rendered you speechless. May I sit down?'

'Of course. Yes, do. Would you like a drink?' George was galvanised into speech and action. The friendliness of her smile and the calm tone of her voice disarmed him and he smiled back tentatively.

'I should love one.' She sat down on his sofa, crossed one bony knee over the other and turned slightly to watch him pour the drinks. 'Thea told me about your little hideaway—you know I've been over to introduce myself?—and I decided to come and see for myself. I like your wife, George. You're a very lucky man.'

George felt faint with relief. It looked as if, after all, everything was going to be all right. He handed her a gin and tonic, overcome by her generosity.

'It all just swept me off my feet, you see,' he began and then hesitated a little. He didn't want to be tactless.

Felicity raised her eyebrows and took a little sip. 'I'm not a bit surprised. She's a real sweetie.' She looked at him as he sat opposite her, a more measuring glance, and he began to feel uncomfortable again. 'You could have told me, you know, George.'

Her voice was reproachful, hurt, and George experienced a wave of guilt.

'It was all so quick . . .' Once again he hurried into speech but she shook her head, made a negative gesture with her free hand and grimaced a little.

'Let's forget it, shall we? All over now. But I'd still like to be friends. We don't have to lose twenty years of friendship just because you're married, do we? After all, I was married for all those years.'

George glanced at her sharply. Was she implying that he could deceive Thea as she had deceived Mark? But Felicity was looking round the room, her expression unreadable.

'Perhaps we could all get together?' he suggested cautiously. 'You must come over for supper.'

'I should love to!' She took him up on it at once. 'In fact I hoped to be invited before now. Thea and I get on very well, you know. Oh, by the way, I don't think we should tell her, do you? About us, I mean. No need to hurt her. She's so young and innocent.'

George's heart expanded with relief and gratitude and he came nearer to loving Felicity at that moment than at any time during the previous twenty years.

'I'd come to that conclusion myself,' he said.

'I'm sure you had.' She was smiling at him and after a moment George smiled back. 'And now'——her tone suggested that all the deception and hurt was behind them and forgotten——'what do you say to taking me out for a bite to eat before the train goes?'

'Oh!' George was taken aback by this direct approach and one or two alarm bells sounded.

'Just a quick snack? For old times' sake?'

She was still smiling at him but now it had an almost wistful quality and George was seized with remorse. He had treated her disgracefully and she was being so forgiving and generous. Surely it wouldn't hurt, just this once, to take her out? After all, Thea need never know. What harm could it possibly do?

'Why not?' He nodded. 'Good idea. Finish up your drink and we'll go round the corner to the little Italian place. Bit rough and ready but it's very good. You always liked Italian food.'

'Oh, George. How sweet of you to remember. Sounds fun. There!' She emptied her glass and stood it on the little coffee table. 'Ready when you are!'

AS THE TRAIN SLID out of Paddington, Felicity settled back into her seat. Her expression was an odd one: bleak, contemptuous, triumphant. It had all gone better than even she had dared to hope but there was some element of satisfaction missing. Of course, she'd sized up George's weaknesses with masterly precision and exploited them shamelessly and now he was trapped, but even so . . . There was one fact that she had failed to take into her calculations, one thing she hadn't allowed for, and that was her own feelings on seeing him after all this time. The sheer power of her own emotions had almost unmanned her and she'd needed all her considerable strength. He'd looked so tall, so very male. In her plottings George had played a pathetic role. She'd seen him as a weak figure to be crushed and humiliated. He had ceased to be flesh and bone and blood and hair but had become, in her imaginings, a puppet to be manipulated. When he had opened the door and she'd looked up at him, she'd felt quite dizzy. He was so real. She remembered how the thick greying hair grew, the texture of his skin under her fingers, his smell. It was an evocative, masculine smell compounded of tobacco, aftershave and George's own particular body smell and she had felt suddenly weak. She'd wanted to seize him, feel his arms round her, wanted to be told that it was all a terrible mistake, that he still belonged to her. She had been obliged to hurry past him, forgoing the enjoyment of his look of horror, shock and fear. She had planned to enjoy that look, to savour it, but weakness had overcome her and she'd had to summon up all her reserves to be able to carry out her plan.

As the train gathered speed, she stared out into the cold, light spring evening remembering how they had chatted during dinner. She had renewed her acquaintance with his hands, long, elegant members with sensitive fingers, that had moved, gestured, clasped, totally indifferent to her whilst she had watched them, mesmerised, longing for their touch. He had kissed her at the end. It seemed the only way to say goodbye that wasn't churlish or simply silly. He had taken her by the upper arms and given her a swift light kiss and, as quickly, released her and put her into the taxi he'd telephoned for from the restaurant.

Now, she sat quite still, containing, controlling her loneliness, calling up her anger and jealousy. Somehow, these fiery emotions which had dominated her waking hours for so long seemed to elude her, swooping and wheeling just outside her consciousness, whilst an aching feeling of loss took hold of her until all she could feel was the grip of his fingers on her arms and the touch of his lips near her mouth. As the train sped westwards she crouched in her corner like a damaged bird, staring out, until the sky beyond the window grew dark and night approached.

Six

THEA SAT ON ONE of the benches on the platform of the Old Station House and watched a robin pecking at the crumbs she had thrown down for him. He was very tame, sometimes hopping after her through the original sliding doors that led into what had once been the waiting room. Thea raised her face, eyes closed against the hot June sun, and the sharp, peppery scent of hawthorn drifted into her nostrils. Beside her stood strips of bedding plants in plastic containers alongside several larger shrubs, presently to be put into the big wooden half-tubs that stood between the seats. The lawnmower had been run down the ramp ready to be pressed into service along the railway track. Still Thea sat on, immobilised, half drugged by the heat of the sun, such a welcome change after a long cold wet spell. She pushed up the sleeves of George's old tattersall shirt and stretched out her long legs in the shabby jeans. Thea had no thought for clothes beyond their ability to keep her warm and decent and she had been delighted to discover a number of old shirts and jerseys amongst George's cast-off possessions that would keep her adequately clothed for some time to come. George, who had never lived with a woman other than his mother but had heard all sorts of stories regarding wives' extravagances and clothes-buying sorties, was rather relieved to find that he had such a frugal wife and thought that she looked charming in his checked shirts with the sleeves rolled up and a cotton scarf at her throat. With her youth and height and glorious hair she could have carried anything she chose. And Thea chose simplicity.

She stirred and drew in her legs and the robin cocked an eye at her and flew away. Thea sighed a little and passed her hands over her face, straining back her hair and stretching a little. There was no doubt that things seemed much better again now. George had lost that rather inward look and the 'quietness' which she had described to Hermione. He had come back one weekend quite his old self, if not more so. There was a kind of expansiveness about him which suggested relief from tension and he had been loving and attentive and happy. Why then was she visited with this feeling of unease? A verse of psalm slipped into her mind. *Why art thou so full of heaviness, O my soul: and why art thou so disquieted within me?* Why indeed? A week or two later when she told George that Felicity had dropped in he had suggested, quite casually, that they should perhaps invite her for lunch one weekend. She might be lonely, he said, as if in explanation, and it might be a kind thing to do. So Felicity had come and everything had been easy and natural and since then she'd been in several times whilst George was at home: for a cup of coffee one Saturday morning and for supper on a Sunday evening. And once she'd come uninvited on a Saturday afternoon bringing a home-made cake. On that occasion she'd seemed slightly tense and George, coming in and finding her unexpectedly in the kitchen, had behaved rather oddly, with a kind of forced jollity, and had disappeared again quite quickly. Felicity had watched him go and continued to stare at the closed door for some moments before Thea gently recalled her attention. She had left soon after, refusing a cup of tea or to share in the cake, and Thea had gone to look for George and found him standing at the window in his dressing room, jingling the coins in his pocket and staring out across the garden to the humped indigo shoulders of the moor, clear-cut against a pale twilight sky. She had slipped her arms round his waist and pressed her cheek against his throat and he had dragged his hands from his pockets and clutched her to him, kissing and touching her with such urgency that they had fallen on to the little bed in the corner and he had made love to her exhaustively, almost desperately.

Thea knew quite well now that Felicity was the married woman with whom George had had his affair but what she did not know was how seriously to regard it. If it was all over it wouldn't matter at all. It was in the past.

That Felicity had been married to another man who was George's friend was a moral issue between the three of them and nothing to do with Thea. If only George had told her they could have laid the ghost together; as it was she could only watch and wait and pray that it was indeed all over and that she had nothing to fear from Felicity. She knew that that was where the danger lay. Despite the fact that George was a kindly man, who would hate to hurt anyone's—and especially a woman's—feelings, Thea felt certain that she could trust him absolutely. However, she feared the effect that Felicity's loneliness, unhappiness and residual power over him might have if she chose to exert it.

Thea felt genuinely sorry for Felicity who, she imagined, had probably expected to marry George after Mark died. Now she was alone, middle-aged, her lover taken by a younger woman. As the woman in possession, as it were, Thea could afford to feel generous but she felt more than that. She would have liked to befriend Felicity but couldn't decide if it were naïve or merely patronising to assume that it could be done. Now, these small incidents were beginning to make Thea wonder if Felicity was using her, Thea's, innocence to come close again to George and she felt fearful and helpless. What could she do, so young and inexperienced, to hold her own against someone like Felicity? She couldn't bear to think of losing George or to think that their happiness could be destroyed. She drew her feet up on to the seat and wrapped her arms around her knees, burying her face in them. What could she do to hold on to all that she had grown to love so much? Panic seized her and she wondered to whom she could turn. If only her cousin Tim, Hermione's grandson, were not so far away. When she was a little girl Tim had been her hero and her champion, the big brother she'd never had, hauling her out of scrapes and taking her part when things went wrong. Later she had been his confidante, boosting his ego through unhappy love affairs. During the years when she had been nursing her mother, Tim had qualified and taken the highly prestigious job in computer programming with a Dallas-based company. They stayed in touch and he had flown over for the wedding but he was too far away for Thea to confide in him as she had in years gone by.

Instinctively she fell back on the teachings and habits of her young life and, emptying her mind of its confusion, tried to pray. The collect for the second Sunday in Lent seemed the most appropriate on which to concentrate.

Almighty God, who seest that we have no power of ourselves to help ourselves: Keep us both outwardly in our bodies, and inwardly in our souls; that we may be defended from all adversities which may happen to the body, and from all evil thoughts which may assault and hurt the soul; through Jesus Christ our Lord. Amen.

The words brought Thea a measure of comfort. After all, as yet her terrors were formless and she knew that she must have faith in George and in their love. Surely it was great enough to overcome anything that might threaten it? She sighed deeply, feeling more hopeful, and, getting up, turned her attention to the bedding plants.

SOME WEEKS LATER, CASS wandered down Tavistock High Street wondering what she should buy for supper. The boys, Oliver and Saul, and Gemma, her twelve-year-old daughter, were home for the holidays and the days seemed to pass in a continuous series of mealtimes. It was lucky that the weather had changed. Meals could be less formal and more haphazardly put together when it was hot. Then there was the lunch party that she and Tom were giving on Sunday to be organised. The usual crowd was coming: Abby and William, Harriet and Michael, Kate, Thea and George. Even as she thought about George, she saw Felicity on the other side of the road staring into the shoeshop window. Cass paused for a moment and then crossed the road and touched her on the shoulder.

'Hello, Felicity. How's it going?'

It was a moment or two before Felicity could grasp the intrinsic difference in Cass's approach and when she did it was as if she had been struck a blow to the stomach. Never in all their acquaintance, since she and Cass had first met at Felicity's own wedding and Mark and George had behaved so foolishly over her, to Felicity's rage, had Cass spoken or looked at her in such a way. Gone was the mocking, measuring glance of the rival, the provocative tone of an old enemy who knew her to be worthy of her steel, and in its place—she felt herself cringe away from it—was pity. If Cass felt sorry for her then her position must indeed be pathetic. Cass's smile was friendly, her tone kindly, and instinctively Felicity's head reared up in pride and total rejection.

'I'm very well, thanks. And you? You're looking tired.'

Cass raised her brows a little as if she acknowledged the hit but was surprised and even faintly amused at it. Her reaction was rather that of one who might look tolerantly, even with admiration, upon an old and toothless dog who barks at a visitor. Metaphorically she patted Felicity's head, refusing to be alarmed or provoked.

'It's the holidays and the children are home. Totally exhausting. What about a cup of coffee?'

No jibes about Felicity's 'barrenness' as Cass had always called it, no remarks about the pleasures of being able to live for oneself. Felicity clenched her fists.

'No time, I'm afraid. I've got people to lunch.'

'Nice for you.'

Felicity knew that Cass was visualising her small circle of cronies, mostly naval wives who, now that their husbands were away less and less, would soon get tired of Felicity dropping in, phoning up. Single women could be a bit of a pain when husbands were around and they made an odd number at dinner parties. Lunch sessions and coffee mornings would be cancelled and more and more she would be left alone except when someone said, 'We really must ask Felicity round, poor old thing. We forget she's all on her own.' Felicity saw all this and more in Cass's eyes. She saw sympathy with the pity, and the humiliation and pain that she felt was nearly as great as that which she'd experienced when she received George's letter announcing his defection. She lifted her chin and stared at Cass.

'And, of course, I go to London very often now.'

'London!' Cass arched her brows as if in amazement that Felicity was still capable of travelling so far and, had she done it in her old manner, Felicity would have seized upon it with fierce satisfaction. But Cass was still regarding her with that friendly kindness, pleased for her that she should have such a treat, and Felicity felt that she would like to rend her with her red pointed nails. She must restore her position of equality and wipe that look from Cass's face.

'Oh, yes. To see George. I'm sure Tom has told you that George is at the Ministry of Defence?'

She had done it and her heart exulted within her. Cass looked at her blankly. 'George?'

It was Felicity's turn to raise her black, much-plucked brows. 'Of course. He's got a flat in London. All on his own of course. I must say that I was a bit surprised when you talked of his sharing with Tom and Tony.' She laughed and shook her head. 'That wouldn't have suited us at all. Anyway. I mustn't keep you from your brood. I must say I'm glad I haven't got all that. Nothing so ageing as children. Look after yourself, Cass. You really mustn't let yourself go. So easy at our ages. See you.'

She turned away, her heart beating so hard and so heavy with bitter satisfaction and pain that she felt it might burst or that she must faint. Cass stood staring after her and then walked quickly away in the opposite direction.

'WELL, ALL I CAN say,' observed Kate on Sunday as she stacked plates on the draining board, 'is, if what you say is true, Thea and George look very happy about it.'

She kept her voice down so that Cass's other lunch guests shouldn't hear and began to scrape the remains of food from the plates into the dog bowl, watched with keen anticipation by the golden retriever, Gus. Kate had bred Gus and he knew that when she came to a meal at the Rectory she could always be counted on to look after his welfare.

'And I can only tell you what Felicity said to me,' hissed Cass and jumped violently as Oliver suddenly materialised behind her.

'What's all the whispering about, girls?' he asked in a normal voice and they both said 'Shush!' together and then burst out laughing.

'Now who were you gossiping about?' he speculated as he went to help fill Gus's bowl.

Kate smiled and slipped an arm around him. 'How do you know it wasn't you?' she asked.

He beamed down at her and put his arm about her shoulders. 'People only gossip about me to my face,' he assured her. 'They always want to be absolutely certain that I know exactly how they feel about me.'

Kate hugged him. She missed her twins terribly and saw them very seldom now that they were in their final year at university. Cass's children had always been almost as dear to her as her own, and Oliver, so like his grandfather the General who had been such a friend to Kate, was especially dear. Incredible to think that he was eighteen years old and yet, in some ways, Oliver had always had something about him that made her feel he was older than all of them.

'What do you think of Thea?' she asked him.

'Now are you trying to throw me off the scent?' he pondered, putting the bowl down for the salivating Gus. 'Or was this the subject of all your whispering? I like her very much. George is a lucky old devil, isn't he? Can't think what these young girls see in these old men.'

'George and your father are the same age,' said Cass repressively, making coffee.

'That's what I mean,' said Oliver, unperturbed. 'Positively ancient. It's almost indecent. She'd be much better off with a young virile chap like me.'

'That's a mistake that young men often make,' said Cass, who had always treated Oliver as an equal rather than her child. 'A girl sometimes prefers an experienced older man to a callow youth who has no idea how to treat her and is only interested in bolstering his own ego.'

'I hope,' said Oliver reprovingly, 'that you are not implying that I am a callow youth?'

Kate burst out laughing. 'She wouldn't have the nerve,' she said. 'None of us would.'

'Well, all I can say is that marriage is doing wonders for old George,' said Oliver. 'Not nearly as boring as he used to be. Speaks to me and Saul as if we're actually members of the human race. He's full of the milk of human kindness and I put this pretty shirt on specially to wind him up. Saul and I took bets on how long it would take him to remark on it. And he hasn't even noticed it. Too busy leering at Thea and trying to hold her hand when nobody's looking. I shall have to pay Saul twenty pence now!'

He picked up the coffee tray and set off towards the dining room. Cass and Kate looked at one another.

'Could Felicity have been trying to wind you up?' asked Kate. 'After all, it must be positively humiliating to lose George after twenty years to a mere child like Thea.'

Cass shrugged. 'All I can say is that she sounded very convincing. And it was you who said that she was biding her time and it would all end in tears. But she might have been. They certainly look happy enough at the moment and I simply can't imagine George running a wife and a mistress and behaving like he is this morning. Come on. We'd better join the mob.'

Seven

WHEN POLLY WICKAM TELEPHONED Thea and suggested that they meet in Exeter for lunch, Thea was delighted to agree. All her fears seemed, after all, to have been unfounded. George was still a loving companion and she hadn't seen Felicity since before Cass's lunch party. This last was a little surprising as Felicity had become a very regular visitor but, after some thought, Thea had decided to let sleeping dogs lie and enjoy her happiness with George. They had spent two peaceful weeks of leave in Shropshire and returned with pleasure to the Old Station House where Thea felt that she had lived for years and which was now so much her home.

On the morning that she was to meet Polly at Coolings, the wine bar behind Queen Street, she drove across the moor to Two Bridges and turned left on to the Moretonhampstead road. It was a clear bright day and the moor was almost gaudy with its stretches of purple heather contrasting with the gold of the autumn-flowering gorse. The berries of the hawthorn and the rowan were ripening and the beech leaves showed a hint of bronze. The bracken was beginning to die away in shades of rust and flame and the whole glowed and dazzled beneath the early-autumn sunshine.

In Exeter, Thea parked the car in the Mary Arches car park and, following Polly's instructions, made her way through narrow streets until she stood outside the wine bar. Suddenly feeling rather shy, she pushed open the door and peered in. It was dark inside after the brightness of the day and Thea stood for a moment, blinking, as her eyes accustomed themselves to the gloom.

'Thea! Hi! Over here.' Polly was gesticulating from a dark corner and Thea smiled with relief and went to join her.

'This is fun.' She slid into the empty chair and looked around her. 'Is it always as busy as this?'

'Well, people come in for coffee, stay on to have a drink and then find that it's lunchtime. I was lucky to get a table. Now you're here I'll go and get us a drink and you can be deciding what you want to eat. The menu's written up on blackboards. See?' Polly gestured to the boards fixed above the bar to the whitewashed walls. 'What will you drink? I generally have the house white. It's cheap and cheerful.'

'Fine. Whatever you usually have.'

She watched Polly threading her way to the bar and noticed that she had meant it when she told Thea not to dress up. Since her marriage to George, Thea had discovered that women did not always strictly mean this and she had turned up in her jeans to find that the other women were looking very smart indeed. Polly, however, was wearing jeans and a sweatshirt and Thea felt almost smart in her best cords and one of George's better jerseys. She felt, suddenly, that it was fun to be sitting here in Coolings with a girlfriend of her own age getting her a drink, surrounded by laughing talking people, while some music with a very strong beat played in the background. She looked around her, alert and interested, and completely unaware that she was arousing a certain amount of interest in one or two quarters. She grinned at Polly when she came back bearing two glasses. Polly grinned back.

'Here's to us.' She raised her glass to Thea. 'So what's the news from the Wild West? I haven't been over to see Harriet for a while. She came here last time. How she can bear to live in that isolated cottage I can't imagine. The silence at night positively terrifies me when I stay with them. And if it isn't creepily quiet there are peculiar sounds that frighten you to death. I remember being woken up with this really weird noise. Terrifying, it was. I lay awake for hours, rigid with fear. When I told Michael in the morning, he said it was a sheep coughing. Jesus! What with that and the owls roaring away, not to mention the foxes screeching, who can possibly hope to rest quiet in their beds? Give me the nice normal sounds of the petrol engine revving and jolly people rolling home drunk in the early hours.'

'I think it's what you're used to,' said Thea, laughing at Polly's description. 'I'm used to the quiet and can't sleep in towns. Do you stay with Harriet and Michael often?'

'Not what you'd call often. Sometimes when Paul's away lecturing on the life cycle of some deadly boring insect. Did you know she's expecting a baby?'

'Harriet? No, I didn't. How lovely for her.'

Polly raised her eyebrows and pulled her mouth down at the corners. 'If you like that sort of thing. She's thrilled. Better not say anything if she hasn't told you. She's loving telling people and I don't want to spoil her fun. I'm to be godmother.' She made another face. 'What a positively terrifying thought. Drink up and we'll get another when we order the food. What do you fancy? The cauliflower cheese is really good.'

Thea found herself being swept along, finding Polly's lighthearted approach refreshing and infectious.

'Do I gather,' she asked cautiously, when they were back at their table with heaped plates of cauliflower cheese and delicious-looking fried potatoes, 'that you and Paul don't want children?'

'Not yet.' Polly attacked her food with enthusiasm. 'I'm not the maternal sort and I simply can't see Paul with a baby. He probably wouldn't notice it. Now if I could give birth to a completely new mayfly . . .'

'Oh, Polly!'

'I mean it. You don't know him. He's always reading or down at the lab. He's hardly aware of my existence. It's lucky that I'm a very self-sufficient person.'

'Sounds a bit lonely,' ventured Thea.

Polly shrugged. 'Could be worse. Look at you. You're alone all week. At least Paul comes home every evening. How do you manage, all alone in that big house? What's it like being a naval wife?'

'Oh, it's not too bad at all. I'm told by the old hands that I don't know I'm born. Apparently having a husband away only five days out of seven is luxury, especially when I could be with him in London. It's nothing to him being away at sea for months on end whilst you're left dealing with sick children, trying to move house and all the other traumas. I've come in on the jammy bit so I can't complain. Mmm! This food is absolutely delicious, Polly! Anyway, I go up midweek to see him and there's an awful lot of garden to keep me busy. And there's lots of really kind people, well, you know them, people like Cass Wivenhoe, who've been so friendly. I'm very lucky.'

'And George, so I hear, is very dishy.'

'Oh, well.' Thea blushed and then laughed. 'Well, I think so. He's quite a bit older than I am, actually.'

Polly, who knew all about George from Harriet, made big eyes across the table at her. 'An attractive, experienced older man sounds pretty good to me. Do you ever lend him out to friends who are in need?'

'Certainly not! I've had quite enough of that with Felicity . . .' Thea stopped abruptly and bit her lip.

Polly's eyebrows shot up and, pushing aside her empty plate, she rested her elbows on the table, glass between her fingers, and looked at Thea quizzically.

'Now that sounds rather interesting. Come on, you can't possibly stop there.'

'It's nothing. Really. Well, at least, it's all over now. It's, oh honestly!' Thea shook her head, laid down her fork and looked at Polly almost beseechingly. 'It's nothing. Honestly.'

'In that case,' said Polly firmly, 'it won't matter if you tell me about it. I'll go and get some coffee and then you can tell me all!'

WHEN FELICITY TURNED UP at the flat in London the second time, just after Cass's party, George was surprised but not nearly so frightened as he had been on that first occasion. She gave the same reason as she had then but her rather strained air made him feel glad that he had an excuse for not being able to offer her hospitality. He was going to dinner with Tom and Tony and there was only time for a quick cup of tea before he said goodbye to her. On the third occasion he was prepared to let her see that he was surprised—and not pleasantly so—but she seemed so dejected that he let her in without demur. She had come up, she said, to visit a friend but there must have been a muddle because the house was empty and no message had been left for her. She looked rather tired and told him that she had one of her 'heads' and George began to feel sorry for her. He took her in and gave her tea and she was very grateful and quiet and George was at a bit of a loss to know how to deal with this subdued, forlorn Felicity. He was very kind to her, remembering that she was all alone now whilst he had Thea. Always in his dealings with Felicity lurked the remains of his guilt at having deceived and abandoned her and he found it quite easy to be gentle with her. She huddled in the corner of his sofa looking so pathetic that he wondered how on earth he was going to turn her out. When the time came, however, she asked him to telephone for a taxi and when it arrived she got up to leave. At the door, however, she gave a little cry and stumbled, clutching her head in both hands and dropping her handbag. She looked so ill that George was obliged to send the taxi away and help her back to the sofa. She rummaged in her bag and found the Ergotamine tablets which were prescribed for her migraines while he went to fetch a glass of water.

When he returned she smiled up at him. Her face was paper-white, her eyes black and enormous, and George looked at her anxiously. 'You can't travel like this,' he said. 'I'm not sure that we can even get you to an hotel. You'd better stop here. I can sleep on the sofa. I'll go and sort the bed out.'

Felicity watched him go and then placed the tablets back inside her handbag and drank the water. She was trembling from head to foot and when he came back and touched her on the shoulder she jumped violently. She stood up and followed him into the bed-room.

'You should be quite comfortable,' he said, a little awkwardly. 'Shout if you want anything.'

He didn't look at her and turned quickly away.

'George.'

Her voice was barely above a whisper but to him it was like a clarion call. He hesitated but didn't turn back to look at her.

'Please, George. Don't leave me. Please.'

It was as if his heart had turned to marble, a great cold weight in his breast, and despair clutched at his entrails. He put a hand out and took hold of the door jamb.

'Please, George.'

She started to cry, hurt, whimpering little noises, and George gave a moan of desperation.

'I can't, Felicity,' he whispered fiercely. 'You know I can't.'

She was close to him, standing behind him. She pressed her face against his back and he felt her hand on his wrist.

'Just this once. Don't leave me alone. I feel so awful and I'm so lonely. Oh, George, I've missed you so much.'

George swallowed hard. She lifted his hand and pressed it to her cheek which was wet with tears and he moaned aloud again in his distraction. She released his hand and began to cry in earnest, holding her hands over her face, and with dragging steps stumbled to the bed. She fell on to it, weeping. George stood quite still, gazing out into the hall and struggling with his conscience. Presently he went out and closed the door quietly but firmly behind him.

HERMIONE SAT IN HER summerhouse watching Thea approaching across the lawn. She knew at once that all was not well with this beloved child and she clasped her hands tightly beneath the shawl in which Mrs Gilchrist had insisted upon wrapping her. The autumn day was dull but warm; nevertheless, in the absence of sunshine Mrs

Gilchrist always feared the worst and Hermione had to be shawled and muffled despite the actual temperature. She struggled a little to release her arms so that she could extend her hands to Thea. She scanned the girl's face anxiously. It had a drawn look with smudgy shadows beneath the brown eyes. Gone was the buoyant vivid look and Hermione felt her heart begin to tap a little faster.

'My darling girl.' She clasped Thea's hand and drew her down to sit in the chair beside her own.

'Something's wrong, G.A.'

It was so like Thea to come directly to the point that Hermione almost smiled.

'I gathered that on the telephone. Can you tell me what it is?'

'I don't quite know what it is.' Thea's face was troubled and unhappy. 'Well. Except that it's George, of course. He's all different. Sort of distant and closed in. He's behaving like a terribly polite stranger and I can't break through. It's horrid. And frightening. I simply don't know what to do.'

'But do you know why he's behaving like this?'

Thea, who had been clutching Hermione's hand, released it and turned to stare out over the lawn. 'It's Felicity,' she said. 'I'm sure of it. Felicity is the woman he had an affair with and I think she's made him go back to her. I think he's seeing her in London.' Her lips shook a little and she swallowed hard.

'My darling girl . . .'

'If I'd known at the beginning, you see, I wouldn't have encouraged her. I could have frozen her out. But I was so sorry for her, losing her husband and her mother, and it was only later that I guessed who she was. I do think that someone might have warned me. Cass or someone.'

Hermione closed her eyes for a moment as she took the unintended rebuke to her heart but, before she could speak, Thea was going on.

'George should have told me himself, of course. If only he'd had more faith in me. I would have understood. And now it's too late.'

'Too late? Do you mean that . . . ?'

'Oh, no. No. We haven't even discussed it. He won't let me near him. But how can I fight if he shuts me out?'

'And what about Felicity?'

'She hasn't been near. That's why I'm so sure now. She wormed her way in and she's got what she wants. What a fool I've been! And we were so happy.'

Thea gave a little sob and Hermione began to struggle out of her chair but they stopped short as a cry alerted them.

'So you've arrived and you never came to tell me!'

Mrs Gilchrist was advancing over the grass and, as one person, Thea and Hermione sat up and presented a united smiling front.

'I thought it was a bit too late for coffee.' Hermione could not help but admire Thea's controlled voice and friendly smile. 'I decided I could wait till lunch. I'm sorry. Have you been holding it back?'

'Nothing to notice. I'll pop back and heat the soup. By the time you've helped Mrs Barrable indoors it'll be waiting for you.'

She smiled upon them both and turned back to the house. Hermione looked at Thea. 'There will be time to talk afterwards,' she said firmly and comfortingly. 'I'm sure that we shall find a solution.' She paused as Thea helped her to struggle to her feet. Once upright she looked into Thea's eyes. 'I'm assuming, of course, that you don't want to give him up?'

'Oh, no!' Thea shook her head miserably. 'But maybe, if he's gone back to her, he won't want me any more. Perhaps he didn't really love me as much as I thought. And I love him so much.'

'Absolute rubbish!' Hermione's fingers dug themselves into Thea's arm. 'It's nothing to do with how much he loves you. I'm sure that there's no question of that. It's just that he's got a conscience and she's exploiting it. I'm sure of it.'

'But what shall I do?'

'Don't know yet. I shall have to think about it. But you mustn't give in. You must go on showing him that you love him.'

'I can't help doing that,' said poor Thea. 'I do.'

'Good,' said Hermione. 'We'll give her a run for her money. And you mustn't get too depressed. I always remember what my dear mother used to say. "Who would want a man that no other woman wants?" Look upon it as a sort of compliment and get ready for battle. After all, you can't know that he's given in. Come along or she'll be out again nattering about the soup.'

They went slowly across the lawn and into the house. In the dining room, Mrs Gilchrist was ladling soup into bowls and smiled at them as they took their seats.

'Have you heard from Tim lately?' Thea knew that there would be little chance for any private talk until afterwards.

'My only grandson,' said Hermione as she unfolded her napkin, 'has written to tell me that he will be coming back from America in the spring. I don't understand all this computer business but he seems very happy doing it. He tells me about "networking" and "software" and "parallel programming" just as he once used to instruct me on cricket. He's coming down to see me when he gets back but his letter was full of some girl he'd just met. He'd just been to an exhibition apparently, by one of our RAs—the name escapes me at the moment—and rather fell for his daughter who was out there with him. He's been asked to visit them in London when he comes over so I have no doubt that I shall be well down on his list of priorities.'

'I should love to see him.' Thea broke her roll and started on her soup while Mrs Gilchrist bustled round making sure that everything was in order as she would continue to do on and off throughout the meal. 'There was so little chance to talk to him at the wedding. We write but it's a bit spasmodic.'

'Well, when he finally turns up you must come over. He'll certainly want to see you.'

'He was my best friend when we were little. We had such lovely holidays here. D'you remember how I used to write endless stories and then we'd act them out in the summerhouse? The only thing we ever really argued about was Percy. Who would have him if you died.'

'There was never any question of that,' said Hermione. 'If anything happens to me, Percy belongs to you. We all know that. And that reminds me. Have you seen your new friend Polly lately? She sounds such fun. We must teach Percy to say "Pretty Polly" ready for when he meets her. The quotes from *The Beggars' Opera* that your great-uncle taught him might be rather inappropriate.'

'She'd love him.' Thea watched Mrs Gilchrist out of the room and turned to Hermione. 'She thinks that I ought to go with George to London during the week. I wondered that, too. If I hadn't left him all alone during the week perhaps this would never have happened. It was just so awful. Those endless days in that poky flat with nothing to do. I know a lot of people think that I must be mad, with all London on the doorstep, but once you've seen all the things that people say you mustn't miss and been to the theatre and some concerts it all gets rather boring. You can't spend your whole life shopping.'

Hermione sipped at her soup thoughtfully. She knew that Thea simply wasn't cut out for city life but Polly had a point.

'And George,' continued Thea, 'got paranoid about the house being broken into while we were away and his mother's things being stolen. A neighbour went in and kept an eye on things but that's not terribly satisfactory. And then he started talking about letting it. I couldn't bear the idea of not having a bolt hole from London and I hated the idea of other people living there.'

Hermione set her spoon down and smiled. 'It's a good job that George has reached the rank he has. You'd have made a dreadful naval wife.'

'I would,' agreed Thea readily. 'I'd have hated all that moving about. Never settled in one spot. Grotty married quarters without your own things round you and having to let your own home to complete strangers. Awful. Cass and Kate were talking about it once and it sounded quite unbearable.'

Hermione opened her mouth and shut it again as Mrs Gilchrist put her head round the door. There was one obvious way to tie George back to Thea's side and she was surprised that Thea hadn't already thought of it. For the moment, however, it would have to wait. Perhaps she could approach the subject after lunch; meanwhile the subject of Tim seemed to be as safe a conversation as any, and for the rest of the meal they stuck firmly to memories of his and Thea's shared childhood holidays.

Eight

FOR THE WHOLE OF the winter, George and Felicity seemed locked together in a battle of wills. It was not enough, now, for Felicity to destroy George's marriage. It was as if, in some way, Cass's pity had underlined what Felicity had discovered for herself on that first visit to George in London: on its own that would be a very empty victory. She saw her own loneliness stretching away into the future and the fear of it made her clutch at George as her only means of escape from it. She knew that at any time she could have gone to Thea and woven the strands of their past relationship together with the fragile threads of the visits to the flat into a fairly sturdy rope for George's neck. Unlike George, however, Felicity felt quite sure that Thea would throw the rope down and trample on it and tell Felicity to go. She found it amazing that George couldn't see this and that he only had to tell Thea the whole truth and he would be free. She rejoiced at his lack of understanding of Thea's character for here was her strongest weapon. It lay in deceit and lies and the guilt that was growing in George, smothering and distorting his natural feelings and reactions. She never let him see what a bitter, crushing wound to her self-esteem his rejection of her had been on the night she had appeared with her 'migraine.' Cass's pity had worked her up to it, spurred her on, and, nervous though she had been, in her secret and innermost heart she had felt certain that George would be overwhelmed by guilt, his innate kindness, the intimacy of past moments, and would give way.

He had not. He had left the flat, taking an overnight case, and gone to a local hotel and she had left early in the morning after a night of humiliating misery; it had taken all her courage to write him a note thanking him for his hospitality which she followed up with another visit. The pain she felt when she saw the complete rejection—almost disgust—in his eyes had to be borne. Somehow she had to get him back. She had deluded herself into believing that if he would only make love to her again all would be well. The past would reinstate itself and he would love her again. But George had never loved her. Nor had she loved him.

In the beginning it had been a joke, harmless fun: George, the best man at the wedding, Mark's closest friend, pretending that if only he'd seen her first Mark wouldn't have stood a chance. It was a joke that went on too long. When Mark's submarine had sailed immediately after the honeymoon he had already asked George to look after her. Felicity had newly moved to Alverstoke, knowing no one, and George had taken her round, introduced her to other submariners and their wives, escorted her to a Ladies Night in *Dolphin,* the submarine base. No one remarked on it. George had a reputation for being a very useful man even in those early days. Men would sigh with relief when George approached their table, knowing that he could be safely left to talk to or dance with their wives while they went off to the bar to talk shop. Husbands and wives alike trusted George.

As time went by Felicity tried to detach him from his gallant ways, hating it when any other woman benefited from his considerable charm. However, the affair that George and Felicity drifted into was a very spasmodic relationship. It could hardly have been anything else with the Navy moving them about like so many chess pieces. Perhaps it was because he had deceived his best friend that George carried on, afraid that if he didn't Felicity might spill the beans. Perhaps it was because he was constitutionally unable to bear the sight of suffering or pain that he had himself inflicted that made it impossible for him to cut himself free. Whatever it was, it was not because he loved her. And to Felicity, George was a possession, a belonging, and, even if she didn't love him, she wanted to keep him. So she continued to turn up, waiting for that moment in which he might weaken. When he grew angry, she pointed out how easy it might be to misconstrue these visits: the dinner at the Italian restaurant, the night spent in his bed and one or two other unheralded arrivals. George's spirit writhed within him. When he had told her that she must never come to the flat again or to the Old Station House she had opened her eyes at him and wondered aloud what Thea would think to find that George had asked her, back in the spring, to invite his mistress to their house. Beside Felicity's rapier-like mind, George's brain was like putty, soft and heavy and only too impressionable.

Thea, meanwhile, had thought deeply about G.A.'s suggestion which would probably solve the problem. It was a simple and obvious one: Thea should start a family. She and George had agreed to give themselves a year or two together first and Thea had decided to abide by that decision even when, during long days and nights alone at the Old Station House, she had begun to wonder whether it wouldn't be rather fun to get on with it. When Polly had told her about Harriet, Thea had felt a fierce envy clutch at her heart, and when G.A. had suggested that it would be the answer to these real or imaginary problems, Thea had longed to believe in it and act upon it.

There was one fact, however, that couldn't be done away with and it was this. At present the fight was between George, Felicity and Thea. A baby would unquestionably weigh on Thea's side and George would be duty-bound to cast Felicity off. This, in Thea's mind, had a grave disadvantage. It meant that she would never know whether George had come back for her or for the baby. George must be hers because he loved her most. At the thought of losing George she felt weak with fear and heavy with misery and it was only with a supreme effort that she could continue to greet him with open and unquestioning affection on Friday evenings, turning away his moods with love and his irritability with good humour.

She guessed, rightly, that these were outward manifestations of his guilt and she therefore feared the worst. However, love, warmth, a happy home, these were her weapons and she used them. She decided that it wouldn't be cheating to make her home even more of a solid bulwark against the threats from outside and when she heard that Harriet was going to get a Newfoundland puppy she was tempted to do the same. A home was even more of a home with animals and she arranged to go with Harriet to have a look at the litter. She had met Harriet and Michael's Newfoundland, Max, and had been completely won over by his great bulk and kindly manners.

'They've got a wonderful temperament,' Harriet told her, 'but you'll have black hairs over everything and they eat an enormous amount, especially when they're young and you want to be building up the bone.'

Max, leaning heavily against the dresser, looked at her reproach-fully.

'Now you've hurt his feelings,' cried Polly, who was over for the day. 'You're worth it, aren't you, Max?'

Max sighed weightily and yawned a little as if to imply that he was used to this sort of treatment and that it was all one to him. Harriet laughed.

'We're dying to see how he reacts to a puppy,' she said. 'We don't want to leave it too late so that it upsets him. I've told Freddie—that's the breeder—that we'll be over this afternoon. And all I can say is: beware. If you can resist a Newfie puppy you're a better man than I am, Gunga Din.'

Thea couldn't resist. She gazed at the big, black fluffy puppies with their enormous paws and flopping ears and fell in love at once. Freddie Spenlow, a broadly built young man with an eager face that was saved from plainness by the variety of expressions that passed so rapidly across it, laughed at her expression.

'They're exactly like bear cubs,' she breathed. 'Oh, I love them.'

'Well, at least I don't have to tell you that they won't stay that size,' he said. 'Not if you've seen Max. That one's yours, Harriet. That big chap at the back. He's got a look of Max about him, I think. Their mother,' he told Thea, 'is Max's litter sister's daughter. Never mind.' He smiled at her blank expression. 'Are you thinking about a dog or a bitch? I imagine you've had dogs before?'

'Oh, yes. We always had dogs at home. Usually crossbreeds that were going to be put down. We could never afford a pedigree.'

'Well, I tell everyone who has one of my puppies the same thing. If you have a problem telephone me first. Vets aren't too used to these big breeds and I can probably help. I was trained as a vet and I know Newfies. If you can't cope, bring the puppy back. Don't give it away or have it put down. Oh, you'd be surprised.' He nodded at her shocked look. 'I've got very cautious since I've been breeding. Anyway. I'll make some coffee and we'll bring Harriet's puppy in so she can have a good look at him. At the moment you could have a bitch or a dog but I've got three couples coming down at the weekend to have a look so you'll have to make your mind up.'

Over coffee, Freddie put all the pros and cons clearly before her and it was obvious that his dogs were very important to him and that he only let his puppies go to homes that had been vetted as thoroughly as possible.

'You remind me of Kate Webster,' said Thea. 'She breeds golden retrievers.'

'Oh, I know Kate,' said Freddie with a smile. 'We're very good friends, Kate and I.'

The next day, Thea went to Freddie's again on her own. She didn't want to be distracted by talk of Harriet's puppy or Polly's cries of delight and amusing observations. She sat in Freddie's muddy kitchen in his unattractive little bungalow with three large Newfoundlands vying for her attention and watched the bitch puppy that she had selected growling and pouncing and playing on the floor. The big dogs looked down in astonishment at this forward creature, lifting their paws politely as she tumbled between their legs and ignoring her as she tugged at them and worried at their tails. Thea sat at the table, her arm round the neck of Freddie's stud dog, Charlie Custard, whose head was nearly on a level with her own, and felt, for the first time for ages, peacefully happy. Here, in this untidy place, she felt as if she had stepped out of her own life with its attendant problems and was just herself: Thea, unattached, uninvolved, free. Freddie pushed a mug of coffee across the cluttered table to her—he made surprisingly good coffee—and sat down opposite. He didn't speak, just sat quietly with her, letting her unwind as she hugged the great dog and rubbed her cheek against his warm, smooth, furry head.

Presently she looked across the table at Freddie and smiled rather ruefully and sighed a little. He smiled back and Thea could see some sort of likeness to Kate. She struggled—for her brain seemed to have become dull and sleepy—to analyse it. She had been to Kate's for coffee and had felt the same peaceful, still quality. Surely it couldn't be because they both bred dogs and wore disgracefully old clothes? Perhaps it was because they lived alone, pleased themselves and had none of the struggles that were automatically involved in relationships. They could be themselves, no self-doubt or guilt. But there was probably a price. Loneliness, perhaps; a lack of love? Did that explain the dogs? Thea shook her head and pulled herself together. Freddie was still smiling at her.

'Got it all worked out?' he asked and she had a suspicion that he had followed her entire thought process.

'No.' She shook her head again and smiled at him. 'Not really. I was just trying to decide why I feel so comfortable and relaxed here.'

'Dogs are nice people,' said Freddie. 'They don't impose on you. Not till dinnertime, anyway.'

Thea burst out laughing and looked at the puppy, who had fallen asleep between the front paws of one of the big dogs. 'I love her,' she said.

'Only way to buy a puppy,' said Freddie. 'Love at first sight. Same with humans, of course. The trouble is, they don't always love you back.'

Thea looked at him quickly but he was looking at the puppy.

'You'll have to help me,' said Thea, not knowing quite what else to say. 'With the puppy. What it eats and things.'

'No problem. I'm not far away.'

'No,' said Thea. 'No, that's true,' and wondered why she found it such a comforting thought.

ONCE AGAIN IT WAS February and once again Hermione was waiting for Thea to arrive. On this occasion, however, there was no fog. A high, blustery wind from the south-west roared and crashed about the house, howling in the chimney and whining round the doors. Hermione pulled her shawl a little closer and looked at Percy, huddled silently in his cage.

'We don't like it, do we, Percy?' she murmured. 'We're getting too old.'

'To me, fair friend, you never can be old,' recited the parrot in Hermione's dead husband's voice. 'For as you were when first your eye I eyed, such seems your beauty still.'

He was silent and the wind howled louder. Hermione stared into the corner where the cage stood. Her chin shook and tears ran down her soft wrinkled cheeks. 'Edward,' she murmured and covered her eyes with her thin, age-mottled hand. 'How I miss you still. Oh, my dear love. How we loved the sonnets.'

She felt weak and old and tired and longed quite desperately for the man who had lived with her and loved her for more than fifty years. They had sat in this very room, he reading aloud to her while she played patience, his voice mingling with the rustle and fall of logs and the flick, flick, flick of the cards. They had taught Percy some of the words, laughing together, delighted when he showed such aptitude. Hermione's tears fell on to her cards and she strove to overcome her weakness lest Thea should come upon her unannounced. She caught her breath suddenly as the niggly little pain in her abdomen gave a sharper twinge than usual. Perhaps, after all, she should get the doctor to give her a check-over. But not just yet. She didn't want to know anything unpleasant until this business with Thea was sorted out. She'd written to Tim, giving him an outline of the situation and asking him to come down as soon as he arrived in the country. He was much more likely to be able to help Thea than she, more or less tied to a chair, and they'd always been such friends. How she loved these two children. She thought of Thea, fighting her battle with courage and love. And Tim, so like Edward to look at, so eager and always ready to lend an arm to the weak. If only he would come. Hermione sighed and wiped away her tears with her handkerchief. She must not weaken now. Tim would be home in a few weeks to help her. She began to deal the cards with trembling hands. Thea should be here at any moment and must find nothing amiss. The wind screamed louder and somewhere a door banged loudly. The parrot shifted uneasily in his cage and Hermione paused, holding the cards, listening. At that moment, the pain struck again with such force that she half rose with a cry, clutching with one hand at her stomach and the other at the table that rocked for a moment and then fell as she did, the tiny cards scattering like leaves. And Edward was there, coming towards her, young and strong, arms outstretched, and she cried out his name, 'Edward', as she died.

Tim fell to his knees beside her, gathering her up, and looked up to see Thea standing beside him, her eyes wide with shock.

'Get the doctor, quickly!' he cried. 'Ask Mrs Gilchrist. Quick!'

Thea fled away and Tim continued to crouch, holding the frail old body close, touching the tears which were still drying on the withered cheeks and, at last, gently closing the eyes which, for that brief second, had blazed at him with hope and love and joy.

Nine

FOR THEA THE ARRIVAL of Percy was the turning point. It was as if the presence of the parrot, talking now in G.A.'s voice, now in Uncle Edward's, gave her new courage and strength to cope not only with George but with Hermione's death. She would never forget that terrible scene. She and Tim had arrived together at Broadhayes and she had followed him into the library expecting G.A. to be overjoyed by the surprise of seeing her beloved grandson unexpectedly. Instead, that cry of 'Edward' and the terrible sight of the overturned card table before Tim had gathered his grandmother up in his arms and told Thea to get the doctor. By the time he arrived she was dead. He had questioned them closely and a sobbing Mrs Gilchrist had told him that Hermione had complained a few times of little pains in the abdomen but that she had refused to seek advice. The doctor knew Hermione far too well to expect that Mrs Gilchrist would have been able to bully her into any course of action she didn't wish to take and comforted her by saying that he suspected it would have done no good even if she had.

'Sounds like an aortic aneurysm,' he told them. 'The lining of the main blood vessel weakens, bit like a balloon, and one day it bursts. If I'm right, she's been living on a time bomb. We couldn't have operated, she was too old. It would have meant a graft. It's a major operation and I doubt she would have survived it. Just as well she didn't know she had it, at least she wasn't worrying about it. I'm afraid there'll have to be a post-mortem to make sure I'm right.'

If Tim had not been there Thea would have been lost indeed, and his presence continued to be comforting during the following days. However, close though they had been throughout their young lives, even Tim could not take G.A.'s place. Thea was quite unable to take him into her confidence and she felt as if she had lost not only the person who had taken over the role—as far as that is ever possible—of her mother but also a confidante and ally. Tim and Mrs Gilchrist were at one in insisting that she should take Percy home with her. Hearing him talk in G.A.'s voice was alternately harrowing and comforting, but he seemed contented enough to be with her and she spent as much time with him as possible. He and the puppy, Jessie, would stare at each other for ages. Jessie would bow down on her front paws, stern in the air, and give a short high yelp, inviting him to play. After a while he learned to yelp back at her whereupon she would sit down at once, ears cocked, gazing at him in amazement. Maggie Tabb, the Cornish girl who came in to help Thea with the spring-cleaning, was enchanted by the odd couple and begged for some of Thea's drawings of them to take home to her small boy, Wayne. The next morning she told Thea that he'd demanded a story to go with the drawings and Thea settled down and wrote a charming tale which delighted Wayne and prompted Maggie to say that she should put it in a book.

After she had gone, Thea sat at the kitchen table thinking very hard. Why shouldn't she write some stories about Percy and illustrate them? After all, she'd always enjoyed writing children's stories. Why not ones about Percy? It would be fun to do and it would help her through these days of waiting and wondering. George had been almost his old self since G.A.'s death. He had comforted and consoled her in her grief but there was still a barrier and she knew that without G.A. to support her it would be much harder to go on without some sort of confrontation. Some instinct warned her against this, told her to hold on a little longer. Hermione's death, however, had brought home to her a realisation of the waste of time and life this muddle was creating and she felt unwilling to let it drag on much longer. Nevertheless, Thea had always trusted her instincts and it occurred to her that if she had something of her own to be thinking about and planning for, maybe she could manage. She decided against telling George about her new idea. It would be her thing, her project, and if anything came of it she would enjoy surprising him. It would be worth waiting for, worth working for.

George, meanwhile, was praying that his appointment to HMS *Warrior* at Northwood, which was the headquarters of the Commander-in-Chief and Fleet Headquarters, was going to be the answer to his problems. He was delighted to be leaving the somewhat pedestrian planning job at Whitehall and looked forward to being back in the more operational, day-to-day life where there was a proper Mess and he could live in. Most officers, having done their obligatory month of living in, couldn't wait to move out and start claiming lodging allowance but George could see many advantages to living in. The most obvious was that Felicity would not be able to turn up on the doorstep. He would hardly need to go outside the base all week and with luck he would be able to avoid her completely. True, Thea wouldn't be able to come to stay but, what with Percy and the puppy, Thea's visits these days were very few and far between. George didn't realise that this was mainly because Thea instinctively preferred to fight the battle on her own territory and Percy and Jessie had given her the excuse to do just that. He missed her midweek visits but latterly he had been so terrified that Felicity might turn up whilst Thea was there that he had been a bundle of nerves, quite unable to enjoy her company. It was almost a relief when she said that she couldn't come. For George, the appointment was the chance he had been looking for, the turning point, and he decided to keep his head down and wait to see what happened.

Tim, on the other hand, had no intention of being so patient. Waiting to see what might turn up was not the way he worked. Tim was like Rabbit. He never let things come to him but always went and fetched them. Hermione's letter had shown that she was very worried about Thea and George and that she expected him to do something about it. She had left him Broadhayes and all that she had;

sorting out Thea was the least he could do to repay her. Apart from that, he was extraordinarily fond of Thea, looking upon her as a younger sister and feeling a sense of responsibility for her. Unfortunately, Hermione's letter had not been too clear for she was intending to tell him the details when he arrived back from America. However, what was clear was that this Felicity Mainwaring was the fly in the ointment and needed to be dealt with, and Tim already had an idea how this might be achieved.

When the funeral was over he went back to London to visit David Porteous, the artist he had met in America with his daughter Miranda, in the hopes of furthering this plan. To Thea he said not a word. He wanted to see the situation for himself, to meet George and to determine just how the land lay. Tim wanted to settle at Broadhayes, run his computer business from home and marry Miranda. However, he felt honour-bound to deal with Thea's problem before he could enter fully into his inheritance and he had no intention of wasting time.

For Felicity, life had narrowed into one thought: to win George back. So obsessional had she become that she couldn't see that her behaviour was much more likely to make George hate her than love her. She lived for her trips to London, planning them in advance, deciding what to wear and inventing series of conversations which she and George would have when she arrived. Back at home she spent hours walking from room to room, staring out of windows, willing the time to pass until the next meeting. She managed to block out the fact that George dreaded the sight of her, convinced that time would bring him to his senses and they would be together again. If only he would touch her. She was sure that once she broke down the physical barrier he would respond to her as he had done in the past. She steadfastly ignored the truth that a man with a twenty-five-year-old wife would be unlikely to prefer a forty-five-year-old mistress. She stuck rigidly to her diets, made regular visits to the hairdresser and clung to the belief that an experienced older woman must be more exciting than an inexperienced young one. In the early spring, she sensed a slight relaxing in George's attitude and began to hope anew. Since he hadn't mentioned his new appointment to her, she had no idea that his move to Northwood was offering him a way out and, naturally, he didn't tell her. So she waited, feeding herself on tiny scraps of comfort, encouraging hope out of words and gestures that she magnified and distorted so as to build up nourishment out of a meagre allowance of the last remains of George's affection for her. So Felicity had survived the winter. Now it seemed that George was beginning to respond and Felicity prepared to redouble her efforts which would bring her the results for which she had schemed and planned for so long.

IT WAS POLLY WHO found Thea the agent through whom she hoped to sell her work. Her illustrated stories of Percy the Parrot were coming on apace and Thea had found great satisfaction and comfort in having something positive to be working at and thinking about. She had let Polly into the secret and Polly had been rendered speechless as she looked at the sketches and read the stories.

'They're delightful,' she said at last. 'Absolutely charming. Honestly, Thea, I wouldn't have believed it. These drawings are so professional. We must get someone to look at them. I'm sure they'll be an absolute hit.'

'D'you really think so?'

'I certainly do. Paul may know someone.'

'Paul? Surely it's not his sort of thing at all?'

'No, no. But he's written lots of papers and a book and heaven knows what, and they all have to be published. He can probably tell us where to start. He may be a boring old turd but he does have occasional uses.'

'He isn't at all boring. When I met him at Hugh's christening I thought he was very nice. You can't fool us any more now that we've met him.'

'Well, naturally he was on his best behaviour in front of Harriet and Michael. Me being godmother to Hugh and so on. You saw his social side. Tremendous effort for him, poor old duck. He had to go to bed for a week afterwards to recover. He starts getting withdrawal symptoms if he can't pore over a microscope at least once an hour.'

'You're hopeless. I thought he was very nice.'

Polly made a face as if execrating Thea's taste and returned to the stories. 'Leave it to me,' she said. 'Honestly. These are terrific.'

A few weeks later she telephoned. 'Thea? Listen. I've found you an agent. I've had a quick chat and described your stuff and he wants to talk to you.'

Thea clutched the receiver. 'Gosh,' she said at last. 'Oh, Polly.'

'I know. Exciting, isn't it? I've got his telephone number here somewhere. Hang on a minute.' Thea could hear paper being shuffled. 'Jesus!'

Polly's voice changed and Thea held her breath in suspense for a moment.

'What is it?'

'My dear.' Polly's voice was awestruck. 'There's a mother blackbird sitting on the fence stuffing the largest worm you ever saw down the throat of one of its young. It's quite incredible.'

'Polly!'

'Yes. Sorry. Quite distracting. Got a pen? Here it is.' She read the name and number twice. 'OK? Get on to him at once. He's expecting a call. Let me know how it goes. 'Bye.'

It had gone better than Thea had dared to hope and she had sent off some work for the agent, Marcus Willby, to see. He was very impressed and started to approach publishers. Thea waited to hear the result; hoping for a miracle, her heart jumped whenever the telephone rang or the postman called. However, when the telephone rang a few weeks after George had gone to Northwood, it was not Marcus but Felicity.

'Hello, Thea,' she said. 'Long time no see. How's everything?'

'Fine.' Thea pulled herself together quickly. 'We're fine.'

'Good. Just thought I'd see how you were. I must pop over some time. I've been so busy. Still. I expect you're glad not to be having to trek up and down to London any more. That awful flat. And that bed!

I've never slept in anything so uncomfortable. Anyway. Glad you're OK. When I've got a moment we'll get together. I'll telephone. See you.'

The line went dead and after a moment Thea replaced the receiver. Felicity's words seemed to go on ringing in her brain. 'And that bed! . . . I've never slept in anything so uncomfortable . . . And that bed! . . .' So it was true. What she had held out against, never really allowed herself to believe, was true. She sat on at the table, quite still, until she realised that she was deadly cold. Rising stiffly, she crossed to the Rayburn and pushed the kettle on to the hotplate. She folded her arms across her breast as though shielding herself from a blow and looked at Percy.

'I always trusted him, you see,' she said. 'Somehow I just couldn't believe he would. I trusted him.'

Percy listened to her consideringly and then spoke in Hermione's voice. 'Put not your trust in princes, nor in any child of man, for there is no help in them.'

Thea's face crumpled and she covered her face with her hands. 'Oh, G.A.,' she whispered. 'How could you die when I needed you?' And she burst into tears.

Ten

AS SPRING PROGRESSED SLOWLY into summer, Tim was not the only person to realise that Thea was very unhappy. He was, however, the first person to take positive action. George found himself at a loss. At last he had managed to shake himself free of Felicity—hadn't seen her for weeks—and suddenly Thea was behaving most strangely. She seemed to be evading him in some subtle way that he found difficult to analyse. She had lost that openness that he had loved and he began to be afraid. It had occurred to him that, if he were to be no longer available to Felicity, she might well turn her attention to Thea but how was he to find out if this were, indeed, the case? So upset was he, however, by Thea's distancing herself from him that he did actually manage to bring himself to the point.

'Seen anything of Felicity lately?' he asked in what he hoped was a light casual tone.

They were sitting on the platform reading the Sunday papers in the warm May sunshine and Thea lowered the Review pages to give him a look of such serious intensity that he almost quailed in his chair.

'I haven't seen her for months.'

She seemed to stress the word 'seen' and his mind flew about wondering what she was implying.

'Neither have I,' he protested quickly. And realised that in making it a protest he had admitted some form of accusation.

She raised her eyebrows a little as if indicating indifference and this detachment was so unlike the warm impulsive girl he had fallen in love with that he couldn't keep back a low inarticulate cry or from stretching a hand to her.

'It's time that you went to fetch your mother,' Thea said quickly, ignoring the gesture. 'She gets so anxious if you're late. I must get on with the lunch.'

She laid her paper aside and went indoors and George sat for a moment, shocked by her rebuff. It was so unlike her, so studied an evasion, that he realised he must take some positive action. It was clear that now was the time to tell her what had happened in the past and in London and to lay Felicity's ghost to rest once and for all. Something had happened to do away with her trust in him and he couldn't afford to lose it—or her. The mere thought of it brought him to his feet and carried him into the kitchen.

'Thea,' he began, his voice loud with fear and hastily summoned courage, then paused.

She was talking to a short thickset man who was making a fuss of Jessie and admiring Percy, who danced excitedly up and down on his perch. She turned to him and the man straightened up and smiled expectantly.

'George, this is Freddie Spenlow. Jessie's breeder. I asked him to pop in and have a drink and run an eye over Jessie. He's going to stay to lunch. Isn't that fun?' She was talking quickly as if to avert or avoid some interruption. 'You must go and get Esme,' she added to George, as the two men shook hands and murmured politely. 'I'll get Freddie a drink.'

She gave George a light kiss and he found himself going out and getting into the car and was halfway to Tavistock before he let himself face the fact that had been apparent from the first moment he'd entered the kitchen. Freddie Spenlow was in love with Thea. George swore under his breath as he drove through the narrow lanes and wondered if this could be the reason for the change in Thea. Had she suspected or been told the truth about Felicity and turned to a younger man? George swore again and struck the wheel with the palm of his hand, cursing himself for not telling her the truth right at the beginning. She had been so loving then, so generous. Why, oh why had he let it all get so out of proportion, let Felicity get her foot in the door? Now, looking at it in retrospect, it all seemed very simple and straightforward and he felt despair that he should have taken risks with Thea's love by behaving in such a dilatory and pathetic way. He pondered on that slightly emphasised word 'seen'. Had Felicity written to Thea? Or telephoned her in her rage and told her everything? It was the risk he'd taken when he'd moved without telling her that he was going. It had been a premeditated rejection and all he could hope was that Felicity would finally accept that the affair was over. He should have known better. He felt quite certain now that, to spite him, Felicity had told Thea about the past affair and her visits to London and probably other things; other things that were not necessarily true but that Thea might believe.

Suddenly George realised that he was sweating and that his palms on the wheel were sticky. Just suppose that Thea, believing whatever calumnies Felicity had chosen to invent, had turned to this dog-breeder, this Freddie? George took a deep breath and made an effort to control his rampaging thoughts. The clear cold calculating part of his brain told him that Thea would never deceive him and, if she were seriously attracted to Freddie, she would hardly invite him to drinks or lunch. Freddie might have fallen in love with Thea but it by no means followed that Thea returned these feelings. Somehow he must put the matter right, tell her the absolute truth about himself and Felicity, explain his fears and failings and then all would be well. Thea was not the sort to love lightly or to throw away all that they had for no good reason. It was his job to make absolutely certain that she knew there was no good reason, no reason at all.

He swung the car into the cul-de-sac where his mother now lived and watched her come hurrying out of the small bungalow. He rejected the thought of unburdening himself to her. It wasn't simply that he felt she shouldn't be worried. He couldn't bear the idea that she should know he'd made a mess of things. He'd been handed heaven on a plate and had practically lost it, given it away. He could imagine her expression and the few well-chosen remarks she would employ and knew that he couldn't cope with them. It was enough to know that he was a fool without other people telling him about it. George straightened his shoulders and arranged a smile on his face as his mother peered at him through the windscreen. Lunch was going to be hell.

TIM, ON THE OTHER hand, was moving into action. He had visited Thea and George and found himself puzzled. George seemed very much the devoted husband and it was Thea who was uncharacteristically brittle, holding them at arm's length, chattering brightly. When she thought herself unobserved her eyes were bleak and Tim could only assume that things must be as his grandmother had written to him but that George and Thea had no intention of letting the outside world see the cracks in what had apparently been a happy relationship. Nevertheless, Tim came away quite sure that George was still in love with Thea and that it was the 'other woman' who was causing the problems. Felicity must be removed. He had no doubts at all about Thea. He could feel her unhappiness behind the façade and he knew her well enough to know that once she loved nothing would change her. And he knew that she loved George. She had written to him in the early stages of the courtship, describing George in glowing terms and her own feelings with an authenticity that had made Tim almost envious. Hermione had confirmed it all in later letters. No, it was Felicity who was causing the rift and she must be dealt with before the damage became irreparable.

Tim was a straightforward young man who disliked muddle. He was by nature a communicator and liked everything open and aboveboard, preferring to sit down and discuss a minute difference or disagreement rather than let it get out of hand. He knew that Thea was like him in this respect and was surprised that she had let things go so far. He considered having the matter out with both of them, bringing it all into the open, but rejected the idea on the grounds that he did not know the background well enough. The fact that he had just fallen in love himself made him rather more sensitive than usual and he decided on a more circuitous route. On his return from London he sent Mrs Gilchrist—who had agreed to stay on to look after him—on a long, well-deserved rest to her sister and sat back to await his guests.

A few days later, David Porteous climbed stiffly out of the little car and stood gazing appreciatively at the small granite manor house that was Tim's inheritance.

'Delightful!' he cried to his daughter, who was emerging from the driving seat. 'Absolutely charming!'

The words could easily have applied to David himself. Not over-tall and a little on the rotund side, he exuded an air of cheerful expectation that life was going to be good to him and if it wasn't scheduled for today, well—you could almost see the shrug, the rueful smile—tomorrow would do just as well. From the top of his silver head to his well-polished shoes he looked ready for action and as Tim hurried out of the front door to greet them his heart lifted almost as much to see David, dressed as usual in very old flannels and an even more ancient navy-blue guernsey and waving enthusiastically, as it did to see Miranda.

'Tim!' David crossed the gravel to shake Tim's hand. 'What a generous invitation! I'm delighted to be here. And what a delightful house!'

'Isn't it? I'm so glad you agreed to come, David. I'm really going to need you to help me sort out this problem I've been left with.'

'My dear chap!' David opened innocent blue eyes. 'Sounds most exciting.'

'He is not to be excited or overtired.' Miranda received Tim's welcome coolly. 'He's had a very bad strain of flu and he must rest.'

David drew down the corners of his mouth in mock gravity at Tim, who winked back.

'Of course he must!' Tim picked up two suitcases which Miranda had produced from the car. 'I've lit the fire in the library in case you find the house cold. These old places never seem to warm up even in the hottest weather. Come on in. I'm sure you're both dying for a drink.' He headed for the front door, followed with alacrity by David.

Miranda shut the car doors and, carrying other pieces of luggage, followed more slowly. Her face wore a troubled expression. She had none of her father's tolerance and optimism and tended to see life in black and white with very few shades of grey. She had fallen quite desperately in love with Tim but was behaving in a very restrained manner towards him until she was absolutely certain of his intentions. She knew that her extremely moral Scottish mother had had one or two problems with her easy-going father and she had no intention of suffering in the same way. Yet it was Tim's very eagerness and enthusiasm, his thick untidy fair hair and twinkling eyes, that had attracted her. What he saw in her she was not yet sure.

In fact, Tim had fallen in love with them both. He added David's charm, generosity and kindness to Miranda's ethereal, fair, fine-boned prettiness and they made a most attractive whole. He had hardly been alone with her as yet and this visit was designed to let everyone get to know each other. However, Thea's problem was very much at the forefront of his mind and, being Tim, he wanted to get it out of the way before he settled down to his own affairs. By the end of the weekend very little else but Tim's idea had been discussed and after supper on Sunday they went into the library to try to finalise it.

'Well, what about it, David? Think you can handle it?' Tim leaned back in a huge armchair, covered with a shabby, faded chintz, and stretched his long legs out to the fire. 'As I see it, we need someone on the inside to find out the exact situation.'

David, sitting forward in a similar chair, had drawn his feet well in, ankles crossed, knees apart. His forearms rested along his thighs and his eyes were fixed on the brandy glass which he turned thoughtfully in his fingers.

'It seems easy enough,' he admitted, 'the way you put it. If somewhat drastic. But I wonder, dear boy, whether you have too much faith in me. Don't get me wrong! I'm flattered. Very! But, you know . . . don't want to let the side down, d'you see?'

'Rubbish!' exclaimed the redoubtable Tim, leaning forward to top up David's glass from the decanter. 'That's quite out of the question! You're absolutely the right man for the job. Isn't he, Mirry?' He appealed to the small figure curled up on the sofa amidst well-worn silk cushions.

'I think that it's all nonsense.' This had been her uncompromising attitude from the start and she had refused to join in with the conspirators. 'You have no right to interfere with other people's relationships, whatever you may suspect.'

'But I've told you umpteen times it's not a question of suspicion or hearsay. Thea actually told Grandmother what was happening. They hadn't been married a year when this woman was trying to get him back. Come on! Surely you have some sympathy for the poor girl!'

'And I've told you, Tim, that it's not a question of sympathy. You're so dramatic. OK. So Thea told your grandmother these things and you, being fond of Thea and being her cousin and all that, automatically assume that she's totally in the right and George is totally in the wrong. Why did George hurry back to his mistress so quickly? If Thea is so delightful and charming why should he go back to a woman who, according to our evidence, is a raddled old cow? You shouldn't interfere. You might do even more damage.'

There was silence. David looked at Tim out of the sides of his eyes, Miranda sat back farther in the corner of her sofa clutching a cushion to her chest and Tim, who had got up to stride about in order to declaim the better, stood for a moment, baffled, thrusting his fingers through his thick fair hair.

'Could she be right?' he demanded.

David shrugged, pulling down the corners of his mouth in his characteristic way. 'Can't say, old boy. Might be. Her mother always was.'

'How very irritating for you!' Tim, jealous for his lovely plan, was only half joking.

'Absolutely! Scottish, you know. John Knox has a great deal to answer for, in my opinion.'

'Oh, honestly!' Miranda cast aside her cushion and stood up. She made her way to the fire and perched on the edge of the big wooden club fender where, in the past, Thea had loved to sit. 'Look! I'm not saying anybody's right or anybody's wrong. All I am saying is, let's not rush in like bulls in a china shop. I know you feel that you can't enter into your inheritance until this is settled . . .'

'I'm not rushing in! I'm sending David to do a recce,' interrupted Tim. 'And it's nothing to do with my inheritance. Not really. It's Thea herself. She's obviously unhappy however she may try to hide it and I'm very fond of her.'

'So you keep saying,' remarked Miranda bleakly.

David looked up. He eyed his daughter thoughtfully and then turned to Tim. 'Got an idea. Before we do anything why don't you get Thea over? For lunch, say. Once we've met the girl we'll probably feel like you do. Always helps to know the people you're talking about, d'you see? What d'you say?'

'Well, I could.' Tim stood, considering. 'I shall have to ask her over soon anyway to meet you. She'll be a bit hurt otherwise . . .'

'Mustn't have that,' observed Miranda somewhat tartly but Tim was too preoccupied to notice.

'OK. We'll back off a little and get Thea over. You'll love her.'

'Naturally,' muttered Miranda as Tim left the room in search of a telephone.

David studied his daughter's bent head. 'Darling!'

'What?'

'It's showing.'

'What's showing?'

'Little green-eyed monster. Not very attractive.'

'I dislike her intensely already.'

'Nonsense. He's just sorry for the poor girl.'

'Oh, don't you start. "Poor girl!" She sounds an absolute wet!'

'Poor darling! You have got it bad.'

'I haven't got anything. And don't patronise me!'

David pretended to duck, throwing up his hands in protection, and after a moment Miranda smiled unwillingly.

Tim was back looking pleased with himself. 'She's coming to lunch on Tuesday. That's great. It means we can get on. Now, who would like another drink?'

Eleven

MAGGIE TABB, THEA'S CORNISH cleaner, emptied the contents of the red plastic bucket into the sink and turned the taps on full. Thea, sitting at the kitchen table trying to read her letters, wished that she'd use the sink in the utility room but knew she'd be wasting her breath suggesting it. When Maggie was in voluble mood nothing stopped the spate. Somehow, since the spring-cleaning, Maggie had continued to come and Thea found that she liked having her around. It was a strange alliance but Thea knew that Maggie was on her side and Maggie knew that if she needed help to fill in official forms or someone to back her up with those in authority, the 'missis' would help her. She poured out her problems to Thea and listening to them helped Thea to keep her own troubles in perspective.

Having filled the bucket, Maggie lifted it with strong muscular arms and stood it on the floor. She pushed back her improbably red, wiry hair, showed Thea her crooked teeth and took breath for the second instalment.

'So I ses to Normin, "Yewer still me 'usbin, never mind thet yew've gone off wiv that ol' surfboard chin." An' now 'e wants me FIS, see! So I tells 'im, "'Twas fer wen 'ee wadden earnin' much," an' I ses, "'tent fer 'ee, 'tes fer me an' ower Wayne, 'tes fer wives an' kids, not fer 'usbins who've gawn off wiv some tart." If et 'adden bin fer me an' Wayne 'e wudden 'ev bin edible fer it, see? If 'e don' wanna ac' like a faither an' a 'usbin any moer 'e don' get no FIS! See!'

'I should think not.' Thea, who had been distracted for a moment by the imprint stamped on one of the envelopes, smiled quickly at Maggie lest she should feel that she wasn't concentrating. That worthy, sensing that she had temporarily lost her audience, smiled back unresentfully.

'Mister's gone, 'n? Well, I'll do the baffroom 'n' clear out 'is dressin' room. What do 'e fink o' thisyere lil ol' burd, 'n?'

'Oh, I think he likes Percy very much, actually. I'm hoping we'll teach him some new sayings.'

' 'E's right priddy, en 'e? Percy, 'n? 'Tis a funny ol' name fer a parrit.'

'I suppose it is. I must admit I hadn't thought about it, I've known him for so long. What would you call a parrot, if you had one?'

'Dunno.' Maggie stared in at Percy, who stared unwinkingly back at her.

'Shall I compare thee to a summer's day?' he asked her suddenly and Maggie burst out laughing.

' 'E's a real laugh, 'n? 'Oo's a priddy boy, 'n? 'Ere! 'ev anuvver grape!'

She passed one through the bars and, collecting dusters and polish, went out leaving Thea to open her letters in peace.

Barely able to contain her excitement, she tore open the envelope that bore her agent's imprint and drew out a letter. She had to read it three times before she took it in and when she had she fled with it to George's little study, shutting the door behind her. She quickly checked the number, dialled and heard a click and then the sound of Marcus Willby's voice. After a moment Thea realised that she was listening to one of the new answering machines and slammed the receiver down in a panic. Feeling that she would burst if she didn't speak to someone, she tried Polly's number, but there was no reply and she replaced the receiver. She read the letter again.

They loved her stories and the drawings, wanted to publish them and asked if she had any thoughts for further work in this direction. She felt a mixture of excitement, terror and a strange new sensation. It was as though a new part of her were emerging, a hitherto unknown Thea, a Thea who could produce something that was viewed with admiration by a body of professionals. The letter implied that she had a future, a career, and that she might become important to them. It was such a revelation that she couldn't take it in and, in the end, was obliged to go outside and walk up and down the platform. She longed to tell George but something made her wait until the thing was finalised. She wanted to produce it as a fait accompli, knowing that it would give her extra strength in the fight against Felicity. She felt quite sure that George had no intention of leaving her for Felicity and, lately, that he had been trying to make an opening to discuss the situation. So far she had held him off. Once she would have welcomed the opportunity to have it all out in the open but that was at the beginning when she felt strong and safe in George's love and had thought that the affair was over. When she realised that he was seeing Felicity again she had felt a terrible fear. If she couldn't hold him at the beginning of the marriage, how could she hope to later? Her confidence was badly dented and, with G.A.'s death on top of it all, she had felt herself lost. Felicity's telephone call had been the last straw. Yet George was behaving as though the whole thing was over. He seemed more relaxed than he had for some while and it was very clear that he still seemed to love her, to need her.

Nevertheless, there was something, some indefinable obstacle that prevented absolute oneness and Thea knew that it must be done away with completely. Now she felt that this could be achieved only when she and George could approach each other on equal terms. At the very beginning Thea had felt that love was the only criterion and that by giving all she had she would automatically defeat any attempts to destroy or undermine their happiness. She had come to believe that this was no longer the case and that she was fighting some shadowy battle with a very clever opponent who never showed herself clearly. But now Felicity had declared herself with all the strength of a twenty-year relationship with George behind her and Thea had only herself, unformed, untried. It was important that she waited until she was in a stronger position before she struck back and now she had something more, something positive to add to her inner strength and faith, and she intended to use it. She stood for some moments, the letter still clutched in her hand, watching the swallows wheeling and diving above her head, and a great feeling of power surged in her. She felt that she had been given her weapons, good weapons: self-worth and achievement added to love and understanding, and she could begin to feel the ground sure and firm beneath her feet.

She went back into the kitchen where Maggie, now employed in dusting the kitchen dresser, turned to look at her enquiringly. Thea grinned at her. She longed to tell Maggie the news but didn't feel that she should mention it to anyone until she had talked to Marcus. However, she couldn't help the happiness that welled inside her overflowing a little and her grin widened. Maggie waited expectantly. Thea shook her head.

'Sorry. Just a letter with some good news. Don't mind me. I'll make some coffee.'

She pushed the kettle on to the hotplate of the Rayburn and assembled the necessary materials, singing to herself in her rich contralto voice.

' 'Er's 'appy,' observed Maggie to Percy, whose cage stood on a bamboo table alongside the dresser. 'Nice, innit?'

'The nicest child I ever knew was Charles Augustus Fortescue,' said the parrot in roundly modulated tones and gave a loud squawk.

'Thet ol' auntie o' yewers musta bin a right caution.' Maggie took down a bone china handpainted cup and cradled it tenderly in her large red hands as she dusted it.

'She was.' Thea smiled at Maggie. She had no fears for her precious things; nothing could have been gentler than those unlikely-looking extremities and Maggie cherished the things as if they were her own. 'I feel that she's here with me at times. Percy says things in her voice and it's quite uncanny. I think that he really brings me good luck. Things are beginning to get better since he arrived.'

Maggie, who knew a great deal about Thea's affairs one way and another, replaced the cup and smiled at Percy. ' 'Ear thet, bwoy? Right lil ol' drop o' sunshine yew be, 'n?'

When Maggie had gone home and Thea had once more, without success, tried to speak to Marcus Willby, she began to gather her belongings together, watched by Percy.

'I can hardly believe it,' she told him. 'It's unbelievable. And it's all because of you, Percy.' She passed him a peanut through the bars. 'You're my good luck mascot. I feel I can do anything with you around! I must dash! I'm going to have lunch with Harriet.' She hurried out.

FELICITY WAS AT HER wits' end. The trip to London, which had led to a complete stranger opening the door of George's flat and telling her that Commander Lampeter had moved without leaving a forwarding address, had been such a shock that she was still trying to recover from it some weeks later. It had been rage, humiliation and sheer fear that had made her telephone Thea and say that unforgivable thing which she hoped would destroy Thea's peace of mind. As for herself, she felt completely adrift and she spent the days once more in endless wanderings: out into the garden, back to the house to make a cup of coffee, upstairs into little-used rooms, staring mindlessly out of the windows. She went on unnecessary shopping trips to Tavistock and telephoned one or two friends, hoping to pass some time in someone else's company. It was unfortunate that so many people were away on holiday and others were tied up with their children home from school. Felicity remembered Cass's look of compassion and her spirit seemed to shrivel within her. One morning, having had a telephone call from Book Stop to say that the book she had ordered had arrived, she decided to drive into Tavistock to collect it and to pass an hour or so.

Felicity's garden gate opened on to a nearly disused track where, having no garage, she parked her car. To her surprise a man was seated to the side of the track with an easel before him and the paraphernalia of the artist around him. He rose to his feet and smiled at her.

'Good morning. I do hope that you don't object.' He gestured at the easel. 'It's such a lovely setting that I simply couldn't resist.'

Felicity nodded rather ungraciously and went to her car, noticing that he'd parked his own car as unobtrusively as possible. She was used to cars slowing in the lane to admire the charm of the cottage, which was an old Devon longhouse set in a background of tall beech trees. There was none of the usual cottage prettiness about it, instead there was an uncompromising austerity about the stone walls and heavy thatch. Felicity had had the good taste to keep the cobbled yard as unadorned as possible and had resisted the hanging baskets and tubs that her friends assured her would 'liven the place up'. The enclosing walls were covered with pennywort and ivy-leaved toadflax and at the back a small lawn, hedged with fuchsia and escallonia, made a perfect, private spot for sunbathing.

Tavistock was fairly quiet on this sunny morning. Felicity collected her book, stopping to browse a little in the bookshop, bought a few things in Crebers and turned her steps to the Bedford Hotel for a cup of coffee. Her heart gave a little plunge when she saw Kate sitting in the corner but she gave her a nod as she went up to the bar to order. There was nothing for it but to join her and Kate smiled welcomingly enough. After all, she and Kate had always been friendly until Kate's marriage had broken up and George had begun to show an interest in her. It had come to nothing but Felicity had never totally trusted her since. The real obstacle to the friendship had always been the fact that Cass and Kate were so close.

Kate had dressed with her usual indifference to style or fashion and Felicity gave an involuntary little click of the tongue, signifying her disapproval.

'How's it going?' Kate, moving her tray so that Felicity could share the table, registered the click with amusement.

'Oh, not too bad. You?'

'Struggling on. Thankful that the boys have taken their finals and might be able to get out and earn some money.'

Felicity looked at her. It had never occurred to her to wonder how Kate coped, all alone except when the boys were home or her brother Chris, who used the house as a base, was in the country. After the divorce, Mark Webster had gone to live in Canada, leaving Kate to fend for herself and the twins, and, quite unexpectedly, Felicity found herself remembering a time when they had all been young together.

'Remember the house in Solent Way?' she asked impulsively and Kate looked at her in surprise.

'I do indeed. You helped me find it. It was like paradise after that ghastly quarter in Eastney.' Kate shook her head and smiled reminiscently. 'It was a good summer, that one.'

'Yes.' Felicity poured herself some coffee. She felt the oddest sensation and one she wasn't at all used to. She wasn't one for looking back or glamorising the past but just for a moment those shared times seemed infinitely precious. She looked at Kate, experiencing again the feelings of that younger Felicity, strong, positive, grabbing at life which seemed, in those days, to be so full, so exciting, not the defeating empty existence that it was now.

Kate was watching her. 'It's the music that gets me,' she said unexpectedly. 'Pop music. You switch the radio on and they're playing something that takes you straight back. Smells, feelings, pain, joy, whatever. It's all there. Noël Coward was right when he said there was nothing so potent as cheap music. It doesn't happen with Mozart or Brahms. I heard Paul McCartney singing "Yesterday" a few days ago and found that I was crying my eyes out.'

'Don't!' said Felicity fiercely. She swallowed hard several times and her lips trembled.

'Sorry.' Kate covered the thin hand with her own. 'But you can't deny the past, Felicity. It's part of us. It's helped make us what we are. How's George?'

The question pulled Felicity together as nothing else could. She and Kate stared at each other.

'It's over,' said Felicity and she pressed her lips together and tears filled her eyes as she continued to stare at Kate. 'Don't tell Cass,' she said desperately and covered her face with her hands as she heard her pathetic plea ringing in her ears.

Kate looked with compassion on the bowed black head and leaning forward topped up the coffee cups.

'It's the last thing that Cass would be thinking about,' she said gently. 'Tom's been appointed to Washington. Captain of British Naval Staff. You knew he'd been promoted? He's off in a couple of weeks. Cass is hanging on to get Gemma off to boarding school and then she's following him out. She's trying to let the Rectory.'

Felicity blotted her eyes carefully and felt an enormous relief. 'You must think me an absolute fool.'

'Of course I don't. Do you realise that we've known each other for twenty years?' Kate smiled at her and, after a moment, Felicity smiled back. 'Must count for something. If you can cope with the twins you're very welcome to come back for lunch. They'll be here in a minute.'

'I'd love to come. But not today. Thanks. Perhaps I could phone.'

'I wish you would. I get lonely, too, you know.'

'Yes.' She accepted Kate's admission, suspecting that it had been offered to help her over that awful moment of weakness earlier, and was grateful. 'Thanks. I'd better be on my way.' She stood up, picked up her bag and the shopping and hesitated. 'Thanks, Kate.'

'Don't forget to phone.'

'No, I won't. I really won't.'

'See you then.'

As she went out she passed a tall dark young man on the steps. He gave her an indifferent glance and Felicity's heart gave a great bump. It was a few moments before she realised that what she had thought was a reincarnation of a youthful Mark Webster must be one of Kate's twins. What must it be like to have such a constant reminder of a not very happy past?

As Felicity parked her car at the end of the track, she saw that the artist was still there. She regarded him more closely this time, noticing that the cord trousers and navy-blue guernsey were good quality, if old, and that he had donned a floppy linen hat to keep the sun off. Their earlier exchange had already elicited the fact that his voice was that of a gentleman and he had charming manners. He seemed to be in his late fifties. He was sitting, now, on his little collapsible chair with his arms folded across his chest, staring at the scene before him. He had evidently made a start although, at this angle, she couldn't judge the results. She had to pass in front of him to get to her gate set in the low stone wall and decided to smile at him pleasantly, if not absolutely welcomingly. His response was gratifying for he raised the hat and made an attempt to rise.

'Please don't get up,' she said at once. 'I don't want to disturb you but I do have to come in and out, you know.'

She was rather surprised at her effort at good humour. She was still feeling very emotional after her meeting with Kate and all she wanted to do was go inside and put her thoughts in some sort of order. She realised that the artist was smiling at her and making some reply to her remark and suddenly she felt afraid of being alone, of brooding, of confronting her future.

'Would you like a cup of coffee?' she asked abruptly. 'You must be getting rather hot sitting there?' Am I mad? she asked herself. Inviting a perfectly strange man in for coffee! He's probably a homicidal maniac! Well, who cares?

'How extraordinarily kind!' He was looking at her in gratified amazement. 'But I really mustn't trespass on your hospitality. I have a flask, you know.'

'Oh, a flask!' She dismissed his flask contemptuously. 'Flask coffee is abominable. Come on in and have a fresh cup. Mind you, I shall demand a look at the finished work!'

He bowed. 'I shall be delighted for you to see it. Perhaps I should introduce myself.' He fumbled in his back pocket, produced a card and handed it to her. She studied it and her eyebrows shot up.

'Well,' she said. 'I am honoured. Come on in and we'll have that coffee.'

Twelve

POLLY SAT AT THE table, eating toast in a desultory way, listening to *Composer of the Week*—the radio was permanently tuned to Radio Three—and thinking about Thea. She was delighted for her, no question about that, but she also felt a sort of envy as though Thea's new-found achievements had underlined a certain lack in her own life. Hitherto, she had been perfectly happy listening to music, reading endlessly and being on the fringe of university life. She loved Exeter and went often to the cathedral to listen to the music and the singing. Polly was an indifferent housewife and her ability to ruin food amounted almost to genius. Paul, who despite his preoccupation with the taxonomy and population distribution of the British *Ephemeroptera* liked a comfortable and well-run home, had decided that help was needed. He discovered, through a colleague, a Mrs Bloge who was prepared to come in and do all that was necessary in the house and, for an extra sum, would prepare meals which could be put in the freezer, thereby providing a staple diet. In between, they lived on cheese and tinned soup and Paul made certain that he had a good lunch. Polly herself was totally indifferent to food and was grateful that he took such a pragmatic view of the situation. All the same, she was beginning to wonder exactly what purpose she was fulfilling in life. It wasn't as if Paul really needed her. He was so wrapped up in his work that Polly wondered whether he noticed her at all although, to be absolutely fair, he always liked to share any new discovery with her. Polly tried not to let him see that she wasn't absolutely riveted by the fact that *Ephemeridae* lay their eggs in water in summer, or that the 'nymphs'—that live underwater for anything up to two years—moult approximately twenty-seven times. She tried to look fascinated when he informed her that the adult never feeds and lives from twelve hours to one week depending on the species, resolutely resisting the urge to say, 'Why bother then?' which was the observation which had sprung most readily to her lips. That was in the early days, when she had been determined to share every tiny fact and statistic with him.

Now, try as she would, the problems surrounding the similarity of the *Leptophlebiidae* and the *Ephemerellidae* had ceased to excite her and latterly she found herself suffering from regular bouts of lockjaw in her determination to stifle her yawns lest he should feel hurt. Since he had become a Reader he had a number of research assistants with whom he could share the progress and excitements of his work. He went on field trips to collect specimens which were brought back to the lab for identification and sometimes he went to lecture at other universities. Lately, on these occasions, Polly hardly noticed that he wasn't around and it was her friendship with Thea that had made her realise what she was missing.

For years she had watched and admired Harriet and Michael's marriage. They were so happy together, so in tune. Of course, they had trained and worked together which was unusual but then the baby, Hugh, had arrived which had seemed to make the bond tighter than ever. Polly loved the way that Michael really cherished Harriet, caring for her, smoothing her way, anticipating her needs. Nevertheless, she had looked upon it as that one-in-a-million relationship that didn't have any bearing on real life. It was wonderful, enviable but a minor miracle that one didn't look for in one's own more mundane experience.

When Thea appeared on the scene, Polly had felt that here was someone to whom she could more closely relate. Her husband was also bound up in his work, committed to something which Thea could not really share. He was away for days at a time and Thea also was thrown on her own company but Polly had begun to realise that

Thea approached it quite differently. She was not content to let herself and George run quietly along on parallel lines that, however close they might be, never actually met. She was determined that the marriage was going to be a lively, important event and not just a background to George's job. Polly was very impressed with the line Thea had taken regarding Felicity. Thea had fought intelligently and now, with her book arousing such interest to give her an extra zest, Polly was quite sure that she would win.

These days when Polly returned from the Old Station House, where an air of busy fulfilment was more and more to be felt, she looked around her own home with a feeling of dissatisfaction. Her peace of mind, her ability to potter endlessly and to feel quietly content, was vanishing and she didn't know how to deal with it.

Polly sighed and began to clear away the breakfast things. She collected up the crumbs for the blackbird and, leaving the washing-up for Mrs Bloge, went to get dressed. Thea was coming up to do some shopping and they had arranged to meet at Coolings. She brushed her long heavy bob of dark hair and put on a simple white shirt with a long thick cotton skirt in an unusual terra-cotta colour. As she slipped her feet into leather sandals and looked around for her bag she kept one eye on her watch. Polly always tried to be on her way out of the house when Mrs Bloge arrived. She felt that she was despised by this tall, thin woman whose nose, chin, bosom, even knee caps jutted forward in an aggressive way. She knew that Mrs Bloge was wondering why she, Polly, couldn't look after the house herself and she felt inadequate under the humourless grey stare.

Often she would escape to a friend, who lived a couple of doors up, thus avoiding the verbal cut and thrust in which Mrs Bloge liked to revel before she got down to work. Even here Mrs Bloge bested her. She had the tact and delicacy of a bull elephant and delivered her observations, based on the obvious and the banal, with the finesse of a steam hammer and the bridling self-satisfaction of one who has just invented a brilliant epigram. This tended to leave Polly feeling even more depressed, so she was delighted to have a good reason to be waiting to leave the minute Mrs Bloge arrived in the kitchen.

Thus it was that she arrived early at Coolings and, having bought herself a drink, was very surprised to see Thea already there, sitting at a table with a dark young man.

'Look who I found in Waterstone's,' she said as Polly approached.

Freddie Spenlow smiled round at her. 'Hello,' he said, getting to his feet. 'I'm not trying to muscle in on your party. Just keeping her company till you turned up.'

'You're very welcome as far as I'm concerned.' Polly bent to kiss Thea, beamed upon Freddie and, sliding into the spare seat, raised her glass to them.

'I've been telling him my news.' Thea looked flushed and happy. 'I've sworn him to secrecy. I don't want George to know until I've signed the contract. It's lucky that he's away all week or I'd never keep it up. But when I saw Freddie I simply burst out with it.'

'I spied her poring over the books in the children's section,' explained Freddie. 'I thought she was going to tell me something else when she said she had some good news.'

Polly laughed and Thea blushed a fiery red. 'I was looking at the competition,' she said defensively. 'I'm euphoric and terrified in turn.'

'You need another drink,' said Freddie. 'Or would you like me to be on my way now?'

The girls looked at each other, eyebrows raised. Thea gave a little shrug and shook her head and Polly nodded agreement.

'You may stay,' she said graciously and Freddie smiled at her.

'Very kind, ma'am. In that case, may I buy you a drink, too?'

'Splendid fellow,' murmured Polly. She emptied her glass promptly. 'I knew that there was an excellent reason for your staying.' She looked at Thea as Freddie threaded his way to the counter. 'So. How's everything?'

'Better.' Thea seemed to think about it and then nodded. 'Yes.

Definitely better. Oh, Polly. It's so exciting. I feel so strong and positive. If Felicity showed her face now I feel I could beat her.'

'Any more telephone calls?'

'Not a word. Nothing. If only I could get that remark she made out of my mind I would say it's all over. But I can't forget it. When I think of George with her like that probably just after I'd left to come home . . .' Thea's hands clasped involuntarily.

'You've either got to forget it or have it out with him.' Polly put her hand on Thea's arm and gave it a little shake. 'I thought you said that you were going to talk to him.'

'It needs to be the right moment. I don't want to be at a disadvantage but I think it will be soon now.' Thea smiled up at Freddie, who had returned carrying three glasses. 'Lovely. Thanks. But I must remember that I've got to drive home.'

'You can come back and sleep it off,' said Polly, taking her glass. 'I'll make you pints of black coffee. We're here to celebrate and that's just what we're going to do! Here's to Thea.' She raised her glass and Freddie followed suit. 'And even more important! Here's to Thea's parrot! To Percy!'

The others said, 'To Percy,' and drank.

'Freddie's got some good news, too,' said Thea. 'We ought to drink to him as well.'

'Oh?' Polly looked at him enquiringly. 'Have you won Crufts?'

'Nothing as exciting as that, I'm afraid.' Freddie looked diffident. 'It's just that I've been taken on by a local panel of vets. When I moved down from upcountry I made quite a bit of money on my house and I've been living on it. It was nice while it lasted but I can't go on. Anyway, they've accepted me. That's all. Nothing to be compared with Thea's news.'

'Certainly it is!' said Polly bracingly. 'Well done. Will you go on breeding your bears?'

'Oh, yes. That's where the fun comes in. That's the jam on the bread and butter.'

'They're wonderful,' said Thea. 'I'm having so much fun with

Jessie. I'm coming to the conclusion that Newfoundlands simply aren't like other dogs.'

'Well, of course they aren't.' Freddie looked at Polly. 'So when are you going to have one?'

'Jesus!' Polly shook her head. 'In our little courtyard? Anyway, Mrs Bloge would have a fit at the thought of dog hairs all over the floor.'

'Who's Mrs Bloge?' asked Freddie.

'My cleaner,' said Polly glumly. 'She's a sort of latter-day Vlad the Impaler. Attila the Hun could have taken her correspondence course and learned a new trick or two.'

Thea laughed. 'Poor old Polly. Can't you sack her and find someone nice? Like my Maggie?'

'Sack her?' Polly looked so horrified that Freddie laughed, too.

'That bad, is she?'

'My dear chap,' Polly lowered her voice, 'I can see that my little word picture hasn't given you an idea of what I'm up against. She's probably the head of some sort of local mafia. If I sacked her she'd send the boys round to smash the windows and empty my dustbin into what, in moments of uncontrolled excitement, I call my garden. Let's not speak of it, please. I have my consolations. After all, Brahms is Composer of the Week. One must count one's blessings.' She looked reproachfully at Thea, who was still laughing.

'We'll think about food instead,' said Freddie comfortingly. 'And, since I've invited myself to this celebration, I insist on it being my treat.'

'I'll drink to that,' said Polly, brightening up at once. 'Oh, dear. It looks as if I have already. Oh, well. Drink up. I'll get the next ones while you decide on what you're going to eat.'

She collected up the glasses and went off. Freddie looked at Thea and, after a moment, she covered his hand with her own.

'Sorry,' he said. 'I shouldn't have come. I just couldn't resist the opportunity. Sorry.'

'Poor Freddie.' The usually lively face looked so forlorn that Thea was almost tempted to stroke the rumpled hair as if he had been one of his own Newfies. 'You mustn't let it show.'

'I know.' He rubbed his hand over his eyes, nodded and sat up straighter. 'OK. Let's concentrate on food. What do you usually have? Whatever it is, I'll have the same. For some reason I don't feel terribly hungry.'

Thirteen

FELICITY WAS HAPPY. SHE could hardly remember a time when she had felt such lightness of spirit, such a positive looking forward to each day, without it being accompanied by some niggling worry or insecurity. This new happiness was free from anxiety and it was David that she had to thank for it. He had come several times to the cottage and during the short chats over cups of coffee she had learned that he was a widower with a grown-up daughter and that he appeared to have no emotional ties. He told her that he would like to work up several sketches of the old longhouse, to do a series of watercolours, and she was delighted to accede to his request. Now, at her insistence, he had begun to join her for lunch and twice had stopped on for supper. He was rather enjoying himself. After each visit he returned to an eager Tim and a slightly scornful Miranda but, so far, there was nothing to report. Felicity never mentioned Thea or George, never seemed to have any visitors and was always pleased to see him. After his fourth visit she suggested, rather tentatively, that if he would like to see some of the countryside she would be only too happy to be his guide. With Dartmoor on the doorstep, she said, there surely must be no end of possibilities for an artist of David's reputation and it was such a pity not to take the opportunity to see it. David was inclined to agree with her and they arranged to spend a morning together exploring the lesser-known beauties of the moor. Felicity insisted on driving. It would, she said, give David chance to soak in the atmosphere and she knew the moor like the back of her hand.

To David, used to the pastoral English scenes of the home counties with their wide slow-running rivers and chalky downs, Dartmoor was a minor revelation. Each time they emerged from between the high Devon hedges and banks on to the austere landscape of the moor David was struck anew by the contrast. So many things caught the eye: a group of tall foxgloves glowing purple against a beautiful stone wall, the arch of an ancient bridge with the sun striking down on to the rushing water beneath, the tiny stunted yellow tormentil growing at the foot of a granite cross. David loved the minutiae. Not for him the great sweeps of heather or the jagged stone fists of the tors. Although he loved to look at them and to marvel at the majestic scenes amidst which they drove, when it came to painting it was the small detail which he preferred to record and their first two trips were mainly taken up in deciding what he would like to do.

By this time, David had almost forgotten his mission and was gathering exciting new ideas for an exhibition. Felicity, on the other hand, was beginning to visualise a future with David in it and began to plan cautiously ahead. It was a novel experience to be with a man who was older than she was—even Mark had been two years younger—and she was enjoying it. David was a charming companion and his ten years' seniority made her feel delightfully young, almost girlish. David liked women. He liked them as people and could understand and empathise with them and, for Felicity, this was a whole wonderful new experience. George was a kind man but David went much further than that and Felicity found herself quite at ease with him, chattering and laughing and behaving as she had probably never behaved before in her whole life. She felt free and relaxed and rather special, deferring to him in a way she had never done with Mark or George, and feeling feminine and pliable when she could give in to him. David had a delightful way of making a woman feel very desirable He managed to imply that he was quite bowled over but would never have the bad taste to suggest anything improper and it was irresistible to Felicity.

This tendency had been one of the many rocks upon which the relationship with his narrow-minded, moralistic wife had foundered but he had never quite managed to conquer it. It was so second nature to him that he rarely thought about it at all. He liked people to be happy and, in the main, women knew the rules and played along quite readily without anyone getting upset or hurt.

Felicity was taken in completely and before long David was occupying her every waking thought and quite a few of her dreams. She had all but forgotten George. Her new-found emotions for David showed her that what she had felt for George was an affection that was part habit and part fear of being alone and, in the excitement of these new sensations, she shed the old outworn passions without a backward glance. She might have been forty-seven by the calendar but at heart and emotionally she was twenty and she glowed and fizzed with love.

To do David justice, he was not aware of the depth of Felicity's feelings and would have been horrified if he'd realised that she was becoming so involved. Because he saw her at her very best he had no difficulty in imagining that she might indeed be a danger to Thea and he hoped that his presence might distract her. He had no idea of taking George's place but her attitude led him to suspect that she was very ready to devote some of her time to him. When he reported this to Tim, that young man agreed that at least it kept her off Thea's back and gave her and George a breathing space. At the moment they could do no more and David, already wrapped up in ideas for his exhibition, felt that Felicity's company was a small price to pay. Far from it, he enjoyed being with someone who treated him as if he were a cross between Turner and Robert Redford and could scarcely be blamed for taking full advantage of the situation. It never occurred to him that she could be hurt. Her reputation had led him to draw various conclusions and he decided to make the most of the next few weeks. Also, it was giving Tim and Miranda time alone to get to know each other without David feeling like a gooseberry. It worried him that Miranda was so like her mother: prickly, ready to take offence and of a jealous disposition. Perhaps Tim would deal with it better than he himself had. Meanwhile, he set off most mornings driving Miranda's little car and looking forward to another day of painting.

GEORGE STOOD ON THE PLATFORM and watched Thea strolling on the track. He had determined that the time had come to tell her the whole truth. He was no longer prepared to waste any more time in misunderstandings and had decided that he must take his chance with Thea's love and generosity. He didn't really fear that she would walk out on him, only that she would love him less. Only! He groaned to himself. Somehow he must get through it. He simply couldn't bear the distances that were stretching between them and longed with all his heart to restore to the relationship the joy and one-ness it had known at the beginning.

He raised his eyes to the hills beyond. On the highest peak a soft mist curled like smoke, forming and re-forming as the warm west wind blew it, shredded it, lifted it. Cloud shadows darkened the slopes and then moved away so that they were once again bathed in bright sunshine. The scene soothed him and quietened his terror. He looked again at Thea, who stooped to pick the wild flowers that grew along-side parts of the track. Jessie followed in her wake, jumping out at the fast-moving shadows and bouncing at bumble bees that lumbered heavily amongst the blooms. As though she guessed his thoughts, Thea turned and looked back. Her hands were full of ox-eye daisies and she stood for a moment, watching him. He raised an arm and waved to her and she made her way back to him, pausing on the track to gaze up at him as he stood above her. He reached a hand down to her and pulled her up rather than letting her use the ramp and then held her, gripping her by the upper arms, the daisies crushed between them.

'Thea.' He looked into the brown eyes nearly on a level with his own and shook his head. 'I've been a fool, Thea. I want to talk to you.'

'Come then.' She disengaged herself gently and led him to one of the seats. She put the flowers at the end and sitting down turned to-wards him as he sat beside her.

'The thing is . . .' He paused to light a cigarette and to marshal his thoughts. 'The thing is that Felicity and I had an affair. It lasted for nearly twenty years and right up to the moment that I met you. When Mark died she expected me to marry her and perhaps I should have. But I didn't want to.'

He inhaled deeply on his cigarette. 'I realised that a spasmodic affair was very different from marriage and I wasn't prepared to commit myself to it. And I didn't love her.' For the first time he looked directly at Thea. 'It's easy to say that, isn't it? It's very easy to deny things when it suits your book to do it. But it's quite true. She doesn't love me either. It had become a habit that started when we were both young. I'm not going to explain or excuse it. It was before you and it's between me and Felicity. The trouble was that I behaved very badly to her when I met you. I should have told her then, of course, but I was so afraid that she might do or say something that would ruin what we had.'

He stirred restlessly, tapping some ash to the ground. 'I behaved like a coward. I hid from her until we were married and then wrote to her. Yes, I know,' as Thea made an involuntary gesture. 'I simply couldn't bear the idea of your knowing, you see. But she came here and met you and then came to the flat in London.' He looked at Thea again. 'Nothing happened, I swear to you. Since I first met you I've never touched her.'

They looked at each other. Presently Thea turned a little, staring out across the track. George took a last lungful of smoke and threw away the stub. He watched her profile, waiting for her to speak.

'Don't you believe me?' he burst out at last. 'I know it was wrong of me. I should have told you everything from the start but honestly, nothing has happened.'

'Why are you telling me now?' asked Thea.

'Because it's between us. We're not like we were at first, like we could be. I've meant to tell you over and over again but I always lost my nerve. I'm very ashamed of myself. I haven't enjoyed facing the fact that I'm a coward.'

Thea turned to him then and touched his knee. 'I guessed anyway. No, not that you're a coward, silly. About Felicity. It didn't matter as long as it was in the past. You should have realised that. It was when I thought that you and she . . .' She stopped.

'But we didn't,' cried George eagerly. 'She turned up at the flat and I was terrified that she'd come when you were there. She tried to blackmail me into going back to her.'

'Blackmail you?'

'Oh, I know it sounds ridiculous. But when she found out that you didn't know about us she hinted at things. Things that would have sounded awful out of context.'

'Like the bed being uncomfortable?'

George stared at Thea, who had turned away again and was look-ing across to the hills. He swallowed and nodded.

'Yes, I see. That's when you changed and became so far away from me. What did she say? Or did she write?'

'She telephoned. She said that she was glad that you'd left that awful flat. That the bed was the worst she'd ever slept in. Did she sleep in it?'

'Yes,' said George flatly and Thea looked at him quickly. 'She turned up one evening saying that she'd gone to see a friend but that there was nobody there. She had one of her heads. Felicity gets these really dreadful migraines and she looked awful. She could barely stand up and I told her that she'd better stay the night. She suggested that I stay with her but I refused and spent the night at the bed and breakfast round the corner. That's the absolute truth. That's what I meant when I said that things sounded awful out of context. What must you have thought? Oh, Thea. I'm so terribly sorry. You do be-lieve me, don't you? I swear to you . . .'

Thea leaned forward and kissed him, her eyes suspiciously bright, and he strained her against him, relief and joy sweeping over him and making him tremble. He buried his lips in her hair and willed himself not to burst into howls of relieved weeping.

'You are a twit.' Thea's voice shook a little. 'It's been so awful. I believed that you'd gone back to her.'

'Oh, my God.' He held her tighter. 'Oh, Thea. I should have told you.'

'Yes, you should. All this wasted time. Oh, George, you should have trusted me.'

'I know. And then I saw you with that man and I could see that he was falling for you. I was so afraid.'

Thea sat back and gazed at him in surprise. 'What man?'

'That Freddie. The dog-breeder. I came into the kitchen that Sunday and he just had that look. I knew he was falling in love with you.'

Thea burst out laughing. 'Oh, poor Freddie. No, no. You've got it quite wrong. He's madly in love with Polly. Apparently it was love at first sight when he met her with Harriet ages ago and she's hardly aware of his existence. He told me in secret and I'm the only one he can talk to about her. He'd just been having a session when you appeared.' She started to laugh again. 'Oh, dear. Poor George. You mustn't breathe a word about it.'

'Oh, Thea. Oh, thank God. I was afraid that he might make you see that I'm just a silly old man . . .'

'No more!' Thea kissed him. 'It's all over. Finished. We're us and I love you.'

They kissed for a long moment and at last George let her go.

'I need a drink,' he said. 'I haven't got the stamina for this sort of thing any more. Would you like one?'

'Yes please. Some wine, please. It's in the fridge. And when you come back I've got something else to tell you, so don't be long.'

When he'd disappeared into the house, with Jessie trotting hopefully at his heels, Thea sighed a sigh of pure happiness and stretched long and mightily. All the feelings of fear, loneliness and depression seemed to slip away from her and she felt whole and happy. Thank God. It was all over and they could start again with no shadow between them. A sentence slipped into her mind. *Heaviness may endure for a night, but joy cometh in the morning.* Thea sent up a prayer of thankfulness and prepared to tell George her exciting news.

fourteen

THE CAR BREASTED THE hill, glided into the verge and stopped.

The young man in the car behind overtook contemptuously, driving in that particular way that some locals do during the holiday season, indicating that they are not tourists but part of the indigenous population. These people gesture impatiently when they are held up by cars from which families hang, oohing and aahing at the sight of moorland ponies or sheep with their young; delight in showing their prowess in backing up in difficult situations; clasp their heads in well-simulated despair when the town-bred visitor, in his shiny new car, hesitates in terror when faced with pulling in close to a thorny hedge or dry-stone wall to let a coach through. This particular young man had been trailing in Felicity's wake for some time unaware, since Felicity had bought her car upcountry and was indeed driving slowly to show David the sights, that he was following someone more local even than himself. Felicity had been born and bred near Tavistock, the young man had moved down from the Midlands only seven years before. He swept past them with a derisory hoot and then slowed down a little, for even he was not yet immune to the panorama that spread itself before him.

Felicity and David didn't even hear him. Rolling countryside stretched away to the sea over to the south beyond Plymouth, into the deep, thickly wooded Tamar valley and down into Cornwall to the high tors of Bodmin Moor which dominated the skyline where bulky white clouds massed. It was very hot. The sheep lay close under the

dry-stone walls in an effort to find some shade as the moor shim-
mered and glittered and ponies gathered under the shelter of the
stunted thorn trees. High above, a lark was singing in the still air, and
David realised that he was holding his breath.

'Terrific,' he murmured. 'It has everything, this county, hasn't it?
The sea, the little fields and lanes and these great hills. What con-
trasts! The lushness of the valleys and the starkness of these moors.
Magnificent. And the weather, never the same for two days running. I
can't thank you enough, Felicity, for showing me all this.' He turned
towards her, obviously moved, and gestured futilely. 'It's too much
to put into words.'

As always she was delighted by his reaction. Mark had preferred
the bright lights to rural pleasures and George never seemed to notice
anything at all unless some repair or correction was needed to improve it.

'I'm glad.' She smiled at him. 'Of course, I've known and loved it
all my life but you never take it for granted somehow. It's so nice to
have someone to share it with.' And feeling that she might be getting
a little emotional, she added, 'What about some coffee?'

It was the first whole day that they were to spend together on the
moor and Felicity had packed a picnic.

'Felicity!' David's tone was reproachful. 'Do I see a flask? I thought
that flask coffee was "abominable"!'

'So it is,' she remarked, unmoved. 'Usually. Mine's special!'

'I believe you.' David turned back to the view as Felicity manipulated flasks and cups. 'What a scene! I envy you having this on your
doorstep. Thanks.' He took the china mug and sipped appreciatively.
'You're right. It's very special.'

They laughed a little and sat in companionable silence, drinking
the coffee and letting their eyes wander over the spectacle before
them. The sun had not yet reached the height of middle day when its
light would absorb the mysterious shadows and the moor would be
exposed to its pitiless glare that emphasised the inhospitable aspects
of its landscape.

'You know,' began Felicity, screwing the top on to a Thermos, 'I've been thinking. Wouldn't it be more sensible if you were to stay overnight while you're getting your material or portfolio or whatever you call it? It seems so silly to spend all that time driving to and fro. The moor is absolutely at its best early and late and we could really take advantage of it.'

David, hearing warning bells for the first time, gazed determinedly at Devon. Devon gazed back. 'It's a most generous offer . . .' he began and knew at once that he had exhibited signs of weakness. He should have begun with a positive word like 'impossible' for Felicity was already saying things like 'not generous at all . . . would love to have you . . . felt rather lonely of late . . .'

'So difficult,' he murmured, 'don't want to hurt feelings, d'you see . . . ?'

'But you said yourself that your friend doesn't mind what you do as long as you enjoy yourself and that he's too busy setting up to work from home to be able to take you around himself. Not,' she added, with a short laugh, 'that he'd know where to take you if he's a newcomer.' For a brief second she was at one with the young man in the car. 'What did you say your friend does?'

'Oh, he's a computer programmer.' David evaded the complexities of Tim's career. 'Look. I'll tell you what. Let me put it to him. But you know what people are—invite you down, ignore you, but get hurt if you pal up with someone else. Don't you find human nature amazing?'

If Felicity did she had no intention of being sidetracked by a discussion about it.

'See what you can do. It would be such fun.' She smiled at him pleadingly and he smiled back at her, feeling a twinge of guilt. 'And it would give you plenty of time to finish your paintings of the cottage. Promise you'll try? Now.' Felicity repacked the hamper, started the car and let in the clutch. 'I'm going to show you Burrator Reservoir and then we'll find a cool shady place for lunch.'

When they arrived back in the early evening, having gone farther than they had intended, David discovered the battery on his car to be as flat as a pancake.

'I left the headlights on,' he exclaimed in despair. 'There was a thick fog over the top this morning and I needed my lights. Forgot to turn them off, d'you see? What a fool I am. Haven't got any jump leads, have you?'

Felicity, seeing events playing into her hands, denied any knowledge of jump leads and insisted that the local garage would be shut. Since she had no near neighbours to come to their assistance the solution was plain. David must stay the night. It was no trouble, she told him, she even had spare pyjamas and shaving-gear which had been her husband's (actually George's from the pre-Thea era) and she always kept several new toothbrushes in case of emergency.

David admitted defeat and followed her into the house. She showed him where the telephone was so that he could phone his friend and went away to resurrect George's proofs of passion. David found his little book, looked up Tim's number and dialled.

'Hello?' He tried to speak quietly. 'Is that you, Tim?'

'Hello, who . . . oh, David!' Tim's voice rang out suddenly in his ear. 'Thank God you've phoned. Look, a crisis has blown up here and I've got to catch the next flight out to the States. We didn't want to both disappear and let you come home to an empty house but I'd like Miranda to come with me if that's OK by you. You're well occupied at the moment, aren't you? It's only a very quick dash. I'll put you on to Mirry, OK?'

David could hear his voice talking to Miranda and then she was on the line.

'Hi, Daddy, thank goodness! Listen, Tim's boss phoned from the States, some crisis with the computer programme or something. He's got to get the next flight out. When will you get here?'

'I can't get there,' said David through lightly gritted teeth. 'I'm stuck. Car's broken down and I'm right out in the wilds.'

'Well, what will you do? Where are you phoning from? Are you at Felicity's?'

Miranda's clear voice had a carrying quality and David cocked a nervous eye at the ceiling. Felicity could be heard scurrying to and fro above like Samuel Whiskers.

'Yes, I am. I'm going to have to stay the night. Does Tim have to go?'

'Absolutely! He's still under contract and it's all terribly hush-hush. Hang on . . .' He could hear them conferring in the background. 'Tim says that we shall be away no more than forty-eight hours, so can you hold the fort?'

'Forty . . . Miranda!' David's howl of anguish was louder than he intended and, turning, he was brought face to face with Felicity who, flushed with her recent exertions, was eyeing him curiously.

'Ha ha.' He attempted a light laugh and grimaced at her, putting his hand over the mouthpiece and whispering, 'Bit of a drama going on.' She passed on into the kitchen.

'Are you still there, Daddy? Look, Tim wants me to go with him. You don't mind, do you? Thank goodness you telephoned. I wouldn't have just gone and left you a note or something but I'd packed just in case you turned up in time. There's plenty of food. You'll manage, won't you? See you, then. Take care. Tim's shouting at me to hurry. We've got to get that flight. 'Bye, then.'

The line went dead and David stood for a moment, breathing heavily through his nose. After a moment he went into the kitchen to break the news to Felicity.

Felicity bore it with remarkable equanimity. She already had a low opinion of David's friend—she had no idea that Tim was Thea's cousin—and this merely confirmed her opinion of him as a thoughtless, selfish young man. To rush off without warning, leaving a guest to fend for himself, was just what was to be expected from such a person. However, it gave her the excellent opportunity to press her case further and persuade David to stop for more than just one night. Once he'd calmed down and had a drink, he began to see the advantages of spending a few days at the longhouse although he felt a little apprehensive. However, Felicity was obviously so delighted to have him there that, as the evening wore on, David found her pleasure contagious and decided that the best thing was to relax and simply enjoy it. This was quite in tune with his temperament and they ate their supper very happily, planning an early start in the morning.

For Felicity the next week was idyllic. David was painting as he hadn't painted for years and he was overjoyed. For him, his work, the moor, Felicity's love, were all woven together in one great tapestry and he didn't separate one strand or colour from another. One evening, delighted with what he had done that day, mellowed by a delicious supper and some good wine, he caught her to him and hugged her and the next moment—afterwards he could never quite remember how—the relationship had moved on to a different level and they were lovers.

The emotional as well as the physical release seemed to add yet another dimension to his painting and he went from strength to strength. The fact that Tim and Miranda seemed to be delayed in America bothered him not at all. Having got his car into working order, he drove to Broadhayes on a day when Felicity had a lunch that she simply couldn't cancel and left a letter on the hall table, explaining that he was staying with Felicity and containing her telephone number, and collected some clothes and a few necessities.

Felicity dared not look ahead. She was living each day as it came to the absolute maximum. To wake with David beside her and to sleep with his arms around her; to lie on a sun-warmed rug beside a river, watching him absorbed and intent, while the light glanced off wet brown stones and a dipper bobbed amongst the rocks; to walk on the turf, whilst the wind pulled and tore at her clothes and a buzzard cried above her, knowing that presently she would go back to find him sheltered behind the dry-stone wall, reproducing with deft, tender strokes the texture of the crumbling stone and the springing cushions of moss that clung to it, was a kind of magic she had never known. These things had become her whole life and she did not look beyond them. David made love as he painted: intent, concentrating, with tender, loving, life-giving touches that made her feel beautiful, desirable, cherished, and she gave back to him everything she had. The moor with its ever-changing scene and majesty seemed to enter into their love until she felt that there was no one left but the two of them and David, at one with his work and the world about him, felt exactly the same.

Felicity, happy and relaxed, seemed to shed years. Her face, softer now that the grim watchful expression had gone, wore a youthful tender expression that caught at David's heart. Her eyes, dark and luminous, gazed into his with so much love that he crushed her to him, almost afraid to see the vulnerability. The sharp, birdlike movements became slow and languid and the fearful urgency which had always dominated her life slowed to a calm, patient waiting.

One morning, stopping in Tavistock to buy some fruit for their picnic, she saw Thea. She thought with shame of how she had tried to destroy Thea's happiness and went up to her and touched her on the arm.

'Felicity.' Thea looked faintly alarmed and then puzzled.

Felicity smiled at her, knowing the reason for that look. She hardly recognised herself these days either.

'Hello, Thea. How are you?'

'Fine.' Thea still looked wary. 'And you? I must say you look very well.'

'I've never felt better in my life. Is George well?'

'Yes, he is.'

Recognising and understanding Thea's hostility, Felicity was overcome by remorse and, overwhelmed as she was by her own happiness, longed to put things right.

'Look, Thea,' she began, tentatively. Apologies had never been much in Felicity's line.

Thea, seeing that she was having difficulties and knowing that she need no longer fear her, smiled a little. 'Spit it out,' she said encouragingly.

'I want to apologise for my behaviour. It was unforgivable to say what I did on the telephone. It wasn't true, you know. I wanted to hurt you because George rejected me.'

'I know.' Even now Thea frowned a little as she remembered the pain. 'George told me everything.'

'Did he? Then try to forgive me. When he met you, he tore me up and threw me away. After twenty years. It was very hard, you know.'

'It must have been. I'm sorry.' Thea smiled again. 'You look happy. I hope you are.'

'Oh, I am. Very happy.'

Felicity shook her head as if in bewilderment at her own happiness and Thea started to laugh. On an impulse the two women hugged each other.

'We'll get together soon,' said Felicity. 'Must dash. Someone's waiting for me. Give my love to George.'

'Yes. I will.' Thea watched her hurry away, still puzzled.

Felicity's heart felt full to overflowing. Everybody could be encompassed in this great love that she had found. She felt that she had discovered the secret of life and now she would never let it go.

fifteen

POLLY STARED AT PAUL across the kitchen table. He was preparing to go on a field trip and her idly expressed wish to accompany him had caused an outburst of irritation which seemed to her to be out of all proportion. Her remark had been only half serious and his reaction surprised her. He pointed out that they had discussed it when they first knew that he was going and she had said quite categorically that she didn't enjoy tagging along on these occasions. Resenting his tone and more to annoy than anything else, Polly said that she thought she might change her mind, and Paul had been moved to comment in a rather outspoken and unflattering way about her mental inconsistencies and abilities.

Now, as she stared at him, he exhaled in exaggerated self-pitying exasperation and stood up. 'Well?' His expression as he looked down at her was one of impatience.

She regarded him dispassionately. How silly and portentous he looked, as though he were a schoolmaster awaiting an explanation from some recalcitrant pupil. Polly felt a wave of dislike which almost bordered on contempt. She felt an urge to fling the contents of her mug all over his shirt front, to slap the faintly sneering lip, to jump up and down on his feet, screaming.

'Fiona will be here at any moment to collect me,' he said. There was an edge of anxiety now. 'What are you going to do? We shan't be able to wait for you, I'm afraid. You'll have to drive yourself over. I don't know where you'll stay at this late date. It's the end of August and the place will be packed.'

Polly continued to look at the long narrow face with its ill-humoured expression. His reddish hair was beginning to thin and she had the startling idea that she was looking at a stranger.

I don't like you a bit, she thought. In fact, I hate you. At this minute I actually hate you. Go and do your silly insect-hunting. I hope you fall in Slapton Ley and drown yourself. And Fiona.

'Oh, I was only joking,' she said casually, wishing that the veneer of civilisation that buried atavistic instinct hadn't prevented the outburst of violence that she had contemplated and would have enjoyed. 'I should be bored rigid.'

She noted the relief in his eyes but, as he drew breath to answer, a car horn sounded. Polly raised her eyebrows. 'Fiona,' she stated. 'Mustn't keep her waiting. Better hurry along.'

Paul's lips thinned a little at her tone and then, with a shrug, he went into the hall and picked up his case. Polly followed behind. 'Don't come out,' he said. 'I'll see you on Sunday.'

He kissed her quickly and hurried down the path. Polly saw an arm stretch across to open the door and watched Paul throw his case on to the back seat. As he got into the passenger seat his face was wreathed in smiles and he did not look back or wave. Polly made a rude face at the disappearing car, shut the door and wandered back to the kitchen, wondering what to do with the days that lay ahead. Schubert was Composer of the Week and she stood listening to a string quartet whilst she drank the rest of her coffee and tried not to think about Fiona, Paul's research assistant. She'd met her once and hadn't really taken a great interest in her. She was quiet and serious, quite pretty, and absolutely immersed in her work with Paul. Just lately, however, Polly had heard her name more frequently on Paul's lips and had begun to take notice. It was when he told her that Fiona was driving him to Slapton while the others were going in the minibus with the equipment that she had been led to make her rash remark. His reaction had been interesting and Polly continued to brood on it with part of her mind while she decided how to spend the day. She knew that Harriet and Michael had taken Hugh upcountry to visit Michael's parents and would be away for a fortnight and she didn't like to bother Thea, who was now very involved in getting the book ready for her publisher. Her friend Suzy, who lived a few doors away, was heavily pregnant and could talk about nothing but this great event and Polly simply didn't feel up to another in-depth discussion on the merits of breast-feeding.

She roamed upstairs and stared out of the bedroom window. The quiet cul-de-sac, which was a short walk from the campus, was tree-lined, the small front gardens of the semi-detached Victorian villas containing the usual quota of lilac and forsythia bushes whose leaves were now a faded dusty green. It was a soft grey day and suddenly she felt profoundly depressed. It seemed as though she were the only person in the world with no aims, no purpose, no point. Even the responsibilities which should have been hers had been delegated to Mrs Bloge.

I'm twenty-six years old, she thought. What am I going to do with the rest of my life?

She saw herself standing at this same window as the years slipped gently past and the thought filled her with a profound panic which she couldn't analyse. After all, her future might look boring but it was hardly frightening. Nevertheless, the feeling persisted and to calm herself she tried to see her life rationally and merely recalled Paul's expression when she said she'd like to go with him to Slap-ton. She tried to remember why she had fallen so madly in love with him and what had made her rush into marriage with him within weeks of passing her finals. It seemed now that they had so little in common and yet, at the time, his serious detachment from the daily round had fascinated her and her lighthearted, easy-going attitude had charmed him. She was reading English and Drama and, after their first meeting, they began to bump into each other, to meet at parties, aware of a mutual attraction, until at last Paul invited her to a dinner party given by a friend and she had returned the compliment by taking him to a production at the Northcott Theatre. She was flattered by the attention of a senior lecturer who was doing so well in his field and he mistook her enthusiasm for his subject for a genuine interest rather than the result of the first flush of infatuation.

After a year or two of marriage they had settled into a pattern. He remained immersed in his work and she was contented with her quiet round, visiting friends, going to concerts, reading. It was Thea who had sowed the seed of discontent, jolted her out of her pleasant rut. She had made Polly feel dissatisfied, as though she were missing out on something. But what to do about it? She had considered getting a job. She might find something in the university which was the obvious place to try. She imagined herself getting up each morning and hurrying off with Paul to spend her day in the library or one of the offices and the thought filled her with lassitude. Why should it be more fulfilling to do an indifferent job than to do exactly as one pleased all day? Of course, to do something that one really loved, as Thea was, would be quite different. But what would she really like to do? Nothing leaped to mind. After a bit she tried to see herself as a mother. She had watched Harriet and Suzy going through the process without the least twinge of broodiness or envy and imagined herself to be entirely lacking in maternal instinct. And now that scene with Paul had unsettled her further. Why should he be so reluctant to have her around for the week? She felt quite certain that it wasn't simply because it might be difficult to find somewhere for her to stay. The old Paul wouldn't have bothered about that. He would have left it for her to arrange and told her vaguely that he'd see her later.

Sighing deeply, Polly turned away from the window. Depression threatened to swamp her and she experienced the desire to crawl back into bed, hide under the quilt and weep gently, quietly, copiously. Or on the other hand, she could bawl loudly and messily and smash every breakable object in sight.

'PMT,' she told herself sternly and went back downstairs.

As she reached the bottom stair the telephone began to ring. She snatched it up with relief.

'Hello, Polly. I hope you don't mind me ringing. It's Freddie.'

'Freddie!' Her surprise sounded in her voice. 'How nice. How are you?'

Freddie, who had been in terror that she might say 'Who?' felt his heart bound with joy. 'I'm fine. Fine. And you?'

'Fearfully fed up. Suicidal. Paul's gone off on some insect hunt and I'm all alone for a week.'

Freddie could scarcely believe his luck. He swallowed once or twice and cleared his throat. 'The thing is,' he lied, 'I've got to pick up the books I ordered from Waterstone's. I wondered if you might be free for a bite to eat or something. I hope you don't think it's a cheek or anything . . .'

'It'd be wonderful,' Polly assured him. 'I'd love it. I was wondering what on earth to do with myself. Shall I meet you in Coolings?'

'That would be marvellous. Say twelve thirty? Would that suit you?'

'Perfect. See you then.'

Polly, her spirits rising, put down the receiver. Her anxiety about her marriage and plans for her future could be postponed for another day, possibly indefinitely, and she ran back up the stairs to change into something suitable for a lunch date.

TIM, DRIVING AT SPEED down the M5, could hardly wait to get home. He wondered now how he could have lived in Dallas for two whole years and his one thought was to get back to his inheritance. Tim was a very English man, a fact that had only truly occurred to him when he met David and Miranda at the party in Dallas. To hear David's Old Wykehamist vowels and to see Miranda's fair English prettiness was, for Tim, a revelation. They represented all that he had been separated from and he suddenly knew just how terribly he had missed it. Miranda—dressed from top to toe in Laura Ashley—had a shy reserve which charmed him at once and he sensed her relief when she realised he was English.

It had been good to go back to America with the fact of Broadhayes solidly behind him and Miranda at his side. Everyone had been delighted for him and Miranda had been made much of and looked after by colleagues' wives whilst he was working. They were staying with Tim's boss and his wife and subtly, accepted by them both without words, they became an official 'couple', neither denying the prospect of a wedding in due course, and accepting the hints and gentle allusions. Miranda was impressed to see that Tim was well thought of and much liked and, although one or two of the younger wives treated him with a proprietorial affection which she resented, there was no talk of girlfriends or anything that implied a libertine temperament. Her mother had brought her up to despise lax morals to an excessive extent. Miranda was enough her mother's daughter to have held these opinions without the added underlining and emphasis to which she was continually exposed. She loved her father but was wary and watchful of him lest he should slip. There had been several such moments and Miranda, schooled by her mother to regard niceness as weakness and kindness as foolishness, had no idea what it must be like for one of David's character to live under such a regime.

Tim, blithely unaware—as David had been before him—of the iron will beneath the pretty shy exterior, blessed his good fortune and his grandmother's generosity. It was wonderful to be going back to Devon with Miranda at his side. He had no fears at all about his ability to earn his living, especially with Grandmother's money tucked away to help out until he really got going. His spirits soared as they turned on to the A30 just west of Exeter.

'Nearly home,' he said and reached out to squeeze Miranda's hand. 'How do you feel to be coming back to Devon?'

It occurred to him that she'd been rather quiet and if he'd thought about it at all he'd put it down to a natural weariness. It would never have dawned on him that it was because he had been overhelpful and friendly to an attractive young mother at Heathrow who had been struggling with a young baby at the carousel. Tim had leaped forward to assist, leaving Miranda to deal with their luggage, and she had been unable to overcome her resentment at his ready charm and the young woman's obvious response. Tim hadn't even noticed and, by the time they were through Customs and had struggled out to the car, his thoughts were already far ahead.

Miranda reasoned with herself. Tim's love and good opinion were too precious to risk and, after all, he'd simply been helping the woman. Later, when they were married, she could point out the un-wisdom of being too friendly and creating the wrong impression so that people, women especially, took advantage. She was aware of the pressure of Tim's hand and the fact that he was glancing at her, con-cerned by her silence.

'I was thinking of Daddy,' she said mendaciously. 'Staying all this time with Felicity.'

They'd been through it several times, ever since they'd been un-able to get a reply from Broadhayes when they telephoned to tell David they would be delayed. It was Tim who'd insisted that they telephone Felicity and Miranda had been horrified to learn that David had decided to stay with her, quite beside herself worrying about what awful temptations he would be led into with a woman of Felic-ity's reputation. Tim had finally succeeded in calming her and since, short of her returning alone, there was nothing Miranda could do she had made the best of it.

'Well, he'll certainly have been keeping George at bay,' observed Tim with somewhat callous optimism. 'We'll telephone as soon as we get in. At least he's been looked after. If only I hadn't sent Mrs Gilchrist off he'd have probably stayed at Broadhayes. Never mind. All over now. Gosh! It's wonderful to be back.'

Sixteen

FELICITY WAS TOO DEEPLY immersed in her happiness to feel any anxiety when Tim telephoned from America to find out if David was with her. Even when she took the call to say that they were back at Broadhayes and David could return she was unmoved. It didn't occur to her that anything could happen that might shake this new wonderful love that had come when she was in such great need of it. Since George's betrayal she had been living in a different world where pain and loneliness had kept an unceasing vigil over her life. She had fought and struggled, jealous and frightened by turns, terrified to look into the future, miserable when she looked into the past. Suddenly, between one moment and the next, David had arrived and it was as if the whole desperate business had been swept away. Resentment, hatred, fear, all had gone as if they had never existed and in their places had come love, happiness, peace. She had been raised from the dark places and they were only distant shadows to her now.

When Kate telephoned and asked her to lunch Felicity refused. She simply couldn't bear to be away from David. Kate belonged to another existence, that other life of dark places, and she had no desire to return to it, even briefly. She had forgotten that Kate might be lonely or have needs and even if she had remembered it would have made no difference. David filled her whole vision and she could spare nothing from him. Summer was beginning to die down into autumn and Felicity longed to show David the glory of the moor when the colours turn to fire and the hills are purple with heather. She wanted to stand with him above Holne at night when the mist, soft and white like milk, lies in the valleys and coombes and the harvest moon rises slowly above the earth, huge and mysterious, bathing the silent moor in its unearthly glow. She wanted to share with him the sight of the rowan berries, brilliant against an early-morning sky, whilst one's breath hangs like steam in the chill air.

Even her house had never seemed so much like a home. Things, possessions, had a different meaning now that the beloved saw them, used them, lived amongst them. Cooking became an art rather than a chore, Felicity forgot to count her calories, and food and drink became yet another gift which she could bestow. Never had she known life so simple and so happy. She hadn't experienced a temperament which lived almost completely for the present and it bewitched her. She saw that David was contented, fulfilled, optimistic and imagined that she was seeing the whole picture.

David knew that this was an interlude, a gift from the gods, and accepted it as such, unquestioning and with no thought for the future. He worked and loved and it was good and he assumed that Felicity was accepting it in the same spirit. It would never have occurred to him that someone of Felicity's age and experience could imagine that life could continue at this magical level. He was merely grateful that such a lull in the hurly-burly of life should be granted to him and enjoyed it as one enjoys the warmth of an Indian summer, the pleasure heightened by the knowledge that winter is not far away.

It was only when David began to talk of his return to Broadhayes that the first breath ruffled her calm sea and gently rocked the boat of her idyllic happiness. Even then she looked upon it as a temporary separation. Naturally he must go and see his friends. Obviously he had his work to do and his house in London to attend to. She hadn't even got so far as to think about how they would live, although she had already decided that to spend some time in London would be fun. Her absolute confidence in their relationship blinded her to all sorts of small signs and when David realised this he was horrified. His work was completed so far as he could go in this setting and he wanted to get back to his studio. His sight was beginning to clear, the midsummer night's dream was over, the magic was fading. When he saw what it meant to Felicity he felt uneasy. He remembered how she had pursued George, had been prepared to stop at nothing to win him back, and his unease bordered on fear. He was very fond of her and was deeply grateful to her. She was part of the miracle, without her it couldn't have happened, but he didn't want to spend the rest of his life with her. When Miranda's mother died he had been ashamed at the degree of relief that was mixed into his grief. He felt light and free and he had no intention of going back into bondage. He told himself that Felicity would get over it once he was gone but his heart was heavy and he was quite incapable of telling her the truth. He told her that he simply had to get back to London, that he'd already been away much longer than he'd intended, that he would be in touch. So confident was she that none of this disturbed her and when he drove away he felt like a murderer.

MAGGIE TABB CLEANED THE kitchen sink industriously, one eye cocked to the window. Outside, Thea and a man whom Maggie had never seen before walked up and down. Thea was gesticulating and talking furiously whilst the man, his head bent to hers, laughed and nodded. Jessie ambled at their heels, pausing for a moment to sit down and scratch at one of her floppy ears. Maggie had noticed the strange car, parked inside the five-bar gate, as soon as she arrived and her curiosity was rife. She stationed herself at the sink where she could observe the nature of their parting.

''N' 'oo c'n 'ee be?' she asked of Percy, as she polished away at the taps. 'I never sin 'im befower.' She sidled over to his cage, one eye on the door. 'C'm'on,' she wheedled. 'Jes' fer Maggie. Say "Normin's a silly ol fewel." Go on. 'Ave a go!'

Percy regarded her solemnly and remained silent. She straightened up and shrugged. 'Misrubble ol' bag o'fevvers,' she said. 'Won' even try, will yer?' She heard an engine start up and, moving quickly to the window, saw Thea waving the car out into the lane. 'Now!' she exclaimed, vexed. 'I didden see if 'e kissed 'er. 'Tis all yer fault.'

'Mademoiselle from Armenteers, hasn't been kissed for forty years,' shrieked Percy. 'Hinky, pinky, parley-voo.'

'What's the matter with Percy this morning?' asked Thea, appearing in the kitchen and beginning to root in the dresser drawer. 'He's been chattering away all morning. He seems to be in a state of high nervous tension.' Various items fell to the floor and she bent to retrieve them. 'Honestly, the things one keeps! We'll have to have a good turnout, Maggie.'

''E'd be fair worked up,' agreed Maggie. 'P'raps 'tis 'avin' strangers in the 'ouse.' She paused invitingly but Thea refused the bait. 'If 'ee tells us wot yewer lookin' fower, us cud 'elp, p'raps.'

'Actually, I'm looking for the Sellotape. Oh, I know. I think I saw it in the study.' Thea had no intention of telling Maggie who Marcus Willby was or that he had called in on his way down to Cornwall in order to discuss the progress of her work. She shut the drawer and made for the study.

'Kettle's boilin',' Maggie bawled after her, disgruntled that her ploy had failed. What was she doing upstairs in her little room? And who was the stranger with whom Thea was so friendly? 'Wan' a cup o' coffee? I'll bring 'n up, eh?'

'Don't worry.' Thea reappeared with the Sellotape. 'I'll make us both one. Then you can get on in the sitting room.'

'Ah, I cud do wiv a cuppa.' Maggie sighed deeply and relinquished her quest for information about Thea's affairs. 'Feelin' right misrubble, I be.'

'Maggie!' Thea, preparing mugs, sounded surprised. She felt guilty that she hadn't taken Maggie into her confidence about the book but she wanted to wait until everything was cut and dried. George had been delighted by her news and was quite ridiculously proud of her achievement and it had been immensely difficult to prevent him from immediately telephoning all their friends to share in the good tidings. She insisted on absolute secrecy until it was certain and once Maggie knew so would everyone else in the surrounding countryside. Since it had been Maggie's idea that stories should go with the pictures that she had drawn for Wayne, Thea had decided to buy her a present as soon as her advance came. 'I thought all was well between you and Norman now.' She poured in milk, stirred and set the mugs on the table. 'Come and have your coffee and tell me what's been going on. You said he was overcome with remorse and wanted to come home.'

'Yeah,'e wus. Didden know 'ow ter get 'isself back, see. 'E phoned up in a turrible takin', cryin' 'n' carryin' on 'e wus. Silly fewel.'

'And what did you do?' Thea stirred in sugar.

'Went 'n' fetched 'e,' said Maggie promptly. 'Banged on the dewer 'n' shouted fer 'e ter get 'isself out or I'd go 'n' get 'is mum ter see wot a dick'ead 'e wus bein'!'

'His mum?' Thea was riveted by this recital.

'Big wumman,'is mum,' said Maggie, reminiscently. 'Scared to deff uv 'er, Normin is. Came boltin' out like a rabbit.'

'So what's the problem now?'

' 'Tes still thet ole surfboard chin. Frien' o' mine saw 'em togevver t'other day. 'Course,'e denied it all. Never seen 'er, never bin near the place. I give 'im a swipe roun' the lug'ole wiv the lid off of 'is san'wich tin. Got reel upset,'e did. 'N' ower Wayne come in 'n' Normin,'e shif' out quick down the boozer.' She took a great gulp of coffee. 'Shitface,' she said moodily. 'Allus sneaks off,'e do. Never 'as it out wiv me.'

'I suppose it's possible,' surmised Thea, to whom these revelations were no longer a shock, 'that your friend could have been mistaken.'

They both paused to listen as a car pulled up outside and a door slammed. Thea stood up to look from the kitchen window. 'It's the vicar,' she exclaimed. 'Apparently he knows my father. He said he'd drop by for a chat.' She went out to greet him.

Maggie swallowed her coffee hurriedly. 'I doan' like 'im,' she confided to Percy as she set her mug on the draining board. ' 'E d'go on about me 'n' Normin summink awful.'

But Percy was whistling 'Lead kindly light, amidst the encircling gloom' quietly to himself from the floor of his cage and didn't seem to hear her.

Seventeen

DAVID STAYED AT BROADHAYES for over a week after he'd left Felicity. Because she thought that he was going straight back to London she had never asked the name of his friend near Moreton-hampstead and he felt that it gave him a breathing space. He was delighted to see Tim and Miranda getting on so well and was interested to see that they both had separate bedrooms. Since Mrs Gilchrist had returned immediately after their return from America, David couldn't decide whether this arrangement was intended to observe the proprieties or was due to Miranda's rather stringent views on sex before marriage. Whatever it was, they both seemed very happy about it and by the time Miranda and David returned to London, Tim had asked and received David's blessing on their union. If David had doubts he kept them to himself. It was possible that their marriage would not be exposed to the strains beneath which his own had bent and buckled and it was no good being pessimistic. He was rather more concerned with his own behaviour towards Felicity and on his last evening, when Miranda had gone up to have a bath, he bared his soul to Tim.

'I feel as if I really used her,' he said as he and Tim sat in the library nursing their after-dinner brandies. 'I simply got carried away, d'you see? It was just one of those moments that come so rarely. Everything was absolutely right.'

'Perhaps she felt the same.'

'No.' David shook his head. 'I thought so, too, at the beginning. By the time I realised that she was taking it seriously it was much too late.

She's sitting there waiting for me to telephone and I feel an A1 swine.'

'Perhaps you should view it all in the light of her past behaviour,' ventured Tim. 'She deceived her husband for years and tried to break up Thea's marriage. Perhaps she deserves a little comeuppance.'

'Perhaps she does.' David shrugged. 'So do we all, I imagine, one way or another. I'd just prefer not to be the person administering it. Mine has not been such a blameless life that I feel qualified to judge. A little dalliance to take her mind off George was one thing. Leading her up the garden path, abusing her hospitality and then walking out on her is quite another.'

'Oh, dear.' Tim looked at David anxiously. 'This has really upset you, hasn't it? I'm sorry, David. It's all my fault. I dreamed up the whole thing and then left you to it. I'm really sorry.'

'It's never been my way, d'you see? I always like to let the ladies think they've cast me out rather than the other way about. That way you keep them as friends.' He grimaced. 'Not that I want you to think I make a habit of it.'

'Of course not.' Tim felt a great surge of affection for David and cast about for some way out of the dilemma. 'Perhaps you could re-main friends with Felicity.'

'I think not, dear boy. Felicity would want a great deal more than that.' He shook his head. 'I don't know what to do about it so doubt-less I shall take the coward's way out and do nothing.'

'Does she know your address in London?'

David frowned a little and then shrugged. 'I don't remember giv-ing her the actual address. She knows it's Chelsea. She's certainly got the telephone number. I had to give her that. But she was just so sure that I was coming back that she didn't really press for my address.' He swallowed his brandy. 'Christ, I feel a shit!'

Tim reached for the decanter and refilled David's glass.

'I don't know what to say. If it's any comfort, it certainly took her mind off George. When Thea telephoned to tell us all about her book she said that they were both terribly happy and that they've decided to start a family. Although that was in confidence, of course. She sounded over the moon. I only wish my grandmother could have heard her. She was really worried, you know, and she wasn't at all the sort of person to panic unnecessarily.'

'Oh, well. That's something at least.' David tried to look more cheerful. 'Let's hope I've got it wrong and Felicity won't be as upset as I fear. We'll have to see how it goes. I'd be delighted to think that we could be friends but I just don't think she sees it like that. Never mind. No good going over and over it. Let's dwell on more cheerful things. So when's the wedding going to be?'

THEA, DRIVING OVER TO have lunch with Harriet and Polly, felt that her cup was full to overflowing. Life seemed to be getting better and better. There was no shadow now on her marriage, George was completely her own, so excited about her work, and even Felicity had looked so young and happy when they'd met that Thea didn't have to feel that she was taking her own happiness at someone else's expense. Then there was all the excitement about the book, the trip to London to the publishers and the plans for a second book and, as if to gild the lily, there was this latest joy. Thea knew without any doubt at all that she was pregnant. It might be only by a matter of weeks but she knew it absolutely. She felt so happy that it was frightening. Why she should have been chosen to have all these blessings whilst there was so much sorrow and misery and violence was beyond her. She rocketed between bliss and terror. Supposing something happened to George or to herself before all these wonders could be fulfilled? She tried to cast such negative thoughts from her and dwell on her joy. Her one sadness was that Hermione had not lived to see these wonderful events. Her faith, however, assured her that Hermione knew of them and was with her in spirit, encouraging her and supporting her, which to Thea was an infinitely comforting thought.

When she arrived, Harriet was upstairs dealing with Hugh and Polly let Thea in. Ozzy, the puppy, bounded to greet her whilst Max

paced slowly behind him looking upon Ozzy's high spirits with benev-
olent tolerance. He'd been young once and he didn't grudge Ozzy his
hour in the sun.

'You're so much bigger than Jessie,' Thea told him as she fended
him off and held out a hand to Max. 'You make her look so small.'
She followed them all into the kitchen.

'You look wonderful,' said Polly enviously. 'Positively glowing. So
what's new?'

'Nothing,' said Thea, hugging her latest secret to herself. 'What
about you?'

'I'm so thrilled I can hardly breathe,' said Polly solemnly. 'Paul
thinks he's discovered a new species of *Siphlonuridae*. My dear, imagine how world-shattering. He's examined its wing veins and its geni-
talia and he's certain that it's a find. I've been praying and fasting. Not
a morsel of food has passed my lips since the great discovery. My life
can never be the same again.'

'Take no notice of her.' Harriet arrived in the kitchen and grinned
at Thea. 'It must be very exciting for Paul.'

'Well, of course, dear Fiona found it,' said Polly. 'Naturally. So
Paul's going to name it after her. That's how it's done. Well, it's only
right. It looks just like her!'

'Poor Polly.' Harriet went to organise the lunch. 'It must be exhausting, living in the rarefied air of scientific discovery.'

'Percy the Parrot's much more my line,' agreed Polly. 'Great stuff!
You'll be able to read it to Huge, Harriet, when he's older.'

'I wish you wouldn't call him that,' said Harriet, piling food on to
the table. 'You are his godmother, after all.'

'Can't resist it,' said Polly, breaking off a corner of cheese. 'He's
so small. Anyway, I shall buy him Percy the Parrot books when he's
older. At least Thea won't have to worry about what to read to her
children, if she has any.'

There was a silence of such an unusual quality that Harriet turned
from her soup-stirring. Both of them looked at Thea.

'You're pregnant,' cried Harriet.

Thea stared back at them, her cheeks turning scarlet and her eyes glowing like stars.

'You are!' cried Harriet. 'Oh, Thea! How wonderful!'

She dropped the soup spoon and fled round the table to hug Thea, who hugged her back, still quite unable to speak for fear that she might cry.

'Jesus wept!' said Polly morosely. 'That's all I needed. Don't say I've got to fork out for another bloody rattle!'

WHEN DAVID ARRIVED BACK in London there were no fewer than six messages from Felicity on his answering machine. It was Miranda who had persuaded him to use this device, which protected him from time-wasters when he was working, and he soon came to rely on it. He tended to sift through the calls at the end of each day, returning some and not others. Miranda was quite ruthless, helping him to decide on the borderline cases, and he was usually happy to give in to her. He hated using the telephone. On this occasion, however, it was he who got to the machine first, listened to the messages and quickly wiped the tape. He did not want to explain in detail to Miranda just how close he and Felicity had become. He and Tim had tacitly allowed her to believe that he had been nothing more than a guest and David knew she would be horrified to know how very intimate the relationship had become. He felt hot with shame as he listened to Felicity's voice becoming more and more anxious as the messages proceeded although, even then, his main feeling was one of relief that he was ex-directory and he thought it was unlikely that she would turn up on the doorstep. He decided that he must write to her, without using his address, and explain. His heart sank at the thought.

Miranda telephoned Tim to tell him of their safe arrival and, when she had finished and was preparing some supper, David turned the machine back on. Even as he did so he wondered what on earth he would do if Felicity were to telephone and Miranda should answer.

His question was answered the next morning. Miranda had contacted her temping agency to advise them that she was back and prepared to work for a week or so before she returned to Devon. When the telephone rang she answered it, hoping that it was an offer of work. She could hardly believe that David had been stupid enough to give Felicity his number and, being Miranda, decided that the thing should be nipped in the bud immediately. She said stiffly that Mr Porteous was working and on no account could be disturbed. Felicity, imagining her to be a housekeeper or secretary, asked if she would give him a message and grudgingly Miranda agreed. The nature of the message was perfectly discreet but implied a degree of relationship which caused Miranda to furrow her brow. There was something going on here and she intended to find out what it was.

AFTER DAVID'S DEPARTURE, SEVERAL days passed before Felicity began to feel uneasy. To begin with she embarked on an orgy of cleaning. During his stay she had somewhat neglected this aspect of life and now she cleaned the whole house from top to bottom. In some ways it was a psychological cleansing. She felt that all her old life was being swept away and she was preparing for a new beginning. By the end of the second day everything positively gleamed and sparkled and Felicity had the beginning of one of her heads. She longed for a drink but knew that alcohol would make it far worse and contented herself with a cup of coffee. She sat in a large comfortable armchair, listening to a concert and thinking about David. Or rather she continued to think about him but in a more conscious way, for he was never out of her thoughts. Despite her physical exhaustion, she felt relaxed, loose, easy, and a deep contentment filled her. She rolled her head against the cushions, stretching out her legs and laughing a little at herself, glad that no one could see her in this state. Love, the genuine, knocked-sideways, authentic emotion, had come very late. It was as though some dammed-up spring had burst and was watering and nourishing all the parched, dried-up areas of her life. Emotions flowered and happiness blossomed and she felt weak and gentle and vulnerable for the first time in her life. There was no self-interest in her love. All her care was for David, his well-being, his happiness.

After forty-eight hours she began to wonder a little that he hadn't telephoned but as much because she was concerned for his safety as for any other reason. At last this anxiety began to take hold and Felicity started to worry. She had been trained in a hard school, used to being unable to hear from Mark—or George—for weeks at a time, never having known the luxury of having either of them at the end of a telephone. You didn't whine and complain, you just got on with it. This, however, was a whole new experience and she didn't yet know the rules. Added to which there was David's career and temperament to take into consideration. She had seen him at work, absorbed, forgetful of everything around him, and she wondered if this might have happened. He had told her that he'd been away far longer than he ought to have been and she didn't want to start off by seeming to be a nagger. Nevertheless, by the end of the third day, she threw caution to the wind and telephoned the London number, unaware that David was still at Broadhayes. Hearing his voice shocked her into stillness for a few seconds before her heart began to bump. She burst into speech and then realised, as David's voice continued, that she was connected to an answering machine. She stopped speaking abruptly, feeling quite unnecessarily foolish and, at the same time, overwhelmed with disappointment. She slammed the receiver down and then wondered if she should have left a message.

She walked away from the telephone, deliberating. Surely there could be no harm in a friendly message, hoping that he was safely back? Why should she feel so nervous about it? It was perfectly reasonable that she should feel concern for him and it was possible that he might have mislaid the piece of paper on which she had carefully written her telephone number. This sudden anxiety made her decide to try again. Fortifying herself with a strong gin and tonic, she redialled and listened to David's voice courteously entreating callers to leave names, telephone numbers, messages, after the tone. Felicity waited for the high-pitched buzz and spoke into the emptiness at the other end. She made her voice light and social, stumbled over her telephone number and replaced the receiver feeling a perfect fool. She finished her drink quickly and went to prepare her supper. Perhaps he might call her later.

At the end of a week, she was feeling desperate. Abandoning pride, she had made several calls and left messages and, on other occasions, talked to a self-possessed-sounding female who told her that David was busy, out, unavailable. She promised to give him Felicity's messages but would not be drawn into conversation. Frustrated, hurt, unhappy, Felicity took to roaming up and down, up and down, gazing out of windows, staring into the darkness at night, remembering the feel of David's arms around her, his lips on her skin, the comfort of his presence. Tears ran unchecked down her cheeks as she huddled beneath the quilt waiting for the dawn, hoping that it would usher in a day during which she would receive an explanation of this terrible muddle. She would not have asked for much: a telephone call, a short note. The Navy had taught her to live alone, contented with the minimum of contact, but she could think of no reason for this unbearable silence.

When Felicity had gone up to bed on the night of David's departure she had found a sketch on her dressing table. It was of a bridge over the River Dart and a part of the bank with a group of foxgloves glowing against the sun-warmed stone. They had spent some happy hours in this place and Felicity caught it up with a cry of delight. It had been lightly colour-washed and the light danced on the water which seemed to flow and splash even as she looked at it. Across the corner David had written, 'Bless you for everything. It's been perfect. With love. D.' She had wept then but her tears were joyous, grateful, happy tears, confident in his love and in their future together. Now she stared at the sketch with eyes that were swollen with quite different tears. It was the last thing she laid down at night and the first thing she picked up in the morning. It was all that she had left of him.

Eighteen

WHEN KATE SAW HER in Tavistock and invited her to lunch, Felicity accepted. She simply couldn't bear another day sitting by a telephone which did not ring. Kate, who imagined that Felicity was still missing George, kept the conversation as impersonal as possible and Felicity, clinging to her pride, tried to appear cheerful. It was evident that Kate was living with great economy and Felicity felt a twinge of remorse that she hadn't thought to bring her some offering towards the meal. She had been too deeply immersed in her own fears to think about it. She looked about the kitchen and at Kate herself, dressed in rubbed cords and an old guernsey. She looked thin and tired and Felicity felt a stronger twinge.

'Are you keeping well, Kate?' she asked, finding a momentary relief in thinking about someone else. 'How do you cope financially? I suppose you never hear from Mark?'

'Not since he went to Canada. None of us hear from him. He never even sends the boys a birthday card or anything at Christmas. Nothing. Can you imagine it? Not that I wanted anything from him. My brother helps out. He uses the house as a base. You've met Chris, haven't you?'

'Yes, I think so. Even so, it must be difficult to make ends meet.'

'I don't,' said Kate simply. 'I should have taken a proper job, of course, rather than trying to make money with breeding and my obedience classes and things. But I wanted to be around when the twins were home for their holidays. Anyway, we've managed so far. My one terror is that Chris meets someone and decides to get married.'

She set a dish containing a shepherd's pie on the table. 'Not very exciting, I'm afraid. I'm not much of a cook, as you probably remember.'

Felicity sat down and stared at the dish. She wasn't hungry, she was simply tired. She felt exhausted. She looked up and met Kate's eyes. It seemed at that moment as though Kate knew everything, although that was impossible.

'Are you OK?' Kate's expression was one of absolute understanding and compassion and Felicity felt her misery rising to the surface. She nodded and fiddled with her fork. Kate watched her for a moment and then began to serve the pie. 'Sorry I couldn't offer you a drink. A proper one, that is. I've got some cheap plonk here if you feel up to it?'

She poured some into the glasses and pushed one towards Felicity. She raised her own and Felicity nodded and lifted hers, trying to smile, before she sipped at it.

'The twins have been taking a year off,' said Kate, deciding that it would be kinder to chat mindlessly and let Felicity relax. 'They've gone off backpacking across Europe. I'm just praying that they'll be OK. At times like these I'm grateful that there are two of them and that they get on so well together.'

'You must miss them.' The thought of Kate's loneliness reminded Felicity of her own and she swallowed once or twice.

'Oh, I do.' Kate smiled a little sadly. 'I thought that they might stay home for a bit but there's not much excitement for them down here and they wanted a holiday before they start work.'

She didn't expect Felicity to ask what work they intended to take up. She knew that Felicity, having no children of her own, had not the least interest in those belonging to other people. She was not prepared, however, for Felicity's next remark.

'Why didn't you marry again?' she asked.

Taken aback, Kate raised her eyebrows and laughed a little. 'It takes two,' she said. 'And nobody asked me.'

'What about that chap from the bookshop?' Felicity drank some more wine in an attempt to wash down the pie which threatened to stick in her throat. 'Alex, wasn't it?'

'Oh, Felicity.' Kate shook her head. 'That's going back a bit. It didn't work out, I'm afraid. I couldn't put him before the twins and he, quite rightly, resented it.'

'But the twins will go away and leave you. They already have by the sound of it. You'll be left alone. You should have thought of that.'

'I did think of it. It didn't seem all that relevant then. At times like that you live so completely in the present.'

'Yes.' Felicity gave up and pushed her plate aside. 'How terribly true that is.'

Kate looked at her thoughtfully. 'I was terribly in love with him,' she said. 'I had no idea that such depths of emotion existed. Nothing mattered but him. It was like I was ill, like an obsession.'

Felicity stared at her. Her breath came quickly, she nodded and her eyes were wide and bright. 'Yes,' she said. 'I know just what you mean.'

'I lived like that for three months until the twins came home for the holidays. And then it began. It was like having a bath of cold water emptied over me. Being torn in two pieces. Alex got tired of it in the end and it finished.' Kate, too, pushed her plate aside and rested her elbows on the table. She looked at Felicity and her eyes were cloudy with memories. 'I can't forget him,' she said. 'Funny, isn't it? It still hurts like hell but I can't get him out of my system. I really loved him, I suppose that's why. Thank God he sold up and moved away. At least I don't have to see him any more.'

'Oh, Kate.' Felicity reached out and took Kate's hand. 'I'm so sorry. I had no idea. At the time I simply didn't understand. And I was so beastly to you.'

Kate came back to the present and looked with surprise at the pain in Felicity's eyes. Their hands gripped for a moment and then Kate reached for the bottle.

'Come on. No good sitting here crying. Has that friend gone that

you had staying with you? Did you say that he was an artist or something?'

'That's right.' Felicity attempted a casual tone. 'He was on a
sketching holiday, getting a portfolio together. It was . . . it was
great fun. I miss him.'

'Nice?' Their eyes met.

'Mmm.' Felicity nodded, not trusting her voice. Her lips trembled a little.

'That nice?'

Felicity swallowed, nodded and began to cry.

'Oh, dear.' Comprehension dawned and Kate grimaced sympathetically. 'Married?'

Felicity shook her head, still crying.

'So what's the problem?'

'He's been gone a week and I haven't heard a word. Not a thing.
He hasn't telephoned. I've left messages but he doesn't reply.' Felicity lowered her head to her arms and began to cry in earnest.

Kate, guessing what a terrible blow this must be coming so soon
after George's rejection, reached across the table and gently stroked
the black hair. She considered and discarded various remarks and sat
in silence, simply stroking. After a while, Felicity raised her head and
began to search for a handkerchief. Kate watched her for a moment
and then shook her head.

'The twins each have a saying at the moment,' she said as Felicity
mopped at her face. 'Guy says, "The light at the end of the tunnel is
always an oncoming train" and Giles says, "Life's a bitch and then you
die." I offer them to you as the only consolation I know. Ah hell! Let's
have another drink.'

When Felicity left, Kate put her arms round her and held her tight.
'Cass's old pa used to say, "When you're up against it, go and look at
yourself in a mirror and imagine all your ancestors all down the cen-
turies standing behind your shoulder willing you onwards and upwards." It does work. You think of all that they might have been

through and you feel you can do it, too. Whatever it is. You feel their support and their strength. You're never truly alone, you know.'

'Thanks, Kate.' Felicity rested for a moment against her and then released herself gently. 'And thanks for the lunch.'

'Any time. Stay in touch.'

Felicity nodded and got into her car. When she looked into the mirror as she reached the bend in the road, Kate was still standing at the gate looking after her As she drove through Whitchurch and into Tavistock she remembered Kate's quote: 'Life's a bitch and then you die.' It occurred to her that were she to die now, crash into a bus or something, no one would care. Except Kate. She knew that Kate would care and a faint ray of comfort touched her sore heart. Suddenly she realised that, should that happen, everything she owned would go to George. So certain had she been, after Mark's death, that they would marry that she had changed her will and left everything to George. As she drove into Tavistock a resolve formed in her mind and seeing a space in the market square she parked the car and hurried into the town.

MIRANDA WAS BECOMING MORE and more suspicious. However, since David quite deliberately shut himself away during the day— she knew better than to disturb him when he was working—and had spent a few evenings with friends, it was several days before she spoke to him about her suspicions. By this time she had taken two more calls from Felicity and listened to several more messages on the answering machine. She cornered him one evening before supper when, pleased with his day's work, he was enjoying a gin and tonic and listening to a concert.

'Daddy.' Miranda stood looking down at his semi-recumbent figure. 'What's going on with you and Felicity Mainwaring?'

'What? How d'you mean?' David hauled himself into a sitting position.

'She keeps phoning. Why did you give her our telephone number?'

'Well, it was difficult not to.' David had learned that a calm rational reply often allayed suspicion. 'I was there for two weeks, you know. Damned awkward.'

If he hoped to awaken sympathy he was to be disappointed.

'But she knew the situation. You said that she was delighted to play hostess to a well-known painter.'

'Perfectly true. Still, she was very kind. Couldn't treat the place like a hotel, d'you see?'

'She seems to think that you're going back.'

David's heart sank. He hadn't realised that Miranda had been monitoring the answering machine or that Felicity's messages were becoming more frequent and less discreet.

'Well'—David's calm slipped a little—'obviously, in two weeks, we became quite friendly. Only to be expected. I might have said things, led her to suppose that I'd drop in if I was in the area.'

'It sounds more than that to me.' Miranda stared at him uncompromisingly. 'I hope you didn't lead her on. You know what a reputation she's got.'

'For heaven's sake, Miranda,' said David testily. 'Don't talk to me as if I were a child. I'm not Tim. He was the one who dropped me in it and I dealt with it as best I could. If there have been misunderstandings I'll deal with them. It's none of your business. And don't speak about Felicity like that. She's a very nice person and I feel very badly that I used her as I did. She was very kind to me.'

Suddenly the remembrance of those magic days engulfed him and he felt a stab of loss. Miranda's face took on a half-contemptuous, half-fearful look that David recognised and dreaded.

'You slept with her, didn't you? She's more or less implied it, anyway, so you needn't lie. Oh, how disgusting! How could you?'

David swallowed his drink and stood up. With an effort he controlled his temper but his hands trembled.

'I have no intention of discussing my private life with you,' he said quietly. 'Yes. Felicity and I made love. It was comforting and generous and moving.'

'At your ages?' Miranda was pale with mortification and disgust. 'It's horrible.'

'Stop this!' David's voice rang with the authentic note of real anger and Miranda, on uncertain ground, backed off a little. David saw it and took advantage. 'I refuse to discuss this any further. It is no business of yours and I will not have you sitting in judgment on me. I had quite enough of that with your mother. Now. Are we having any supper this evening?'

At the mention of her mother, Miranda flushed a dark red and, biting her lip, fled from the room. David sighed a deep sigh and finding that he was still shaking poured himself another drink. He heard the telephone ringing and the noise cut off short as Miranda answered it. Perhaps it was Tim and she was pouring out her heart to him. Well, good luck to her. He knew that Tim would be on his side but prayed that he knew better than to let Miranda know it.

Supper was a very quiet affair. Miranda was behaving rather oddly, which didn't particularly surprise him, but she wore an air of triumphant defiance which puzzled him a little. It was only when supper was over and he was back in the drawing room that he thought to ask her if it had been Tim who had telephoned earlier. She shook her head and set his coffee down beside his chair.

'Who was it then?'

She looked at him, still with that strange expression. 'It was Felicity,' she said at last. 'I told her that you didn't want to speak to her.'

David opened his mouth and shut it again. After all, what could he say? He had been going out of his way not to speak to Felicity for nearly two weeks. Miranda stared at him and David shrugged and turned away. The second half of the concert on the radio was just starting—Sibelius's First Symphony. He sat down and picked up his coffee. He must have dozed a little for he had disturbing dreams and then Miranda was leaning over him and saying that she was going up to bed. After she had gone, David got up and stretched a little and then went to pour himself a brandy and soda. As the music of the last movement filled the room, he had a sudden vision of Felicity. He stood quite still on the hearthrug and stared unseeingly ahead of him. She was walking on the moor. The wind had whipped her hair over her eyes and she was laughing at him, her eyes alight with love. Clouds streamed across the granite peaks behind her and the sky in the west gleamed with golden light. Other intimate scenes formed and re-formed in his mind's eye. His heart beat a little faster and he knew himself for a fool. As the symphony's last notes died away, David swore quietly to himself, set down his glass and, going upstairs to his studio, found Felicity's number and picked up the telephone receiver.

WHEN FELICITY WOKE ON the morning after her lunch with Kate she felt so deeply depressed that she could barely find the will to get out of bed. She went downstairs feeling miserable and when she cracked her favourite cup on the tap she felt a wave of such black despair that she had to clutch at the sink. The day went from bad to worse. She dropped a bag of sugar that exploded all over the flagstones on the larder floor and banged her head on the low beam in the bathroom as she stepped back from opening the window. Suddenly she found herself screaming.

'Bloody thing!' She struck uselessly at the beam. 'Bloody, bloody thing!'

The screams became sobs and she collapsed on to the loo seat, weeping uncontrollably and nursing her bruised hand. Forgetting that during the last year her monthly cycle had become a very difficult time to live through, she imagined that she must be going mad, that life simply wasn't worth living. Exhausted physically through lack of sleep, emotionally drained, it didn't occur to her that she had felt rather like this every month of her adult life nor that for the last year it had got progressively worse, the depression blacker, the anger more violent. The possibility that she was in the grip of menopausal despair did not suggest itself to her.

By the evening she had decided that she would take one more chance. If David refused to speak to her she would know that it was

all over and she would never bother him again. She hadn't eaten since
the few mouthfuls of shepherd's pie at Kate's and her head was beginning to throb but she poured herself a large gin and tonic to boost her
courage and settled herself at her bureau. She felt her heart give its
usual jolt when the ringing tone was replaced by the click and the
voice gave the number.

'Hello.' Felicity felt breathless and her voice had a tremulous quality. 'Oh, hello. May I speak to David Porteous please?'

'It's Mrs Mainwaring, isn't it?' The young voice was cool. 'I've just
been talking to my father about you. I have a message from him. It is
Mrs Mainwaring, isn't it?'

'Yes. Yes, it is.' Felicity clutched the receiver in her trembling
hand. Her heart jumped in her breast as hope flamed joyfully within it.

'He doesn't want to speak to you. He says he's sorry if he gave the
wrong impression whilst he was staying with you but he assumed you
understood the situation and felt as he did. That it was just a bit of
fun. He knew your reputation, you see. My fiancé is Thea's cousin,
that's who my father was staying with, so he knew that you were a
woman of the world and how you'd tried to break up Thea's marriage and all that. He's behaved rather badly, I'm afraid, but that's
how he is. I'm sure you'll be able to understand that. He made my
mother very unhappy so really you're well out of it. Anyway, he's
made it quite clear that he doesn't want to communicate with you, so
I would be glad if you'd leave us alone now.'

There was a long silence and then the little click and the familiar
buzzing sound. Felicity sat on, clutching the receiver, her eyes tight
shut against the appalling things that tried to show themselves to her:
David knowing about George, knowing how she had behaved to
Thea, using her when she thought that he was loving her. Her heart
beat with thick heavy strokes and the shock and pain seemed to create
a huge lump in her chest, threatening to suffocate her. Presently she
put the receiver down and picked up her glass. She drank the gin back
as though it were water and stood up. Things seemed to move and
rock around her and she steadied herself before she made her way to

the cupboard and poured herself another drink. Her head pounded rhythmically and she knew that she must take some of her tablets. She gulped back some more gin and made a noise that was somewhere between a sob and a cry. The cool voice seemed to have got inside her head. '. . . knew your reputation . . . woman of the world . . . break up Thea's marriage . . . that's how he is . . .' She shook her head to try to dislodge the voice and winced at the pain. Mustn't think about that voice saying those dreadful things. Think about something else. Tablets. Must get some tablets.

The carpet seemed to be rocking up and down as she stumbled across it to the kitchen. She opened the cupboard, almost hanging on to the doors for support, and seized the bottle. After some difficulty with the lid, she shook out two tablets and looked around. Lightning seemed to flash behind her eyes and she saw that a glass of water was standing at hand. She took the tablets, washed them down with the gin and made a wry face. Oh, dear. Not water after all. She staggered back into the sitting room still clutching the glass and collapsed on to the sofa. The voice started up again. '. . . doesn't want to communicate . . . just a bit of fun.' Felicity began to weep. He had never loved her. She had imagined it all. He had known about her and George and had thought her fair game. She cried out, 'Oh, no,' at the thought of it and, getting up, went to the drinks cupboard. She seemed to be holding a glass in her hand already and she sloshed the gin in untidily, spilling it. She poured in some tonic and staggered back to the sofa. The voice muttered in her ear. '. . . made my mother very unhappy . . . very unhappy.' Mustn't think about it. Think about something else. She closed her eyes against the pain in her head and tried to concentrate on the music. The second half of the concert had started. Sibelius's First Symphony. She must listen, let it calm her. If only her head would stop. She simply couldn't bear the pain. She must take some tablets. Yes. That's what she had meant to do.

She took another gulp from her glass and scrambled up. On her way to the kitchen the pieces of furniture seemed to come out of their places, looming up at her, bumping her knees. She stood for some time in the kitchen, leaning against the wall. Presently she opened her eyes and saw the tablets standing on the working surface. That's it. That's what she'd come for. She must have taken them out of the cupboard without realising it. She shook some out and took two. Oh, how her head hurt! She might just take one extra one, perhaps a few extra, and then she could sleep. She washed them back with the gin and staggered back into the sitting room, collapsing on to the sofa. '. . . just a bit of fun . . . a bit of fun.' Don't listen to the voice. Listen to the music. It filled her ears and rolled around the room. She saw herself with David on the moor, she could feel the wind blowing her hair and he was smiling at her, waving, and she was going towards him. He would take her in his arms and she would never be lonely again. She began to weep soundlessly, her mouth stretched open, tears streaming down her face. It seemed as though her head would burst and she felt sick. She found that she was clutching a glass in one hand and the bottle of tablets in the other. Had she taken them yet? Surely not. Her head wouldn't be such agony if she had. She took some more, finished off the gin and lay back, closing her eyes, dimly aware of the last movement of the symphony. It lulled her and she began to lose consciousness.

After a while the music stopped and another sound took its place: an insistent, rhythmic shrilling. The noise went on and on, penetrating Felicity's drugged torpor. With an immense effort she tried to drag herself back to wakefulness. Her lids fluttered a little and she tried to raise herself but she was too tired, too heavy, too peaceful to care about it. Her hand swung clear of the chair and the empty glass rolled away over the carpet. Her snoring breaths grew slower and presently the telephone stopped ringing and there was silence.

'. . . AND EVEN NOW, WITH the funeral over, I can't believe it,' Kate wrote to Cass. 'I keep thinking of things I might have done or said. Oh, Cass, she lay there for two days. Isn't it dreadful? To get over George and then have some other guy kick you in the teeth. Nobody knows about that but me so don't breathe a word, not even to

Tom. Thea and George are away on holiday so they don't know yet and there were only a few people at the crematorium, mainly Navy. She didn't seem to have any family. It was terribly depressing. I kept remembering things when we were all young. Parties and balls and things. Awful. I still can't believe she did it on purpose. Her GP says that so many of these deaths are accidents, that people have a few drinks and then forget how many tablets they've taken and just take more and more. Felicity of all people! She was so tough, so hard. But when she came to lunch it was as if something had broken, like she'd been encased in a hard shell all those years and it had been smashed by her love for this man and she was left all tender and vulnerable and unprotected. You felt that there was another Felicity who had been there all the time and none of us knew it. God! The sadness of it. I can't help thinking of those last awful hours when she was all alone and how desperately unhappy she must have been. But even more amazing, totally unbelievable! You'll never believe this, never in a million years! She changed her will the day before she died, almost as if she knew. Cass, she left everything she had to me . . .'

Nineteen

IT WAS KATE WHO told George. Anxious lest he or Thea should hear of it from one of Felicity's cronies—who might feel that in some way George was to blame—she discovered from Maggie Tabb the date of their return from holiday and telephoned the following morning. It was sheer good fortune that George answered. Thea, he explained, was wrestling with the washing machine and two weeks of dirty washing and when Kate told him that she had something very important that she wanted to say to him privately his tone became puzzled and a little wary.

'Come on, George.' Kate's nervousness and horror at the task in store lent an edge of impatience to her voice. 'It's really serious or I wouldn't ask. You know me well enough for that. Surely there's some shopping Thea needs. You could offer to get it while she's busy.'

With a certain amount of reluctance George agreed to the meeting place which Kate had already decided on, well away from prying eyes and wagging tongues: a lane that ran beside a pine wood just beyond Princetown. It led on to the army ranges and wasn't much used by anyone else but there were two lay-bys placed at intervals and Kate parked in the second one. It was a wild blowy day and Kate remained huddled in the car watching for George's Rover. She was already beginning to question her choice of locality in which to tell George the tragic news. When she knew that she was going to have to be the one to tell him she had imagined a series of encounters, none of which had seemed suitable. For Kate, the moor had always been a healing place. The high tors, the sweeping grasslands, the great elemental force of it all must surely help him to assimilate and bear the things that she had to say to him. Now, she began to wonder. Had she been attributing her own emotions to George? Panic seized her. Well, it was too late now and, although it was windy, at least it wasn't raining. Perhaps they could sit inside the car. Even as the thought occurred to her she instinctively rejected it. The cramped interior of a car was not the place for this. At length, in the rear-view mirror, she saw George's car approach and watched it pull in behind. George waved and, as he got out, she left her own car and went to meet him. He held out both hands to her and she took them and kissed him on the cheek. The wind roared round them, buffeting them as they stood together, howling through the wood.

'Hello, George.' She held on to his hands and smiled at him and had to raise her voice above the gale. 'Sorry about the secrecy and silence stuff. I've got some bad news, I'm afraid. Felicity's dead.' She said it quickly, holding his hands tightly against her breast. 'She died of an overdose of her migraine tablets but her GP is quite certain it was an accident.'

She registered his expression of disbelief and horror and felt that it was important to keep talking. Or rather shouting. It was awful to be saying these terrible things at the top of her voice whilst the wind snatched the words from her lips and whirled them into the grey void.

'She'd met another man during the last few weeks and had been quite swept off her feet by him. She came to see me. So I know that it's true. She told me so herself. She was in a desperate state. They'd been lovers and then he'd gone off without a word and she was terribly unhappy.' She felt the convulsive start that George gave and guessed that he was drawing the parallels between his own behaviour and this unknown man's. She gripped his hands and shook them, determined to make her point. 'It was nothing to do with you, George. She was waiting to hear from him, you see, and the doctor thinks that she got into a state and took some tablets after she'd been drinking. They found the glass.'

'Felicity never took her tablets when she'd been drinking,' said George flatly and Kate strained to hear his words. He squeezed her hands, released them and began to feel for his cigarettes. 'You know that. It was an absolute rule. She must have been in a very bad state, or it was intentional.'

His expression was bleak and Kate folded her arms across her breast as the wind screamed through the tops of the pines and the trees creaked beneath its force.

'George.' Kate realised that her teeth were chattering and that she was shivering but whether from cold or nerves she couldn't tell. 'Honestly, George. It was nothing to do with you. She told me all about this man. She was completely head over heels in love with him. I'd never seen Felicity like that before.' She bit her lip as she realised that she'd been tactless and then decided to let it stand. 'She was almost unbalanced by it. Perhaps that was the trouble. Why she took the tablets when she'd been drinking. She was in a terrible state when I saw her.'

George turned from her, trying to light a cigarette in the shelter of his jacket. When he'd succeeded he inhaled deeply, greedily, and then turned back to her.

'When did it happen?'

'Over a week ago. Accidental death was decided and she's . . . they took her to the crematorium in Plymouth. Where her mum went.' For some reason Kate couldn't get her tongue round the word 'cremated'. It seemed worse, somehow, than 'buried'. 'I was there and one or two of her friends. Pat. And Barbara. Oh, George. I'm sorry.'

George, who had been staring over the moor watching the tall fading grasses flatten beneath the wind, looked down at her. He tried to smile.

'Sorry. Dreadful shock.' He shook his head. 'Bless you, Kate. For everything. For telling me. And being there. You know. Look, don't think I'm being rude but if you don't mind I'd like to be on my own for a bit.'

'Yes, of course.' Kate hesitated. 'You'll be OK?'

He nodded and, leaning forward, he kissed her. She put her arms around him, hugged him and then left him, the wind tearing and dragging at her, and climbed with relief into the shelter of her car. Her eyes were watering and, dashing her sleeve across them, she peered in the mirror at him as she started the car. He was still standing quite still, smoking his cigarette. Helplessly she pulled out of the lay-by and drove slowly back to the main road. He raised a hand to her as she passed him and she drove on wondering if she'd handled it properly. How on earth did you tell a man that his mistress of twenty years' standing had died of an overdose? Chilled to the bone, trembling like a dog, Kate turned the heater to maximum and pulled on to the main road.

George watched her go and then turned back to his contemplation of the moor. The whole thing was unbelievable. Felicity dead. He shook his head, frowning out on the grey forbidding landscape, and, flinging away his cigarette, thrust his hands deep into his pockets. Felicity dead. It seemed unreal. That anyone as vitally alive, as forceful, as positive as Felicity should have passed into a mere handful of dust was inconceivable. He remembered her biting tongue and caustic wit, her fierce glance—judgmental, condemnatory—and her passion. He recalled the black hair, the flashing eyes, her sharp features and the overall impression of speed and movement: a bird in flight or, more recently, a bird of prey. George felt a stab of remorse and shame. During these last two years he had feared her, hated her, wanted her out of his life. And now she was. Permanently removed, gone for ever. He swallowed and, wrapping his arms across his chest, dropped his head. He remembered when Mark had first introduced her to him at a party. She'd been wearing one of the new mini-skirts and was as brown as a gypsy. He'd taken the thin fingers and raised them to his lips and she'd laughed, raising her black-winged brows.

'How fearfully French,' she'd mocked and her black eyes had danced and flashed, captivating his stolid, very English heart. 'Not a Frog, are you?' What a long road it had been from that gay beginning to this lonely end. He thought of her, pleading with him in London, desperate, lonely, and him, forgetful of their shared love that had spanned twenty years, caring only for his new love, mindful of a new life and indifferent to her misery. He lifted his head and felt the first drops of rain, cold on his face. Suddenly, he longed to be back at the Old Station House, feeling Thea's warmth, rejoicing in the knowledge of their unborn child, their offering to a hopeful future. No use to dwell upon the past and all the mistakes that it contained. Thea would help him to bear the pain of it, to see it in proportion.

He stumbled to the car and lowered himself into the driving seat, taking his handkerchief from his pocket and wiping the rain from his face. He drove back to the road and turned towards Tavistock, switching on the windscreen wipers and huddling into his coat. Several times he wiped the moisture from his face and it wasn't until he was nearly home that he realised it was not rain upon his cheeks but tears that slipped unbidden from his eyes and, though he tried, would not be checked.

ON THE FOLLOWING MONDAY George returned to Northwood and in the evening Thea telephoned Polly and told her the whole story. Polly was shocked into silence and Thea was able to pour out her own horror, which she had not been able to do with George. He had needed comfort and support and Thea thanked God that she had seen Felicity, changed out of all recognition by her happiness, and that they had had that moment of reconciliation and understanding. She had been able to tell George about that, confirming Kate's story of another man, and it had helped George in his attempt to come to terms with the tragedy. Thea remembered how she and Felicity had hugged each other and felt grateful. She said all this to Polly several times before she hung up, exhausted, but comforted and relieved to get it all out of her system.

Polly replaced the receiver thoughtfully and Paul glanced up from his book.

'So what was that all about?'

'Awful.' Polly shivered a little. 'A friend of Thea's has died. She fell in love with a man who didn't care for her that much and when he left her she took an overdose.'

Paul's expression indicated a faint contempt for the irrationality of female behaviour. 'Bit extreme, isn't it?'

Polly pulled herself together and regarded him. 'Depends on how strong your feelings are, I suppose,' she said, deliberately omitting to tell him that Felicity's death was viewed as an accident.

Paul shrugged. 'Or how weak your intellect.'

Remembering the great drama which had surrounded Fiona's recent discovery, Polly raised her eyebrows. 'Perhaps it's simply that you've never experienced any great emotion outside a laboratory,' she suggested.

Paul stared at her. A contemptuous look curled his lip a little. 'Perhaps you're right,' he said and picked up his book.

It was only later that Polly noticed the possible ambiguity in Paul's answer. After all, Fiona spent a great deal of time with him in the laboratory.

WHEN DAVID CONTINUED TO get no reply from Felicity's telephone number he decided to go down to see her. He thought of writing to her but felt, on reflection, that it would be better to have it out face to face. It was only right to talk the whole thing through thoroughly and then, if Felicity were prepared to take the chance, they would take up the threads and go on together. He was still very much in two minds as to whether the relationship would work but he was, by now, deeply ashamed of his behaviour and wanted to make amends. He was very fond of her and the more he thought about it the more he thought it was worth a try. Things were still very strained with Miranda and he was glad to leave her with Tim at Broadhayes and drive the well-known road to Mary Tavy.

Felicity's car was in the track but there was no reply to his ring and the place seemed deserted. He wandered round peering in at the windows and then gave up and drove away, wondering what to do with himself until he could go back and try again. Of course, she might have gone away. He remembered that she sometimes took a taxi to the station if she intended to be away for any length of time and he pulled in at the local garage from which this service was run.

The young man who operated the pumps raised a hand to him, recognising him from his previous visit, and David, who had filled the car up at Moretonhampstead, pulled well over on the forecourt and got out.

'Hello there. How are you? I'm trying to find Mrs Mainwaring. Don't happen to know if she's away, do you?'

The young man's shocked expression alerted him and he felt his heart give a little tick.

'You 'aven't 'eard then, sir? Oh,'twas terrible. The poor lady's dead. Took too many of 'er tablets, seemin'ly. Lyin' dead she was fer two days before anyone found 'er. Shockin', isn't it, sir?'

David felt for the car behind him and leaned back against it. The young man looked at him closely. 'You all right, sir?'

David nodded. 'When . . . when did she . . . die?'

The young man shook his head consideringly. ''Twas a few days ago now. Might be a week. Funeral was yesterday. Sorry to give you such a shock, sir. Fancy you not knowin'.'

'I . . . I've been away. I had no idea . . .'

''Course,'er 'usband'd died recently, so I 'eard. 'Spect you knew all about that.'

'Yes. Yes I knew about that.'

'Kept 'erself very privit, she did. Didn't use us much. Took 'er car down to the Citroën garage in Plymouth. Filled up 'ere sometimes, she did. Used the taxi but she weren't one to chat. Poor soul. Terrible thing. Sure you're all right, sir?'

'Nobody knows why she should . . . why she did such a thing?'

The young man pursed his lips and shook his head. 'P'raps she couldn't get over 'er 'usband. Navy 'e was. You didn't know 'er too well then, sir?'

'Not too well. Friend of a friend.'

A car pulled in at the pumps and the young man nodded and turned away. After a moment David opened the car door and got in. He sat for a moment and then, with a tremendous effort, started the engine and pulled away, raising a hand to the young man. Presently he found himself on the open moor and turned off the road as soon as he could. He switched off the ignition with a trembling hand and gazed out over the misty uplands. Surely, surely it could not be true? He thought of her happiness, her response to his love, the way that she had given all of herself. He remembered her voice on his answering machine and how it had changed from from friendly enquiries to desperate pleadings. He recalled Miranda saying, 'I told her that you didn't want to speak to her,' and gripped the steering wheel in both hands as a wave of anguish engulfed him. He had killed her. She had loved him and trusted him and he had killed her. Never mind what she had been or done before; to him she had shown love, generosity, passion, and he had taken it all, used it and then flung it back in her face. Too cowardly to tell her the truth, he had left her imagining that he would return and then let her discover, quite brutally, that it was all over. Shame and grief wrenched at his breast and resting his forehead on the wheel he began to cry.

Presently, exhausted by the great tearing sobs that shook him, he raised his head and leaned his forehead against the cool glass of the window beside him. Tiredly he stared out over the quiet indifferent landscape and finally a small measure of calm returned. He felt numbed, beyond thought or reason, and, when he could sit no longer and there seemed nothing else to do, he started up the engine and drove back to Broadhayes.

Twenty

IN THE END, MIRANDA agreed to be married from Broad-hayes in the local church. It was such a perfect house to be married from and, unlike her home in Chelsea, there was room to put up their relations and friends. Anyway, David, at this time, would have made an indifferent host. Even by Christmas he still seemed unable to recover from the shock of Felicity's death. Naturally, none of them felt able to mention it to Thea and she, sublimely unaware that they knew of Felicity's existence, never mentioned her to them. They had none of the comfort of being able to tell themselves that her death had been accidental and even if David had known this to be the case he would have been unable to accept it. His whole being shrank from the horror of what he had done and when he came face to face with himself in the looking-glass each morning as he shaved, he saw the visage of a murderer.

Miranda, shocked and frightened at her part in it, thrust it deep down inside and refused to look at it at all. Even she was unable to say with conviction that Felicity had got what she asked for or that it was a just retribution. She pushed it out of sight and was glad when David returned to London and she no longer had to see his tortured eyes looking out of the carefully schooled mask that had become his face.

Tim fared best. Horrified though he was, he steadfastly refused to believe that Felicity had killed herself. Everything that they knew of her, he argued, went against that. Much more likely to have been accidental and, because of his love for Thea, he was able to remember what Felicity had been prepared to do to harm his cousin and could

harden his heart. As the new year wore on, he was far too busy setting up his business and organising his new home to think of it at all
and it sank gently into the recesses of his mind.

As the months went by they saw very little of David, who was
busy with an exhibition in London, and Tim, alone at last with Miranda, was beginning to find that marriage was not quite the joy he
had hoped for. Miranda's tendencies to unexplained silences and
prickly irritability worried him. It was borne slowly in upon him that
she preferred them to live an almost reclusive life, where there could
be no cause for jealousy or suspicion, and Tim, who had imagined
them using Broadhayes to its maximum advantage—giving parties,
keeping open house—was disappointed and puzzled. He spent more
and more time in his office with his computers and made the most of
his business trips to see friends and fulfil the naturally gregarious side
of his personality and, although she hated it when he went away, Miranda seemed content enough to keep herself occupied with her own
pursuits.

GEORGE'S GRIEF WAS VIOLENT but as proportionately short.
Thea talked him through it as he had hoped she would, comforting
him, guiding him kindly but firmly away from the boggy paths of
guilt and self-pity and leading him to the higher paths where he could
look back and remember Felicity with gratitude and affection. Perhaps she made it too easy for him to disown any responsibility but it
was not in her interest—or his—to have him obsessed by remorse.
She had no past memories to mourn over but a much more recent
memory of a glowing, youthful-looking Felicity which she could de-
scribe to George, assuring and reassuring him that her death was an
accident. George was only too ready to be convinced, to put it all behind him and to look forward to a life which seemed to have no cloud
on its horizon.

In June when Thea gave birth to a daughter, Amelia, even she let the
tragedy of Felicity's unhappiness and death slide away. It was as though
she had taken the pain from George to be dealt with in her own way and

she mourned Felicity in a completely different manner. She mourned the sadness and unhappiness that had been Felicity's lot by virtue of her character. What a blessing it is to be born with a happy, loving, generous disposition; what a handicap to start life with a tendency towards self-seeking and selfishness, an indifference to the well-being of others. Thea brooded on the ability to change oneself, to train and encourage the character towards a discipline that brought contentment and fulfilment. It depended upon so many things and it was impossible to judge the capabilities of others. The frailty of human nature and life itself weighed upon her soul and she sought her usual reassurance. The collect for the fourth Sunday after Epiphany brought her comfort.

O God, who knowest us to be set in the midst of so many and great dangers, that by reason of the frailty of our nature we cannot always stand upright: Grant to us such strength and protection, as may support us in all dangers, and carry us through all temptations; through Jesus Christ our Lord. Amen.

She left the care of Felicity's soul in higher hands and turned her attention to her own household.

AS IN THE PAST, Kate's mourning took place on the great open spaces of the moor. She looked back over the twenty years that she had known Felicity and her heart was heavy. She wondered if Felicity had ever experienced real happiness. It seemed that this unknown man had shown her something, enabled her to experience some depth of feeling hitherto unknown to her. How cruel, then, to have it snatched away. Kate remembered how Felicity had sat at her kitchen table and wept and she knew that none of them had really known her. Perhaps Felicity had never truly known herself. As usual Kate's fears and depression were soothed in the face of this great timeless world but they could not entirely be done away with.

I'm getting old, she thought and remembered Cass's last letter.

Cass had felt it almost impossible to believe that her old enemy and sparring partner was dead. She still couldn't take it in.

'. . . It's too awful, Kate,' she'd written. 'It sounds so terribly un-like her, if you know what I mean. I simply can't imagine her keeling over or giving in just for a mere man. It must have been an accident. Those awful heads she used to get. Perhaps she didn't know what she was doing, especially if she'd been drinking. Oh, God! When I think of all that Felicity-baiting I used to do I feel very small and mean. I'm so glad you and she were together just before the end. That's a com-fort somehow. I wish I could have the chance to say I'm sorry. I was rotten to her sometimes. Oh dear. I'm crying now. She was an old cow, wasn't she? But even so, she was part of us, part of all our pasts, and I'd give anything to see her again. She could be as rude as she liked! And when I think that she left everything to you I'm speechless! I could forgive her anything. Oh, Kate. Isn't life hell? I think I must be getting old! Thank God we shall be home for Christmas . . .'

Kate, too, still felt a spasm of shock when she woke each morning to the fact that Felicity had smoothed her path financially. It was such a very great blessing, to be eased from the pinching and saving of the day to day, but Kate felt uneasy at receiving such benefit in such a manner and her thoughts of Felicity were troubled and grateful in equal measure.

DAVID SIMPLY COULDN'T COME to terms with it. His mind played and replayed the same scene: Felicity dying. He saw this scene a hundred different ways while trying desperately to cling to Tim's theory. Sometimes this seemed very reasonable. Felicity had been no neurotic, no unbalanced clinging female. She was a strong, forceful personality. Look how she had fought for George. At this point, David would remember that George, too, had rejected her and that even the most balanced of people can only take so much punishment. Even so . . . And so on and so on. His mind would tread the same well-worn circular path until he was exhausted.

His exhibition was a tremendous success but each painting was a reminder, a memory, a little stab to the heart, and he was glad to put it behind him. He visited Tim and Miranda as seldom as he could, afraid of resurrecting emotions or being obliged to talk about Felicity. If he had but known it there was no risk of that. At Broadhayes the subject was taboo by mutual consent but, at present, the mere presence of Tim and Miranda would have been too much for him. Anyway, he was enjoying his freedom. He hadn't been alone for years and he found it soothing to potter quietly when the day's work was done, listening to music, reading, inviting one or two of his closest friends to supper. Slowly the pain receded a little but the guilt lived on, fresh and new each morning, and he suspected that he would never be free of it.

EVEN POLLY, THOUGH SHE had never known Felicity, was affected by her death. Thea often talked of it with her, going over the mysterious circumstances, describing George's reaction, reporting on his progress through the months. Polly was strangely moved by the idea of the lonely, unwanted woman, dying alone in the empty house. Had she regretted it when it became too late? Tried to raise help? What had been her last thoughts? She was moved to make greater efforts with Paul, who was even more deeply immersed in his work and—Polly suspected—Fiona. However, these efforts seemed to go unnoticed and, with the arrival of Amelia, Polly was often at the Old Station House and life gradually slipped back into its old pattern.

THE YEAR WORE ON and the anniversary of Felicity's death arrived and passed. Those who had known her turned their eyes towards Christmas and a new year but they had all, in some way, been touched and changed and Felicity herself would have been surprised to know how often she was remembered, mourned, loved. Too late now, these emotions, to be of use to her, but they would go on working in other hearts and breasts and, because of her, thoughts and actions would be differently shaped and lives changed.

Twenty-one

ALBAN BERG WAS COMPOSER of the Week the day that Polly's husband went off with Fiona.

The day started like any other. Paul had risen early but this was not unusual. He was in the habit of waking at about six o'clock, making coffee and vanishing into his study to put in a few hours' work before he went off to the university. Two or three times each week he and Polly didn't see each other until the evening, for she found mornings difficult. The thought of light conversation across the muesli was anathema to her; the bleared eye above the stubble was inimical to her well-being so early in the day. Apart from which she doubted that Paul would have noticed her presence since he tended to spend breakfast time with his head in a book, his eyes rarely lifted from the printed page.

By the time Polly arrived downstairs, on the day in question, Radio Three was well into Berg and the kitchen showed the usual signs of disorder. Automatically she began to clear the table and saw, mid-yawn, the note propped against the butter dish.

Paul's tiny crabbed handwriting was almost illegible and broken phrases presented themselves to Polly's dazed eyes. '. . . bit of a shock . . . can't let her down . . . inevitable . . . be in touch . . .' with 'Fiona' scattered about at intervals like sultanas in a scone.

Polly, her nerves on edge, switched off the Seven Early Songs and wondered what to do next. What was the form when one's husband took off with his assistant, leaving a farewell note and mentioning in passing that he'd be in touch?

She looked again at the note. Nothing had prepared her for it, no warning, no discussion, no opportunities to put things right. It was true that during the last two years they had tended to drift a little further apart. Polly had become deeply involved in the launching of the Percy the Parrot books and had encouraged Thea through her pregnancy and the birth of her daughter, Amelia. She knew that this was living life rather vicariously through someone else's achievements and joys but it was harmless and fun and Paul seemed to be spending more and more time wrapped up in his work. There had been no rows or arguments and he had accepted with total equanimity her friendship with Freddie. It had, so far, been a perfectly harmless friendship just as she had imagined Paul's had been with Fiona. Perhaps she had been naïve but Paul didn't seem to have the temperament of a deceiver. And how very odd of him to come to such an important decision about their marriage all in a rush, between, as it were, one insect and the next! But what was in his mind for the future? What did he intend? Obviously he intended that she, Polly, should stay put while he sorted his life out with Fiona. Then, no doubt, he would 'be in touch.'

Polly felt a sudden surge of anger. She'd be damned if she would sit here, tamely waiting to hear what had been planned for her and how her future had been organised! Leaving the table in its disorder, she gathered up the note and went upstairs. A recce of Paul's dressing room showed that he had taken very little with him. His weekend bag had gone and his shaving things from the bathroom but she saw from the bedroom window that the car stood in its usual place by the kerb. She also saw Mrs Bloge coming down the road. This solved one problem. Nothing useful could be attempted with her in the house. Polly couldn't have borne for her to know. She hurried round collecting her keys, bag and jacket and went back downstairs.

'Can't stop this morning, Mrs Bloge,' she called. 'Got to dash. Shan't be back till after lunch. See you next week.'

'What about me wages?' Mrs Bloge issued from the kitchen, heavy with disapproval.

'Heavens!' Polly gave a feeble laugh. 'Yes, of course, it's Friday, isn't it?'

She scrabbled in her purse, brought out the amount in the back section which was designated 'Bloge' and, passing it over, hurried out into the bleak January day. A few yards up the road, she turned in at the gate of a semi-detached villa almost identical to her own but in rather better repair. Round the side of the house she went, through the back door and into the kitchen.

'Hi,' she shouted. 'Hello. Only me. Anyone in?'

She could hear scufflings and voices off and, in the upper regions of the house, the sound of a French horn. The inner door opened and her friend Suzy appeared, a small child growing out of her hip like a Siamese twin and another clinging to her leg. She came in, dragging the leg with the child on it.

'Thank goodness it's you,' she said with her sweet smile. 'Simon is having one of his insecure days and Daniel's got a bit of a temperature. Put the kettle on, there's a duck.'

'Jake's home, I hear.' Polly jerked her head French hornwards and went to fill the kettle.

'He's got a concert in Bristol next week.' Suzy laid the smaller child in a carrycot on the sofa under the window and swung Simon up and into his high chair at the table. He clung to her as if she were a lifebelt and he a drowning man. Polly knew just how he felt.

'Paul's left me.' She couldn't keep it back another second.

'Paul? Left you?'

Even Simon, sensing drama, let go of Suzy and gazed at Polly.

'He's gone off with Fiona.'

'With Fiona?'

'He left me a note. On the table.'

'Left a note?'

Polly looked around for the echo whilst Suzy thrust a plastic drinking mug into Simon's open but unresisting mouth and gave Polly her undivided attention.

'I don't believe it. It doesn't sound a bit like Paul. He doesn't like women. And with Fiona of all people.'

'Why "of all people"? If he's going to run off with anyone surely she's the most likely candidate? They have masses in common, she's young, pretty . . .'

Saying the words made the situation a great deal more real and, quite suddenly, Polly began to howl. Loudly and luxuriously, she broke down and howled without restraint.

Simon took his mug out of his mouth and his face began to crumple. Ominous noises came from the carrycot. Even the French horn stopped. So did Polly. She couldn't face an irate Jake roaring in demanding, 'What the bloody hell is going on now? Can't I ever get to practise in peace?' and so on.

Suzy soothed the baby and replaced Simon's mug whilst Polly sniffed and snuffled and tried to pull herself together. After a moment. Suzy pushed a mug under her nose. Polly gave her the note to read and morosely piled sugar into her mug.

'What dreadful writing,' observed Suzy. 'He should have been a doctor.'

'He *is* a doctor.'

'You know what I mean—a real doctor. I can't read a word of this.' She screwed up her eyes, turning the paper this way and that, and passed it back. 'I'll take your word for it. What are you going to do?'

'I've no idea. There's no address, no telephone number. He doesn't seem to have taken very much with him and the car's still there. I think I'm supposed to sit and wait until he contacts me. At the end it says "be in touch". I don't know what to do.' Polly felt like blubbing again but the French horn was back in full flood and Simon had a glazed look, so she didn't like to. She took a huge swig from the mug and choked violently.

'Jesus!' she spluttered. 'What the hell is this?' She coughed frenziedly.

'It's wild raspberry tea. It's very good for stress.' Suzy once again patted the baby and restored Simon's mug. Luckily the French horn hadn't been disturbed this time. 'Listen, I've had an idea.'

'So have I.' Polly held the mug out. 'I'd like some coffee.'

'Know what I think?' Suzy ignored her. 'I think it would be a very bad idea to sit waiting for Paul to take all the decisions. You're always so easy-going. And he seems to spend half his spare time in the lab with Fiona. Let's face it. You've handed it to him on a plate. I expect she flatters him and it's gone to his head. I can't believe it's serious.'

'But what can I do?'

'I don't know. Anything. Visit friends. Get a dog. Have a haircut. Get a job. Anything. It doesn't matter so much what you do as long as you do something. You don't want to sit about moping, do you?'

'Yes,' said Polly, sulkily. 'As it happens, I do. I think it's intolerable that he should explode this bombshell and then expect me to wait patiently until he decides to get in touch. I want to sit and think about it and realise how much I hate him. And her.'

'It's a pity you haven't got children,' mused Suzy, ignoring this excursion into self-pity. 'Children keep you occupied, stop you thinking too much. It's a mistake to do anything dramatic. Mmm. Yes. Perhaps a dog's a bit much and jobs aren't that easy to come by but at least you can go and get your hair done. It will keep your morale up and make you feel better. Now will you go?'

Polly shrugged. She felt that her problem was being made light of and she didn't want to make it too easy. 'I might.'

'After all, it's a start, isn't it? There's a super place just off Queen Street I go to when life gets too much for me. Hang on, I'll see if I can make an appointment with Tony for you.'

'Who's Tony?' Polly asked listlessly.

'He's the owner. He does my hair. Hang on.'

She went into the hall and Polly heard the telephone being used. Simon stirred in his chair and she eyed him cautiously. Sometimes she could deal with him, sometimes not. Simon and Suzy had a real Oedipus and Jocasta thing going and Polly simply wasn't in the mood for it. She gave him a biscuit. He placed it carefully on the tray of his high chair and proceeded to smash it into crumbs with his mug. Fair enough. Polly shrugged. At least it was keeping him quiet.

'Great!' Suzy came in beaming. 'He's had a cancellation and he can fit you in at twelve o'clock. I'll tell you where he is. You've simply got to stay positive! I remember when Jake had a thing with a violinist, I just kept going, did my own thing. He soon packed it in. You remember? That's when we started Daniel. He was our reconciliation. I'm sure that this is just a flash in the pan. Don't weaken. That's the great thing.'

Polly sighed. The last thing she needed was bracing talks and raspberry tea. If only there had been time to telephone Harriet or Thea. She stood up and collected her things. At least she might get a decent cup of coffee at the hairdresser's.

THE SALON WAS MORE like a bistro than a hairdressing establishment. The walls were whitewashed stone, the lighting flattering, and at one end people drinking coffee sat on painted wooden chairs at scrubbed pine tables. A large blackboard hung on the wall listing exotic dishes and there was a little bar in one corner.

Polly announced herself to the receptionist, who looked about twelve, and the girl vanished through a curtain at the back, no doubt in order to summon Tony. Polly looked around; there were only two basins, cleverly concealed in an alcove, and two padded chairs, set at angles away from each other, before huge mirrors with heavy wooden frames.

'You must be Polly!'

Polly swung round. Tony was an old Harrovian, tall and tanned—he was just back from a skiing holiday in Austria—with blond hair cut short around his ears and neck but left long on top. He wore his old school tie round the collar of a cream raw silk shirt which was tucked into green cords.

'Hello.' They shook hands. 'And you must be Tony.'

'Absolutely. Suzy told me what happened and I think that it's very brave of you to come.'

'Suzy told you? On the phone?' Polly was shocked.

Tony ushered her to one of the chairs. 'Certainly. Very sensible of her. Then we all know where we are, you see. The thing is to take your mind off things until you've calmed down a bit. Amazing the things that people do when they've had a shock. Now then.'

He lifted bits of her hair and rubbed them in his fingers, staring at her in the mirror with narrowed eyes.

'All this off, I think. Yes? Short, straight, sleek. Yes?'

'My husband likes it long,' protested Polly feebly, huddling nervously in her chair and still feeling unsettled by the fact that this stranger knew all about her private life.

'My dear girl'—Tony bent close and their eyes met in the mirror—'does that matter in your present circumstances?'

Polly stared at him mesmerised. He gave a sharp nod and called for a minion. Another girl appeared, looking even younger than the first. She was dressed from head to foot in black: black polo neck, brief black skirt, long black woollen legs, flat black pumps. She took away Polly's jacket, wrapped her in waterproof garments and led her to one of the basins.

'Lean back, that's it. Head comfortable? Tell me if the water gets too hot.'

It was impossible to nod so Polly gargled assent and closed her eyes. She loved having her hair washed: the warm water, the massaging fingers, the smell of shampoo and then the warm fluffy towels. Bliss. Far too soon it was over and she was sitting once more in the padded chair. The girl smiled encouragingly at her. 'Coffee?' she asked.

'Oh, yes please,' said Polly fervently, remembering the wild raspberry tea.

Tony appeared. He combed her hair, picked up his scissors and smiled. 'Ready?'

Polly nodded.

'Want to talk?'

Polly shook her head.

'Off we go then.'

He snipped away, twisting great swatches of hair on to the top of her head and holding them in place with enormous, brightly coloured bulldog clips. Her coffee came. It was delicious and she drank it quietly, co-ordinating with his cutting so that she didn't spill any. Presently he laid aside his scissors and went to work with a hairdryer and brush. A woman came to sit in the other chair and a very superior girl started to perform the same sort of rites upon her. It was all very peaceful and relaxing and, try though she might, Polly couldn't bring her mind to concentrate on the disaster that had befallen her.

'There!' Tony laid aside the tools of his trade.

Polly could barely believe her eyes. Silky shining brown hair fell smooth and sleek to her jawline. She looked much more sophisticated but, oddly, younger. Tony swung a hand mirror to and fro behind her head so that she could see the back.

'Amazing!' She shook her head, lost for words. 'You're brilliant.'

'Well, we all know that, lovey.' He took away the towels, brushed her off and gestured to his minion who hurried off to find Polly's jacket. As she followed him to the reception desk, Cass emerged from the café corner, smiled at her vaguely and then stopped in her tracks.

'Polly! It is Polly, isn't it? I'm Cass Wivenhoe. Remember me? Harriet brought you over to lunch and then we met at Thea's. And then at Hugh's christening. How are you?'

'Not at all well at the moment,' Tony answered for Polly. 'Her husband's run away with his assistant, silly man, and Polly's all of a doodah, poor duck.' Polly was horrified. She glared at Tony, who winked back at her as he passed her the bill. 'She needs to be taken out and given a good lunch.'

'My dear.' Cass was staring at her in consternation. 'I'm dreadfully sorry . . .'

'Please.' Polly searched for her chequebook, blushing furiously.

'Honestly . . .' She began to write the cheque as though her life depended on it.

Cass's eyes met Tony's questioningly and he gave a little nod.

'Well, look. Why not?' Cass rose swiftly to the occasion. 'I've had my hair done and now I'm at a loose end. I'd love it if you could spare the time. I've come all this way to let this terrible man have his way with my head and it seems such a pity to waste the result by driving tamely home again.'

'The transformation I wrought on you definitely needs celebrating,' said Tony firmly to Polly, who seemed to have lost her powers of speech.

'He's right!' Cass was delighted at the suggestion. 'And I've had another thought. I'm having a party tomorrow evening and it would be wonderful if you could come. Harriet and Michael will be there and Thea and George. All the old mob. We've been out in the States for the last two years and we're belatedly celebrating our twenty-fifth wedding anniversary. It's a few months late but we haven't been back long. It will be great fun! You simply must come. I absolutely insist. We'll go and have lunch and talk about it.'

Taking Polly firmly by the arm, lest in her despair she should fling herself beneath the wheels of a passing bus, Cass swept her off into the town.

'THE TROUBLE IS, I can't seem to take it in.' Polly had drunk two large gins and she was feeling loquacious and even euphoric. 'I can't get it into my head that he's gone. You know? It's like trying to meditate. Or pray. Every time you start your mind slips off somewhere else. It's like that.'

'Well, I think that's a very good thing. It means that you won't be doing anything silly in a rush. And who knows? He may feel a bit silly himself in a day or two and come hurrying back to you.' Cass set the menu aside and waved to a passing waitress.

Polly examined this idea. To her surprise she wasn't as pleased as she might have been at the thought of it.

'He's a pompous prick!' she announced. The waitress looked surprised and Polly took another glop of gin. 'Well, he is,' she muttered defensively.

Cass gave their order, unmoved by this somewhat public revelation. 'D'you know, I've been thinking,' she said. 'Why don't you drive over this afternoon and stay with us for the whole weekend? Well, as long as you like. I think it's a bit much for you to be stuck waiting for Paul to deign to contact you. It'll be horrid for you. We could drive down in tandem when we've finished shopping. We'll go back to your place, pick up your car and drive down to the car park to fetch mine. You can come home again when you feel like it, when you've pulled yourself together and got a plan of action. I don't see why he should have it quite all his own way. Now, why don't you? You'd be among friends and I'd love it. It's such a dreary time of year to be on your own. What do you say?'

'Sounds wonderful!' Polly finished her gin and grinned broadly. She didn't mean to but she couldn't control her face. She could feel the grin plastered there but could do nothing about it. She rarely drank spirits and generally behaved badly when she did.

'Good,' Cass exclaimed. 'Now what sort of dress for the party, I wonder?' She looked at Polly appraisingly. Polly continued to grin. 'Something long and elegant, I think—and stunning. Yes, definitely stunning.'

Polly pondered this suggestion but before she could ask Cass to elaborate the food arrived and the moment passed. To Polly it seemed as if they were eating for hours. Delicious food came and went and, after a bit, she felt more normal as the effect of the gin wore off. Before she could pass into the maudlin state that so often follows, however, Cass had whisked her off again.

Shopping with Cass was an experience Polly was unlikely ever to forget. In and out of shops they whirled and Polly undressed, tried on and re-dressed until, finally, Cass was satisfied.

'You're so slim! I really can't think why you wear those floppy, baggy clothes. So unflattering.'

Polly stared into the looking-glass at her new image clothed in a long soft clinging garment. 'Are you sure it's me?' she asked cautiously.

'Absolutely certain!' cried Cass firmly. 'And while we're here . . .'

They left with bulging bags and took a hopper back to Polly's house so that she could pack. She was, by now, subject to severe twinges of guilt, quite certain that this was not how abandoned wives behaved. Cass, sensing her change of mood, clung to her side barely giving her a chance to pack and reminding her to cancel the milk and papers.

After telephoning Mrs Bloge and Suzy, Polly picked up her case. 'I'm ready,' she said. 'Suzy, my friend up the road, will keep an eye on things. She's got a spare key.'

She looked round the hall—what on earth was she doing?—and then at Cass. Alarm seized her.

'Splendid!' Cass beamed at her. 'Then all you need to do is look forward to a jolly weekend. I really don't see why you shouldn't have some fun, too.'

It was the 'too' that decided Polly. After all, who knew what Paul and Fiona might be up to, going off into the blue, while she had to sit alone waiting to hear her fate? Panic receded and defiance returned.

'Neither do I,' she said firmly.

Twenty-two

POLLY HAD NO IDEA where Cass lived on Dartmoor. Had she been visiting Harriet, she would have taken the A30 to Okehampton and turned on to the Tavistock road across the moor. As it was, Cass left the city and drove to the A38 where she followed the signs to Plymouth.

Polly, sticking firmly on her tail, was terrified lest she should lose sight of her rear lights and wished she'd asked Cass for directions. In the gathering gloom it was difficult to distinguish one car from another and Polly heaved a deep sigh of relief when the indicator light on Cass's car started winking and she followed her off the main road. Through Ivybridge they went, past the farmland behind the town and, finally, on to the moorland road.

Now Polly was well and truly lost, her headlights showing up stone walls, stunted trees and the white coat of the occasional sheep. Just as she had decided that she and Cass would be crossing the moor for the rest of their lives—rather like two terrestrial flying Dutchmen—the indicator in front of her started to wink once more and she found herself passing between two stone pillars and following Cass up a bush-lined drive. Cass drove past the house where the light over the door glowed welcomingly after the endless darkness of the moor and round to some outbuildings where she parked. Thankful, Polly pulled in beside her and switched off the engine.

Cass was already out of her car and hurrying round to Polly shouting words of praise and encouragement, as though Polly had been first past the chequered flag at Le Mans instead of having driven probably less than forty miles in fairly normal conditions. Polly liked it. Rarely did she have her achievements viewed with anything more than a tepid tolerance and Cass's approbation was a very pleasant change. She preened a bit and shrugged off her cleverness.

'It was nothing,' she said modestly. 'I just followed your rear lights.'

'Even so'—Cass was helping to gather her case and belongings—'some people are very nervous of driving on the moor in the dark if they're not used to it. No street lights and the narrow roads, not to mention the sheep and the ponies leaping out at you. You were rattling along behind me like an old hand.'

Polly felt that perhaps, on reflection, she had been rather brave. Fearless, even. Her spirits rising, she followed Cass down the path and up the steps of the large Georgian house.

'It used to be the Rectory'—Cass opened the front door which didn't appear to be locked—'but the Church Commissioners sold it off and the Tanners live in a ghastly modern place in the village, poor old things. I feel really sorry for today's clergy. The only perk they had was being able to live in lovely old houses. Now they live in horrid modern boxes.' She shut the door behind them. 'It's a bit big when all the children are away but when everyone's at home we really need the space. It's a devil to heat, of course. I hope you'll be warm enough.'

Polly, still feeling rather brave, took in the square hall with its wellproportioned staircase and murmured that she was sure she would be.

A door opened and a man emerged into the hall. 'So there you are!' he exclaimed. 'I was beginning to worry.' His eye fell on Polly. 'Hello, there,' he added in a different tone. 'Who's this?'

He came forward and Polly recognised the dark, rather stocky man she had met at Harriet's wedding and again at the christening.

'It's Polly.' Cass made it sound as if she had produced a delicious delicacy for his tea. 'You remember, Harriet's friend. I met her at Tony's. She's all on her own for the weekend so I persuaded her to come to the party. Isn't that nice?'

'It certainly is!' Tom took Polly's hand and smiled at her. 'D'you know, I couldn't place you for a moment.'

'That's because she's had her hair cut and she looks quite different,' explained Cass. 'Now she's got to unpack her things. No, I'll take the case, Tom. You go and put the kettle on whilst we sort out a bedroom and then we'll have some tea.'

Tom gave Polly another smile. 'See you later,' he said and she followed Cass up the stairs.

'In here, I think.' Cass opened one of the doors on the large landing and, going into the bedroom, turned on the bedside lamp. 'It'll probably be the warmest one and you've got the bathroom next door. You'll have it to yourself. We turned one of the small bedrooms into a connecting bathroom for ourselves and Gemma's got a tiny one off her room. Well?' Cass looked round the room. 'What do you think?'

'I think it's lovely.' Polly spoke quite truthfully. The room glowed with warm soft colours: the velvet curtains a dark ruby, the carpet a mixture of faded blues and reds, the patchwork quilt thrown across the wide bed a brilliant spot of colour. Old, well-polished wood gleamed dimly and the brass bedhead shone in the lamplight. 'It's really super. And it feels quite warm to me.'

'You're above the kitchen, you see.' Cass crossed the room and pulled the curtains across the blackness of the night. 'We never let the Aga out so this wall is always warm. I'll get you an electric radiator, though, just to give it a boost. Shall I leave you to unpack?'

'Thank you. Cass?' Polly hesitated and Cass paused at the door. 'Shall you tell Tom about Paul?'

'Not if you don't want me to,' replied Cass promptly. 'But if people know what's happened you won't have to behave as though nothing's wrong.' She smiled. 'Everyone will be nicer to you. And if you behave badly, they'll make allowances.'

Polly began to smile, too, remembering the gin at lunchtime. 'What makes you think I'll behave badly?' she asked.

'My dear!' Cass looked shocked. 'I don't think anything of the kind. I just believe in leaving all one's options open.' She gave Polly a tiny wink. 'Don't you?'

'Perhaps you're right. OK. I'll leave it to you.'

'You can trust me. Come down when you've finished and we'll have tea by the fire.'

The door closed quietly behind her and Polly slipped off her out-door coat, heaved her suitcase on to the bed and snapped open the clasps. As she passed between bed and wardrobe she caught sight of herself in the looking-glass inside the wardrobe door and experi-enced a little shock of non-recognition. Going close, she peered at her hair, turning her head from side to side. Yes, it certainly suited her and she wasn't at all surprised that Tom hadn't recognised her. She put the empty suitcase in the bottom of the wardrobe, picked up her sponge bag and towel and, opening the door, stepped out-side. The landing stretched away, dim and shadowy: the closed doors blank-faced and secretive. All was quiet. Slowly she became aware of the stately ticking of the grandfather clock in the hall below and some measure of panic returned. She went into the bathroom, laid her things out, had a pee, washed her hands and hurried down-stairs.

COLD EARLY-MORNING LIGHT POURED into Harriet's bed-room where she lay dreaming. Max had just had puppies. He was staring in consternation at these bear-cub-like creatures—they all seemed to have been born at a full six weeks old—and then turned a reproachful gaze upon her.

'You should have warned me,' he seemed to say, 'that this sort of thing could happen to an elderly dog.'

'It's amazing!' Harriet said to Michael, who had now appeared in the dream with them. 'Max has had babies! It's incredible! Fancy us not realising after all this time that Max is a bitch!'

'Honestly, Harriet!' Michael, for one reason or another, seemed to be a bit impatient. 'For goodness' sake!' His voice was getting louder. 'Harriet!' Now he had her by the shoulder and was shaking her. 'Harriet! Wake up!'

'What? What is it?' Harriet woke to find Michael bending over her. She clasped his arm convulsively. 'Oh, Michael, where are the babies?'

'Babies?' Michael stood upright. 'Only one baby, I hope. And that's where it was when we went to bed last night. I think I'd have noticed if you'd had it in the night. What are you talking about? If you've been keeping it from me that you're about to drop twins, Harriet, I shall be very upset.'

'Oh, Michael.' Harriet, struggling into a sitting position, began to laugh. 'I dreamed that Max had had puppies. You should have seen his face!'

'I can imagine it only too well. Poor old Max. And at his great age, too! I woke you because Polly's been on the telephone. Apparently she's staying with Cass.'

'With Cass? What's she doing with Cass? They hardly know each other.'

Michael shrugged. 'I've no idea. She didn't confide in me. She's there for the party tonight and she phoned to see if you were going to be up to it. She said that the house is in an uproar and Cass suggested that she pop over to see you. That's why I woke you up. I said that you'd phone back.'

'Oh.' Harriet looked puzzled. 'How strange. I didn't realise that she was so friendly with Cass. Well, it'll be lovely to see her. I think we'll go tonight, don't you?'

'If you feel up to it.' Michael helped to haul her into a standing position. 'But not for too long.'

'It'll be good.' Harriet gave him a kiss. 'I'll get dressed and be right down. Good grief! It's nearly ten o'clock!'

'Well, you've been sleeping so badly I thought a lie-in would do you good. Everything's under control. I shall pop into the office later on but there's no hurry. I've even given Hugh his breakfast. Need any help?'

'No, I'll manage. Bless you, darling. I'll be down in a sec.'

Michael returned to the kitchen where Hugh had arranged assorted toys under the table and was kneeling amongst them, talking to them in a low monotone. Max lay stretched out before the Aga. Ozzy was asleep in the utility room but, in his old age, Max had begun to appreciate the warmth and comfort of the kitchen. Michael bent to stroke him and he opened one eye and sighed deeply.

'I hate to tell you this, old chap,' murmured Michael, 'but you've just become a mother.'

AS POLLY, CLOSELY FOLLOWING Cass's instructions, set out across the moor to Harriet, fitful gleams of sunshine lit up the craggy landscape. At the end of several weeks of nearly continuous rain, Dartmoor was looking exactly what it was: a giant sponge. Things dripped and squelched and even the sheep looked deeply depressed. They stood in clumps looking like so many sheepskin rugs that had been left out in the rain for weeks.

Poor old things, thought Polly, steering her way carefully between several who had taken up positions in the middle of the road and showed no disposition to move. It looks as if it would be a kindness to put them out of their misery and have them for lunch!

She reached the Princetown road and looked with awe upon the gloomy aspect of the prison, grey and forbidding. A working party moved to and fro in one of the fields and Polly shivered and set her foot more firmly on the accelerator. She turned left out of Princetown and headed towards Tavistock. Once through Merrivale, she kept her eyes open for the turning off on to the narrow road across the open moorland which led to Lower Barton and on to a farm.

Minutes later she was driving up the track to Harriet and Michael's cottage. It was, in fact, a converted barn standing in an isolated position at the side of the track which wound on past the little garden to another open-fronted barn which Michael used as a garage and wood store. As Polly parked by the gate into the garden, the front door opened and Harriet was hurrying out to meet her.

Polly sprang from the car and hugged as much of Harriet as she could get her arms round. 'Goodness, Harriet!' she cried. 'It looks as if it could be at any moment. Are you sure you ought to come tonight?'

'Another week yet,' said Harriet comfortably, kissing her old friend. 'You've had your hair cut! Looks great! And what on earth are you doing with Cass? Come and tell me all and say hello to your godson.'

She led the way through to the kitchen where Hugh was kneeling beside the recumbent Max with a row of toy animals perched on Max's furry side. A large teddy bear, wearing a fetching tinsel scarf, sat astride his neck.

'They're all on an outing to see Father Christmas,' explained Harriet. 'Max is the coach and teddy's the driver.'

Polly crouched to give Hugh a hug and Max a pat. 'Don't get up,' she said quickly to Max, who had shown no signs of expending such a vast amount of energy, 'or there'll be a dreadful accident. Hello, Huge.'

Hugh gave her a sidelong glance. 'Sing!' he commanded and Polly looked taken aback.

'We were having a singsong on the coach,' explained Harriet. 'We went up to Exeter to see Father Christmas with the playschool and everyone sang songs. So now it's the in-thing. Tell you what, Hugh, I think the coach has stopped so that everyone can stretch their legs and have some coffee. Why don't we have something, too, and then Polly can sing afterwards when she's wet her whistle?'

Hugh looked doubtfully at the passengers and then at Polly, who smiled at him. 'Shall we do "row, row, row your boat" while Mummy gets the kettle on?' she suggested. 'And then we'll all stop and have a coffee break. The coach must be getting pretty exhausted, too.'

Hugh's face cleared. 'Sing!' he shouted.

They sang. When, or so it seemed to Polly, they had rowed the full length of the Thames, Harriet announced that coffee was ready and the passengers were allowed off the coach to stretch their legs. Max pulled himself into a sitting position and rolled an eye towards the biscuit tin.

'Looks like the coach needs some petrol,' said Harriet, giving Max a biscuit. She sat Hugh in an armchair near the Aga, piled in the passengers and gave him his feeding mug and a small bowl with some biscuit and a few nuts and raisins in it. 'There you are. Share them round,' she told him. 'And now,' she said, subsiding at the table, 'tell me how you come to be staying with Cass.'

'Oh, Harriet,' Polly sighed. 'You simply won't believe this.'

Harriet stared at her aghast, as the recital proceeded. 'Gone off with Fiona? Left a note?'

Polly looked at her in alarm. Harriet was beginning to sound Suzy-ish. If she suggested she bought a dog or offered her raspberry tea Polly felt that she might hit her with a blunt instrument, pregnant or not.

'I don't know what to do,' she said and drank some coffee, smelling at it cautiously first.

'I'm not surprised!' Harriet sounded indignant. 'What a perfectly foul thing to do. Thank goodness you met up with Cass. She's just what you need in this sort of crisis. But do you really mean that you had no suspicion at all?'

'Well, I didn't. But you must remember, Harriet, that our married life isn't like most people's. Paul is often stuck in the laboratory or in his study and he's not terribly social. I'm not complaining. I'm very happy doing my own thing and I'd hate always to be gadding about to parties and things. I'm useless, domestically, you know that. I like pottering about, reading and listening to music and going out for walks. We're both very boring people, which is why we suit each other. We're not what you'd call madly passionate but I hadn't noticed any change in that respect or in anything else.' Polly shook her head. 'All I can assume is that, as he's been working so closely with Fiona, they've fallen madly in love and it's sort of sent him off his head. He's probably gone off to assimilate the facts, examine the data and write a short treatise on it,' she added morosely. 'Then he'll decide how to react. Meanwhile, I have to sit and wait for the results.'

Harriet stared at her across the table and then burst into an uncontrollable fit of mirth. 'I'm sorry,' she moaned. 'I'm truly sorry. It was just the way you said it. Oh, God. Sorry, Polly.' She mopped her eyes on a tea towel.

'Don't mind me.' Polly finished her coffee. 'I like to give people a good laugh.'

'No, no.' Harriet showed signs of breaking out again but controlled herself. 'It's not at all funny. And I'm really glad you're here. But look, you mustn't go home after the party. Come and stay with us for a bit. I certainly don't think you should be sitting at home alone, waiting at the end of the telephone.'

'Cass has told me I can stay as long as I like and, to be honest, Harriet, you don't look as if you're in a fit state to have guests. It's not as if I'm wonderfully practical and could cook terrific meals and be helpful to you. I'd probably be a pain in the neck. I'm sure Michael would think so. Where is he, by the way?'

'At the office. Ozzy's gone with him. And that's all rubbish and you know it. It would be lovely to have you. After all, Michael's cousin Jon is supposed to be arriving at any moment. He's in the Foreign Office and he's been abroad so much I've never even met him. If I can cope with him I can cope with you. It might even be a help. Anyway, see how you feel after the weekend.'

'Thanks. Huge has gone to sleep. What do you do with him when you go into hospital? Can I be of any help with that?'

'Well, everything's very well organised at the moment. Michael will simply take some time off from the office. He's fantastic at a time like this. Not at all the helpless male and he's super with Hugh. If there's a problem I'll shout. You'll stay and have some lunch?'

'Oh. Yes, please. Cass said that the longer I was out of the way the better. She's nice. And Tom . . .' Polly paused. 'You had a thing about Tom once, didn't you?'

'Oh, God. Don't talk about it. It's not a time that I'm particularly proud about. Yes, I did. I had an affair with him in the end. You probably remember. Why do you ask?'

'Well, it's just that they seem very well suited. Very easy-going and happy with each other. Didn't they have a child that died?'

'Don't talk about it.' Harriet stood up and went to the sleeping Hugh. 'I still feel so guilty. Tom and I were having an affair and Cass was running around with a married man and nobody really knows whether Charlotte—that was the little girl—found out and killed herself. It was awful. I've never forgiven myself.' She looked down at her sleeping son. 'How terrible to lose a child.'

'Well, at least it seems to have brought them back together.'

'It was quite a few years ago.' Harriet sighed and shook her head. 'What a terrible price to pay. Tom adored Charlotte and she absolutely worshipped him. Gemma isn't the same sort of child at all, very self-contained and aware of herself, and, of course, the boys are growing up and pushing out the boundaries, which is never easy for a father. He loves all his children and he's very proud of them but he must miss Charlotte dreadfully. Oh, Polly! I've come over all melancholy. Get us a drink, there's a love. You know where it is.'

'Jesus,' said Polly, getting up and going into the larder. 'I can tell that it's going to be one of those days. Thank goodness we've got a party to look forward to!'

Twenty-three

IN THE SURROUNDING COUNTRYSIDE, people were getting ready for the party.

As Kate got older she found herself becoming less and less sociable. She could see no advantages in leaving her fireside to venture out in totally unsuitable clothing into a cold January night to mouth banalities at people she saw regularly. Cass's twenty-fifth anniversary was obviously a special event but the thought of it had rather depressed her. The remembrance of those twenty-five years—Charlotte's death, her own divorce and her affair with Alex and now, more recently, Felicity's tragic accident—lowered her spirits. The legacy that Kate had received from Felicity had made an enormous difference to her life. She no longer had to scrape by, grateful to her brother Chris for his generous contributions, but was able to indulge herself a little and to feel more independent. Nevertheless, the lean years had made their mark and she found it difficult to be extravagant.

She had missed Cass terribly whilst she had been in America and was delighted to have her back but the thought of this evening's celebration gave her very mixed feelings. Chris, back in the country for a few weeks' holiday, watched her sympathetically. He was pleased that Felicity's legacy had given her much more security but he knew that now the twins had left home she was finding the middle years rather a struggle against loneliness and a tendency to brood.

'It's incredible to think that I've been going to Cass's parties for twenty-five years,' she said as they sat by the fire willing themselves to make a move. 'Unbelievable.' She gave herself a mental shake and smiled at him. 'Well. I suppose we'd better go and change. We haven't actually got to dress up though. I know it's a special occasion but Cass said that we can be casual.'

'Just as well,' said Chris as he climbed the stairs behind her. 'Everyone knows us far too well to expect us to be smart.'

THEA AND GEORGE, HAVING farther to drive, were already dressed. They were looking forward to the evening. The last year had been a happy, fulfilling one for both of them and the year-old Amelia had set the seal on their happiness. George had been made up to Captain, scraping in by the skin of his teeth, but now there was talk of a posting to NATO, probably Brussels. Thea was finding it difficult to come to terms with this. She couldn't bear the idea of leaving Jessie and Percy, not to mention the Old Station House, for two years but nor did she want to be apart from George. The conflicting interests and emotions of naval life had come late to her and she didn't know how to handle them. She thought of Cass, letting the Rectory, arranging for her children to be flown out to America during holidays, passing Gus over to Abby Hope-Latymer, and felt ashamed at her own dilatoriness. Added to these anxieties was the knowledge that she was pregnant again. She hadn't told George yet but the thought of going through the pregnancy in a foreign country with foreign doctors was a dreadful one. Despite her physique and youth, the birth of her daughter had been long and painful and Thea felt that she could only cope with this second pregnancy in the surroundings she loved.

She hoped that the party would take her mind off her worries. Polly had telephoned her from Harriet's that morning to tell her that Paul had gone off with Fiona and that she was coming to the party that evening. Thea was upset by the news but not terribly surprised. During the last year, she had had plenty of opportunity to observe Paul and Polly's relationship and it was not difficult to see that they were drifting further and further apart. She had been anxious that Polly might turn to Freddie for more than the easy-going, lighthearted companionship that they shared but Freddie seemed reluctant to break up the marriage and was content to bide his time. Thea, who assumed that Polly was staying with Harriet, decided to ask her to stay for a few days. Harriet was about to have the baby and Polly would need someone to talk to. At least it would distract Thea from her own problems even if there wasn't much that she could do for Polly.

George went to get the car out whilst Thea, having settled Amelia, was talking to the babysitter. Percy watched the proceedings with approval and crooned the 'Skye Boat Song' to himself. He liked the babysitter who fed him grapes and, unbeknownst to George, let him out of his cage to explore the kitchen. 'Speed bonny boat,' he whistled, hintingly, and Thea said that she must be going.

'Don't hurry back,' said the babysitter, who couldn't stand children but loved parrots. 'We'll be fine. Enjoy yourselves.'

HARRIET, HAVING SETTLED HUGH and wearing what appeared at first sight to be a navy-blue tent, talked to the babysitter whilst Michael went to fetch the car. Ozzy, propped against the bookcase, and Max, stretched before the fire, watched approvingly. They liked the babysitter who spoiled them with treats and let Max hog the fire. They looked meaningly at the door and sighed. Harriet took the hint and said she must be going.

'Don't hurry back,' said the babysitter, who couldn't stand children but adored dogs. 'We'll be fine. Enjoy yourselves.'

MEANWHILE, SOME MILES AWAY at Tiverton, Oliver was stopping off on his journey down from Cambridge, where he was at the university.

He pulled up outside the Victorian brick boarding houses of Blundell's School and went up the path to the side door of Petergate. As he reached it, it opened and his younger brother Saul nearly fell into his arms.

'This is great, Ollie,' he said. 'Do they know we're coming?'

'No.' Oliver took Saul's bag and flung it into the back of his old and rather battered Fiat Panda. 'I thought we'd be a nice surprise. Come on. We've got to get a move on. How's it going?'

'Oh. All right.' Saul's initial enthusiasm seemed to wane a little. He sighed.

'Spit it out,' said Oliver encouragingly. 'Still got a crush on what's-her-name? Got anywhere?'

'No chance. She likes really cool men. Thinks I'm too young. She's only a couple of months older than I am, too. Makes me sound as if I'm a kid. After all, I've passed my driving test. I may just give it all up.'

'Faint heart never won fair lady,' said Oliver as they fled towards Exeter. 'Your turn will come, never fear. Cheer up, old son!'

ANNABEL AND WILLIAM HOPE-LATYMER, up at the Manor, were both looking forward to the party. Land-rich they might be but, with two boys at preparatory school and a fourteen-year-old daughter at Sherborne School for Girls, they were, just at present, extremely cash-poor. They knew that the food and drink would be of the highest quality and even Abby, who hated dressing up, went up to change quite willingly.

'Good thinking to have a party now,' observed William, hunting for a clean shirt. 'There's always a whole spate of them at Christmas and over the New Year but it's now when everything's dark and drear that people need cheering up.'

'How right you are,' agreed Abby, who knew perfectly well that William didn't have a clean shirt and was wondering how to break the news to him. 'I thought we might not be quite so formal and stuffy tonight, darling. Why not wear that super rollneck Sophie gave you for Christmas and your new cords? You'll look very dashing!'

'You mean I haven't got a clean shirt,' said William, with a re-signed sigh. 'Will that do for a party?'

'It's not a dinner or anything,' said Abby, 'just a good thrash, Cass said. A late twenty-fifth wedding anniversary. Let's be different. You don't always have to wear a collar and tie, you know.'

'It just seems right,' grumbled William, going to find the said jersey. 'I bet Tom will be wearing a collar and tie.'

'That's because he's as stuffy as you are,' said Abby lightly. 'All those naval rules and regs. Break out! Be different!'

She left William in her dressing room and went into her daughter's bedroom, humming. Dear old William! What a dinosaur he was! She began to look through Sophie's clothes for something different and exciting.

POLLY, TOO, WAS PREPARING for the party. She had enjoyed her day with Harriet and on returning to the Old Rectory had had tea with Cass and Tom in the drawing room. It seemed to have twice as many chairs as the evening before, a log fire roared up the chimney and the furniture gleamed and shone from polishing. It looked welcoming and cosy. As she passed through the hall on her way upstairs, Polly saw that the dining-room table was laid out with a buffet supper and the sideboard creaked beneath its weight of bottles. She hurried on to her bath feeling both excited and nervous.

Now, as she moved around the bedroom, she felt just nervous. She peered at herself in the looking-glass. Her hair was still looking good and the new dress, high at the neck, long in the sleeve and very clinging, was unbelievably flattering. She could have passed for twenty-four.

Polly sat down on the bed. Do I want to pass for twenty-four? she thought. What am I doing here, all dressed up to kill?

Even as she thought about Paul, part of her mind thrust the problem away. She simply didn't want to confront the reality of his departure or attempt to come to terms with the situation. She felt as though she were in some kind of limbo, a protective deadening cocoon, which prevented the need for thought or action. At that moment she heard the sound of vehicles coming up the drive and passing beneath her window. The bell rang, the front door opened and voices were heard exclaiming. Polly's hands clutched together convulsively. More wheels, more exclaimings. She sat, silently listening.

After quite a few more arrivals Polly stood up. Before she could move to the door, a car could be heard approaching at far greater speed than the others. The vehicle stopped at the bottom of the steps. A door slammed, then another. The front door opened and there was a loud cry.

Polly went out on to the landing and looked over the balustrade. In the hall Cass was trying to embrace two young men at once. The taller of the two was as fair as Cass herself. The younger was darker and sturdier and Polly guessed at once that these were her two sons.

'Darlings!' she was crying with delight. 'What a wonderful surprise! Tom!' she called. 'Look who's here!'

Polly started to descend the stairs, hoping to make her entrance under cover of this family reunion. Saul, released from Cass's embrace, turned and caught sight of Polly. His eyes widened and his mouth dropped open. Oliver, taking in the situation at a glance and feeling that his brother was doing himself no great favour in giving a fair imitation of something on a fishmonger's slab, gave Saul a sharp nudge. Saul gulped, his teeth meeting with a sharp click, and pulled himself together.

'Oh, Polly,' said Cass, as Polly, reached the bottom of the stairs. 'Isn't this a wonderful surprise! These are my sons. This is Oliver and this is Saul.' She put an arm round each of them. 'I had simply no idea they were coming. This is Polly. She's staying with us for a few days. You must make sure she has a lovely time. I must tell Tom you're here.' She hurried off.

The boys shook hands with Polly, who smiled at them warmly. 'How nice to meet you,' she said, 'and what a lovely surprise for Cass. Have you come far?'

'No,' croaked Saul whilst Oliver said: 'From Cambridge.'

'Goodness,' said Polly, 'I should have thought that was quite far enough!'

'I picked Saul up from Tiverton on the way down,' explained Oliver. He herded them towards the drawing room where they were met in the doorway by Tom, who looked less delighted to see them, and Polly sensed that Saul was rather anxious regarding his reception. Oliver beamed at his parent.

'Hi, Pa. The usual mob, I see. Don't worry, we're looking after Polly. Saul's going to get her a drink.'

'Just wine,' said Polly quickly. 'A glass of white wine would be super.'

'Right.' Saul disappeared with remarkable alacrity, avoiding his father's eye. Tom looked at Oliver.

'How did he manage permission to come out of school?' he asked. 'It's not an exeat.'

'Oh, it was no problem,' said Oliver airily. 'It's a special occasion, after all. Unfortunately, Gemma's housemistress didn't agree or she would have been here, too.'

'You had no right to pull Saul out of school. He simply can't afford distractions at the moment. He has to work hard. And it's not even an official twenty-fifth anniversary party. We had that out in the States.'

'Don't get out of your pram, Pa,' said Oliver. 'One weekend isn't the end of the world. Look! I think someone's trying to attract your attention.'

Tom, hailed by a passing guest, moved reluctantly away and Oliver blew out his lips in relief. 'Pa's being very heavy-handed with poor old Saul at the moment,' he explained. 'Worrying about his A levels. Just what he doesn't need, poor kid. He's been rejected by a rather horrid girl and she's really knocked his confidence.'

'Oh, how sad,' Polly cried. 'Poor Saul.'

'Don't let on that I told you. He's got his pride. I shall have to keep the aged parent off his back, though. Thinks he's not working hard enough and shouldn't let himself be distracted by girls. Shall we go and meet people?'

POLLY, PERCHED ON A low stool, was beginning to enjoy herself. She'd had a long chat with Thea, who tried to persuade her to come back to the Old Station House afterwards. Polly felt that it would be rather rude after Cass's kindness but agreed to go on Monday and, at this point, Harriet joined them. Polly found that being the centre of so much attention was rather pleasant and worried that she wasn't feeling more upset. It all seemed so unreal and as the party progressed there was an air of the problem being shelved for the time being. Polly was quite happy. She'd drunk enough but not too much and the supper was delicious. Saul hovered solicitously and one of Tom's fellow officers, a man called Tony Whelan, had joined them. He had a lighthearted, bantering style of conversation which was just the sort of thing she felt up to at present.

'Where's Oliver?' she asked, realising that she hadn't seen him for some time.

'He's suddenly vanished away, as is Oliver's wont at these functions,' said Tony, who had sat down beside her on the floor to eat his supper.

'"He had softly and suddenly vanished away, for the Snark was a Boojum you see,"' said Polly, forking up some salmon mousse.

Saul looked surprised and Tony laughed to see his expression. 'Don't you know your Lewis Carroll?' he asked and Saul looked even more surprised. Tony shook his head sadly. 'Nobody reads any more.'

'I never stop reading,' said Saul indignantly. 'You want to try doing History A levels!'

'You're not to be horrid to Saul,' said Polly to Tony. 'He's looked after me all evening. He's the nicest boy I've met for ages.' She put down her plate and picked up a bowl of chocolate pudding. '"The nicest child I ever knew was Charles Augustus Fortescue,"' she recited and smiled ravishingly at Saul. 'Don't you love Belloc?'

'He's never heard of him,' said Tony teasingly. 'No good lying, Saul, I can tell!'

'"Matilda told such dreadful lies, it made one gasp and stretch one's eyes." I shall read him to you, Saul,' said Polly dreamily. 'We'll read him together. Just you and me.'

Saul began to think that things were looking up a bit and cast a rather cheeky look at Tony. 'Sounds good to me,' he said and felt daring and manly. 'When do we start?'

.   .   .

CASS GATHERED UP SOME plates and went into the kitchen to organise coffee. Oliver was sitting at the kitchen table. He smiled up at
her as she came in.

'The kettles are on,' he said. 'I imagine you'll want both of them?'

'Oh, Ollie! Bless you,' said Cass. 'What are you doing out here on
your own?'

'Don't worry. I've done the social bit. I shall go back with the coffee. No one will miss me. I was just thinking about Gus.'

'Oh, Ollie,' said Cass again but with a different inflection. 'Oh, I
know. He was always here to greet you when you came back, wasn't
he? Rushing round to find something to bring you. Oh, I miss him,
too, but we couldn't take him to the States and then he got that tu-
mour and Abby had to have him put down. I felt so badly about him.'

'Sorry, Ma.' Oliver came round the table and put his arm around
her. 'Didn't mean to upset you.'

They stood for a moment, embracing, but they had ceased to think
about Gus. Instead they thought of Charlotte. Both knew the other's
thoughts and, though neither of them spoke, they both felt comforted.

POLLY WOKE LATE ON Sunday morning. Unused to the excitement and the stimulation of the previous evening, she had passed a
disturbed and restless night and had then fallen into a heavy sleep in
the early morning.

She came round slowly, dozing in fitful jerks and finally coming to
full consciousness just after eleven o'clock. Her head was buzzing
slightly and she was very thirsty. After a moment, she rolled out of
bed, pulled on her dressing gown and, opening her bedroom door,
stood for a moment, listening. Silence.

She slipped into the bathroom, made a hasty toilet and went back
to dress. It was very cold, the sky overcast and louring. Polly pulled
on her cords and her thick, baggy jersey and went downstairs. Simultaneously, Saul appeared from the kitchen door and Tom emerged
from the drawing room.

'Good morning,' they said.

'Hi,' said Polly. 'I'm sorry I'm so late.'

'Have some coffee,' offered Saul, seizing his advantage at being nearest to the kitchen. 'I'm sure you're dying for some.'

'Ooh, yes please!' Polly's tone was heartfelt. 'I'd kill for a mug of coffee.'

'What about breakfast?' Tom was not to be written off so easily. 'I do a very good fry-up.' He strolled behind them into the kitchen.

'I don't think I could,' said Polly, to whom the thought was appalling. 'Just some coffee would be terrific.'

Saul already had the kettle on and was dealing with mugs. 'Milk and sugar?' he asked her. 'Do you want some, Pa?'

'Yes, please,' said Tom easily, sitting beside Polly, who had subsided on to a chair at the huge old kitchen table.

'Both for me, please,' said Polly. 'How cosy it is in here. It was a lovely party, wasn't it? Where's Cass?'

'Oliver's taken her into the village to get the papers and a few supplies,' said Tom. 'It's not much of a walk but it's bitterly cold and Oliver wanted to fill the car up. He's got an early start tomorrow morning.'

'So you've got today off?' Polly smiled up at Saul as he put her coffee in front of her. 'Thank you, that looks perfect.'

'As long as I'm back in time for my first lesson tomorrow morning.' Saul passed his father a mug. 'Oliver will drop me off on the way up.'

'You shouldn't be here at all, really,' said Tom, stirring in sugar. 'It's not officially an exeat,' he explained to Polly. 'Apparently Oliver telephoned Saul's housemaster and told him that it was a very special family occasion and Saul would be the only family member not present.' He shook his head. 'Children get away with murder these days.'

Saul shot him a look of resentment but, as he opened his mouth to retort, the telephone in the hall rang. Nobody moved.

'Go on, Saul,' said Tom, impatiently. 'You're on your feet. It's probably for you anyway. Get on with it.'

Reluctantly, Saul left the kitchen. They heard his voice answering and Tom smiled at Polly.

'For you, Pa.'

Saul reappeared and Tom sighed and got to his feet. Polly smiled at Saul. She felt all the frustration that he was feeling and wondered how she could help him.

'I was just wondering,' she said to him, 'whether it's too cold for a bit of a walk or a drive. You know. Blow the cobwebs away. What's that place you were telling me about last night? Some reservoir?'

Saul's face lit up. 'Oh yes,' he said. 'Burrator. I'd love to. You'll need a coat, though.'

'Hang on a minute!' protested Tom, returning from the telephone, as Polly passed him in the doorway and ran up the stairs and Saul started to unhook a coat from behind the kitchen door. 'What's all this? Where are you going?'

'I suggested showing her Burrator Reservoir,' said Saul. 'It should be wonderful after all the rain we've had. The water will be roaring over the dam. Polly's never seen it.'

'It'll be freezing up there.' Tom looked annoyed. 'Honestly, Saul! It's crazy to take her up there on a morning like this.'

'I'm sure it would be for you, Pa!' Saul's happiness buoyed him up and lent him a certain recklessness. 'But we're not old like you. We've got our young blood to keep us warm!'

And with a grin of malice mingled with triumph, he hurried out to meet Polly as she came down the stairs.

MICHAEL WAS READING HUGH his bedtime story—*The Tale of Samuel Whiskers*—which was Hugh's favourite. Michael did a different voice for each character, which delighted Hugh and sent him into paroxysms of mirth.

'"I fear that we shall be obliged to leave this pudding,"' he read. '"But I am persuaded that the knots would have proved indigestible, whatever you may urge to the contrary."'

The bedroom door opened and Harriet put her head round. 'All done?' she asked, rather more brightly than usual.

Hugh shook his head furiously and Michael looked at her sharply. She came across and gave Hugh a hug. 'Good night, darling,' she said and kissed him, holding him a little longer than usual. 'God bless.' She went to the door and glanced back at Michael, making a little grimace.

'Very nearly finished,' said Michael and she went out and along to her bedroom where he joined her a few minutes later.

'What is it?' he asked. 'Has it started?'

Harriet nodded wordlessly. She was gathering up her overnight case and various belongings.

'Oh, hell!' said Michael. 'I hoped we'd get through the night at the very least. I knew that blasted party would be too much for you.'

'Oh, don't fuss, darling, please. There's plenty of time. I've phoned the hospital and told them we're on our way.' She smiled at him and then gave a little gasp of pain. 'Oooh!'

'Oh, Harriet.' He went to her and put his arms around her. 'I love you. Don't worry, we'll manage. I suppose we'll have to get Hugh up and take him with us. I'll go and get him organised.'

'No, wait.' Harriet felt another stab of pain and sat down on the side of the bed. 'I was thinking about that downstairs. Why don't we phone Polly? It's real luck that she's with Cass. She can be over in half an hour and I would be much happier if she's here. Hugh adores her and she'll be quite happy to come. Ooooh!' and poor Harriet gave another gasp. 'Go and phone, darling, please. I'll get a list ready for her. I'll have to warn her that your cousin may turn up but with luck you'll be home by morning. Ooooh!' She swallowed and then chuckled. 'Get a move on, Michael. Our next child seems to be in a bit of a hurry to get out!'

SAUL WAS HAVING A wonderful day. Polly, rather recklessly, had let him drive her car up to Burrator where they had watched the water thundering and roaring down between the stone ramparts of the dam. They had walked down through the trees and stared up at it, deafened by the noise and covered by its spray. It had been almost frightening in its power and Polly had imagined how it might be if the ramparts crumbled and the dam collapsed, the whole weight of the water pouring down into the valley. We'd be swept away like rag dolls, she thought, and shivered with a delicious terror.

'Getting cold?' Saul bellowed into her ear and she nodded and clutched his arm as they toiled back up to the road.

'Want to go back?' he asked, when they reached the car. For one glorious moment he imagined that it was summer so that they could go walking off into the heart of the moor and he could do wonderful, exciting, unspeakable things to her in the bracken. He sighed and returned to frustrating reality. 'Or shall we go and have a sandwich in the pub?'

'Oh, yes!' cried Polly enthusiastically. 'Is there a pub?'

'There's the Old Oak down at Meavy,' said Saul. 'Let's go and get warmed up.'

When they had their sandwiches before them—Polly with coffee, Saul with a pint—he told her how the reservoir looked during a drought summer, the crumbling cottages and homesteads showing above the water. Polly hung flatteringly on his words and laughed infectiously at his jokes. Saul began to wonder if he'd died and gone to Heaven without realising it. He noticed one or two men glancing sideways at Polly and how their eyes followed her when she went to the loo and he could feel his chest expanding and his stature being added unto by the minute, despite Holy Writ claiming it as a physical impossibility.

When they finally arrived back at the Rectory it was to find Cass and Tom dozing before the fire and Oliver watching a film on the television in the study. Leaving Cass and Tom to their somnolence, the other three gathered up the necessary requirements for a nursery tea, carried them into the study and had a wonderful time round the fire, toasting crumpets and thoroughly enjoying each other's company.

When the telephone rang, none of them took any notice. Presently Cass poked her head round the door. 'Ah, there you are, Polly,' she said. 'It's Harriet. Well, it's Michael actually. Harriet seems ready to pop and he's about to take her into hospital. She's asked if you'll go and look after Hugh tonight so that they don't have to drag him out. Can you come and have a word?'

'Oh, God!' Polly leaped to her feet. 'Yes, of course.' She hurried into the hall.

'Will she be all right driving over in the dark?' asked Saul anxiously. 'After all, she doesn't really know the road. I think that I should go with her.'

'Rubbish!' Tom strolled into the study. 'You've got to be off first thing in the morning, young man. I'll go over. I can stay the night and bring her back tomorrow. I'll be in plenty of time for my train.'

'Nonsense, darling,' said Cass calmly, quelling Saul with a look. 'It may not happen all that quickly for Harriet. She spent days having Hugh. You have to be in London tomorrow. Polly may have to stay for a few days and she'll certainly need her car while she's there.'

'The obvious thing is for her to follow me across,' said Oliver, who had moved to the window and was looking out into the winter's dusk. 'That way we'll know that she'll arrive safely. Saul can come with us. He can travel with Polly to give her company on the way and come back with me. But we ought to get a move on and not just because of Harriet. It's just started to snow.'

Twenty-four

POLLY SAT DOWN IN an armchair and stretched her legs to the log fire that hissed and crackled in the wood-burning stove. On either side of it two huge wicker baskets, filled to the brim with logs, stood witness to Michael's last act of thoughtfulness. When she had finished speaking to him on the telephone she had fled upstairs, thrown her warmest things into her case and rushed down again to where Oliver and Saul were waiting. She hugged Cass warmly and listened whilst Tom gave her advice and they both told her to come back as soon as she could. Meanwhile, Oliver was already in his car and revving the engine as Saul, grasping her case in one hand and her arm in the other, almost ran her round to the stable block and her car. White flakes whirled and danced in the darkness around them and Polly felt a thrill of fear.

'I've never driven in snow before,' she said, struggling to unlock the car door. 'I'm glad you and Oliver are coming with me.'

'It'll be OK,' said Saul, his new-found confidence positively surging and bubbling inside him. 'It's barely settling. I'll drive you if you like.'

'No, no. Better not.' Polly settled herself in the driving seat. 'I shouldn't really have let you this morning. Although you're probably a better driver than I am.'

Peering out of the rear window into the falling snow, she reversed out of the stable expecting at any moment to back into something solid and unforgiving.

'Left hand down a bit,' said Saul. 'Then you'll be OK.'

Following his instructions, she edged back until she was able to pull forward and make her way round to the front of the house. At the front door, where Cass and Tom stood waving, Oliver's car moved out in front of her and they set off in procession down the drive.

Although the snow had yet to settle, visibility was very poor and Polly, gripping the steering wheel tightly, was grateful for Oliver's rear lights glowing out in the darkness and Saul's instructions.

'Bit of a left-hand bend coming up here,' Saul advised. 'Drops down into a dip here with a bit of a climb the other side, better change down. We'll be turning right in a few minutes.'

'You know the road awfully well.' Polly took a deep breath and relaxed her grip on the wheel for a moment, easing her shoulder muscles.

'I was at prep school just outside Tavistock,' he said, his eyes fixed on the road ahead and Oliver's lights. 'We drove across this road a dozen times a term for five years. I ought to know it. Yes, this is it. Turn right here. We're on the main Princetown road now. Of course, Harriet and Michael are very high where they are but I expect they'll be well prepared for a bit of bad weather.'

'Yes, they are.' Polly's eyes strained to keep sight of Oliver's car as the snow seemed to fall thicker and more blindingly. 'Harriet was showing me on Saturday.' Jesus! she thought, was that only yesterday? 'They've got enough food in to withstand a couple of years' siege and a great pile of logs in that shed. I suppose it's quite sensible.'

'Definitely,' said Saul. 'It's not often that bad up here but it's best to be ready for it. Now, we shall be turning left any minute. We're coming into Princetown.'

Polly remembered the grey gloomy bulk of the prison. What must it look like on a night like this? She shuddered a little.

At last, after what seemed several years, Polly was bumping up the familiar track and Michael was hurrying out to greet them. He directed her past the garden gate and round into the open-fronted barn where the log pile stood. She stopped thankfully and Michael opened her car door.

'Well done,' he said, with great relief. 'And I see you've got plenty of support. How very wise! I was beginning to panic that you might lose your way in the dark.'

He took her case and the three of them went back towards the cottage. Oliver had turned his car at the bottom of the track.

'Come in,' said Michael. 'Harriet's got some last-minute instructions. I've told you about my cousin Jon, haven't I? He won't be a bother, terribly jolly chap. He should arrive at any minute. Shove him in the boxroom. Harriet had made up the spare room ready for him but you'll be in there. Anyway, with luck I'll be back.' He turned to Saul as Oliver reached the gate from the track. 'I imagine that you two will want to be getting back?'

' 'Fraid we must,' said Oliver, who knew that Saul would have liked to stay until the last possible second. 'It's blowing a bit over the top. We ought to be on our way.'

'Yes you must,' said Polly at once. 'It would be terrible if you got stuck.' She engulfed Saul in a warm hug. 'I'd never have managed without you,' she told him. 'Thank you for a lovely day. Phone me when you get home, won't you? I'll want to know that you're both safe.'

He nodded, hesitated, then gave her another hug, his mouth briefly finding her lips. She kissed him firmly and turned to Oliver. 'Bless you,' she said. 'Please drive carefully,' and giving him, too, a quick hug, she followed Michael into the cottage.

A few minutes later, Harriet and Michael had gone, too, Harriet still shouting last-minute instructions and Michael urging her to hurry. Finally, he had bundled her into the car and they had set off, vanishing into the still falling snow which had now begun to cover the ground. Polly made her way to the sitting room and collapsed in the armchair by the fire.

Presently she stirred. Nursery tea in the study at the Rectory seemed some time ago and she decided to go and forage in the kitchen. Harriet's list lay on the table and Polly smiled at the minute instructions for Hugh's welfare.

'I've told him we're going,' Harriet had explained to Polly, 'and he knows that when he wakes up in the morning you'll be here. I thought it might be a bit of a shock otherwise. He's quite happy about it.'

This was perfectly true. Harriet had represented Polly to him as a cross between Peter Pan and Father Christmas and had outlined the days ahead as one long glorious game. Polly would have quailed had she known. Hugh, however, listening wide-eyed to the treats in store for him and remembering Polly's willingness on Saturday to join in with a will, nodded acquiescently and agreed to be a good boy and try to go to sleep. In the morning, Harriet promised him, Polly would have a lovely surprise for him. He could hardly wait for her to go and collect this new brother or sister so that the good life could get under way.

Polly, sublimely unaware of her part in this programme of dissipation, studied the list while she heated some soup and made toast.

'Really good staff work, this,' she told Ozzy, who had followed her into the kitchen and now lolled hopefully against the dresser. Max, who moved as little as he could these days, had remained by the fire. 'She's hidden presents all over the house so that Huge can have a treasure hunt every day. Brilliant, isn't it? I'd never think of a thing like that. She's even made a list of the places in case he can't find them. Even better. Imagine the frustration! Knowing they were there but not finding them! You're on the list, too. That's how I know that you've been fed, so it's no good looking pathetic.'

Ozzy sighed. It was the story of his life—foiled and bested at every turn. He lay down but kept his eye on Polly's movements, confident that the odd toast crust would come his way. Ozzy knew a sucker when he saw one.

Blessing the comfort of the Aga, Polly settled at the table with her supper and, for the first time for forty-eight hours, began to unwind. The shrilling of the telephone bell caught her unawares and she banged the spoon against her teeth. Sighing, she got up and went to the wall telephone. Saul's voice burst out of the receiver.

'Are you OK? We've just got back. It's really bad up on the top now. The wind's getting up and it's already starting to drift. Are you sure you'll be all right on your own? I'm sure I should have stayed with you.'

Polly reassured him as to her well-being, promising that they would speak on the morrow, had a word with Cass and returned to her soup.

Later, as Ozzy was licking the empty bowl and munching a few crusts, the telephone rang again. It was Michael this time. Everything was OK but he would certainly be staying the night with Harriet. He would phone her again in the morning and, with some detailed instructions on how to keep the wood-burner on overnight and promising to give her love to Harriet, he rang off.

'IF YOU'D GOT AWAY yesterday, instead of fooling about going to see reservoirs, you'd both have been back by now.' Tom, eating some party leftovers—Cass always refused to cook until everything had been eaten up—was feeling grumpy. His weekend had been, in some indefinable way, unsatisfactory.

'Oh, do stop droning on, Pa,' begged Oliver, who seemed, as usual, to have bagged all the best remains. 'And anyway, I certainly wouldn't have been back yet. It may be far worse upcountry and Saul and I might have been stuck for days in a snowdrift.'

For a moment, Tom allowed himself to play with all the delightful possibilities of that scenario. He sighed wistfully.

'And anyway,' continued Oliver, 'I should have thought that you'd be delighted to have your two sons here with you. You must just relax and enjoy us.'

Saul grinned and continued to eat sausage rolls.

'I'd be much more delighted to know that you were getting on with your work,' said Tom as he watched his elder son eat the last of the profiteroles. 'You're coming up to your finals, Saul's got his A levels in a few months. It's a very important time. I don't want to see all the money that's been spent on educating the pair of you go flowing down the drain.'

'Oh, honestly, darling.' Cass felt that it was time she intervened. 'They'll probably only lose a few days' work. They're both quite capable of catching up. And, after all, it's another five months to their exams. Nothing to worry about.'

'Oh, well, I'd naturally expect you to take their side,' said Tom morosely. 'Don't mind me, I'm only the breadwinner. Hang on a minute, is that the last of that smoked cheese?'

'It is.' Oliver ate it and beamed at his father. 'And very nice it was, too.'

Before Tom could react, Cass got to her feet. 'Come on, darling,' she said to Tom. 'We'll leave these two to get on with the washing-up and then they can bring us some coffee. You mustn't let them wind you up,' she said when they reached the drawing room. 'They don't mean any harm. Can't you remember how you and your old pa used to argue?'

'I suppose so.' Tom sank into an armchair. 'They make me feel so old. I'm sure I was never as lazy as they are.'

'Well, you were at Dartmouth so it was a bit different. And you were very proud when Oliver got a place at Cambridge.'

'Of course I was. They're great kids. It's just that I sometimes feel too tired to cope.'

'You and me both.'

Oliver appeared with a tray and grinned at them. 'Coffee,' he announced. 'Saul's washing up but I thought you might be gasping. Oh, and we found these.'

'These' were the special after-dinner Belgian chocolates that they all loved and Tom raised his eyebrows in amazement. Oliver placed them on the table by his chair and went out. Tom looked up, met Cass's eye and burst out laughing.

'You win,' he said.

POLLY CARRIED HER COFFEE into the sitting room and sank back into the armchair, Max at her feet. She opened the door of the wood-burning stove, enjoying the friendly settling and crackling of the fire. She gazed mesmerised at the flames and, after a while, began to nod. Her dreams were a confused jumble of the events of the last few days. Much later she came awake with a jolt and glanced at her watch. Bedtime.

She rose and called the dogs, who padded behind her into the hall and waited whilst she opened the door into the porch. The snow was already blowing against the porch door and she stared out into a white world.

'Go on, Max. And you, Ozzy,' said Polly, shivering. 'Go and have a pee!'

The dogs turned amazed looks upon her. They had been right about her being a sucker. Now they knew that she was potty as well. After a moment, Ozzy strolled out and sniffed cautiously at the snow. Max sat down firmly. He was too old for these games.

'You're a pain, Max.' Polly pushed her feet into a pair of gumboots that stood in the porch. 'Come on then! Out we go! Pee time!'

Max watched in alarm from the safety of the porch whilst Polly gambolled in the snow. She returned and lugged him forcibly out of the door. Ah well. All alike, these humans! Had to do everything in group movements. Couldn't even go for a walk, some of them, unless their dogs had them on the end of a piece of string. Max knew his duty. He strolled over to a bush that was fast disappearing beneath a covering of snow, lifted his leg briefly and hurried back to the porch. May as well humour her!

Polly gave a sigh of relief and called to Ozzy, who had now decided that he liked the snow so much that he would sleep out in it. After a battle of wills, Polly got him back inside, settled them beside the Aga with a couple of biscuits, locked up, checked on Hugh and went gratefully to bed.

Twenty-five

POLLY WAS DREAMING. SHE and Saul were stuck in a snowdrift and Max was trying to rescue them. The trouble was that he would keep singing, a strange high droning noise that was horrible to listen to and was impeding the rescue.

'Do shut up, Max,' she kept shouting but he wouldn't listen and she was sinking farther into the snow with Saul clinging to her. She gave a great heave to save herself and woke up.

She lay for a moment feeling an enormous sense of relief and then realised that the high droning song was still going on somewhere in the distance. She struggled up and stared round Harriet's spare room, remembered the events of the last forty-eight hours and fell back on the pillows.

'Jesus wept!' she muttered.

Raising her arm, she peered at her wristwatch and hastily shut her eyes. Could it really only be a quarter past seven! She thought about Paul and wondered where he was. Ever since she had read his note, events had been whirling her along at such a pace that she felt she no longer had any control over her life. Even now, Paul might be trying to get in touch, wondering where she was, getting no reply. Would he worry? Decide that he must return? Telephone the police? She groaned aloud and began to feel a sense of desperation. The toneless keening was suddenly more than she could bear. Leaping from the bed, she threw open the door. As she drew in breath to shout, she realised that it was Hugh singing and stopped short. Hugh! For a moment she had forgotten all about him.

Dashing back into the bedroom, she grabbed her dressing gown, thrust her feet into sheepskin slippers and hurried along the passage. Hugh was sitting up in bed surrounded by a strange assortment of toys to whom he was singing. He held a book in his hand from which he appeared to be reading what could only be the words of his song, since there was certainly no tune. Polly relaxed and smiled at him. 'Morning, Huge,' she said.

He glanced at her, nodded rather curtly and turned a page. Whilst she waited for the concert to end, Polly glanced round his little room which Michael had painted a pale apricot so that the sun always seemed to be shining here. This morning, however, a ghostly glow pervaded the room and Polly wandered over to the window and opened the curtains. She caught her breath, delighted, for the land-scape was unrecognisable; the snow had blown and drifted into huge hills and cliffs which transformed the garden and the moor beyond into the sort of magic land that one had imagined in one's childhood. A gleam of early sunshine caused the snow to sparkle and flash and the long shadows in its folds were ink-blue.

'Huge!' she cried. 'Oh, look!'

Fortunately, the concert seemed to have come to its natural close and Hugh, having bowed to his audience, scrambled to his feet and raised his arms to be lifted. His little bed had a drop side but Polly whisked him up and over the top and stood him on the broad window seat.

'Look, Huge,' she said again. 'Look at the snow.'

Hugh stared out. 'Snow,' he repeated quietly to himself. 'Snow.'

Polly, her arm round him to keep him warm, tried to remember what it was like to see something for the first time and to have no idea what it was, what it felt like, tasted like, how it behaved, whether it was to be welcomed or feared. She groped after a fleeting sensation but it eluded her, moving just outside her memory. She gazed at Hugh's rapt face trying, through him, to regain the magic. It was no use. It was beyond her. She sighed, feeling for a brief moment that she had lost something indefinably precious.

'Come on, Huge,' she said, lifting him to the floor and kneeling before him. 'We'll get dressed and, after breakfast, we'll make a snowman.'

'What's a snowman?' he asked, allowing himself to be divested of his pyjamas.

'You wait and see,' promised Polly, who felt that to explain was just impossible. 'Now, what do you wear?'

Hugh pointed to the little chair on which his clothes were piled and Polly bundled him into warm layers, sending up a heartfelt prayer of relief that he was now out of nappies.

'There!' she said. 'You're ready. Mummy's left a lovely present for you. She's hidden it somewhere as a surprise. Can you find it while I get dressed?'

Back in her room she shivered. Hugh's room and the bathroom were kept warm by radiators run from the Aga, as was Harriet's bedroom. But the spare room and the boxroom had no form of heating and Polly had never dressed so quickly. Out on the landing she listened for Hugh. He seemed to be rooting about in the bathroom.

'Found it?' she cried and he appeared in the doorway, beaming happily and clutching a gaily wrapped parcel. 'Well done, Huge.'

They went down the stairs hand in hand, one step at a time, and into the kitchen. Max waved his tail a little but didn't move. Ozzy got up, stretched mightily and sat down again, unwilling at present to extend himself too far. Who knew what this strange woman might not feel it incumbent upon him to perform? He felt it wise to conserve his energy.

Polly swung Hugh into his high chair and he started to unwrap his present. She studied Harriet's list.

Ready Brek, she read. Toast. Honey or marmalade. Yes. This was well within her scope. 'Max has four biscuits for breakfast,' she read on aloud. Max's ears pricked up. This was more like it. 'Ozzy has six. And occasionally a beaten egg.' She went into the utility room where the dogs' food was stored and took down the biscuit tin. They watched from the doorway.

'Here we are.' She put the biscuits on the flagged floor and, wondering if they might need to go outside, went to the door and opened it with difficulty. Snow stood piled as high as her thighs and formed a barrier across the doorway. The earlier gleam of sunshine had disappeared and snowflakes fell softly but insistently from a leaden sky. 'Gracious!' she exclaimed. 'How are you going to get through that, chaps?'

Ozzy finished his breakfast, shouldered his way through the snow and disappeared but Max, having taken one look, finished his biscuits and hurried back into the kitchen.

OLIVER PEERED WITH DISTASTE into a saucepan containing the remains of some porridge, flexed a slice of rather tired-looking toast and felt the cooling teapot. He sighed. It seemed that he would have to prepare his own breakfast. Perhaps, if he waited a little longer, Saul would be down and he could con him into making it for them both. Saul was quite a decent cook. Oliver had learned very early on that it was a great mistake to own to being good at things. People then expected you to perform, to be helpful, and Oliver did so hate to disappoint people. The telephone rang.

'Telephone,' he bellowed, after a moment.

The ringing ceased and Oliver could hear his mother speaking in the hall. Tom appeared in the doorway.

'Has it ever occurred to you to answer the phone yourself, instead of shouting at people?'

Oliver grinned at him. 'What a brilliant idea, Pa. I wonder why I never thought of that. Want some coffee?'

'No thanks. I had my breakfast approximately'—Tom looked ostentatiously at his watch—'an hour ago.'

'Poor old thing,' sympathised Oliver. 'Must be all those years as a jolly jack tar that makes it impossible for you to sleep later than seven o'clock in the morning. Still, that doesn't stop you from having some coffee. Ah! Here's Saul. He can make it for us.'

'Make what?' Saul came yawning into the kitchen dressed in the

ancient tracksuit that he wore as pyjamas in very cold weather. He sat
down at the table. His dark hair stood on end and his eyes were heavy
with sleep.

'You've been selected from a host of applicants to make breakfast,' Oliver told him kindly. 'Two lightly grilled rashers and some
scrambled eggs will do beautifully for me.'

Saul told him, briefly and succinctly, what he could do with himself.

'Really! Your language!' mourned Oliver. 'And in front of your father, too. I hope you're not going to let him get away with that, Pa.
When I was his age you would have thrashed me.'

'Oh, very funny.' Tom laughed mirthlessly. 'If I'd been allowed to
knock some sense into you, you'd be twice the man you are now.
Can't even cook your own breakfast!'

Oliver winked at his brother, who grinned unwillingly. 'OK, I'll
do it,' said Saul with a resigned sigh. 'But you can jolly well make me
some coffee first.'

'On its way, dear boy. Sure you won't have some, Pa?'

'I've said I don't want any,' said Tom, testily. 'And why you should
give in to him, Saul, I really don't know. All his life people have been
at his beck and call . . .'

Cass appeared and took in the scene at a glance. 'Whatever's going
on?' she asked. 'You'll have a heart attack if you bellow like that, darling. That was Thea asking for Polly. She was supposed to be going
over there today. Oh, Ollie, darling. Is that for me? Is the sugar in?
Lovely. Now, out of the way while I cook you a nice big breakfast.'

WHEN SHE PUT DOWN the receiver after speaking to Cass, Thea
immediately lifted it again and dialled Harriet's number. The line was
engaged. She went back to washing up the breakfast things, thinking
about Polly. She wondered how she was reacting to being up on the
moor all on her own—as it were—at Lower Barton. Nobody knew
better than Thea how Polly hated the isolation of the cottage. It was
not that Polly minded being alone but she hated being cut off from

civilisation. At least she had Ozzy and Max to look after her and Hugh would prove a distracting influence. With luck she'd have her hands too full to think about her loneliness and perhaps Michael would be back later. Thea glanced out of the window. The snow lay thick and George had not attempted to get up to London. It would be too awful if poor Polly were to be stuck up there for days. A thought occurred to her. She finished the washing-up and went to find George, pausing on the way to try Harriet's number again. Still engaged.

George was shovelling the snow away on the platform. He stopped as Thea approached and blew out his lips. 'More to come if you ask me,' he said. 'Get the kettle on, darling. I'd kill for a cup of coffee.'

'It's on,' said Thea. 'George, I've just been speaking to Cass. Michael's taken Harriet in to have the baby and Polly's all on her own at Lower Barton. If Michael can't get back she'll be frightened up there on her own. I suppose there's no chance of me getting up there? I could stay with her till Michael's back. Or better still, we could fetch them all down here.'

'Out of the question.' George shook his head. 'Honestly, darling. Look at it. There's no chance of making it up there. It would be madness to try.'

'D'you think that Michael will be able to get back from Plymouth then?'

'Difficult to say. The main roads will be cleared but there's no way I'd risk going out on the lanes.' He saw her face fall and spoke more bracingly. 'I'm sure that Michael will get through. He'll come straight out on the main road and he'd think nothing of walking the last few miles. But I'm not risking these back roads. Don't worry, Michael will make it. Now, how about that coffee?'

Thea went back to the kitchen. At least she could telephone Polly and see how she was coping. She'd give George his coffee and then they could have a nice long chat, assuming that whoever had been talking to Polly had now finished and the line was free.

·   ·   ·

IT WAS MICHAEL WHO had telephoned.

'It's another boy, Polly!' He sounded jubilant. 'And they're both doing well. He's a big fellow—nearly eight pounds—and poor Harriet is exhausted. But everyone's very pleased with her and he's beautiful. Dark, well, he would be with both Harriet's and my colouring . . .'

Polly listened patiently while he delivered a eulogy about the baby and Harriet and sent all sorts of messages to Hugh, and she accepted with equanimity the news that he would be staying at the hospital. 'I doubt if you could get up the track, even if you wanted to,' she told him. 'It's really thick up here.'

'Mmm.' Michael sounded thoughtful, as if he had just returned with a bump to the practicalities of life. 'Yes, it would be. You never get the same idea of it in the town, of course. Listen, Polly. This is very important. My worry is that you may lose the power and probably the telephone. I can't do much about the telephone but at least with the Aga you'll continue to have something to cook on, hot water and heat upstairs. It runs on oil, the tank's full and it needs no electricity to keep it going. If you get a power cut, move into our bedroom where it's warmer.

'Now, light. I don't feel happy at the thought of you fiddling about with the paraffin lamps but in the utility room, up on the high shelf above the dogs' food, are three Gaz lamps. I want you to go and get one while I'm still on the phone. Go on, I'll hang on.'

Polly hurried out into the utility room and looked round. Three odd-shaped lamps stood in a row on the high shelf. Standing on tiptoe she reached one down, went back into the kitchen and picked up the receiver.

'Got it,' she said. 'It's jolly heavy, I nearly dropped it.'

'Right. Now I'm going to explain how to light it. Damn! You'll need matches. Right-hand drawer of the dresser.'

Polly dashed over to the dresser, seized the matches and grabbed the phone again.

Feeling that she was taking part in some sort of assault course,

Polly obeyed Michael's instructions. She jumped as it roared to life, dropping the glass shade and trapping the still burning match. Gingerly she lifted the shade again and retrieved the match, burning her fingers before she was able to blow it out.

'Right,' she said, when she had retrieved the phone.

'Now, don't use all the lamps at once. Always have one at hand with the matches, wherever you are after dark, in case the lights go out suddenly. There's a torch on the windowsill behind the sink. See it? Right, keep that handy, too. Oh, hell! We would have weather like this, wouldn't we? I hope you'll be OK.'

Polly stoutly assured him that they would manage perfectly well and passed the receiver to Hugh, who had been watching the proceedings from his high chair.

Presently, Michael, having told Polly to get in as many logs as she could—if she could—from the emergency pile in the outhouse, hung up, promising to phone again that evening.

A little later, Polly and Hugh, both well wrapped up, ventured out. A few snowflakes twirled idly down from the grey uniformity of the sky and Hugh stared in silence at the absolute transformation of his familiar world. Polly realised that she would have to dig her way out. She remembered seeing a spade in the utility room and silently blessed Michael for his forethought. She went back through the house, trailed by Hugh and Ozzy, found the spade and returned to the porch.

'OK, Huge,' she said. 'I'm going to make a path. Stay close behind me.'

She began to dig a path along the front of the cottage to the outhouse at the end of the building. It was hot work and she wasn't very good at it. Hugh staggered in her wake, the cold stinging his cheeks to a bright poppy red, and Ozzy made plunges into the drifts while Max watched cautiously from the doorway to see what madness might now ensue. Fortunately for Polly the outhouse door opened inwards and she was able to take armfuls of logs along to the front porch where she stacked them against the wall inside. After a few trips she stopped to draw breath and to watch Hugh, who was taking fistfuls of snow and flinging them into the air. Max had now ventured out and was sniffing at this strange white stuff. Polly had the sensation that the four of them were the only creatures left in the world and the real effect of her isolation was borne in upon her. She stared out upon the unfamiliar, desolate landscape and felt a deep atavistic fear. She could be trapped here for days, with just a child and two dogs, helpless and alone. A tremor shook her and, quite suddenly, she abandoned all ideas of snowmen and the like and her one desire was to get back into the house.

'Come on, Hugh!' she cried, her voice high and nervous. 'You'll be getting cold. Let's go in and have a hot cup of tea.'

Max had already gone back in and Hugh came to her willingly. She called to Ozzy, who had gone to attend to his own business, and felt an immeasurable relief when he appeared, tail wagging; now they could all go inside and she could shut the door.

Twenty-six

DURING ELEVENSES IT OCCURRED to Polly that she should have telephoned Thea to tell her that she wouldn't be going over to stay and also to impart the good news about the baby. It seemed very unlikely that Michael would have done so. Now that she came to think of it, she was rather surprised that Cass, or at least Saul, hadn't telephoned her to see how she was coping. She decided that she felt a little hurt. In fact, by the time she had finished her coffee, she had worked herself up into that 'nobody cares about me' state of mind that is so injurious to our well-being. Nevertheless, she decided, it was only right that she should inform Cass that Harriet was safe and well and delivered of a new son and then telephone Thea for a good long chat.

She settled Hugh with his new colouring book and crayons, gave the dogs a biscuit each and picked up the receiver. Silence. She pressed the rest a few times and peered to check that the plug was firmly in. It was. How odd, thought Polly, jiggling the rest a few more times.

After a moment, she left the kitchen and went into the sitting room to try the phone there. More silence. Polly stood frowning. Michael had rung earlier and it was fine then . . . Slowly a dreadful thought crept into her mind. The telephone had been cut off. The snow must have brought down the lines since Michael's call. In a sudden panic, Polly banged the rest up and down again. Nothing. Very slowly she replaced the receiver and stared about her. She was cut off, alone. If there were to be an emergency she would be able to contact nobody. No one would come to her aid. Her heart gave a great somersault of terror and she strove for calmness. Hugh must not suspect that anything was wrong. Be calm, she told herself and took several deep breaths. There's nothing to fear. We have food and heat . . . Another thought struck her and galvanised her into action. She leaped for the light switch and pressed it down. Nothing. She switched it up and down furiously, ran across to the television and pushed the 'on' knob. The screen remained blank.

Polly stood up and pressed both hands to her mouth. They were completely cut off. What Michael had feared had happened. Thank God he'd been able to tell her what to do about lamps. Polly stood for a little longer trying to pull herself together before she crossed to the wood-burning stove to pile on more logs. The flames leaped up, warming and encouraging her. She must get more logs in from the porch before it got dark and she must put the Gaz lamps ready. Preparing her face in what she hoped was an 'isn't this all fun?' expression but which in fact looked more like the death rictus of a homicidal maniac, she went back to the kitchen.

'Look!' cried Hugh. He brandished his colouring book. 'I done a picture of Mummy and Daddy and the new bruvver.'

Polly went to look. It was a picture of the Holy Family. 'Lovely,' she said automatically, ignoring the fact that Mary had become Negroid, Joseph Chinese and the infant Jesus bright blue. Perhaps he's feeling cold there, lying in a manger with no clothes on, thought Polly and pulled herself up sharply. 'It's smashing, Huge,' she said. 'Mummy will love it. Now you must do one for Daddy.'

'No.' Hugh was bored with colouring. 'He can share. Get down.'

Polly sighed and lifted him out of his high chair. He went to Max, who lay before the Aga, and knelt beside him. Bending his head so that it rested on the big dog's back, he took some of his own hair and some of Max's between his fingers and began to twiddle it. His face took on a dreamy expression and he began to suck his thumb. Presently he slid sideways and closed his eyes.

Polly left him to it and went to fetch the lamps. She put one on the kitchen table to light as soon as it should become necessary and took another through to the sitting room with a spare box of matches. She remembered that Michael had told her not to light them all at once and felt another thrill of terror at the thought of all three lamps running out of gas and she and Hugh and the dogs left alone in the dark.

Stop it! she told herself fiercely. Michael would get here somehow, she was sure, even if he had to walk all the way. He would try to telephone again and would realise what had happened. There was really no need to panic. If only his cousin would arrive. Perhaps he'd been caught in the snow himself and was lost on the moor. She found herself wishing that she'd let Saul stay after all and then remembered that she had to get the logs in.

Leaving Hugh and Max fast asleep, she went into the hall and opened the door into the porch. Taking armfuls of logs, she went to and fro until the two wicker baskets were full to the brim. Perhaps it would be sensible to get some more logs into the porch in case the snow kept on falling. She pushed her feet into gumboots, pulled on her coat and, opening the porch door, stood looking out.

The snow still fell; slowly, silently, inexorably covering the garden so that it now merged in one long stretch with the moor beyond. The path that she had so laboriously dug had virtually disappeared and there was no sign of Ozzy's tracks from his earlier expedition. Polly realised there was a world of difference between the Christmas card version of snow with blue skies and jolly robins and this cold, bleak white-out with its eerie silence.

She shivered and then gasped. Out of the white landscape a figure loomed beyond the snow-covered wall. Polly's heart gave a leap upwards. Could Michael possibly have . . . ? She hurried out of the porch, wading and kicking her way through the snow and calling to the figure who was still partially obscured by the falling snow.

'Hi! Hello!' she called. 'Can you find the gate? How did you get here?'

The figure remained quite still.

At this point she reached up against the barrier of the gate and found herself looking at a man who was certainly not Michael. 'Oh,' she said, nonplussed and feeling rather foolish. 'I thought you were Michael.'

He was staring at her, too, as if in amazement and then, as realisation dawned, her face cleared and she laughed.

'Of course!' she cried, relief flooding through her. 'You're cousin Jon and you're wondering who on earth I am. Michael's taken Harriet in to have the baby and he can't get back because of the snow. They've got another boy. I'm Hugh's godmother, Polly Wickam. We've never met because you've always been abroad but I've been expecting you. I'm delighted to see you. I'm all on my own with Hugh, and a three-year-old isn't exactly a comfort in these conditions. For heaven's sake, climb over the wall and come in.'

After a moment, the man did as she suggested and followed her back to the cottage.

'Goodness,' she said, as they stood in the porch together. 'You're soaked. Have you walked miles? Take off that coat and your shoes and get into the warm. I suppose you've had to abandon your car and your luggage. Never mind, Michael's got loads of stuff.'

He took off his coat and, with some difficulty, prised his soaking shoes from his frozen feet. The lower legs of his trousers were caked in snow. He was as tall and as dark as Michael but there any resemblance ended. He was pale and in need of a shave and he looked desperately tired.

'I'm sorry,' said Polly, overcome with remorse at her garrulity. 'You must be exhausted and I'm rattling on at you. The thing is, we're totally cut off. No electricity. No telephone. And the relief of seeing another human being was too much.' She held out her hand. 'In case you didn't grasp it all before, I'm an old friend of Harriet's and Hugh's godmother, Polly Wickam, and you're Michael's cousin, Jon. How d'you do?'

After a moment, Jon put his hand in hers. 'Sorry,' he said. 'I'm a bit punch-drunk. I seem to have been walking for hours.'

His voice was husky with weariness and Polly opened the inner door. 'Come in and get some dry clothes on while I heat up some soup,' she said, 'and then you can meet Hugh and Max and Ozzy.'

He hesitated, frowning. 'Max and who?'

'Ozzy. You know? Michael's Newfoundland dogs? I'm sure you've heard about Max and Ozzy.'

'Oh, yes.' Jon shut the door behind him. 'Yes, of course.'

'Clothes first,' said Polly briskly. 'I'll show you where everything is and then I'll get some soup on the go. Would you like a bath?'

'You can't possibly imagine how wonderful that would be,' said Jon.

'OK, then,' said Polly. 'Follow me.'

TOM CAME INTO THE kitchen and regarded his sons with irritation. His trousers were tucked into thick socks and he wore the superior air of one who was busy whilst those around him remained idle.

'Good grief!' he exclaimed. 'Aren't you finished yet? It'll be lunchtime before you two even finish breakfast.' He pushed the kettle on to the hotplate. 'We've got to dig a path to the woodshed or we shall be out of logs. I've made a start but I don't see why I should do all the hard work when there are two able-bodied young men around. Although I suppose it's a triumph of hope over experience to imagine that you two will do anything useful while I'm here to do it for you!'

Saul rolled his eyes ceilingwards and Oliver sniffed the air with loud deliberation. He leaned towards Saul. 'Do I smell a martyr burning?' he suggested.

'Oh, very funny!' said Tom, making himself some coffee.

'What's funny?' asked Cass, coming into the kitchen. 'It doesn't seem to be getting any better, does it? Has anyone seen a weather forecast?'

Tom was understood to say that he'd been far too busy to watch television but the other three ignored him.

'I'll go and see if there's anything on,' said Oliver, pushing back his chair and thereby neatly avoiding the washing-up.

'And then come on out!' Tom shouted after him. 'Don't think you're going to lounge in there watching the box while I work!'

Saul sighed and began to pile the plates together. He had just finished when Oliver reappeared looking, for Oliver, rather ruffled.

'What's the matter?' said Cass at once. 'Have you seen a forecast?'

'Not as such,' said Oliver. He glanced at Saul and back at Cass.

'What is it?' asked Saul, surprised at Oliver's reticence. 'What's happened?'

'There's been a breakout from Princetown,' said Oliver. 'A prisoner escaped last night.'

The other three stared at him in silence.

'Oh, God!' Saul burst out. 'And Polly's all on her own.' He plunged out into the hall and everyone started to speak at once.

'He won't get far in this weather, the police will soon bring him back . . .'

'Polly will be terrified . . .'

'Listen. Before Saul gets back . . .'

But Saul was already back, brandishing Cass's address book. He looked quite wild, his hair on end and his eyes wide with anxiety.

'What's Harriet's surname?' he cried. 'I can't remember her bloody surname.'

'Wait!' said Tom. His voice was quiet but years of authority in the Navy gave it a quality that made the others turn to look at him. 'Let's be calm, shall we?' he said. 'A prisoner has escaped. It's a well-known fact that any prisoner escaping from the moor has very little chance unless it's a set-up job with help from outside.' He turned to Oliver. 'Was any mention made of that?'

'Yes,' said Oliver. 'The spokesman said that it was, without question, set up with outside help.'

'Right,' said Tom. 'That means that a car with clothes in it will have been left at a prearranged spot and, in normal conditions, the prisoner would be well away from the moor in no time. Obviously, the snow will probably put a stop to that. But if he broke out last night, he might have got some distance before he ran into trouble.' Here, Oliver opened his mouth as if to speak but closed it again. Tom raised his eyebrows. Oliver shook his head. 'I think that we can safely assume that he's at least well away from Princetown and, therefore, from Polly. But, even if he weren't, there's no point at all in telephoning her and frightening her to death. There was no mention of the escape on the television last night so there's every chance that she knows nothing about it. In fact, I'm perfectly certain that if she'd heard anything she'd have been on to us like a shot.'

'I'm sure that's true,' agreed Cass. 'Tom's quite right. You mustn't frighten her, Saul.'

'By all means phone and have a chat with her,' said Tom. 'But keep calm. She's got Max and Ozzy, after all.'

'Oh, the Newfies!' said Saul contemptuously.

'Yes. The Newfies.' Tom nodded at Saul. 'We may all know them as lazy great bundles. But to anyone who doesn't know them, they're bloody big brutes and, what's more, very protective when it comes to Hugh.'

'That's true,' said Cass again. 'They're very wary of strangers around Hugh. Go and get dressed, Saul, and then we'll phone Polly and see how she is. Go on,' she said firmly as Saul hesitated, 'a few minutes won't make any difference and you're beginning to shiver.'

Saul went, reluctantly, and Cass, waiting until she heard him reach the top of the stairs, pushed the kitchen door to and turned to Oliver.

'OK,' she said. 'What haven't you told us?'

Oliver grimaced. 'In the first place,' he said, 'the man's a murderer. And in the second they had the snowploughs out this morning and found what they believe to be his escape car. It seems he ran off the road near Merrivale quarry.'

There was a complete silence.

'That's only a few miles from Lower Barton,' said Cass at last.

'Quite,' said Oliver.

'It still means nothing,' said Tom. 'The last thing that escaped prisoners want is to go straight back inside. They stay away from human habitation for as long as possible. It would be different if he'd been on the loose for days in these conditions and was starving and frozen.'

'That's all very well,' said Oliver, 'but which way would he go? He'd probably want to get away from the road and he'd want to get as far from the prison as he could. What happens if you go up behind the quarry?'

'Well. There's a bridlepath from the quarry that leads straight past Michael's place as it happens,' said Tom, rather reluctantly, 'but it would be covered by snow and not that obvious.'

'Oh, Tom. A murderer!' Cass looked frightened. 'I wish one of you had stayed with her.'

With great restraint, Tom refrained from pointing out that he'd offered to do just that. The situation was too serious for cheap victory. He put an arm round Cass's shoulder and looked at Oliver. 'Did they say what sort . . .' he began but stopped as they heard Saul on the stairs. 'When he's phoned Polly,' he said, quietly but urgently, 'get him out digging and I'll phone the police to tell them that Polly's on her own. I don't want any silly mercy dashes so that we have to rescue him as well.'

The door opened. 'OK,' said Saul. 'What's the number, Ma?' Cass and he went out into the hall.

'What sort of murderer?' asked Tom.

'Killed his wife,' said Oliver succinctly. 'She neglected their kid or something and it died so he did her in. I didn't get it all. Apparently, ever since, he's had a grudge against women.'

'That's all we need,' said Tom, and turned as Cass and Saul reappeared.

'Oh, Tom,' said Cass. 'There's no reply.'

'Did you give her time to answer?' asked Oliver.

'She doesn't mean that,' said Saul. He rubbed his face with his hands and gazed round rather desperately. 'There's just silence. No ringing tone. Nothing. I think their phone has been cut off.'

There was a long silence and then Cass looked at Tom.

'Do you think we ought to telephone the police, just to warn them that Polly's all on her own?' she asked.

Tom nodded. He went into the hall but returned almost immediately.

'Bloody marvellous!' he said. 'The phone's dead! We're cut off, too!'

'GEORGE.' THEA PUT HER head round the sitting-room door where George was watching television, hoping to catch a forecast. 'I can't make the telephone work and I'm still trying . . .'

She broke off as the announcer's words caught her attention and moved to stand behind the sofa, staring at the photograph on the screen of the prisoner who had broken out of Dartmoor the night before. His name, it seemed, was John Middleton, he was an astrophysicist and a murderer and now he was at large on the moor.

'Now don't get worked up,' said George, wishing that he'd heard her coming so that he could have switched the television off. 'They'll have him back inside in no time. He hasn't got a hope.'

'Oh, George. Polly will be mad with terror. She'll die of fright. Oh, can't we possibly get to her?'

'Now darling, you simply must be sensible.' George hauled himself out of the armchair, went to her and took her hands in his. 'It's not going to do Polly any good if we all set off and get stuck in a snowdrift. For all we know Michael's back by now. She'll be OK.'

Thea sighed, her heart heavy. 'I suppose you're right,' she said. 'We couldn't both go, anyway. I couldn't take Amelia.'

'Of course not.' He drew her close and kissed her. 'Now stop worrying. At least Mother's all right. She's got plenty of food in and Mr Ellis was going round clearing paths and things.' George had telephoned Esme as soon as he had got up and seen the snow. 'To be honest I think she was enjoying it.'

Thea smiled a little. 'She probably is. I wish I could think Polly is, too.'

'Now, now. No good dwelling on it. Let's think about lunch. I think I can hear Amelia. Go and bring her down and we'll have a drink.'

Thea nodded and he hugged her tightly before she went away to fetch Amelia.

'George.' Her voice floated back to him. 'Try the telephone, will you? It's making a funny noise. I'd like to be able to speak to Polly and find out if Michael's back.'

George rubbed his hand thoughtfully over his jaw. He had already guessed from Thea's earlier remark that the lines were down and the telephone cut off but he had hoped to divert her by talking of lunch and Amelia. It would take Thea two seconds to realise that if they were cut off then so was Polly, and probably more than just by the telephone. George swore softly to himself and went into the kitchen. He could probably bluff a little longer; say that he'd spoken to the engineers about a fault and so on. He poured himself a drink and, hearing Thea approaching, arranged his face in an appropriate expression for lying.

Twenty-seven

FREDDIE POTTERED HAPPILY IN his kitchen, talking quietly to the dogs. Up early, as was his habit, he had already dug a way through to the kennels, dealt with the dogs and made his breakfast porridge. He sat down, wondering what conditions up on the main road were like. He had no doubt that the snowploughs would be out so it should be quite possible to get into Tavistock. The snow had taken him by surprise and his provisions were low. He was looking forward to trying out his new Fourtrak, justifying the expenditure with the excuse that he might be called out to the outlying farms in any weather, night or day, and it was the sensible vehicle to have.

As he ate, he thought—as he generally did in his idle moments—of Polly. He longed for the courage to throw caution to the winds and tell her of his love. He was still uncertain as to the exact state of her marriage. She always made light of Paul's obsession with his work and had never shown Freddie the least encouragement. She seemed pleased to see him, was easy and relaxed with him, always parted from him with an affectionate hug, but at no time in the past two years had she ever stepped over the line of friendship.

He got up and went to switch the kettle on. The sensible thing would be to make a comprehensive shopping list just in case the conditions got worse. He pushed the thoughts of Polly away and had been scribbling away for some time on the back of an old envelope before it was borne in on his consciousness that the kettle wasn't boiling. He touched the kettle, which was still cold, and fiddled with the plug. Everything seemed in order. An idea occurred to him and he pressed the light switch up and down a few times.

'Power cut,' said Freddie to himself. 'Damn and blast.'

He rooted round for the telephone which lived on the kitchen table under a pile of miscellaneous odds and ends. 'And the telephone lines are down,' he muttered to himself, having pressed the rest up and down a few times. 'I must try to get into Tavistock if I can.'

Charlie Custard watched him, alert, sensing that something was wrong, but Freddie shook his head at him. 'Not this time, old chap. If I get stuck I don't want you with me.'

He gathered up his belongings, shut the dog in the kitchen and went out. He felt confident that he could get up to the main road in the tracks of the tractor that had passed along earlier and, having cleared a path to the garage, he backed cautiously into the lane and set off. White walls of snow showed the passing of a snowplough on the Okehampton road but the surface was icy and, as he approached Kelly College, he saw that a car had skidded nose first into a bank of snow and the driver was standing helplessly beside it. Freddie slowed and the man waved gratefully. The Fourtrak stopped and Freddie leaned over and opened the passenger door.

'Good of you to stop.' The tall dark man smiled in at him. 'I just lost control and in she went. I was about to start walking. I don't think we can do much about it, do you?'

Leaving the engine running, Freddie climbed down and, walking carefully, went round to look at the situation.

'Not a chance, I'm afraid. But I can give you a lift into Tavistock. Any good?'

'To tell you the truth, I'm not too sure where I am,' said the man. 'It was a hell of a trip down. I'm not supposed to be on this road but it was the only possibility.'

Freddie smiled and held out his hand. 'I'm Freddie Spenlow,' he said. 'You're just outside Peter Tavy on the Okehampton road not far from Tavistock. Does that mean anything to you?'

'Not a thing!' said the man cheerfully. 'My name's Jonathan Thompson. I'm on my way to visit my cousin near Merrivale. His name's Michael Barrett-Thompson.' He raised his eyebrows. 'Does that mean anything to you?'

'It certainly does!' cried Freddie. 'How amazing. I know Michael and Harriet very well. They've got two of my dogs.'

Jon shook his head disbelievingly. 'Definitely my lucky day. Am I anywhere near them?'

'Not too far. Get your stuff in here and I'll take you into Tavistock. We'll see how things are looking.'

The roads were clearer in the town, although here and there cars had been abandoned. People with shovels were clearing the pavements and council workers were heaving the snow into lorries to be taken and tipped out of the way. There was a general air of camaraderie and bustle.

Freddie pulled up outside the Bedford Hotel. 'Now,' he said, 'I've got to do some shopping. You could book in here or, when I've finished, we could take a little trip.'

Jon looked surprised. 'Trip?'

'Mmm.' Freddie nodded. 'If the snowploughs have been out on the Okehampton road they'll almost certainly have been over to Princetown. Michael's cottage isn't too far up that road. Getting along the lane to it might be a bit tricky but we won't know till we try. Shall we have a go?'

'I'm game if you are,' said Jon. 'Great!'

POLLY BUSTLED TO AND fro collecting towels from the airing cupboard and spare clothes from Michael's dressing room while Jon looked on. She felt that Michael would have no objection but was careful to select a rather ancient-looking pair of cords and a sweater that had seen better days. She didn't feel up to going into the intricacies of underwear but she did find a pair of very thick socks. He'd have to make do with his own underwear and shirt, which might not be too clean but certainly wouldn't be soaked through with the snow.

'There we are,' she said, dumping them on a chair in the bathroom.

His face, she thought, was curiously impassive. It had a still, watchful expression that gave nothing away. After a moment he smiled at her. The smile narrowed his eyes but barely touched the corners of his mouth. 'This is all very unexpected,' he said.

His voice, too, was characterless if well educated and Polly was aware that the relief she had felt at the sight of another human being was beginning to fade. It seemed that Michael's cousin might be a bit of a stick and the thought of being mewed up for days with him suddenly depressed her.

'Well,' she said, brightly, rather too brightly, 'you've got everything you need.'

There was no doubt that he looked very tired and a fit of compunction overtook her. One could hardly expect him, in the present circumstances, to be the life and soul of the party.

Perhaps, thought Polly, as she went downstairs having provided him with a couple of Harriet's Bic razors, it was being in the Foreign Office that did it. She envisaged him, stuck in strange countries where people jabbered in unknown tongues, dealing with all sorts of crises—monsoons, malaria, outbreaks of typhoid, civil war. You needed the strong, silent type for that sort of thing, no doubt. Jolly, lighthearted, anything-for-a-laugh types probably wouldn't go down very well in those outposts of civilisation. But Polly sighed a little as she opened the kitchen door. Just at the moment she would have sold her soul for a jolly, lighthearted, anything-for-a-laugh type.

Hugh and Max both stirred as she came in and she went to pick Hugh up, holding his warm, relaxed body close to hers. She pressed her cheek against his silky hair and kissed the soft cheek, rosy with sleep. He remained for some moments lying sleepily against her and sucking his thumb. She rocked him a little, staring out of the window and wondering what on earth she was doing in Harriet's kitchen, cuddling her child, completely cut off from the outside world and with a strange man having a bath upstairs. Ozzy stretched languidly and got to his feet. He came to stand beside her, pushing his heavy head against her thigh. He imparted a sense of strength and comfort to her and, shifting Hugh a little, she freed a hand to stroke his ears.

'Good boy,' she murmured, though she was not sure to which of them she spoke. 'Good boy, then.'

The movement seemed to disturb Hugh and he struggled a little. 'Down,' he commanded, and when Polly set him on the floor he crawled under the kitchen table where he kept his box of toys and started to rummage.

Polly sighed, the spell broken, and gave Ozzy a last pat. 'Shall we have some lunch?'

Ozzy looked keen and alert and even Max stirred and opened his eyes as Polly went to look at Harriet's list. Hugh started to converse with his toys in a low monotone and Ozzy watched with interest as Polly set the table, put the saucepan of soup on to heat and prepared Hugh's lunch.

Presently she heard the sound of water gushing away. 'Come on, Huge,' she said. 'Time to eat. We've got a visitor. It's your Uncle Jon, or is he your uncle?' she went on, speaking more to herself as she helped Hugh out from under the table and swung him into his high chair. 'If he's Michael's cousin he's probably more your second cousin once removed or something. Anyway. His name's Jon. Can you say Jon, Huge?'

'Don,' said Hugh obligingly, picking up his spoon. 'Don.' He squashed some potato into the gravy and Polly turned as she heard footsteps on the stairs.

'We're in here,' she called and went to open the door. Several things happened at once as Jon appeared in the doorway. His gaze fell on Hugh and he stopped short. Hugh gazed back, his spoon suspended in mid-air, and Max got to his feet and gave a long, low, menacing growl. Ozzy stood up, ears pricked.

'Max!' cried Polly reproachfully, aware of some tension in the atmosphere but unable to see what it was. 'Really, Max!'

Max flattened his ears and waved his tail a little but as John took a step forward he growled again.

'Honestly, I'm really sorry.' Polly hurried over to stroke Max and remonstrate with him. 'He's usually the gentlest of animals but he's always very protective of Hugh and, of course, with Michael and Harriet away he probably feels especially in charge.'

'Quite right, too.' Jon had remained where he was at the second growl but his pale grey eyes were still fixed on Hugh. 'Is he likely to do more than growl?' He stayed quite still.

'I shouldn't think so,' said Polly, but rather doubtfully. 'I've never seen him quite like this before. I should think that if you don't come near Hugh it'll be OK. I'm awfully sorry.'

'Perhaps you could put him outside?'

For some reason, the quiet suggestion put Polly's hackles up almost as far as Max's. The thought of poor old Max, who, after all, was only doing his job, shut out in the cold utility room was rather too much.

'Easier said than done.' Polly gave a light laugh. 'You've obviously never tried to make a Newfie do something it doesn't want to do.' She pretended to tug at Max, who stood firm and uttered another rumble although turning his head to give Polly a quick lick as if to imply that it wasn't directed at her.

Polly shrugged. 'Nothing doing,' she said. 'You'd better sit down at the end of the table and we'll eat. I'm sure he'll be fine. He just needs to get used to you. Ozzy seems to be OK.'

Jon edged his way to the chair indicated and sat down. Polly continued to stroke Max for a moment and then went to fetch the soup. Jon's curiously light eyes were still fixed on Hugh. Hugh stared back. Polly felt that she wanted to do something violent to break the tension and distract Jon's attention.

'Food,' she said loudly. 'You must be starving. Bread?' She banged things on to the table and smiled at Jon determinedly. 'Eat up and after lunch we'll persuade Hugh to do you one of his pictures.'

.   .   .

'THE LEAST WE CAN do is try to get to a telephone,' said Tom. 'The whole village is off so the best thing is to strike across to Yelverton. We could try going via Meavy in case they're on. This sort of thing can be very local and they may be luckier there. We can at least warn the police that Polly is alone with a small child. They can probably get someone out to her.'

'It could take you hours to get to Meavy, let alone Yelverton, in these conditions,' said Cass, who was filling two flasks with hot coffee. 'Oh, how dreadful it all is. You don't think it would be better to let the two boys go and you stay here?'

'No, I don't!' Tom pulled a heavy sweater over his ordinary clothes. 'I've agreed that Saul can come because I think he might try something silly if I leave him behind. But I'm damned if I trust him not to try something off his own bat if he's only got Oliver with him.'

'You're probably right.' Cass began packing the flasks with some sandwiches into a knapsack. 'Oh, do be careful, darling. I shall be out of my mind. It's so awful to be totally cut off. I shan't know where you are.'

'Well, at least you'll have Oliver if there's some sort of drama. Let's hope he can cope if there is!'

'Have no fear, dear Father.' Oliver had come into the kitchen unheard. 'I'm quite up to a psychopathic killer, should one turn up on the doorstep, and, although I haven't done the Ten Tors and won the Duke of Edinburgh's Award like dear old Saul, I shall probably cope with carrying some logs in and keeping the home fires burning.'

Tom snorted. 'Ten Tors! He'll probably break his ankle going down the drive! Have you dug out those waterproof trousers, Cass?'

'They're all here.' She indicated a pile of garments on the table. 'Thank goodness I'm tall. Saul should be able to wear mine quite comfortably.'

Tom, having put his waterproofs on, was sitting tackling his walking boots when Saul appeared, looking white and tense, dressed in some sort of camouflage boiler suit, black laced-up boots and a woollen hat pulled on over his dark hair.

'Heavens!' remarked Oliver. 'Where are you going? Are they filming the siege of the Iranian Embassy? You look just like an extra!'

'You must put on some waterproofs, darling,' said Cass, holding up the remaining trousers, 'you'd be soaked through in five minutes dressed like that.'

'I know.' Saul took them from her and prepared to put them on.

Tom shrugged himself into his waterproof jacket. 'Saul can take the rucksack,' he said. 'I want to find a good stout stick.' He went out into the hall.

'Real *Boys' Own Paper* stuff,' observed Oliver, attempting to lighten the atmosphere a little. 'You'll have to watch him, Saul. Thinks he's Bulldog Drummond, I shouldn't wonder.'

Saul stepped into the trousers and sat down again to deal with his boots.

'Will you be all right?' Cass asked Saul, concerned by his silence.

Saul, wrestling with his laces, nodded and then glancing up at her gave her a quick grin. Cass saw at once that, besides his concern for Polly, he was filled with a blazing excitement. This was all his fantasies, the old war films and James Bond rolled into one and he was loving every minute of it. Cass, taken aback for a second, had a strong feeling that there was more in Saul's mind than merely going in search of the nearest telephone. She had a terrible twinge of misgiving.

'Saul,' she began but, as she spoke, Tom could be heard shouting from the hall.

'Come on, Saul. We really must be off!'

Saul stood up, hauled on the jacket, swung the knapsack on to his back and gave Cass a quick kiss. 'See you, Ma,' he said and he was gone.

MICHAEL STOOD LOOKING DOWN at Harriet, asleep in her hospital bed. This birth had been easier than Hugh's but she looked tired and pale.

No more, thought Michael. Two is more than enough. She'll be forty in a year or two and Hugh's a handful on his own without this new one. He sighed. His thoughts moved to Polly. He'd just heard that there'd been a breakout from Princetown and that the prisoner's escape car had been abandoned at Merrivale. It was a chance in a thousand that he would turn up at Lower Barton but Michael felt that he must try to get back. He wondered whether to tell Harriet the truth, although it would worry her, or pretend that he wanted to get back to check on Hugh and pick up some stuff for himself. As he debated with himself, Harriet's eyes opened and she smiled up at him.

'Hello,' she said. 'What's wrong?'

'Nothing's wrong.' He'd made up his mind. 'Do you think you could cope if I went home to pick up a few things? I'd love a bath and some clean clothes and I could say hello to Hugh and tell him about his new brother. What do you think?'

Harriet turned dreamy eyes to the window. 'Would you make it in the snow?'

'Oh, that's no problem,' said Michael easily. 'The snowploughs have been right through but you mustn't panic if you don't hear from me at once. The telephone lines are down.'

'Oh, dear.' Harriet looked concerned and started to struggle into a more upright position. 'Oh, in that case you'd better go. Poor Polly will be so worried.'

'No she won't. At least, not yet. I've already spoken to her this morning, remember. But it might be a good idea to check up on things. I'll try to get back this evening.'

'No, no. Don't do that. I'm perfectly OK and so is the baby. We're quite safe here. I'd rather you were with Hugh. If the telephone is off, the electricity may be off, too, and poor old Polly will be in a right two-and-eight. I shall be happier knowing that you're there. I don't want you driving back here in the dark.'

'OK. But you must promise not to worry if you don't hear from me. I'm sure I shall get there quite safely but I shan't be able to tell you that I have.' He bent to kiss her. 'I'll be in bright and early tomorrow morning. Might even bring Hugh.'

'Oh, that would be lovely.' She reached up to return his kiss. 'But only if it's absolutely safe.'

'Of course. Don't worry, I shan't take any risks.'

POLLY WAS FEELING ILL at ease. It was, as much as anything, Max's behaviour that was beginning to unnerve her. He barely took his eyes from Jon and when Hugh, after lunch, went to sit in the armchair beside the Aga, Max got up, too. He sat in front of the armchair with Hugh's slippered toes digging into his big furry neck and continued to stare at Jon.

'He's always been like this with Huge,' lied Polly, trying to laugh. 'It's rather touching, really.' She wanted to go and check the fire in the sitting room but for some reason felt afraid to leave them. Ozzy, sensing Max's antagonism, was watchful and alert without being openly hostile. This is silly! she said to herself. He's Michael's cousin, for goodness' sake! But still she sat on at the table, cradling her coffee mug in her hands.

Jon made no attempt to approach Hugh or even to speak to him. He just continued to watch the child who, always cautious with strangers at the best of times, ignored him completely. He sat now, surrounded by stuffed animals, thumb in his mouth, absorbed in a picture book.

'Do you think he's like Michael?' asked Polly. 'He's dark, of course, but then both Harriet and Michael are, too. I forget whether you've met Harriet?' Jon shook his head, his eyes still on Hugh. 'He's got Michael's brown eyes and he's a very quiet child . . .' She stopped speaking, listening to her voice dying away in the silence. 'More coffee?' she asked desperately.

'Thank you.' Jon pushed his mug towards her.

Polly got to her feet. She filled a jug with water and topped up the heavy Aga kettle. Whilst she waited for it to boil, she turned and rested against the rail of the Aga and looked at Jon. She thought that she had never seen a man sit so still. He's like one of those waxwork figures in Madame Tussauds, she thought, lifelike enough for you to go up and ask where the loos are but with an inhuman look. Or, she thought, letting her imagination have its head, like a robot from a *Star Trek* movie: on the outside a real human being but on the inside nothing but a machine.

'Are you married?' asked Polly, unable to stand her thoughts and the silence another moment. 'Have you any children?'

For the first time since he had entered the kitchen, Jon turned his light gaze upon her. 'My wife and child are dead,' he said. 'They died in an accident.'

Polly's hands gripped the Aga rail and she found herself quite unable to utter even the conventional words of regret or sympathy. She swallowed once or twice and shook her head slightly. Jon watched her. After a moment, that change of expression which passed for a smile touched his eyes. It had a chilling effect.

'How . . . how ghastly,' she stammered and turned with relief to make the coffee. Perhaps, she thought, her hands shaking slightly as she measured the coffee granules into the mugs, perhaps that's why he stares so. Perhaps his child looked like Hugh. Oh, God! What on earth does one say or do now?

That problem was answered for her by Jon himself. 'I need a leak,' he said, and stood up. So did Max. Ozzy raised his head from his paws. Polly put the mugs of coffee on the kitchen table and went to Max.

'Oh, dear,' she said, in as light a tone as she could manage. He's being a pain, isn't he?' She ruffled Max's hair.

'Never mind,' said Jon, in the same light tone. 'He'll need to go himself some time, won't he?' He slipped out of the kitchen while Polly was still taking in what he'd said and she heard him going upstairs.

He reappeared a few minutes later. ' Come and have your coffee,' she said in her 'bright' voice, 'and then, since you must be exhausted after all your traumas, I was wondering if you ought to go and have a sleep? I'm sure it would do you good.'

They both sat down again at the table and Max resumed his position in front of Hugh's chair.

'I might at that,' said Jon. He took a sip of coffee.

Presently his glance slid round until it rested once again on Hugh.

Twenty-eight

AT THE BOTTOM OF the drive—which Saul negotiated without breaking his ankle—they met William Hope-Latymer in his Land Rover.

'Just coming to see if you're OK,' he called, keeping the engine running. 'Jack Halliwell's been out with the tractor, taking some feed out, so I thought I'd chance it. I imagine you're cut off, too? Jack reckons the worst's over.' Suddenly he took in their dress and Saul's rucksack. 'What are you two up to? Off to do the Ten Tors?'

Saul grinned but Tom took charge. 'Did you see that there's a prisoner on the run?' he asked. 'That girl we had staying—you know? Polly?—is over at Harriet's all on her own with their kid.' Too late he remembered Cass's injunction that Saul should not know the details and he prayed that William wouldn't know them either.

'Christ!' William looked shocked. 'I saw it on the news just before we lost the juice. They said he killed his wife because she went out leaving their kid on his own and he got up and set the house on fire, or something. Died of burns. Only three years old. I gather that he took a hatchet to his wife and he's got an obsession about kids and hates women. Bloody hell! And they found his car off the road at Merrivale. That's not far from their place, is it?'

Tom glanced quickly at Saul, took in his horrified expression and looked at William. 'Do you think Meavy will be on?' he asked, ignoring William's question. 'Any chance of a lift that far? Do you think this thing will get through?' he added, hammering his fist on the bonnet.

'Have a bloody good try!' replied William cheerfully. 'If Jack's got out, we can follow along. In you get.'

Tom and Saul hurried round to squeeze in the front with William and he started off gingerly. Saul sat in silence, adjusting his ideas. Some of the pure excitement had gone out of the adventure but an iron determination had entered in its place.

'Jack's got stock out on Lynch Common,' William was saying. 'So we should be OK that far, at least. It's getting down the hill and over the bridge that worries me. Still, we'll have a go.'

Sure enough, at the turning towards Sheepstor the tractor's tyre marks bore away to the right and the Land Rover continued slowly and cautiously towards Meavy. The road started to fall away to the bridge and the three of them sat barely breathing as, slipping and sliding, they began to descend. The snow had drifted into the narrowing valley and was soon piling up in front of the Land Rover. At the bottom of the hill, the road swings round to the right and left again over the narrow stone bridge which spans the River Meavy but, at this point, the Land Rover showed no inclination to remain with it. Despite William wrestling with the wheel—and Tom's shouted instructions—it left the road to follow the old track which led to the now generally unused ford. William decided that if he could not make the turn towards the bridge he would try to use the ford instead.

'Hold tight, chaps,' he said as he straightened the wheel and gently accelerated. The wheels gripped and the Land Rover picked up speed as they followed the old track until suddenly there was a loud crash and they came to an abrupt halt.

'Damn and blast!' cried William. 'Now what? Can you get out, Tom?'

They all scrambled out and waded through the snow round to the front of the Land Rover. The nearside front wheel had hit a pile of stones hidden by the snow and the hiss of air announced that the tyre had punctured.

'We'll have to change that wheel if we can. Have to move her back up a bit to get at it,' said William. 'You two shove and we'll see what we can do. It's worth a try.'

With William in the driving seat, Tom and Saul heaved and strained but all to no avail. There was no prospect of moving it without more help.

'Forget it,' said William, switching off the engine and joining the others. 'Why don't you two go on and try and find a phone? See if you can get someone with a tractor to come and give me a pull out. You needn't worry about me, I'll be all right.'

'OK,' said Tom. 'Don't forget the rucksack, Saul,' he added as he set off to cross the ford. The words had hardly left his lips when, slipping on a stone, he fell with a great splash into the icy cold water.

William went down to help him. 'Come on. Give me your hand.'

'Christ!' groaned Tom as William hauled him to his feet. 'I've twisted my bloody ankle—or broken it!'

'Hang on, don't put any weight on it. Come on, Saul, you take that side and we'll try to get him back to the Land Rover.'

Between them they helped him to hop and hobble to the Land Rover, water cascading from inside his waterproof clothing, and up on to the front seat, his face clenched with pain.

'We'd better get his boot off,' said Saul, 'in case it starts swelling. Look, the best thing is for me to get on up into the village and try to find some help. It's no good,' he said firmly, as Tom began to protest. 'You can't go any further like that and it doesn't need both of us to go for help. I'll find a telephone even if I have to go on to Yelverton. If I don't come back with the rescue party, you'll know that Meavy's off and I've pressed on.' He reached for the rucksack, took out one of the flasks and divided up the sandwiches, keeping for himself the slab of chocolate that Cass had put in.

'He's quite right, Tom.' William was already struggling with the soaking laces of Tom's boot.

'I've left you a flask,' said Saul, shouldering the rucksack. 'I'll be back in a minute if the telephones are on. If not . . .' he shrugged, 'see you when I see you.'

'Well, for God's sake take care,' said Tom and cried out with pain as William started to ease the boot from his swelling ankle. 'Christ, William!'

'Sorry, old chap. It's got to be done. Hang on!'

'And no silly heroics!' shouted Tom after his son.

But Saul was already climbing the hill to the village and continued on his way without a backward glance.

MICHAEL HAD NO DIFFICULTY in getting out of Plymouth. The lorries had been through behind the snowploughs, salting and gritting, and the traffic had made sure that the main roads were kept open. But, when he passed through Roborough and away from the shelter of the buildings and hedges, conditions rapidly deteriorated as the wind drifted snow on to the road and all signs of grit and salt had long since gone.

As the open moor came into view, he caught his breath. The great white waste stretched as far as the eye could see in every direction, all landmarks obliterated. He could have been crossing a desert. It had stopped snowing but the sky was as white as the snow itself and Michael felt a sense of desolation.

If Hell wasn't supposed to be hot, one could imagine it to be something like this: endless emptiness. Cold, bleak, featureless and oneself doomed to travel on in it for all eternity.

He pulled himself together and switched on the car radio. '. . . is still at large. People in the area have been warned not to approach him as he is known to be dangerous. The severe weather conditions are hampering the police in their search . . .' Michael switched it off and pushed his horn-rimmed spectacles more firmly on to his nose. He did not know the full details of the case, having heard of it second-hand from one of the nursing staff. Even so, he was beginning to feel very anxious. 'Bloody hell,' he muttered to himself. 'It would all have to happen together. If only I'd insisted on bringing Hugh with us!' He pushed a tape into the slot and switched the radio back on. Hummel's Piano Concerto Number One filled his ears and he tried to relax.

He crawled on, passing a number of abandoned cars. As he approached the outskirts of Tavistock a car appeared, travelling in the opposite direction. It grew closer, seemed to waver and then started to slide towards him.

'For God's sake!' cried Michael. 'Get over, you blasted idiot!' He steered as close to the left as he could but the other vehicle struck his front wing. Michael had a glimpse of the set terrified face of an elderly woman before his own car slid out of control to plunge head-first into a great wall of snow at the side of the road.

'Hell and damnation!' shouted Michael. He got out of the car but the woman was continuing on her way, veering first this way and then that, without a backward glance.

Michael shut his eyes for a moment as various choice phrases concerning women drivers passed through his mind, then he opened them and looked at his car. It was obvious there was no possibility of returning the heavy Volvo estate to the road without the help of a number of strong men or another vehicle. He glanced round. For the first time he realised that he was almost opposite the turning that led down to Whitchurch—and in Whitchurch lived Kate and Chris. Without hesitation he switched off the engine, changed his shoes for gumboots, took his Barbour from the back of the car and, locking up, set off for Whitchurch.

'I MUST SAY,' SAID Jon, putting down his spoon and fork with a sigh, 'it was a very good idea of yours to get stoked up first. I really enjoyed that.'

'I didn't think that it was very sensible to risk life and limb on an empty stomach,' said Freddie, leaning back in his chair and glancing around the bar. 'Thank God that the Bedford still has its electricity on. You must have been starving.'

Jon stretched out his long legs to the fire while Freddie went to get some coffee. If the truth be told, he was rather enjoying his adventure. He usually took his holidays fishing in Scotland and this was his first trip to the West Country for many years. He'd been back in the

London office for just long enough to enjoy this rumpus and he was looking forward to his first sight of Dartmoor, even if it were under several feet of snow.

Freddie returned with a tray on which stood a large pot of coffee. 'Chap's been telling me that there's been a breakout.'

Jon looked puzzled. He received his cup of steaming coffee and piled sugar in. 'Sorry?' he asked, taking a gulp. 'Breakout? I'm not with you.'

'A breakout from Princetown,' explained Freddie. 'The prison up on Dartmoor. It's only a few miles away. Not far from your relations' place. A car was left for him but he didn't get far in it. Ran it off the road at Merrivale.'

'Merrivale?' Jon wrinkled his brow thoughtfully. 'That rings a bell. I think Michael said something about Merrivale.'

He paused. 'That's right. He said that if I came over the moor I would come through Merrivale and then I was to turn off to the right just after a cattle grid.' He looked at Freddie. 'Does that sound about right?'

'Absolutely.' Freddie nodded. 'Well, it looks as if we might find your cousin having tea with an escaped prisoner.' He laughed and swallowed the last of his coffee. 'All set then? Fancy a man-hunt?'

'Lead me to it!' said Jon enthusiastically and gathering up their belongings they went out of the bar, down the steps and into the street.

'IT'S NO GOOD.' CASS threw her book down. 'I simply can't concentrate. I wonder how far they've got. It's awful to be so completely out of touch.'

'No good getting in a state, Ma,' advised Oliver. 'They could be hours yet. It's a long haul over to Yelverton in these conditions.'

'I know, I know.' Cass got to her feet and wandered over to the fire. Crouching beside it, she poked at it aimlessly and then put another log amongst the flames. 'It must have been perfectly ghastly in the old days. No television, no radio, no telephone, no lights. I can't imagine how they filled the hours. And that reminds me. It's getting on and I'd better get the paraffin lamps down. I hope they'll be home before dark.'

As she straightened up, the front doorbell pealed several times. Cass clutched at her heart and stared at Oliver. 'Who . . . ? Could it be . . . ?'

'Only one way to find out.' Oliver pulled himself out of his chair. 'And that's to go and answer it.'

'Oh, Oliver. Be careful. If only we still had Gus. He was such a good guard dog.'

'Come on, Ma. Get a grip. Homicidal maniacs don't go about ringing on doorbells. Perhaps it's Saul and Pa back already.'

He went out into the hall and, after a moment, Cass picked up the heavy brass poker and followed him. As they went down the hall, the doorbell rang again.

Oliver pulled back the bolt which Cass had earlier put across and opened the door. Abby Hope-Latymer stood on the doorstep, her eyes wide and frightened in her small face as she hurried past Oliver into the hall.

'Abby!' cried Cass, trying to hide the poker. 'How lovely. But should you be out on your own? Haven't you heard . . . ?'

'I certainly have!' interrupted Abby. Her eyes fell on the poker. 'And so, I see, have you. My God, Cass! William went out hours ago and he hasn't come back. I waited and waited but I'm all on my own up there and my nerve finally cracked. I started to hear footsteps and doors opening. Jesus! What a man! Did you see what he did to his wife? She only went out for a drink with some chums. She wasn't to know that the blasted kid would get up and burn the house down! Anyway. I decided to come down to you. Have you seen him?'

Cass pulled herself together and, in the face of Abby's panic, felt a slight sense of superiority. 'Well, hardly.' She gave a little laugh and attempted a joke. 'I know my reputation is pretty widespread but even so I hardly feel that he'd make straight for me.'

'I think she's talking about William, Ma,' said Oliver, grinning at Abby's puzzled expression. 'Not the escaped prisoner.'

'For God's sake, Oliver, go and find me a drink,' begged Abby.

'I've never run so fast in all my life and I had William's gun with me, too.'

A look of respect crept into Cass's eyes. 'A gun?' she said. 'Gosh, Abby! Makes my poker look pretty silly. Do you know how to use it?'

'Haven't a clue!' Abby broke into hysterical laughter. 'Which is just as well. I'd have probably shot anyone if I'd come upon them un-expectedly.'

'But where is it now?' Cass looked at Abby's empty hands.

'On the doorstep.' Abby opened the front door again and picked up the shotgun. 'It seemed a bit, well, unfriendly standing on your step and brandishing a shotgun. Apart from which, if you're as ner-vous as I am, you might have batted me one with your poker.'

They went up the passage together and into the sitting room where Oliver greeted them with large gin and tonics.

'Wonderful!' Abby leaned the gun against the sofa, seized the glass and took a great gulp. 'I imagine that neither of you have seen William. Where's Tom?'

'Well, that's the point.' Cass sat down with her drink and motioned Abby to sit beside her. 'Michael took Harriet into hospital last night to have the baby and Polly went over to look after Hugh and she's stuck up there all on her own with the prisoner loose. Tom and Saul have gone off to try to find a telephone so they can warn the police.'

'My God!' Abby's eyes had been growing larger and larger throughout this recital and she seemed to shrink back into the corner of the sofa. 'Poor, poor Polly,' she whispered. 'What a nightmare.' She began to search her pockets for her cigarettes. 'She must be out of her mind with terror.'

'It's possible that she doesn't know,' said Oliver, perching on a stool by the fire. 'It depends if she's been watching the television. She's probably been too busy with Hugh.'

'Let's hope, for her sake, that she doesn't know.' Abby inhaled deeply on her cigarette. 'Otherwise she'll probably be dead from fright by the time they get to her. And where the hell is William?'

'Where was he heading for?' asked Oliver.

'He went out in the Land Rover to check on one or two of the oldies. Mrs Hampton and a few others. Just to make sure they could cope. He said he wouldn't be long and that was two hours ago.'

'I'm sure he's fine,' said Cass. 'You know William. Someone'll keep him talking and he'll have forgotten the time. He'll probably panic when he gets back and finds you're gone. He'll think that the prisoner's popped in and kidnapped you.'

'Too bad,' said Abby firmly. 'There's no way I'm going back there alone. And suppose he's not there and doesn't come back for ages? I'm not staying up there on my own in the dark.'

'No.' Cass shuddered involuntarily at the thought. 'You must stay here with us. You didn't think to leave William a note?'

Abby shook her head and took another gulp. 'I just grabbed his gun and legged it,' she said.

'Oh well.' Cass glanced out of the window. 'It won't be dark for a few hours yet. William will probably guess where you are. We won't panic. Let's have another drink.'

Twenty-nine

BY THE TIME THAT Saul had left the village behind and set his face towards Yelverton, his mind was made up. He would forget the whole business of finding a telephone and make straight for Polly, all on her own at Lower Barton.

After all, he reasoned with himself on the long trudge up the back road to Yelverton, the police might not be able to do anything. They'll probably go out and check that she's OK but they're hardly likely to leave anyone on guard. The prisoner could turn up at any moment. I can stay with her until he's caught or until Michael can get back.

He was lucky that some farm vehicle had done the trip earlier and he plodded along in a tyre track, his eyes fixed on the lane ahead, his mind full of his plans, trying to picture his arrival at Lower Barton. After a while, it seemed that his world had dwindled to this endless white lane, merging with an endless white sky. At least it had stopped snowing. Secretly he was delighted that Tom had twisted his ankle. He felt free, purposeful and excited. It was always better in times of crisis to be up and doing.

Half an hour later, he was passing through the outskirts of Yelverton and heading for the main road, his conscience eased by a shouted conversation to a local, who was clearing his drive, which elicited the information that Yelverton had no power and that the telephones were off, too.

At the roundabout, Saul looked around him. Very little was moving. One or two locals were about, some of the shops looked open and there was a group of children embattled in a snowball fight. There were several abandoned vehicles dotted about and one or two creeping gently along the road. It was obvious that the ploughs had been through and Saul's spirits rose. With luck he might get a lift into Tavistock. He crossed the road and, sticking out his thumb to any passing car, set off again. He was well beyond the turning to Horra-bridge before anyone took the chance of stopping but, just when he had decided that people might be afraid to pick up a hitchhiker with a prisoner on the loose, a van slowed beside him and the passenger window was wound down.

'Where're you goin', mate?'

Saul leaned down and peered in. The driver was a young man, wearing overalls, a cigarette hanging from his lips. The back of the van was full of tools and equipment.

'Tavistock.'

'Yer in luck. 'Op in.'

Removing his rucksack, Saul opened the door and slid in gratefully. 'Thanks,' he said. 'Where are you going?'

'Up to Mount 'Ouse School. They've gotta burst pipe. Where d'you want ter be dropped orf?'

'To tell you the truth,' said Saul, his excitement growing, 'Mount House will be perfect. I want to get up on to the moor by Cox Tor, just behind it.'

'You wanna wotchit, mate,' said the van driver, with a grimace. 'That escaped prisoner's prob'ly roamin' around up there.'

'I know. The problem is, a friend of mine, a young woman, is stuck up there in a cottage all on her own.'

The young man let out a low whistle.

'Quite!' said Saul. 'I want to get up there as quickly as I can. I'm really grateful that you stopped.'

'Sorry I can't go no quicker, mate. But we'll get there. You're on yer own arter that.'

'Don't worry,' said Saul, as they drove through the town and out on to the Princetown road, 'I'll manage.'

'This road's not so good,' said the driver. 'You won't find much movin' up here.'

'I shan't use the road,' explained Saul as they turned through the gates. 'I know a short cut up the back.'

As the van chugged up the drive, he stared out at the snow-covered playing fields. Small boys ran to and fro, throwing snowballs, building snowmen and generally enjoying themselves.

At the top of the drive, as the van swung to the right, Saul gazed up at the great house where he had passed five years of his life. Today, it seemed like several lifetimes ago. Boys thronged, cheering, round the slowly moving van and there was a soft thud as a snowball hit the back door.

'Glad someone's enjoyin' it,' observed the van driver as he pulled into the car park. 'This do you?'

'Perfect,' said Saul, who did not want to be seen by anyone who just might recognise him. 'I'm really grateful.'

' 'Ope yer girlfriend's OK,' said the young man. 'Take care.'

'I will.' Saul got out and shouldered his rucksack. 'Thanks a lot.'

He hastened away down the back drive before some of the older boys could question him and let himself out through the gate. Unfortunately, here he had no tractor tracks to walk in and he knew it would be hard going from now on. Stopping to have a pee and to refresh himself with a sandwich washed down with coffee, he straightened his shoulders, took a deep breath and set off towards the moor.

CHRIS WAS EXTREMELY SURPRISED to see Michael standing on the doorstep. 'Good heavens!' he said. 'Michael! Whatever are you doing here? Oh Lord, it's not Harriet or . . .'

'No, nothing like that.' Michael was kicking off his boots while fending off the friendly attention of two large golden retrievers who had accompanied Chris to the front door. 'Harriet and the baby are fine. Is your phone still on, Chris?'

Chris stepped back to let Michael into the hall. The dogs followed

him. ' 'Fraid not,' he said, closing the front door. 'It went off just after you phoned this morning to tell us about the baby. What's the
problem?'

'What I didn't tell you this morning was that Polly came over last
night to look after Hugh while I took Harriet into Plymouth. And
now she's all on her own up there with this wretched prisoner on the
loose.'

'Ah.' Chris led the way into the large warm untidy kitchen and the
dogs went back to their positions by the Rayburn. 'Yes, I see. I suppose, if I thought about it at all, I'd have assumed that you'd taken
Hugh with you.'

'I wish to hell we had!' said Michael feelingly. 'Harriet knows
nothing about the prisoner yet and I'm praying that nobody tells her.
She'll go spare. I was hoping to get home and sort things out but I'm
stuck now. Some bloody fool woman driver pushed me off the road
by Anderton Farm.'

The kitchen door opened and Kate came in. She wore her usual old
guernsey and a tweed skirt that had seen better days. 'Who was that,
Chris?' she asked. 'Good grief! Michael! Whatever are you doing
here. It's not Harriet . . . ?'

With a sense of déjà vu, Michael reassured her and explained.

'Oh, Michael. How awful,' said Kate. She looked worried. 'And
he sounds such a horrid man, too. And his car was found at Merrivale.
Oh, dear, this is very bad.' She looked grave. 'What shall we do?'

'To tell you the truth,' said Michael, looking uneasily at their anxious faces, 'I don't know much about him. I've only heard about it
second-hand. What's the exact story?'

By the time they had finished explaining, Michael was looking as
worried as they did. 'Yes, I see,' he said. 'This makes things much
worse. Oh, hell! If I'd had any sense I'd have phoned the police in
Plymouth and they could have got someone straight out.'

'If they can get out,' said Kate. 'The roads will be impassable up
there, surely?'

'Well, I'm going to have to try,' said Michael firmly. 'Even if I have to walk, I must get there somehow. If Polly's seen the television, she'll be terrified.'

'What about Phil's Range Rover?' Chris looked at Kate. 'He's always telling us how bloody wonderful it is. That might get us up there. What do you think?'

'Worth a try,' said Kate.

'But would this Phil just lend it to you?' asked Michael. 'Perhaps he'll want to come.'

Kate shook her head. 'He's just getting over flu,' she said. 'Tell him,' she shouted after the departing Chris, 'that if he'll let us borrow it he can have a free puppy from the next litter!'

She smiled as the front door slammed behind Chris. 'That'll get him!' she said. 'Now, I'm going to make you a hot drink while we wait for Chris. Did you get any lunch?'

'No. But I'm not hungry. Some coffee would be wonderful. Oh, God, Kate. What a thing to happen!'

'It's bloody,' agreed Kate, pushing the kettle on to the Rayburn's hotplate, 'but don't panic yet. Polly may not have even seen the television. We were cut off quite early and she would probably have had her hands full with Hugh, and even if the prisoner turns up, which is most unlikely, she's got Max and Ozzy.'

'Mmm.' Michael didn't sound convinced. 'I'm not sure how good they might be in that situation.'

'Oh, well. You know how I feel about that. I've been telling you for years that you should get yourself decent dogs instead of overweight asthmatic hearthrugs. I'll book you one from my next litter.'

This was an old, much-enjoyed argument and Michael smiled. 'First this Phil, now me. If you go on giving puppies away at this rate, you won't make anything at all out of your next litter.'

'Who said anything about giving?' countered Kate. 'I wish you'd eat something.'

'I really couldn't but I wouldn't mind a pee.'

'Well, you know where it is.'

Kate made the coffee, her face thoughtful. As she poured in the milk she thought she heard the sound of an engine. She hurried up the hall and opened the door. Sure enough, there at the gate was Chris with the Range Rover. He grinned triumphantly as he climbed out. 'Only too willing to help,' he called to her. 'Didn't even have to bribe him with a puppy. He was just cross that he wasn't well enough to come with us. Margaret put her foot down. Just as well, he looks terrible.'

'Brilliant!' Michael spoke over Kate's shoulder. 'That's brilliant, Chris. Bless you. Do I gather from your conversation that you're going to come with me?'

'Of course he's coming!'

'Try to stop me!' said Chris. 'Just let me get some sensible gear on.'

'You can drink your coffee while he's doing it,' said Kate, steering Michael firmly back into the kitchen.

'Look, Kate. I'll have to get back to the hospital tonight. If anyone's told Harriet about this man she'll be having fits and it's not even as though I can phone her to tell her we're all safe. Can I bring Polly and Hugh back to you?'

'Of course you can! You don't have to ask!'

'Ready?' Chris appeared dressed in all-weather gear. 'Let's get on while we've got the light with us.'

The dogs got up, tails wagging, hoping for a walk, but Kate shut them firmly in the kitchen and followed the two men out.

'Be careful,' she said, as Michael put on his boots.

'I know you'll be quite safe with the dogs,' Chris said to her, 'but when we've gone, go in and lock the doors and don't let the dogs go out again. We'll be as quick as we can.'

FROM THE WINDOW OF her workroom Thea stared out to the moor. The sky was lightening from the west and the snow gleamed gold on the shoulders of the hills. She could not keep bothering George with her fears for Polly. He had been very patient and understanding but she could sense that both these emotions would begin to wear thin if she kept talking about it. So she had come away on the pretext of getting on with some work but in reality she was thinking about Polly and wondering how she was coping. Thea suspected that she would, by now, be totally cut off and could imagine how frightening it must be for her. She was also weighed down by a sense of foreboding that was better dealt with alone.

She saw George below her on the platform. He had Amelia, well wrapped up, in his arms and was walking up and down with her. She could see Amelia's fists waving and her cries of excitement floated up, mingling with George's deeper rumble. Jessie ran ahead, sniffing at the snow and making forays into the deeper drifts. Thea's own happiness and security seemed selfish in the face of what Polly might be going through and she told herself for the hundredth time that Michael was almost certainly with her. So why this feeling of unease—even dread? The depth of her affection for Polly quite surprised her. They had become so close, such good friends, and she simply couldn't bear the idea of her frightened and alone.

After a while she realised that her anxious worryings were fruitless and resorted to the comfort she always sought in times of stress or fear. She took some deep breaths and calmed her mind. The Ninety-first Psalm was the one her father had always recommended for times such as this. She couldn't remember it all but some of the verses slipped quietly into her thoughts . . . *I will say unto the Lord, Thou art my hope . . . in Him will I trust. For He shall deliver thee from the snare of the hunter . . . He shall defend thee under His wings . . . thou shalt not be afraid for any terror by night . . . it shall not come nigh thee . . . He shall give his angels charge over thee . . . they shall bear thee in their hands . . .*

She added a prayer for Polly's safety and realised that she was cold and that George and Amelia were no longer to be seen. She shivered, wrapping her arms about herself, and looked again to the moor where strong winds were blowing the snow in drifts like smoke across the granite tops. Golden light from the west filled the sky and her heart lifted a little and she turned and hurried downstairs.

WHEN JON COULD KEEP his eyes open no longer and agreed to go upstairs to sleep, Polly felt a great sense of relief. He had sat for some while, looking more and more exhausted, until his watchful stare had begun to glaze and his head to nod.

'Why don't you go and have a rest,' asked Polly. 'I'll read Huge a story and we'll do a picture for Michael. When you wake up we'll have some tea.'

At last, reluctantly, he agreed and went slowly upstairs. Polly drew a deep breath. Her nerves were at full stretch. She realised that, since Friday morning, she had barely been alone for a second and, for someone who spent most of her days alone, she was beginning to feel the strain that the company of others imposes. Hugh, who had been playing under the kitchen table, crawled out and looked at her. She summoned up a smile. After all, he was being very good with both his parents gone, the snow keeping him penned up inside all day and, to top it all, a strange cousin who hardly spoke but stared all the time turning up on the doorstep. Polly knelt down and pulled him to her.

'What would you like to do, Huge?' she asked him. 'Like to do a picture for Daddy? Or would you like me to read you a story?'

'No,' said Hugh who, although a quiet child, always knew his own mind. 'Want to make a snowman.'

Polly sat back on her heels and looked at him in surprise. Obviously he had stored up her earlier words and remembered them.

'Oh, but Huge . . .' she began, glancing out of the window, and then stopped. The grey dullness had cleared and she noticed for the first time that there were bursts of sunshine between the hurrying clouds. Suddenly she felt a great urge to be outside, to feel the wind on her cheeks and to see the sun on the snow. 'Why not?' she said, giving him a quick hug. 'Let's get our things on and go out. The dogs can come, too. We'll all go together but we must be very quiet till we're outside. We don't want to wake Jon, do we?'

Hugh shook his head, the brown eyes so like Michael's, fixed on her face.

'Come on then.'

Max was waiting for them and they went through the kitchen, crossing the hall quietly, with the dogs following behind. In the porch, with the door to the house firmly closed, Polly perched Hugh on the little bench, took off his slippers and inserted his chubby little feet into his red gumboots. Standing him down again, she helped him into his warm jacket and pulled up the hood. 'No gloves, Huge,' she said. 'They'd get soaking wet with snow.'

She opened the outside door and Hugh waded into the garden; Ozzy, his tail waving, padded behind him. Max followed more slowly. Polly pulled on Harriet's gumboots and took down a sheepskin coat. There was a woolly hat in one of the pockets and she dragged it down over her ears and picked up the spade.

'OK,' she said, joining Hugh. 'First we must make the snowman's big round body.'

She cleared a space with her spade and began to make a start. Hugh, who really had no idea what she meant, gathered snow between his hands and then threw it up into the wind, chuckling with glee when it landed on Max's surprised head. Polly patted her snow into a big round ball and banged it firm with the spade. Then she started on a smaller ball for the head, stopping every now and then to watch Hugh, who seemed to be enjoying himself immensely. She put the head in place, giving it a few thumps to wedge it firmly, and nodded. Now all it needed was a few features to give it character. In the porch she found one of Michael's caps on a peg, and took it out to perch it on the head. The problem was that the wind kept blowing it off and finally Polly was obliged to take off her own hat—or rather, Harriet's—and pull it over the snowman's cold head. She stuffed Michael's cap in her pocket and stood back to survey the result. 'Huge!' she called. 'Come and look.'

Hugh came to look. He stood for a moment. 'Mummy's hat,' he said at last.

'That's right,' said Polly and then grinned. 'It's a snow mummy,' she said.

Hugh continued to stare. 'I haven't finished it yet,' Polly told him. 'She's got to have a nose and some eyes. Come and help me find some eyes.'

Hugh, however, still not understanding, went back to his own games and Polly wondered whether some chippings of wood might be the answer. It was while she was collecting up some pieces of the right shape that she heard Hugh's wails. He had jumped into a drift of snow and tumbled over. He was frightened rather than hurt but his roars gave the impression that he was half killed. Still clutching her pieces of wood, Polly ran out of the shed but, even as she did so, the front door opened and Jon appeared. He had put on his wet shoes but had no coat. He raced across the snowy garden to pick Hugh up. Hugh screamed even louder at this and Polly hurried up the little path that she had dug earlier.

'Huge!' she cried. 'Are you OK? What have you done?'

'You stupid bloody woman!' said Jon quietly. 'Don't you know how to look after a small child?'

The controlled iciness of his anger was in direct contrast to Hugh's penetrating screams and empurpled face and Polly felt fear and her heart beat fast. Hugh, kicking furiously, stretched his arms towards her and Jon was forced to put him down lest he should twist from his grasp and fall. Hugh ran to her and she fell to her knees and gathered him to her.

'I don't think that he's really hurt,' she said, staring up at Jon. Her voice was high and thin. 'He's just frightened. We were making a snowman.'

'You shouldn't have left him.' Jon's voice was flat and Polly had the oddest sensation that he wasn't speaking to her at all. 'You shouldn't have gone off and left him.'

He looked about him and saw the spade. For a moment his eyes widened and then creased into that peculiar spasm of feature that seemed to pass for a smile. A great wave of terror engulfed Polly. She clutched Hugh, whose sobbing had subsided, and felt herself to be trembling uncontrollably.

'He's all right,' she cried in the same high voice and then she swallowed convulsively. 'He's perfectly all right now. He was frightened, that's all.'

Jon bent down and picked up the spade. 'You'll have to be taught a lesson,' he said. He looked at her. 'You know that.'

Polly stared back. Jon lifted the spade above his head and took a step towards her.

'Let the child go,' he said softly and, as he spoke, two things happened at once. Max, who had been pottering round at the back of the cottage, reappeared. Seeing Jon, he started to bark as he floundered through the snow towards him. But Ozzy was quicker. As he bounded towards them a vehicle's horn sounded a fanfare from the bottom of the track. Jon whirled round to face Ozzy and Polly screamed. Two figures had now appeared on the track and again Polly screamed. Jon glanced round, dropped the spade and bolted into the porch with Ozzy on his heels. He slammed the porch door in Ozzy's face and Hugh began to cry again.

Freddie and Jon vaulted the wall and waded through the snow to Polly, who stared up at them in terror.

'Polly!' cried Freddie, hauling her to her feet and holding her tightly for a moment. 'What is it? What's the matter? What on earth are you doing here? Are you all right? Why were you screaming? Where did Michael go?'

Polly, shivering from head to foot, stared from him to Jon and tried to control her shaking lips. Freddie released her and bent down to pick up Hugh.

'Hello, old chap,' he said. 'You remember Freddie, don't you? Where are Harriet and Michael?' he asked Polly.

Polly shook her head and bit her lips. 'They're not here. Harriet's having the baby but Michael's cousin came, only he's very . . . he's very odd.' Her voice cracked and she put out her hand and clutched Freddie's sleeve. He seized her other hand. 'I thought he was going to hit me with that spade.' She swallowed.

'Michael's cousin?' It was the other man who spoke and Polly looked at him, her eyes enormous. She nodded.

'They were expecting him. He turned up this morning. He'd been lost in the snow. He's . . . odd. And when Hugh fell over and started crying he . . .' She shook her head again.

'Where is he now?' asked Freddie. 'Was it him we saw go into the house? I thought it was Michael.'

Polly shook her head. 'Ozzy went for him,' she said, indicating the still barking Ozzy who had now been joined by Max.

'Come on, let's go in and meet this cousin,' said Jon.

He looked at Freddie over Polly's head and they glanced towards the cottage. Polly gave a little cry. 'Look, what's he doing?'

Jon had emerged from the utility-room door and, as they watched, he reached the garden wall in great bounds, leaped over it and ran off down the track.

'Freddie!' cried Jon. 'Your car! Did you leave the keys in?'

'Christ!' Freddie thrust Hugh into Polly's arms. With Jon in close pursuit, he fled across the garden.

'Oh, no!' cried Polly desperately. 'Don't go! Please don't leave me!'

Even as her cry died away she heard an engine kick into life. She stood straining to hear but the wind carried the noise in eddies around her and she couldn't begin to imagine what might be happening.

'Go in,' said Hugh tearfully. He pushed his knees into her waist as though to urge her towards the house. 'Go in.'

Ozzy, who had followed Freddie and Jon as far as the wall, came up to her, wagging his tail, and Hugh leaned down to him. 'Max and Ozzy come too,' he said.

'Yes.' Polly tried to pull herself together. What could possibly be going on? What were Freddie and that strange man doing at Lower Barton in this weather? Why had Jon run away? Did he fear that the other two had seen him threatening her? Even though she had seen him leave, Polly felt a terrible reluctance to go inside. She shuddered. Supposing he came back! The mere thought was enough to send her hurrying inside. Setting Hugh down, she locked the porch door, and when they'd struggled out of their outdoor clothes and boots, they went into the hall and she locked the inner door behind her. She ran through the kitchen to the utility room. The outer door stood open and she slammed it shut and locked that, too. She was trembling from head to foot. The dogs had followed her into the kitchen and were sitting by the Aga; Hugh stood in the middle of the floor gazing at her. He looked very small and vulnerable and Polly felt her own fear recede a little in the face of his.

'Want Mummy,' he said.

'Oh, Huge,' she said and, going to him swiftly, she gathered him up, shut the kitchen door and sat down with him in the armchair by the Aga. 'It's all over now, let's have a cuddle and then we'll have some tea.'

He must not see how frightened she was. Somebody would come soon. They must! Polly rocked Hugh in her arms and felt him begin to relax. She droned a little tune to him whilst her mind ran and reran the events of the last few hours. She wondered what she would do if Jon ran over the other two with the car that Freddie had left at the bottom of the track and then came back to kill her. Why should he want to kill her? She remembered his face when he'd told her that his wife and child had died in an accident. What sort of accident? The doors were locked, but what if he broke a window? She glanced at the window in terror, half imagining his face peering in with that spine-chilling smile. Suppose it got dark before anyone came? At the thought of a night alone in the cottage, her heart seemed as if it must fail and she could barely breathe. Her thoughts fled and whirled, hither and thither, like a mouse trapped behind a wainscot with its exits blocked. Her lips kept silently forming the words 'Help me. Help me,' but no one came and presently Hugh slept.

Thirty

SAUL WAS DELIGHTED TO see the change in the weather. It had been heavy going along the lane past the two farms and up to Tortown. His legs ached with the effort of wading through the snow and he was tired and hot. When he reached the edge of the open moor he breathed a great sigh of relief and stretched his aching back, throwing his arms wide. Pulling off his woolly hat, he let the wind tug at his hair. He stuffed the hat into his pocket and debated as to whether he should remove his jacket. The trouble with wet-weather gear was that it made you feel so hot and sticky but he knew the danger of getting overheated and then cooling down too quickly. He decided that he would rest for a moment to get his breath before the steep pull up to the lane and, taking off his rucksack, he finished the last of the coffee and the sandwiches.

He stood for a moment, watching the sky, enjoying the clear golden light and then, turning his back on the glory in the west, he started to climb to the lane. The wind was cold and he was glad that he hadn't removed his jacket. He should, with luck, come out almost opposite the small track leading to the cottage. Not long now! His heart bounded up with excitement and then he paused, staring up at the lane. He could hear the sound of an engine revving. He strained his eyes. Yes, there it was! A Fourtrak at the bottom of Lower Barton track. The driver was attempting to turn it and it slid and kicked as though he were unused to handling it. Saul started forward. The Fourtrak had achieved its turn and started back along the lane. As it did so, two figures appeared, running down the track waving and shouting, but the Fourtrak didn't stop.

Saul raced up the last few feet. He gained the lane just ahead of the Fourtrak and flung himself at the driver's door. The man was a complete stranger to him and as Saul wrenched the door open he struck out, cursing as the vehicle skidded. Saul stumbled and swung outwards with the door but managed to retain his grip. The engine roared as the driver pressed his foot full down on the accelerator and the wheels screamed as they skidded on the snow. Cursing, the driver took his foot off the accelerator, and the tyres suddenly gripped the snow so that the door swung in again. Saul managed to gain a foothold and seize the man, who struck him full across the face. Saul lost his footing and the door swung out again. Saul hung on for dear life as his feet began dragging through the snow and he was towed along, the door half open. The stranger shouted as he saw the Range Rover coming towards him and he turned the wheel. The Fourtrak left the road to bump and jolt over the rock-strewn moor until coming to an abrupt stop as it rammed a larger boulder. Saul was thrown forward, his shoulder crashing into the half-open door. Pain lanced down his arm and he let go of the door to fall, semiconscious, into the snow.

MICHAEL AND CHRIS WERE out of their vehicle in moments, Chris's feet sliding from under him so that he ended up on his hands and knees. Freddie and Jon panted towards them, shouting.

'. . . prisoner . . . stop him!' gasped Freddie. 'Christ!' He paused for a second to drag in some breath. 'He's getting away . . .'

Michael, trying to take in the fact that Freddie was here and that Jon was with him, turned to join in the race across to the Fourtrak where John, staggering from the driver's seat, stood for a moment as though stunned before setting off over the moor. It was Jon who brought him down. Redoubling his efforts he sprinted ahead and caught him round the legs in a traditional rugby tackle. The others were close behind and Freddie flung himself down, seizing John's arms and doubling them up behind his back. He lay perfectly still and his arms were limp.

'I think he's knocked himself out,' said Freddie.

'Serve him right!' Jon stood up and eased his back. 'I'm getting too old for this sort of thing. Roll him over. Let's have a look at him.'

Cautiously, Freddie rolled the man over. His eyes were closed and a trickle of blood ran down from his forehead.

'That's him!' said Chris.

'Who, the prisoner?' Michael stared down at him. 'How can you be so sure?'

'They showed his picture on television. It's definitely him. Is he all right?'

'Hit his head as he went down. I think he'll be OK,' said Jon, who was still rather breathless. 'Anyone got anything we can tie him up with?'

'There's some binder twine in the back of my wagon,' said Freddie. 'That'll do for now.'

'Hello, Michael.' Jon grinned at his cousin. 'Fancy meeting you here!'

Michael smiled a little but his face was white. 'I might have guessed you'd be here. You always did enjoy a scrap,' he said as Freddie went for the binder twine. 'What the devil's going on? Are Hugh and Polly OK?'

Jon nodded. 'Quite safe and unhurt.' He pointed to the man on the ground. 'He was at the cottage but we turned up before he could do anything. He pinched Freddie's Fourtrak and tried to make a getaway. And then that chap appeared from nowhere and saved the day.' He nodded towards Saul, who had rolled on to his knees and was trying to rise.

Michael gave an exclamation and hurried over to him. 'Saul! Where the devil have you sprung from? What's wrong with your arm?'

Saul was holding his left shoulder with his right hand. He tried to smile. 'I think I've bust my collarbone. Is it the prisoner? Is Polly OK?'

'It seems so. I don't really know what's going on. I gather he pinched Freddie's Fourtrak.' He assisted Saul to his feet as best he could. 'We must get you up to the cottage. Jon says that Polly and

Hugh are OK but they must be absolutely terrified. Let's get you into the car and home.'

Jon and Freddie could be seen, on their knees, tying the prisoner securely. Chris came over to Saul and Michael. 'OK? What's he done?'

'Broken his collarbone, he thinks,' said Michael briefly. 'Can you get us up to the cottage? I must see Polly and Hugh and see what we can do for Saul. We may need to get him to a doctor.'

'I'll go and get her started.' Chris ran back to the lane.

'I want to see him first.'

Michael hesitated. 'OK,' he said. 'If you must. He's knocked himself out.'

As they approached, Freddie got to his feet and came to meet them. 'I couldn't believe my eyes when I saw you, young man,' he said to Saul. 'Where on earth did you spring from? If you hadn't clung on like that he'd have got away.' He looked more closely at Saul. 'My goodness, your face looks sore. Did he do that?'

Saul nodded and grimaced. 'Tried to dislodge me. Can I have a look at him?'

They reached Jon and the man on the ground and Saul stared curiously down at him. A large discoloured lump was rising on his forehead, his face was very pale and his breathing laboured.

'I think he must have hit a rock when he went down,' said Jon, who continued to kneel beside him. 'Doesn't look too healthy to me.'

'Come on, we ought to hand him over.' Freddie turned to Michael. 'There was a police Land Rover patrolling earlier. We'll try to catch it. Otherwise it means going into Tavistock.'

'Are we still mobile, Freddie?' asked Jon.

'I should think so. He hit a rock so all he'll have done is bend the bumper a bit. I'll go and start her up but you'll have to carry him over. I'm not risking coming down here. You can't see what's under the snow.'

Presently both vehicles were under way. Freddie's, carrying the prisoner with Jon in attendance, bumping slowly down to the road and Chris, Michael and Saul in the other, heading for the cottage.

. . .

THE KITCHEN WINDOWS LOOKED away to the moor at the back of the cottage and so Polly didn't see Michael arrive. Because she had thrust the bolts across, Michael was unable to open the front door with his key. He hesitated. He guessed what she had done and also guessed that she had done it because she was frightened. What would she do if he rang the bell? Or should he go round to the back of the cottage and see if she was in the kitchen? Michael was both sensitive and imaginative and he could foresee the effect on a nervous person if she were to see someone looming up at the window without warning. Better to hammer on the door and ring the bell. At least she could peer out from either the sitting room or the study and see who it was. He rang the bell in several short bursts—having some idea that this might sound less threatening than one long peal—beat a tattoo on the glass window of the porch door and shouted at the same time.

'Polly! It's OK, Polly! It's Michael. Everything's all right now!'

At the first sharp trill of the bell Polly gave a strangled shriek, jerking upright in her chair and waking Hugh, who stared up at her. Max struggled up from his deathlike sleep and Ozzy started to bark. Before Hugh could remember the traumas of the day, he heard the knocking and ringing. Scrambling down, he ran towards the door.

'Mummy!' he cried. 'Mummy's home!'

'Wait, Huge!' shrieked Polly and the tone of her voice made him hesitate and stare at her. 'Wait,' she said more calmly as she tried to smile normally.

The door to the porch was made of solid oak, so she couldn't see who was outside although she could hear a man's voice shouting. Catching Hugh's hand, her heart thudding, Polly went through the hall—followed by the dogs who remained there to bark—and into the sitting room. She edged up to the window, watched by a puzzled Hugh, and peered cautiously out. Her heart bounded gloriously upwards. 'Michael,' she cried and he heard her and turned to wave reassuringly to her, indicating that he couldn't get in, but Polly had gone.

'It's Daddy!' she cried to Hugh. 'Daddy's here!' And panting with relief she flung herself at the bolts and the locks, dragging back the doors until she could see him—and how tall and strong and safe he looked—and then he was inside, picking up Hugh in one arm and holding Polly with the other.

He managed to get into the kitchen despite the fact that Hugh had both arms round his neck in a stranglehold and Polly was clinging to him, crying and laughing at the same time as the dogs led the way, tails wagging.

'Everything's quite all right,' he said, sitting down at the table with Hugh on his lap. He smiled at Hugh, who was chattering about brothers and presents and pictures and snowmen and something called Don. 'Sounds wonderful, old chap,' he said. 'Mummy sends her love and so does your new brother.'

Hugh got down to find the picture he had coloured and Michael looked at Polly.

'Oh, Michael,' she said shakily. 'What happened? Freddie was here. And then they all ran off and left me on my own. I was so frightened. Where is he now?'

'Don't worry a bit. We caught him further down the road. He tried to get away in Freddie's Fourtrak. Freddie's taking him down to the police station. He got knocked out when we tackled him but I think he'll live.'

Polly stared at him with round horrified eyes. 'The police?' she whispered. 'Oh, Michael. I suppose so but how awful for you. Why didn't you warn me about him?'

Michael was studying the picture of the multicoloured Holy Family. 'It's lovely, Hugh. I shall take it to show Mummy.' He glanced up at Polly. 'But I didn't know, either. And by the time I found out, the telephone lines were all down.'

Polly looked surprised. 'Didn't know . . . ?' she began, but before she could get any further there was a commotion in the hall and Chris appeared supporting a pale but smiling Saul. Polly's mouth dropped open.

'Saul!' she said in disbelief.

'Hello, Polly,' he said. 'Are you OK?'

She nodded, quite unable to utter a sound.

'He's been very brave,' said Michael, getting up. 'He walked nearly all the way here to make sure that you were safe and then found himself in the middle of a fight, saved the day and got wounded for his pains.'

'Oh, no!' Polly looked horrified. 'Oh, Saul. Your face! Did he attack you, too?'

'He did. I think my collarbone's bust.' He looked exhausted.

'Come on,' said Chris. 'Got a first-aid kit, Michael? I want to have a look at him and get him bandaged up. Don't worry,' he smiled at Saul, 'I've done the course. At least I should be able to make you comfortable if Michael's got some bandages.'

Michael took a box down from a cupboard. 'Should find all you need in here. Want any help?'

'I'll give a shout if we do. We'll use the bathroom, if that's all right with you. A cup of coffee or hot tea would probably be a good idea.'

'Of course.' Michael went to fill the kettle. 'Give him a couple of painkillers while you're up there.'

They went out and Polly shook her head as if to clear her mind.

'Drink!' said Hugh. 'Want drink.'

Mechanically, Polly stood up, swung him into his high chair and put his colouring book and his crayons on the tray.

'Why not do a picture for Daddy,' she suggested, 'while I make us a cup of tea? Michael . . .' She turned to him. 'What did you mean when you said you didn't know? And what difference did it make the phones being off? Didn't you know that your cousin's wife and child had died in an accident?'

'What?' It was Michael's turn to look amazed. 'Wife and child? Do you mean Jon? He's not married, never has been!'

'But he told me himself!' cried Polly. 'He said that they'd died in an accident. I thought that's why he was so peculiar and why he was going to hit me with the spade when Huge fell over.'

'Going to hit you with a spade? Jon?'

'Yes—but Freddie arrived. He would have done except he saw Freddie and ran indoors.'

'Wait a minute, Polly.' Michael held up his hands. 'Let me get this quite straight. Jon told you that he had a wife and child who'd died in an accident and then threatened you with a spade?'

'Well, not quite like that,' admitted Polly. 'He told me earlier about his wife and child. And then, when Huge fell over and started to cry, he said I wasn't fit to look after him. He picked up the spade . . .'

'Hang on. What is all this about a spade? What spade?'

'Hugh and I were making a snowman.'

'I can't believe this! When did Jon arrive?'

'Just before lunch. He'd had to abandon the car and had been walking for hours.'

'Well, if he was here then, when did . . . ?' He broke off as the doorbell pealed and Max started to bark. 'That'll be Freddie and Jon,' he said. 'Now I can get to the bottom of this.' He went out looking rather grim, not noticing that Polly had turned pale.

'. . . met the Land Rover at the end of the lane,' she heard Freddie say. 'Gave the fuzz a bit of a turn.' He came into the kitchen and smiled at Polly. 'Are you all right?' he asked. 'What a perfectly dreadful experience. Thank God we were in time. Sorry we rushed off and left you like that.' He went to her and put his arm round her, uncaring of what anyone might think. 'All over now.'

Polly stared at him and then looked past him as Michael appeared with Jon, who smiled at her. 'Hello,' he said.

She smiled mechanically at him but turned to Michael. 'I thought you said . . .' She paused. 'Where is he?'

'Who?'

'Jon!' said Polly, looking scared.

Michael frowned, puzzled. 'But this is Jon. My cousin Jon.'

'What! But that's *not* Jon,' said Polly.

As all three men gazed at Polly, the door opened and Chris ushered in Saul, whose arm now reposed in a very professional-looking sling.

'That's a bit better,' said Chris. 'Let him sit down comfortably. Got that tea ready?'

'No.' Michael looked distractedly at the boiling kettle. 'Hang on a minute. Polly, what do you mean? This man is my cousin Jon. Isn't he the man you said came before lunch, told you his wife and child died in an accident and threatened you with a spade?'

Everyone now stared at Jon, who looked quite nonplussed.

'No, it wasn't him,' said Polly, her voice rising with panic. 'It was the man you chased.' She looked at Freddie. 'You saw him. He was going to hit me with the spade.'

Freddie nodded. 'That was the escaped murderer,' he said gently. 'Got out of Princetown last night. Sheer luck we turned up when we did.'

Polly opened her mouth once or twice but no words came. Her lips framed the word 'murderer' and Michael pushed her gently into a chair by the table. He began to make the tea.

'You obviously didn't know about the escaped prisoner,' he said, keeping his voice level. 'He got out last night and his car went off the road at Merrivale. Do I take it that the man Freddie and Jon chased was the man who turned up here?'

Polly nodded. The five men watched her in silence.

'He was standing at the gate,' she said at last. 'The phone and electricity had gone off. I thought you might come, if you phoned and couldn't get through. And I thought it was you. It was snowing and I couldn't see that clearly. I called to him.' She paused and swallowed, her eyes grew huge with terror. 'Dear God! I actually asked him in!'

'But what made you think he was Jon?' Michael placed a mug of hot sweet tea in Saul's good hand but he was too riveted by Polly's narrative to even thank him.

'He said he was!' cried Polly. 'He said his car had gone off the road and he'd been walking for hours.'

'And he actually said he was my cousin Jon?' Michael put Hugh's beaker of tea on his tray and gently ruffled his hair. Hugh looked up from his colouring and smiled; Michael gave him a tiny wink and nodded reassuringly.

'Yes!' cried Polly. 'No.' She shook her head, making a terrific effort to remember. 'I called to him and when he wasn't you I said . . . Oh, my God! Yes. I said you must be Jon, or something, and he seemed quite surprised.'

'He probably was,' put in Chris. 'His name actually is John. John Middleton, I think. Must have given him quite a turn.'

'That was it!' Polly was remembering now. 'Only, you see, I thought he was surprised to see me here. So I immediately explained that you and Harriet were in Plymouth and I was all on my own.' She shut her eyes and shivered. 'Jesus! I dragged him in and made him have a bath!'

All five men reacted simultaneously. She opened her eyes and stared at them. Michael pulled himself together and put a mug of coffee beside her.

'Drink up,' he said quietly. 'What happened then?'

Polly obediently took a great gulp of coffee and stared at him tragically. 'I gave him your clothes to wear,' she said.

This was too much for Michael. He put his hands over his face and then he began to laugh. 'Sorry, love,' he said, still laughing, 'but you've got to admit it's got its lighter side. You are the only woman of my acquaintance who would drag a convicted murderer in, run him a bath, give him your host's clothes and then cook him lunch. You did give him lunch?'

Polly nodded glumly. 'Soup. Soup and bread and cheese. And coffee.' But, somehow, Michael's laughter had taken much of the horror out of the story and the colour began to come back into her face, although when she told them about the spade she still shuddered. 'Max hated him. I couldn't understand it. He growled and growled. But it was Ozzy who went for him. Max would have done but he was slower.'

Everyone looked at Max, who yawned in a casual manner and looked rather deprecating.

Thirty-one

TOM SAT BY THE drawing-room fire, his bandaged ankle resting on a footstool, and wondered what had happened to Saul. He was feeling a little less touchy than he had been on his return, which had been humiliating to say the least. After his denigrating observations regarding Saul's abilities, it was too embarrassing that it had to be he, rather than his son, brought home on a tractor having sprained his ankle. Tom felt a measure of irritation returning as he recalled his reception. The tractor driver had driven up the drive and jumped down from the cab to press the front doorbell before going back to help Tom out of the link box. Cass and Abby had opened the door brandishing, respectively, a poker and a shotgun and had dissolved into fits of giggles when they saw Tom with his arm round Dave's neck. Unfortunately, Tom had left his boot, together with his walking stick, in William's Land Rover and had been obliged to hop, supported by Dave, into the house.

The two women, taking over from Dave, helped him into the drawing room where they deposited him in an armchair. Cass went in search of bandages whilst Abby, still giggling, sloshed large quantities of gin—and an infinitesimal spot of tonic—into a glass which she pressed into his hand.

'Drink up,' she urged. 'You've got lots of catching up to do. Cass and I were too frightened to move so we've just been sitting here getting pissed. I've lost William, you see, so I came down here for company and now I'm too scared to go back. Oliver's gone to leave a note for William to tell him where I am. He's been gone for hours.'

So whilst Cass bandaged his ankle, Tom explained what had happened and where William was and, shortly after, William arrived and took Abby away, leaving the others to worry about Saul.

Tom, still smarting from the unseemly levity and unguarded and unflattering remarks surrounding his homecoming, was half inclined to get his own back by hinting at accidents and disasters of numerous varieties to increase Cass's anxiety. However, having survived variously the traumas of the death of her eldest child, three children away at school and a husband almost continually at sea, Cass was hardened to minor disasters and not easily stampeded into panic. She was still concerned for Polly but didn't seriously consider Saul to be in any great danger from the prisoner and more than capable of looking after himself in any other situation that might arise. She had gone off, accompanied by wafts of gin, to cook some supper, giving thanks for the Aga yet again, and Oliver had disappeared on a candle hunt.

Tom sat on, nursing his glass and wondering if Saul had found a telephone and where he could be. Despite his occasional antagonism to both his sons, he dearly loved them. However, they could never take the place of the daughter he'd lost. Charlotte—who had looked so like himself, who had loved him so much—would always take first place in his affections. The dead have advantages over the living. Their faults are forgotten or bathed in an attractive light and they do not irritate and annoy us. Tom imagined a pretty, loving, attentive daughter, surrounded by admiring men but looking always to him first. She would not have tested and challenged him as the boys did. As for Gemma, she had always been so self-contained, so poised for her age, that he was almost frightened of her. Blonde and beautiful like Cass, she had never shown a need of him as Charlotte had. His life was saddened and diminished by her death and he suddenly felt old and tired.

He glanced out of the window. The short winter day, brighter now with gleams of golden light from the west, was drawing in, Tom thought of Saul alone on the moor in the dark and grimaced. No, best not to frighten Cass who, when the effect of the gin had worn off, might realise the dangers for herself. He stirred uneasily. Where the devil could he be?

SAUL WAS SITTING IN the armchair by the Aga waiting for his fate to be decided. The euphoria of his journey, the excitement of catching the prisoner and the sweetness of Polly's admiration and gratitude were all beginning to fade in the face of pain and exhaustion. Michael, having noticed this, was firm in his decision that Saul should come with him back to the hospital. He could be checked over, stay the night there and, if all was well, be taken home the next day. Michael's real dilemma was whether to take Polly and Hugh to Kate's, leaving Jon in situ, or to leave all three of them at the cottage. While he was debating, Polly thought of another problem.

'What about Cass?' she asked. 'She'll be worried to death if she doesn't hear from Saul. How can we let her know?'

'Oh, hell,' said Michael. 'I hadn't thought of that. How on earth can we get a message to them? Even if their telephone is back on, ours isn't. We could try from the hospital, I suppose.'

'Yes, but if Cass's isn't back on, what would you do then?' asked Chris. 'One of us will have to try to get over there.'

'I'll have a go, if you like,' said Freddie, wondering what Polly would be doing. 'Should manage it in the old beast but I must admit it would be nice to have someone with me, just in case.'

'I'll come,' offered Saul.

'You most certainly will not!' said Michael, whose dilemma had now been solved. 'You're coming with me. OK. What I suggest is this. Freddie and Jon go off to Cass's and, if Freddie has no objection, Jon goes back to his place for tonight. Saul, Hugh and Polly come with Chris and me. We drop them off with Kate while Chris and I get my car out of the snow and then Saul and I go on to the hospital. I'll come back to you tonight, Chris, when I've settled Saul and seen Harriet, and tomorrow—well, we'll sort tomorrow out when it comes. How does that suit everybody?'

Everyone nodded. Polly was so relieved at not having to spend another night at the cottage alone with Hugh that she would have agreed to almost anything and she went off to pack for Hugh and herself. She would have to come back for her car, of course, but she would worry about that later. She went round finding all the presents that Harriet had hidden for Hugh and packing them up to take with them. By the time she got back to the kitchen, Freddie and Jon had already set off and the others were ready to go.

Michael checked round, locked up, and the five of them and the dogs went out of the cottage and into the snowy winter evening.

TWO DAYS LATER, POLLY removed herself to the Old Station House. Weather conditions had improved and Hugh was now back in Michael's care. Kate had been very kind and Polly had found her a soothing companion after such a traumatic experience. She had allowed Polly to go over and over the horror of the last few days and had comforted and consoled her. However, as soon as the telephones were working again, Thea had tracked Polly down and urged her to come to stay and Polly felt that she needed to be with someone who knew her whole situation and to whom she could open her heart about Paul. Thea was horrified to hear of all that Polly had been through. They went over it again and again until, at last, it began to recede from the forefront of Polly's mind and she could sleep without nightmares.

'It would have been worse if I'd known he was a murderer,' she told Thea as they sat before the fire one evening with Amelia tucked up in bed and George, who was back at the MOD, in London. 'As it was, I just thought he was Michael's cousin and that he was a bit odd. The spade thing was truly terrifying but by the time I found out he was a murderer, it was all over.'

'Well, it *is* all over,' said Thea, who felt that Polly should begin to put it all behind her and look to the future. 'And now you've got to decide what you're going to do. I still think it's awful of Paul just to go off like that. Unbelievable.'

'I don't know what to do,' said Polly.

'You don't feel that you want to make a fight of it?'

Polly reflected for a moment and then shook her head. 'I don't see the point. I've always come a poor second and, since Fiona came on the scene, I seem to have moved down to third. It's partly my fault. I don't seem to have the energy to make a stand. We've just drifted along and I can't blame him if he wants to stop drifting. I've envied you and George. Your relationship is so strong and secure.'

'Well, I hope you're right.' Thea came to sit beside Polly on the sofa. 'It's going to need to be.'

Polly raised her eyebrows and Thea made a little face. 'It's this Brussels thing. I don't want to go. I haven't told George yet. He just assumes that Amelia and I are going but I hate the idea. I can't bear the idea of leaving Jessie and Percy and this house and I feel so ashamed when I see people like Cass taking this sort of thing in her stride.'

'Well, of course, she's been doing it for so long, hasn't she?'

'Yes, but she had to start. I just assumed that I'd never have to do all the moving around because George was so much older.'

Polly looked at Thea. She had always seemed so strong and confident and Polly was surprised to see her uncertain and afraid.

'What about your writing?'

Thea shrugged. 'George says I can do that anywhere and of course he's right. But I don't want to do it anywhere. I want to do it here.'

'How will he react if you say you don't want to go?'

'He'll be very hurt.' Thea stared at the fire. 'The thing is,' she said slowly, 'I've got a very good excuse but it's a bit cheating to use it.'

'Whatever can it be?' Polly stared at Thea's sombre profile.

'I'm pregnant.' Thea turned her head and smiled at her.

'Thea!'

'I know.' Thea nodded, smiling. 'And the thing is that George is the sort of man who would understand that a woman in that state likes to be amongst her own people. Especially when I had such a bad time with Amelia. And he would let me stay and go on his own, although he would worry like mad about me.'

'Yes, I see.' Polly sighed. 'Oh, dear.'

'Yes.' Thea sighed, too, and then pulled herself together. 'Sorry. I don't mean to be selfish. I've got everything going for me and all I do is whine because I may have to go and live in Brussels. Most people would be thrilled.'

'If it was just Percy and Jessie, I could look after them,' said Polly thoughtfully. 'After all, if Paul and I separate the house will be sold, I suppose. I could come and house-sit for you, then you wouldn't have to let it and you could come home towards the end of your pregnancy and have the baby here. I'm sure George would understand that. It's a compromise.'

Thea gazed at her with such intensity that Polly felt nervous.

'Polly, you're brilliant! Would you really do that? It wouldn't be nearly so bad if I thought you were here and I could come home when I wanted to. I hate the idea of letting it and we couldn't leave it empty for two years. I could fly over for the odd weekend and Percy and Jessie wouldn't have to go to strangers. Oh, Polly! Would you really?'

'Well,' said Polly, taken aback by Thea's reaction, 'I don't see why not. I've got to live somewhere and I'm very fond of Jessie and Percy.'

'Bless you. Oh, you've no idea how you've relieved my mind. I can come home to have the baby and decide if I need to go back out afterwards. Oh, it would be too wonderful for words. I think I need a drink. Stay there. I'll go and open a bottle of wine.'

Polly sat on, staring at the fire and feeling as if she'd unleashed a whirlwind. It seemed her new role was to be whisked from pillar to post with no time or thought for her own life. She had hardly expected Thea to leap at her idle proposition so readily and felt stirrings of panic. What on earth was she doing, offering to look after a large Newfoundland dog and a garrulous parrot in the depths of the country? She thought of being here alone and the panic threatened to become terror. Not that the Old Station House was as isolated as Lower Barton, being on the edge of a village, but nevertheless . . . Thea was back with bottle and glasses and accompanied by Jessie, who immediately collapsed into a deep slumber before the fire.

'You can't imagine what a weight you've lifted from my mind,' said Thea, kneeling beside Polly and pouring wine. 'Here you are. Now you're absolutely sure that you mean it? You have thought it through?'

Polly looked into Thea's radiant face and her heart sank. 'Oh, yes,' she lied bravely. 'It's the answer for me, too. I couldn't bear to go home and sit and wait for everything to collapse around me. Much better for me to be here being useful.'

'Bless you.' Thea stood the bottle on the floor. 'I'll go and phone George in a minute and tell him. He's been getting so cross with me because I should have been getting the house let and so on.' She let out an enormous sigh of relief and raised her glass. 'Here's to us. Let's hope that things work out right for both of us.'

Polly raised her glass and drank. Life was becoming much too complicated and she simply didn't trust her voice.

A few days later she returned home. She felt that by this time Paul would have come to some conclusion and might be kind enough to share it with her. She was in the kitchen before she realised that there were signs of habitation and before she could take it in, she heard the key in the door and Paul came in.

'So you're back at last,' he said. 'Had a good time? I was beginning to worry but Suzy said that you'd gone off to stay with a friend and the weather's been so awful that I wondered if you'd got snowed in.'

Polly stared at him in amazement and after a moment he raised his eyebrows at her silence and went to fill the kettle.

'What's wrong?' he said when she continued to stare at him. 'You look half-witted. Where have you been?'

'Where have *you* been? That's more to the point, surely,' she burst out at last. 'When did you come back?'

'As soon as the weather cleared. All flights out of Edinburgh were cancelled for a few days.'

'Edinburgh?'

'I told you in my note,' he said impatiently. 'Fiona was giving her paper there and then we heard that someone else was giving a paper

on the same thing. I know there's no point in going into details because you won't be interested but it was important that I was there to
give her moral support. As it happens it all went very well but when
I knew that we were going to be delayed I tried to phone and got no
reply.'

Dazed, Polly watched him make coffee. 'You said in your note that
you'd gone off with Fiona.'

'Well, so I did. I've just told you. D'you want some coffee?'

Polly shook her head. 'I thought you meant really gone. Left me.
For Fiona.'

Paul fiddled with the sugar spoon, his back turned to her. 'Why
should you think that?'

'Because it's true,' said Polly slowly. 'Oh, perhaps I read the note
wrong but instinctively I got it right. You have left me for Fiona,
haven't you? You may live here with me but you love her and you've
slept with her, haven't you?'

Paul kept his back turned and made a great business of pouring the
milk. Polly watched him. She was filled with a huge, overwhelming
sadness. There was simply nothing left of the young Polly or the Paul
who had been charmed by her. The tiny flame had flickered and gone
out and there was barely a trace of smoke to mark its passing. She
watched him deciding how to parry her question and felt quite suddenly impatient, almost angry. She wondered how he would react if
she described the events of the past few days and knew that she
couldn't be bothered to tell him. He simply wouldn't be interested.

'It doesn't matter,' she said. 'I know you have and it really doesn't
matter. I was a fool not to see it before. I've been living half a life and
I'm not going to do it any longer.'

He turned now to look at her and she regarded him dispassionately.

'What do you mean?' he asked. 'What are you going to do?'

'You left me ages ago,' she said. 'The note simply confirmed it, underlined it. Made me really think about it. I'm going to Thea's to
house-sit for a while. She and George are going to Brussels and I'm

going to look after Jessie and Percy. I'd like to keep some of my things and you'll have to continue to support me for a bit until I get my act together. But you'll probably think that it's worth it to get rid of me.'

A variety of emotions passed across Paul's face: relief, shame and something else which could have been annoyance.

Perhaps he wanted to be the one to pull the rug, thought Polly. He's annoyed that I've pipped him to the post and wrong-footed him.

'Don't you think you're being a bit drastic?' he asked.

'Am I?' Polly raised her eyebrows. 'What do you suggest? The mixture as before? Me sitting here like a lemon while you have it off with Fiona at the lab?'

Paul assumed an expression of distaste and Polly smiled. 'Sorry,' she said. 'Is that a bit too crude for the finer emotions that you share with her? Well, too bad. Or are you insisting that your relationship with her is purely a platonic one and all you share with her is a microscope?' She nodded at his silence. 'Quite. Well, that's it, isn't it? We'll have to decide whether we want to sell the house or whether you intend to move Fiona into it and buy me out.'

Paul stirred uneasily. 'I don't think that anything should be decided in a hurry,' he said. 'Since you've brought it up, I agree that our relationship has been a rather empty one for some time now. Obviously I shall continue to support you and if you've arranged to go to your friends I shall probably go on living here for the time being. You'd better take the car'—Polly bowed ironically—'and anything that you particularly value. Naturally I shall consult you before I take any definite steps.'

'Naturally.' Polly nodded. 'In that case, I shall go back to Thea's tomorrow, taking as much as I can, and if I want to come back to fetch anything I shall phone first. We'll sort the furniture out at some later date.'

'Very well.' Paul hesitated. 'I'm sorry,' he began and paused.

'Forget it. What about tonight?'

'I'll disappear,' he said quickly. 'Best thing all round I should think. I'll go and pack a bag.'

He went out and Polly turned and walked over to the sink. She poured the untouched coffee into the sink and then stared at her reflection in the window.

He didn't even notice my hair, she thought.

A spasm of pain caught at her heart and, with a sharp movement, she leaned forward and dragged the curtains together against the winter's night.

Thirty-two

THEA AND GEORGE WERE so delighted to have their problem dealt with that they welcomed Polly back with open arms, comforted her and made her feel loved and needed. This was just as well because a few days after her confrontation with Paul, she suffered a reaction against all the events of the past two weeks and had a minor breakdown. She felt deeply depressed and suffered bouts of uncontrolled weeping, and Thea and George enclosed her in a net of love and security until she was able to face her life and take the reins into her own hands once more. A few weeks more and they had gone and she was left alone with Percy and Jessie and the weekly visits of Maggie Tabb. Maggie, who had been told the bare facts of Polly's marriage by Thea, looked upon Polly as a fellow victim. Norman had finally left her for 'ol' surfboard chin' and she felt in Polly a kindred spirit. They got along in a companionable, easy-going way and Polly took over where Thea had left off in assisting Maggie in her ongoing battle to keep the maintenance payments coming and to take advantage of all the benefits available to her. Maggie could barely read and much time was taken up by working through forms and writing or telephoning to those in authority. Maggie repaid this by working late, making special dishes for Polly and sending her young brother over to help in the garden.

Freddie was already a regular visitor. When Thea had telephoned to tell him of Polly's separation from Paul he had felt suffused with a joy so all-encompassing that he had been unable to speak and, when he had seen her in the depths of despair, he had been terrified that she might regret her decision and return to Paul. This had not happened and now he was proceeding cautiously, warned by Thea not to rush things as Polly was in a delicate emotional state. Freddie needed no such warning. He had waited far too long to ruin things now by hasty action. Apart from which, his whole concern was for Polly's well-being and happiness and he was perfectly ready to set his own needs aside for the time being.

For the first time since she left university Polly found herself with a daily routine, thanks to the animals, as well as a social life. Harriet, Kate and Cass took her into their lives and she found herself happily occupied and content. Two other visitors were Tim and Miranda.

Tim sometimes felt that a blight was gradually destroying his marriage. He had come to accept that Miranda was of a jealous disposition and made sure that no action of his, no look or word, could give rise to suspicion or cause her distress. It was tiring for one of his naturally friendly, easy-going nature but he still loved Miranda and wanted to make her feel safe. He hoped that eventually she would learn to trust him and that things would improve. However, this in itself was not enough. Miranda, if anything, grew quieter, more touchy, obsessed with keeping Broadhayes spotless and feeding them on healthy, homegrown food. When he confronted her with her moodiness she became tearful and, for a while, remorseful. Short periods of self-recrimination and shows of physical passion exhausted them both so that Tim was almost relieved when things slowly returned to what he had come to accept as normal.

Much to Tim's sadness Mrs Gilchrist gave in her notice and would not be persuaded to stay. She was very emotional but adamant, saying that it had perhaps been too much to ask of either Miranda or herself to go on together. She had been so long with dear Mrs Barrable that she was set in her ways and she was getting older . . . Tim was quite capable of reading between the lines and knew that it would be cruel to press her to stay or ask for her real reasons. She went off to her sister, promising to stay in touch and with a handsome present and one or two keepsakes about which Miranda knew nothing. Tim hugged her goodbye, promised that he would ask Thea to go to see her when she came home and put the matter to the back of his mind. With Mrs Gilchrist gone Miranda became ever busier and Tim, looking at her drawn face with its inward expression, felt that he was married to a girl he didn't know at all.

One afternoon, finding himself near the Old Station House, he dropped in to see how Percy was faring and introduce himself to Polly. It turned out to be a tremendous success. Percy, carried away by the excitement, positively outdid himself in quotations and recitations, Jessie took to him at once and he found Polly's easy-going humour a wonderful relief after the rules and regulations at Broadhayes. She persuaded him to stop for supper and since Tim was not expected back until later he agreed. It was a magic evening. All four of them were on top form and it was with a real effort that Tim finally dragged himself away. He drove slowly home rehearsing the manner in which he intended to tell Miranda about the evening. He knew that if he were ever to be able to go to the Old School House again or to invite Polly to Broadhayes he must be very careful how he spoke of her or described her.

It took Miranda approximately three minutes to discover that she might have something to fear in Polly and she decided that it would be wise to see for herself so when Tim suggested that they should visit Polly together Miranda agreed and they went to lunch on a glorious Sunday in late spring.

Polly, getting it right for once, had invited Freddie and the day went very well. There was none of the magic of the evening that she and Tim had shared but Freddie and Tim got along splendidly and Miranda, assuming that Polly was seriously involved with Freddie, tolerated her scattiness. On the way home, however, she was careful to point out to Tim her faults and failings and to imply that Paul must have been the injured party and Tim was careful to agree with her. He majored on Freddie and how much he had enjoyed his company and Miranda was lulled far enough into a false sense of security to agree that it would be only proper to invite them back.

Polly was perfectly happy to go and Freddie was overjoyed. To appear publicly linked to Polly gave him enormous happiness and so ebullient was he that even Polly began to see that his friendship was hiding a great deal more. Suddenly her eyes, which had been blind for so long, saw quite clearly exactly how he felt about her. Her first feeling was alarm. She had grown used to Freddie being around and looked upon him as a brother with whom she could joke and relax and in whom she could confide. In a stroke, that was all done away with and her second feeling was a sort of revulsion. Polly was the kind of woman who couldn't bear men to have a hopeless passion for her. Even as a girl she had hated it. It made them ridiculous in her eyes, pathetic and unmanly, and it was why she had always preferred older men whom she could hero-worship and who treated her with an experienced, confident manner. It was this which had attracted her to Paul and it was his charming, lighthearted unavailability that drew her to Tim. Freddie had behaved so perfectly that she had half thought he was in love with Thea but now, unable to dissemble any longer and feeling that he had reason to hope, he dropped his guard.

He relaxed to such an extent that on the way back from Broadhayes Polly was brittle and nervous. She knew that she simply couldn't bear it if he were to attempt to kiss her and, in the end, took refuge in a headache—which her terror had brought on—and he seemed much more concerned that she should hurry in and go to bed than in pursuing his own desires. Polly escaped half mad with relief and guilt and spent the next hour wandering up and down the track with Jessie, the cool night air caressing her hot head, and wondering how she should deal with this new anxiety in her life. At last she went inside and pushed the kettle on to the hotplate. Jessie slumped down as usual and Polly looked at Percy, who drowsed sleepily on his perch.

'What shall I do, Percy?' she asked him. 'It was all so nice and comfortable and now it's been spoilt. I don't want him to be in love with me.'

Percy regarded her thoughtfully. 'Much ado there was, God wot,' he quoted in Great-uncle Edward's voice. 'He would love and she would not.'

'I don't want there to be much ado,' said Polly crossly as she made some coffee. 'I want it to be like it was before. And if that's the best you can do you might as well shut up.'

FREDDIE WENT HOME AND let the dogs out. He, too, walked in the cool night air in his adjoining paddock, his thoughts jumbled and confused. For more than two years he had been in love with Polly, worshipping from afar, and now it looked as though his hopes and dreams might be realised. Why then this surge of anxiety? He loved being with Polly, enjoyed her company more than that of any other woman he had ever known, but when the relationship looked set to move into a more serious and physical stage he had the most terrible attack of cold feet. The thought that she might be expecting him to kiss her had filled him with such terror that when she had said she had a headache he had been visited with the most exquisite relief.

He walked the boundary of his field, unaware of the owls hunting in the woods below him or of the eerie silver light shed by a cold white moon. Perhaps, he consoled himself, it was simply because it had been so long since he had been involved with a woman that he felt so nervous and even then it hadn't been a marked success. He didn't have much sexual drive and an anxiety that he might not perform adequately always hindered him further. But surely with Polly it would all be different?

Freddie sighed deeply, called to the dogs and turned back towards the house. He simply didn't know how to go forward. Cravenly he wondered if he might let the next move come from Polly and shook his head in amazement and despair.

'I'm mad,' he said. 'Quite mad.'

The dogs came up to him, tails wagging, and he stroked their great heads and felt comforted. Perhaps it was a perfectly ordinary attack of nerves and in the morning he would feel differently. He watched the bats for a moment, darting and wheeling over his head, then went inside to make some coffee.

WHEN FREDDIE TELEPHONED A few days later to say that Jon Thompson was coming down to stay for a holiday and that he'd be a bit tied up for a week or so, Polly felt first relieved and then, illogically, hurt. She had worked herself up to feeling capable of telling him kindly but firmly that there was no question of a romantic entanglement and, after all, there seemed no need. She felt rather foolish and let down and went about slamming drawers and cupboard doors and muttering to herself. Jessie withdrew to the garden and Percy, who was enjoying a grape, kept a beady eye cocked in her direction.

'A trick that everyone abhors in little girls is slamming doors,' he observed suddenly.

Polly stared at him in surprise and then burst out laughing and they were in the middle of reciting Belloc's 'Rebecca who slammed doors for fun and perished miserably' when she became aware of someone standing at the open door from the utility room watching them. She gave a cry of alarm and the man raised his hands in apology and explanation.

'I'm terribly sorry,' he said. 'It was too good to interrupt. I'm Marcus Willby. Thea told me that you were staying here and I thought I'd drop in and meet you. It was a very happy day for me when you telephoned and told me about Thea and her parrot.' He held his hand out. 'You are Polly, I imagine. Or have I made a blunder?'

'No, no.' Polly took his hand. 'How nice to meet you. It's all been wonderfully exciting, hasn't it?'

'It certainly has. I've met Percy, of course. How d'you do?' he asked the parrot.

Percy stared at him but remained silent and Polly laughed. 'He's going to go all grand and silent on us now,' she said. 'How nice of you to drop in. I hope that you're going to stay to lunch? I was just feeling terribly unwanted.'

'Heavens!' Marcus's eyebrows shot up. 'The local male population must be dreadfully lacking. I should love to.'

'I have to warn you that I'm the world's worst cook,' said Polly, liking the look of Marcus with his long legs and elegant carriage. He was well into his forties and she felt immediately at ease with his quiet confidence and easy charm.

'Well, I could always take you to the Elephant's Nest, if you prefer?' he offered. 'Thea took me there once. It's very pleasant.'

'No, no. Thank you,' she said hastily. That was one of Freddie's haunts and she didn't want to risk bumping into him today. 'I've got some nice elderly quiche and an ageing lettuce. You must be content with that. Would you like a drink?'

'At least let me deal with that side of things. I'm on my way to Cornwall to visit my mother and I have to take my own drink as self-preservation. I've got a nice hock that will liven up the quiche a bit.'

He went out and Polly watched him go. She turned and made a face at Percy. 'Well, well,' she murmured. 'Lucky old Thea. What d'you think of him then?'

But Percy had returned to his grape and wouldn't answer.

When Marcus had gone, Polly felt in a quite different frame of mind. She felt lighthearted and confident and began to wonder if perhaps she had upset Freddie and acted too hastily in deciding to reject him. She decided to suggest that he bring Jon over to supper. It would be nice to see Jon again in less harrowing circumstances and there would be no risk of Freddie becoming too affectionate with a third person present. She was still surprised that Freddie was prepared to let so much time elapse before seeing her again. He had been such a very regular visitor and she was quite certain that she had not imagined his feelings for her. Perhaps he had seen through her 'headache' after all and been hurt and she decided to see how he reacted at their next meeting.

In fact, he was much as he had always been. Jon's presence allowed them to be perfectly natural together with no chances of intimacy, and the evening was a very happy one. They were able to laugh about

Polly's dreadful experiences at Lower Barton and Jon entertained them with stories of life in the Foreign Office. He and Freddie arranged to take her to the Elephant's Nest as a return run and they parted with hugs and great relief on the part of Freddie and Polly, both of whom were now convinced that they had been overreacting and that, given time, things might well work out after all.

The summer passed quickly. George and Thea came home for occasional weekends and Miranda and Tim drove over regularly for supper or a Sunday lunch. Freddie always made up the foursome and still any really intimate behaviour between him and Polly was held at bay. Because both were afraid of it they had drifted into a close affectionate relationship in which sex seemed to be entirely left out. Pondering on this, Polly found it very strange. She liked Freddie enormously but physically she wasn't interested and on the few occasions—generally when she had had too much to drink—that she decided to let the barriers down a little, she felt that his response was almost automatic: rather as if he thought she expected it rather than because he desired it. Once, when he made a voluntary approach, all her feelings of revulsion rose to the surface and she turned it away as best she could without hurting his feelings.

They were happiest in the company of others and Tim and Miranda were delighted to oblige. Polly was the only young woman of their acquaintance with whom Miranda felt that Tim could be trusted and she was always happy to go to the Old Station House and to have Polly and Freddie back to Broadhayes. Between Tim and Polly a secret, tacitly understood flirtation arose consisting of private little caresses and long looks. It was quite harmless but they enjoyed it and it lent spice to the rare moments they had alone. They exchanged no words but let each other know by glances and touching that, were things different, it would all go a great deal further. So discreet were they that not even Miranda suspected anything and Freddie saw nothing at all. Sometimes Tim dropped in on Polly and then, after a happy hour or two of relaxing nonsense and a few glasses of wine, they treated themselves to a lingering embrace, a long exciting kiss, before

Tim left. They both felt pleasurably heated and uplifted by their shared attraction and comforted as well. It allowed them to feel that, given the right circumstances, they could be happy and fulfilled and it helped them to come to terms with the failures they were experiencing in their other relationships. Neither looked further than their stolen kisses or admitted that there might be danger in their affection for each other.

In August Thea came home with Amelia to prepare for the birth of her baby. She was delighted to be back in her beloved home with Jessie and Percy and she and Polly settled into a quiet, happy period together. They pursued a gentle peaceful routine of unhurried days, tended by Maggie, who brooded over Thea like a mother and looked after all of them with an unusual tenderness. In the hot, heavy afternoons they sat beneath the shade of the old beech trees, whilst Amelia played with Jessie at their feet, and talked softly or gazed languidly into the green foliage moving and rustling above them. Sunlight dropped in gold coins on to the rug where Amelia lay, curled now in sleep, and on to Jessie's broad back. Sometimes Harriet came over with Hugh and the baby, James, and it began to feel that they would be locked for ever into this timeless enclosed world. Even Freddie did not attempt to intrude upon them, finding the atmosphere strangely distressing, the concentrated essence of woman and motherhood, almost claustrophobic.

At the beginning of September, calmly and easily, Thea produced her second daughter, Julia. George flew home for a few days and for a while there was upheaval, his voice seeming loud, his footsteps heavy, in this household of women and children, and, when he left, the four of them settled back quite gratefully again into their ordered existence. So the summer died away into autumn and Christmas approached when George would return and, after the festivities, take Thea and his daughters back to Brussels.

Thirty-three

IN THE SPRING, WHEN Polly had been at the Old Station House for just over a year, several things happened that made her think long and hard about her life. Thus far, she felt that all decisions concerning her future could be postponed until George and Thea returned, which was still a year away, and she had settled very happily into this strange way of living with a parrot and a dog, having a boyfriend whom she did not desire and conducting a flirtation with another woman's husband. Marcus Willby dropped by from time to time and once, after a very long boozy lunch, she told him the whole story of her life. He had laughed and laughed and called it the History of Mrs Polly and she had been very hurt and then had laughed with him. She enjoyed his visits, which had none of the brotherly flavour of her relationship with Freddie or the 'living on the edge' sensation she experienced with Tim. Marcus was so complete, so together, so relaxed. She had discovered that he was divorced, had a son at university, and that he lived in Richmond, but generally they talked about her and about Percy's growing reputation. Thea's books were doing very well indeed and 'Percy the Parrot' soft toys, T-shirts, china and other things were under discussion.

It was Marcus that Polly thought of first on the sunny May morning when she opened the letter that came from Paul asking her for a divorce. He told her that he wished to marry Fiona and suggested that they should meet to discuss the situation: perhaps she would like to come to Exeter for the day? Her heart jumped and bumped in alarm as she stared at the letter. She folded it, pushed it back into its envelope, took it out again and reread it. Divorce! Well, it was hardly a surprise. She had never thought that Paul would want her back and even if he did she wouldn't want to go. Nevertheless, it made her face the future, wonder what would happen to her when Thea and George came back and needed her no longer. She went out on to the platform and sat on the seat where Thea had sat six years before wondering if George would go back to Felicity. Jessie wandered out behind her and pottered off down the track. Polly felt a great sense of loss. It occurred to her at that moment how desperately she would miss the Old Station House, her chats with Percy, the comforting presence of Jessie's considerable bulk and Maggie's friendship. She was overwhelmed by a stab of jealousy. How lucky Thea was to have all this as well as George and two beautiful daughters! Why should some people have good fortune thrust into their hands and others continually miss the boat? Striving to be just, she remembered how Thea had fought Felicity, holding on to all that she held dear, and remembered how easily she, Polly, had surrendered Paul to Fiona. She, too, had had a home and a husband and could have had children if she had so wished. She tried to tell herself that it wasn't the same but suspected that she envied all these things simply because they belonged to someone else and if suddenly, magically, they became hers, they would lose their charm.

So what did she want? She thought about Freddie, wishing that she could find him as physically attractive as she found Tim, and sighed heavily. First things first. She must see Paul and talk about divorce. Her stomach churned nervously as she imagined the scene. Where would it take place? Would Fiona be there? At the mere thought of it Polly rose to her feet and began to pace the platform. She wished it were a Maggie morning. Maggie would display solidarity and lend support but Maggie could not show her a future. Where would she go and what would she do? She attempted to stop this flight into panic by reminding herself that it was another year before George and Thea would be home for good. The important thing was to take advice regarding this proposed meeting but whom should she ask? Freddie would be at the clinic or out on call at this time of the morning but it might be possible to talk to Tim. He had given her the number of his business line as well as his private number and she decided that she would try to have a word with him without involving Miranda. He answered at once, sounding so preoccupied and businesslike that Polly floundered a little. As soon as he realised who it was his voice changed and became much more intimate. Somewhat incoherently she explained her dilemma.

'Don't go to the house,' said Tim at once. 'You must meet him on neutral ground, just the two of you. And don't let him talk you into things. Look, we can't discuss this over the telephone. I've got to come down to Plymouth tomorrow afternoon. I'll come in on the way back.' He hesitated for a moment. 'I shan't say anything to Miranda,' he said. 'See you tomorrow. Fiveish.'

He hung up and Polly was left wondering whether he meant that he wouldn't tell her about Paul's letter or the fact that he intended to visit the Old Station House, although she knew perfectly well in her heart that by ringing him on his business line she had tacitly indicated that this was between her and Tim. She felt strangely nervous and found herself unable to relax, wandering to and fro, up and down, until she could bear her own company no longer and telephoned Freddie, who had just got in. She told him about the letter without mentioning Tim and he agreed at once that she should have some plan before she met Paul. He asked if she would like him to come over but she felt so jumpy that she decided a walk would do her good and she arranged to be with him in an hour or so.

Freddie replaced the receiver and stood in a brown study. He felt as if something momentous had occurred and that he now stood at the edge of a precipice. But why a precipice? He loved Polly, he was sure of it. So why these feelings of terror? Perhaps they would both be happier if they were committed to each other instead of continuing with this rather odd relationship they'd drifted into during the last year. He swallowed once or twice and took several deep breaths. He must offer her the support she would need now to face divorce proceedings and her own future. Freddie hurried into the kitchen, went to the cupboard and poured himself a large Scotch. He gulped it down and poured another, watched with interest by Charlie Custard.

'It's all right for you, old man,' muttered Freddie. 'God, wish I was a dog!'

WHEN TIM ARRIVED THE following afternoon, Polly was still reeling from her session with Freddie who, fortified with several large Scotches, had proposed to her in ringing, positive tones and implied that if she didn't accept he would know that she'd been leading him on and playing with his affections. After several drinks she had found herself agreeing with him and only when he put his arms around her and, puffing great breaths of whisky in her face, attempted to kiss her did her old fears return. They were both rather relieved when Charlie Custard, assuming that Polly was attacking Freddie, started to bark so excitedly that they were obliged to draw apart. Polly, fearing further approaches might be forthcoming and seeing that Freddie was in no fit state to give her any sensible advice, said that she must get back and promised to telephone in the morning. When the morning came she lost her nerve and was pacing restlessly up and down the platform when Tim arrived.

He came towards her looking vital and alive, gave her a hug and then caught her close and kissed her. Ever since she had telephoned an idea had been growing in his mind. A different man might long since have followed up Polly's readiness to flirt with him and the unspoken acceptance of mutual attraction with a suggestion that they become lovers. It would have been easy enough with Polly alone at the Old Station House. Tim, however, was no philanderer. Nevertheless, he was so infatuated by all the qualities about her that were so un-Miranda-like that he felt suddenly inclined to throw caution to the winds.

'Oh, Polly,' he said. 'I've been thinking and thinking. If there were some way round it without hurting Miranda too much, d'you think you might marry me? She's been so strange lately that I'm beginning to wonder if she wishes that we'd never met. I know she isn't happy and nothing I do can seem to put it right. I'd have to talk to her, of course. I've thought of nothing else since you telephoned. You don't have to answer now. You'll have lots on your mind for the moment. I just wanted you to know how I feel.' He kissed her again whilst she stood limp and unresisting in his arms. 'Poor Polly. You're exhausted. Let's talk about this meeting with Paul and how you must approach it. You haven't got a drink somewhere, have you?'

Stunned by Tim's declaration, mesmerised by his concise explanations and instructions on how she must approach Paul and having drunk almost a whole bottle of wine, she agreed to everything and it was only when she crawled into bed that she realised she had now agreed to marry both Tim and Freddie as soon as she had obtained a divorce from Paul.

The next morning, after a night spent in sleepless anxiety, she did what she had meant to do in the first place. She telephoned Marcus Willby.

'What shall I do?' she wailed, having poured out the whole sorry tale. 'I've got to meet Paul and talk about divorce without letting him bully me and now I've agreed to marry Tim and Freddie.'

His roars of laughter, even at such a distance, comforted her. 'You're lucky that it's a Friday,' he told her. 'I'll drive down this evening. I'll book a room at the Bedford and be with you in the morning. And don't speak to anyone else until I get there.'

Polly replaced the receiver feeling comforted. She wasn't quite certain what Marcus would do but she felt much better and decided to spend as much of the day as possible out of the house.

'I shall go and see Kate,' she told Percy. 'I like Kate.'

'Plain Kate and bonny Kate and sometimes Kate the curst,' quoted Percy glumly and gave a loud squawk.

'It's no good, Percy. I daren't stay in. Tim or Freddie might telephone and I don't want to speak to either of them at the moment. I promise I won't be too long and Maggie'll be here in a minute.'

She telephoned Kate, who told her to come straight over, and, fearing that talking even to Maggie might confuse her further and that it was wise to take Marcus's advice, she collected her things and hurried out to the car.

WHEN JON TELEPHONED EARLY on Friday morning and asked if he could come for the weekend, Freddie felt an overwhelming sense of relief. He could barely remember what he had said to Polly, having decided to finish the bottle of Scotch after her departure. He woke the next morning feeling terribly ill and with the strong presentiment that he was a doomed man and wondered what the next step would be. He spent the day with a hangover and in the evening took the dogs for a long walk while he tried to sort out the appalling jumble in his head.

The thought that Jon was coming enabled him to struggle through the day and when he saw the now familiar car pulling in through the gate he hurried out accompanied by Charlie Custard.

'I can't tell you how glad I am to see you,' he said, relieving Jon of his overnight bag. 'Come on in. Kettle's on. Or would you prefer a drink?'

'I'd kill for some coffee,' said Jon, pausing to give Charlie Custard a hug. 'You sound a touch fraught. What's been going on?'

'Oh well.' Freddie put Jon's bag down on a chair and shrugged, feeling slightly embarrassed. 'It's been one of those weeks. You know.'

Jon looked round the cluttered friendly kitchen and smiled a little. 'I do indeed. I can't tell you how nice it is to be back. It's very good of you to let me escape to you like this. Makes London possible.'

'You're always welcome,' began Freddie, making coffee, and then paused.

It struck him that if he married Polly and brought her here, his weekends with Jon—lazing about, endless chats, going for long walks, evenings at the pub—would be a thing of the past and he suddenly knew that he would miss them dreadfully.

'What's the trouble?' Jon was sitting at the table with Charlie Custard leaning heavily against his leg.

Freddie continued to make the coffee, his movements slow and heavy. 'I've been an idiot,' he said at last. 'I've proposed marriage to Polly and I've just realised that it's a ghastly mistake.'

'Has she accepted you?' Jon's voice was calm and he continued to stroke the great dog beside him.

'I think so.' Freddie gave a short mirthless laugh. 'I had to get my-self tanked up to do it and I can't remember much about it. I shouted a bit so as not to lose my nerve.'

He put a mug of coffee beside Jon and shook his head in despair.

'Poor Freddie.' Jon reached for his mug. 'You are in a muddle, aren't you?'

'I thought I loved her,' explained Freddie, sitting opposite with his own mug, 'but when it comes to anything physical it doesn't seem to work. I'm just not very good with women. And don't tell me it's be-cause I haven't met the right one.'

'I wouldn't dream of telling you anything of the sort. It's much simpler than that.'

'Is it?'

Freddie looked up and across at Jon and suddenly it all became very simple indeed. He flushed a dark red but kept his eyes on Jon, who continued to smile at him. The world shifted a little and clicked into place. They sat quite still looking at one another and Freddie felt a great tide of peace and happiness slowly engulfing him.

'How did you know?' he asked at last.

Jon shrugged. 'I don't know. I just did. Does it matter?'

'No. Oh, no. Only I might have . . . How awful if I'd married Polly!'

'Disastrous, I should think,' said Jon cheerfully. 'Not that I'd have let you, of course. I was hoping that you might come to it yourself but I was beginning to despair. I decided I'd have to tell you how I felt and risk getting thrown out.'

Freddie looked shy, pleased and rather overwhelmed. 'When did you know?' he asked bravely.

'When you got out of your Fourtrak and introduced yourself,' said

Jon. 'I remember thinking how wonderful it would be if we got snowed up together.'

'Well,' said Freddie, blushing furiously again, 'you had a start on me there. I've got some catching up to do.' Joy and excitement were crashing over him like golden waves.

'No hurry,' said Jon, drinking his coffee. 'It takes a while to adjust. And we've got the rest of our lives.'

The thought of that made Freddie feel so happy that he feared he might weep. He swallowed, nodded, picked up his mug and put it down again.

'I don't know what to do or say,' he admitted. 'It's such a shock and such an enormous relief. And frightening.'

'I know.' Jon pushed Charlie Custard off and stood up. 'I think a drink might not be a bad idea after all. In the cupboard? OK if I get them?'

As he passed behind his chair he touched Freddie's head lightly.

Freddie nodded, not trusting himself to speak as all the sensations that had been missing in past relations began to make themselves deliciously manifest. Jon poured two stiff drinks and passed a glass to Freddie.

'To us,' he said.

WHEN MIRANDA TOLD TIM that David was coming for the weekend he gave a great sigh of relief. As he'd driven home from the Old Station House his euphoria had gradually waned and at the sight of Miranda his resolve had weakened. He seemed to have been visited with a fit of madness and suddenly saw clearly all the difficulties which would result if he should take the step he had outlined to Polly. Miranda was quiet and edgy and he wondered if she had guessed that something was afoot. Her behaviour was quite different from the way she usually was if she suspected him of philandering. There was something vulnerable about her that made him see just how difficult it would be to hurt her.

She said that she was going out on Friday afternoon and Tim hung about watching for David. He was actually on the telephone when David arrived and when he finally came out of his office it was to find David putting down his bag in the hall. At the sight of the comforting figure of his father-in-law, he ran across and flung his arms round him.

'Gracious!' beamed David. 'Now that's what I call a welcome. Will you think me a cynic if I ask whatever can be the matter?'

'It's lovely to see you,' laughed Tim. 'It really is. But I'm in a frightful muddle, to tell you the truth.'

'Guessed as much,' said David cheerfully. 'Is my dear daughter to blame? Where is she?'

'She's had to go out. Don't know where. Said she wouldn't be long. Come into the library and have a drink.'

'Sounds a splendid idea.' David followed readily. 'So what have you been up to? A woman, is it?'

'How did you guess?' said Tim, busy with the decanters.

'Always is, my dear fellow,' said David gloomily. 'That or money. If Miranda's like her mother it's probably the former.'

'How d'you mean?' Tim gave David a glass and they sat down.

'Both very jealous people, d'you see? Insecure. They see even the most innocent approach to the opposite sex as something to be feared.' David sighed and shook his head. 'It's very sad. I tried to understand it but sometimes the fact that I was being treated like some hardened libertine made me want to behave badly. Being constantly watched and questioned is very tiring and the company of an easy-going woman sometimes went to my head, I'm afraid.' He looked at Tim and raised his eyebrows. 'Ring a bell?'

'Oh, David. Yes. What a comfort you are. The trouble is, I've let it get out of hand.'

'Aaah,' said David thoughtfully and drank deeply.

'No, no,' said Tim quickly. 'It's not what you're thinking. I haven't slept with her. Nothing like that.'

'Then what's the problem?' David looked puzzled.

'I've proposed marriage to her,' said Tim wretchedly.

'My dear boy!' David nearly spilled his drink.

'I know. I know. It's just we've had this sort of flirtation going. She's great fun, quite scatty, and it was a sort of relief. Like you said just now. And she had this problem, divorcing her husband and so on, and I got carried away and asked her to marry me. Miranda's been so odd these last few weeks. To tell the truth, I wonder whether she's regretting marrying me. I'm not sure I make her happy. Oh, hell!'

'The thing is . . .' began David and paused to listen as a door slammed.

Miranda's voice could be heard calling them and the next second the door was flung open and she stood confronting them. Both men rose to their feet as though hauled up by strings and stared at her. Her face was flushed, her usually neat hair was rumpled and she looked young and happy.

'Oh, Daddy! How lovely to see you,' she cried. 'Oh, I'm glad you're here. Oh, Tim! It's so wonderful. You'll never guess.' She shook her head, her hair flying about her face, and stretched out her arms to them. 'You'll never believe it. Oh, Tim, I'm pregnant. It's been confirmed. Isn't it amazing? Oh, I'm so happy.'

And she collapsed on to the nearest chair and burst into tears.

Thirty-four

WHEN MARCUS ARRIVED AT the Old Station House, instead of knocking at the front door or going round to the side door to the kitchen, he walked directly out on to the platform. Polly was standing in the sunshine staring up at the swallows. Her hair had grown again and was tied back casually and she wore jeans and a baggy jersey. When Jessie hauled herself up and went wagging up to Marcus she glanced round and then smiled.

'I've become so aware of the passing of the seasons since I lived here,' she said. 'I noticed it a bit in the town, of course, but nothing like I do now.'

They sat by unspoken mutual consent on one of the seats and Marcus looked about him as he lit a cigarette.

'It's lovely here,' he agreed. 'But I couldn't cope with it on a full-time basis. I need the bustle and movement of the city. Going to concerts and the theatre and the cinema. I get withdrawal symptoms if I stay away too long.'

'I can understand that.' Polly leaned forward to stroke Jessie, who came to sit between her knees. 'I dash up to Exeter when I can and walk about the streets enjoying the noise and watching the people. Then I feel that I'm a member of the human race again. I like to sit in a wine bar and watch life go by and go into shops and smell the heavenly smell of new clothes hanging on their hangers.'

'So you won't really mind leaving this when Thea comes back?'

'I shall miss it. Percy and Jessie and Maggie and the house. But they're not mine, you see. I want something of my own.'

'Yes. Well, I think I can help you there.' Marcus leaned forward, resting his forearms along his thighs. 'As you know, Percy the Parrot is becoming quite big business and I've managed to get a television producer interested in a children's series. Seriously interested. The format's being discussed. We might do stories using the drawings with a narrator—as in *Jackanory*—or perhaps puppets, but still with a narrator like it was in *The Magic Roundabout*. Whichever, I want that voice to be yours. Ever since I heard you reciting "Rebecca" with Percy I've had the idea. However Percy is presented—and I think he's going to have quite a television career—I want you to be the person doing it. We've even discussed a birthdays and requests slot during children's television and on Saturday mornings. That would have to be a puppet, of course, like Basil Brush or Roland Rat. So we've got lots to think about. I shall act as your agent, of course, and we're in a very strong position with the television rights. Quite strong enough to make my own suggestions. What do you think?'

Birdsong mingled with the sound of a strimmer droning like an ir- ritable outsize bee and a dog could be heard, barking with the falsetto shriek of the farm collie.

'You mean not marry Tim or Freddie?' asked Polly at last.

Marcus threw back his head and roared with laughter. 'My dear girl, certainly not! Marry Tim or Freddie! Tim's married already and is probably even now wondering how on earth he's going to wriggle out of his proposal and as for Freddie . . .' Marcus shook his head and inhaled on his cigarette. 'If he needs to get himself drunk to sug- gest marriage having known you for how long?—three years?—take it from me, he's got problems. Forget them. You don't need them. Think about this new career that I'm offering you. Come on. No pre- varicating. What d'you think?'

'It sounds so unbelievable that I can't take it in.' Polly shook her head. 'Why me? There must be millions of experienced people that could do it better than I could.'

'I don't think so.' Marcus threw the butt of his cigarette away. 'I've got a very strong hunch about you, Polly.'

Polly stared at him and he smiled at her reassuringly. 'I'm not kidding you. And you're not a raw beginner. You got a degree in Drama and English and you told me about all your experiences with amateur dramatics before you were married. Trust me. After all, what have you got to lose? Tim and Freddie?'

He burst out laughing again and this time Polly laughed with him.

'But I don't know anything about . . . well, anything,' she protested at last. 'I'd be terrified.'

'Not with me behind you,' said Marcus comfortably. 'Trust me.'

'But where would I live? I'd have to come to London, I suppose?'

Marcus shrugged. 'You wouldn't have to but it would be sensible. Convenient. And I've got an idea about that, too. I've got a little flat at the top of my house'—Polly's heart began to thump nervously—'which has been used by a student friend of my son. He's leaving at the end of this summer and you could move in there.' He caught sight of her face and chuckled. 'Fear not. This is not a devious attempt on your honour'—Polly blushed furiously—'or some con trick to get you into my clutches. You can live there cheaply till your career takes off. Don't worry. I'll block up the internal door. You can use the other entrance which opens on to the fire escape.'

'I wasn't . . . I didn't mean . . .' Polly floundered to a halt.

'Forget it. This is a business deal. I'm going to make lots of money out of you. It's going to take time to get it all set up, of course, which is just as well since you've got to be here for a while. But I want you to do some recordings for me and then I'll need you to come up to town and meet a few people. Well?' He looked at her. 'What d'you say? I want a definite answer. No dithering.'

'It sounds wonderful. Terrifying but wonderful. I can't really take it in, but yes. Yes please. I'd love to have a try.'

'That's my girl.'

Marcus gave her a brief hug but Polly still had another worry. 'What about Paul?' she asked anxiously. 'I've got to meet him. Tim says . . .'

'Oh, balls!' said Marcus impatiently. 'Of course you don't have to meet him. What rubbish! He had the affair, he was unfaithful. He admitted it. And he's been living with his mistress in your home. Isn't that what you said?'

'Apparently.' Polly nodded. 'Suzy tells me that Fiona moved in as soon as I came here.'

'Well then. You deal with it through a solicitor. You can use my chap if you haven't got one. He'll write to Paul telling him that you're divorcing him for adultery and we'll go from there. There's nothing to worry about.'

'I haven't got to see him?'

'Certainly not. Unless you want to. No point.'

Polly looked at him in awe. 'D'you always organise people's lives like this?'

'Not always.' Marcus gave her a tiny wink. 'Only if I think that they're going to make me lots of money. Now. I think we should celebrate and having tasted your cooking I think we'll go out to do it.'

'But I'll have to tell Tim and Freddie, won't I?' Polly looked worried again. 'They ought to know that I'm not going to marry them.'

Marcus got to his feet, pulling her up with him, and looked at her for a moment. 'I usually shake hands with new clients,' he said, 'but in your case I'm going to make an exception.' And he bent his head and kissed her. 'Now go and telephone Freddie and tell him that you've had an offer you can't resist and that you must refuse his generous proposal. Start with him and see how it goes.'

He watched her go into the house and sat down again on the seat, stretching out his long legs and wondering whether he should have kissed her. He was delighted that she'd accepted his offer. He knew he was taking a tremendous chance in promoting someone with no experience but he felt absolutely confident that Polly had an enormous potential in the areas he'd outlined to her. She simply needed to be motivated and pushed in the right direction. When he had discussed it with Thea on the telephone she had been in complete agreement with him and he felt excited at the prospect before him. Smiling to himself, he lit another cigarette and fondled Jessie's ears. A few minutes later Polly reappeared. She looked radiant with relief and Marcus felt his heart move a little in his breast.

'He didn't mind a bit,' she cried. 'He was wonderful about it.' She sank down beside him on the seat. 'Oh, thank goodness. Now it's just Tim.'

'Shall you do him next?'

'It's a bit difficult.' Polly frowned out over the garden. 'Saturday morning, you see. He won't be in his office and if I get Miranda she'll wonder why I want to speak to Tim. She's a very jealous person and I don't want to upset her.'

'Not now, anyway,' murmured Marcus.

'What d'you mean?'

'You'd have probably upset her quite a bit if you'd married Tim.'

'I know. I don't think I ever really meant to.' Polly looked guilty.

'Let's put Tim on hold,' suggested Marcus. 'Put him out of your mind. We'll go and have some lunch and celebrate our new partnership. Yes?'

'Yes.' Polly nodded and smiled at him. 'If you're sure you want to go out?'

'Oh, yes,' said Marcus firmly. 'I don't want to remember this day as the day I got food poisoning. I'll come and say hello to Percy while you get your things.'

ON MONDAY MORNING, DAVID drove slowly across the moor remembering vistas and scenes that he had seen with Felicity and had never wanted to look at since. It was a still day, the thin grey uniform cloud suffused with a golden glow that promised sunshine. The hills unfolded gently before him, horizon upon horizon, and his heart was filled with melancholy. Four years ago, Felicity had been beside him and because of that she had died a terrible, lonely death, and he would never be able to forgive himself. Would they have found happiness together? It was a question he had never been able to answer. He knew that he hadn't loved her in the way that she had loved him and he simply didn't know whether her love would have been enough. At the moment when he'd listened to the Sibelius and imagined her walking on the moor, he had been prepared to take the chance, to have a try at it even though he feared that the magic wouldn't last. It had been too late. David groaned with the shame and pain which even now assailed him and, following his map, headed for Mary Tavy. He had taken it upon himself to seek out Polly and talk to her. Tim had telephoned her that morning and, with one ear cocked for Miranda's footsteps, had talked briefly about Miranda's pregnancy and his resolution to stay with her. He told David afterwards that Polly was perfectly happy about it, even relieved. David, however, had visions of Polly lying on the floor, overcome with sleeping tablets, and decided to see for himself.

The Old Station House was easy enough to find and David left the car in the lane and opened the five-bar gate. He approached an open door and stood for some moments, just outside on the tarmac, listening to a strange conversation.

'. . . 'n' us ain't got time to lissen to 'ee all mornin' . . .'

'Gather ye rosebuds while ye may,' advised a well-educated plummy voice, 'old Time is still a-flying.'

'Yew cudden 'ev said a trewer word, my 'ansome. 'N' us 'even't done the 'ooverin' yet.'

'The glorious lamp of heaven, the sun . . .' Obviously the owner of the plummy voice knew his Herrick.

'Jes' shut up, 'n' get back in yewer cage. Shudden never've let 'ee out. Polly'll kill us.'

'Our Polly is a sad slut,' grieved the plummy voice, abruptly abandoning Herrick for John Gay, 'nor heeds what we have taught her. I wonder any man alive will ever rear a daughter.'

'Yew misrubble ol' bag of fevvers. Get off thet theyer chair 'n' get in 'ere.'

There was a loud squawk and, consumed with curiosity, David knocked loudly and went through a small utility room into the kitchen beyond. There was a flash of feathers and a louder squawk and a large African Grey parrot scrambled through the open door of his cage and turning round on his perch glared beadily at David.

A large red-haired young woman slammed shut the door and wiped her brow with a muscular arm. 'Thet were roight good timin', mister,' she said, smiling at him. ' 'E weren't never goin' back. Lass time us lets 'im out. Ol' bugger.'

'He's a beautiful chap, isn't he?' David smiled at her. 'And very well educated.'

The young woman pushed up her sleeves and shook her head. 'Thet were the missis's ol' aunt 'n' uncle. Gabblin' away all day they must've bin. Doan' unnerstan' 'alf 'e ses. But 'e's a reel laff. So wot c'n us dew fer 'ee?'

'I wanted to see Polly. I'm staying with Thea's cousin Tim Barrable. He's married to my daughter, d'you see?'

' 'Er's out. 'Er's gone over ter see Kate.'

'Plain Kate and bonny Kate and sometimes Kate the crust,' said the parrot sulkily.

The red-haired woman let out a loud squawk which rivalled the parrot's best efforts and David winced involuntarily.

' 'E's bin like thet all mornin',' she said. 'Jew want Kate's address? Yew cud ketch 'er up. 'Er wus poppin' in 'n' then goin' in ter Tavistock. Yew cud tek 'er out ter lunch. Got good noos, 'er 'as. Reel 'appy.'

An enormous black dog appeared at the other door into the kitchen and the parrot, to David's alarm, began to bark. The dog pricked its ears, wagged its tail languidly and yawned. The parrot growled fiercely.

'Yes,' said David hastily. 'That sounds like an excellent idea. If you think Kate won't mind and you think I'll be there in time to catch Polly.'

' 'Er's not long gone.' The young woman was scrabbling about by the telephone. ' 'Ang on. 'Ere 'tis. 'Er wus phonin' on'y a minit since.' She looked a little self-conscious. 'Jew wanna read it, mister?'

With one eye on the huge dog, who was now sitting leaning

against the door jamb with its tongue lolling out, David hastened over to read the name and address in the book that was held out to him. Kate Webster. He wrote the details into a little notebook and smiled at her. 'It's been delightful to meet you all,' he said courteously. 'Thank you.'

And with a last look at the parrot and the dog, he went back to his car.

POLLY, DRIVING AWAY FROM Kate's, decided to see if Harriet was in. There had been no reply earlier but she might be there now and Polly simply couldn't keep her good news to herself. She thought about Freddie. He had sounded so relieved that she was, to be absolutely truthful, a tiny bit hurt. Never mind. She took the bend a little wide and narrowly missed a car coming in the opposite direction. The driver, a man in his fifties, looked as though he were unsure of where he was going. Polly drove on. Tim hadn't sounded relieved. The conversation had been so hurried, so muted, that it was difficult to know exactly what he was feeling. Perhaps motherhood would mellow Miranda and they would be happy. Polly hoped so but her own happiness and excitement were so great that she couldn't dwell on Tim for long. She had her own life to look forward to. What an incredible parrot Percy was! And Marcus . . . A huge grin began to creep across Polly's face.

I hope, she thought as she turned on to the open moor and headed for Lower Barton, that he doesn't block up that interior door!

Thirty-five

KATE FLUNG THE LAST of the clothes into the washing machine, slammed the door, twiddled the knobs and dashed to answer the front doorbell.

'Yes?' she asked breathlessly.

David stood looking at her rather anxiously. 'I'm hoping that you're Kate Webster,' he said, somewhat diffidently. 'And that Polly is still with you?'

'Sorry. You've missed her. Can I help?'

'It was a vain hope.' David shook his head. 'Thea Lampeter is my son-in-law's cousin.' He grimaced. 'Bit convoluted, isn't it? I missed Polly at the Old Station House and a rather incredible young woman with improbably red hair, a parrot and a huge dog told me that I might catch up with her here.'

'That's Maggie,' Kate told him. 'And Percy and Jessie.' She shrugged. 'Bad luck. But now you're here, would you like some coffee? I'm just having some. I'm still recovering from the news that Thea's agent is going to make Polly a television star. With Percy, of course. Come in.'

'Good heavens! How exciting.' David followed her through the hall into the kitchen. 'Then perhaps my journey wasn't necessary. She's pleased?'

'Euphoric.' Kate indicated a chair and pushed the kettle on to the hotplate of the Rayburn. 'Quite beside herself. She was rushing off to tell as many people as possible, I should imagine. You know that feeling? When life's so wonderful you simply can't sit still?'

'I think I can just remember the hint of such an emotion,' said David cautiously. 'A very long time ago.'

'Oh, dear.' Kate laughed. 'Bad as that?'

As the silence lengthened, she glanced round from her coffee-making. David was standing quite motionless, his hand still on the back of the chair, staring at a framed watercolour on the wall opposite. Puzzled, Kate glanced at the painting and back at David.

'May I ask where you got that?' he asked at last.

His voice was strained and his breath came quickly. Kate put the mugs of coffee on the table and sat down.

'It was left to me when a friend of mine died,' she said. 'Why?'

David moved the chair back and sat down, his eyes still on the painting. 'I painted it,' he said simply. 'I painted it for her.'

'For Felicity?'

David nodded and looked at Kate. Then he lowered his head and rubbed his face with his fingers. 'This is so strange,' he said almost inaudibly. 'I've been thinking of her so much today. And then to come into this room and see that . . .' He rested his elbow on the table and shaded his eyes with his hand.

'You were the artist,' said Kate gently. 'You stayed with her that summer.'

David nodded.

'She told me about you.' Kate put her elbows on the table and cradled her mug in her hands. 'She loved you so much and you left her without a word.'

David made an involuntary gesture but made no effort to defend himself.

'Yes, that's how it seemed.' He corrected himself. 'That's how it was. But it was never intended to be like that. It all started out quite differently and then it changed and I thought she understood. Felt the same. It was like a holiday affair, a shipboard romance, d'you see? Lovely and exciting and tender, but not lasting. And I was a coward. When I realised how she felt, I left her to it. She telephoned and my daughter began to suspect. She told Felicity that I didn't want to talk

to her and by the time I came to my senses it was too late. Too late!'
He stared at Kate, his face fierce with grief and self-condemnation.
'She was dead. She killed herself, all alone in that house whilst I was
in London hiding behind my daughter's skirts.' His mouth twisted
uglily and his eyes went to the painting.

'She didn't kill herself.' Kate's voice was calm. 'Her GP was
quite sure of that. He said that she'd been drinking heavily and then
took her headache tablets. Did you know that she suffered terribly
from migraine? He said that she would have forgotten how many
tablets she'd taken but that it wasn't intentional. He was quite definite.'

'But why was she drinking so heavily? Because I left her. Because I
allowed my daughter to tell her to stop bothering me. What difference does it make?'

Kate shook her head and was silent.

'The sad thing,' said David, after a while, 'was that I don't think
we should have been happy. It worked for that moment in time but
we were such different characters. I would have driven her mad. Or
do I say that to console myself? Well'—he gave a mirthless laugh—'I
shall never know.'

'I'd known Felicity for twenty years,' said Kate thoughtfully, 'and
I'd never seen that side of her. I never knew it existed. She was hard
and ruthless and would have certainly wrecked Thea's marriage to get
George back and that's how we all knew her. When she came for
lunch that day and talked about you, I saw a completely different Felicity. Soft, loving, vulnerable. I think that, with you, she was happy
as she had never been before in this life. Perhaps that's something. At
least you gave her that.'

'And took it away from her,' said David grimly. 'And her life along
with it.'

'At least she had it.' Kate shrugged. 'She had you. When her life
had crumbled and there was nothing left, she had that time with you.
What might it have gone on to? Disillusionment? More emptiness and
loneliness?'

'You make it sound as if I had the right to judge. As if I did her a favour by killing her. I can't see it like that.'

'Felicity wasn't a happy person,' said Kate. 'Even when she was young, with a successful husband and George dancing attendance, she was never happy. I think you made her happy. You gave her something that stilled and contented her restless grasping soul. I don't think it would have lasted either. But at least she had it. And died before she could wreck it herself.'

'You are trying to comfort me and in some strange way you have succeeded. Some of the pain has gone.' David looked at her. 'I'm glad you have the painting.'

'So am I. Perhaps I should offer it back to you but I'm not going to. I keep it as a memorial to Felicity and to remind me that it is better to cut your bare feet on the glass than never to feel the sand between your toes.'

'Then keep it.' David had tears in his eyes. 'I shall never know now whether I missed something wonderful. Perhaps it may prevent some such thing in your life.'

'I think I had my chance. I had my moment, too, and, like you, I had to make the decision to finish it or go on with terrible difficulties. I felt I made the only decision open to me at that time. Now I wonder. And like you I shall never know.'

'Where do you find your comfort?'

Kate shook her head. 'You should know that there is no comfort in knowing that you are existing instead of living. For a short while I lived. It was wonderful and agony. Bliss and pain. But I knew that I was living. I can tell the difference. Perhaps the only really contented people are those who have never lived at all. But I keep the painting to remind me that just once I took off my shoes and felt the sand between my toes.'

David held out his hand across the table and, after a moment, Kate put hers into it.

'Thank you,' he said. 'You cannot imagine how much you've helped me.'

'You've helped me, too,' she said. 'I'd imagined you very differently.'

'I can believe that.' David grimaced and released her hand. He stared at the cold coffee. 'I suppose I must be on my way.'

'Why did you say that your visit to Polly wasn't necessary?'

David hesitated, looking profoundly uncomfortable. 'You'll think I'm a fool.'

'I doubt it.'

'She and my son-in-law had a bit of a flirtation going and he got carried away and asked her to marry him. Then he discovered that my daughter is pregnant and he told Polly that it was all off. He said that she was quite happy about it but . . . Well, if you must know, I had visions of her lying on the floor with an empty pill bottle in her hand so I thought I'd check. I wanted to be absolutely certain, d'you see? That's why I followed her here.'

Kate laughed. 'I can promise you that Polly has no intention of taking an overdose. She's out of her mind with joy. What a nice man you are. How glad I am that you came. And I don't even know your name.'

'It's David. Porteous,' he mumbled as an afterthought.

Kate's eyebrows shot up. 'Do you tell me that I have a Porteous on my kitchen wall? I'm very honoured. But I'll have to increase my contents insurance. Damn!'

David laughed and got to his feet. 'I can't thank you enough,' he said. 'You seem to have taken away the sting. The grief I can live with.'

'Must you go?' Kate stood up, too. 'You haven't even drunk your coffee. Let me make you some more.'

David stood deep in thought and then looked at her. 'Will you understand if I go now? I want to walk on the moor for a time and think about things. Things as they were and as they are now. But I should so like to come back afterwards. May I?'

'Of course you may. I understand.'

'Yes.' David heaved a great sigh. 'I think you do. Thank you.'

'Come back any time.' Kate escorted him to the door. 'Turn right out of the gate and you're practically on the moor. I'll see you later.'

'I don't quite know how long.'

'You'll need as long as it takes,' said Kate gently. 'I'll be here.'

'Definitely "Kate of my consolation," not "Kate the curst,"' said David.

Kate laughed. 'You've been listening to Thea's parrot,' she said and went back inside and closed the door.

DAVID GOT BACK TO Broadhayes late that evening. When he returned to Kate, she invited him to stay on to supper and he telephoned to tell Miranda that he'd met an old friend and didn't know quite what time he would be back. In a way it was true. Kate's long acquaintance with Felicity made her feel like an old friend. As he walked on the moor and drove across familiar roads, he thought of all that Kate had said. He had no intention of telling her how he had come to be at Felicity's house in the first place but the way that Kate had talked of her seemed to tie together with Tim's information about her affair with George. He, David, had known another side of her, a different Felicity, and, allowing himself to remember that summer, he felt glad and rather humble.

During the evening, Kate told him much more. She painted in the background of their lives as girls and as naval wives and, as she talked, a whole picture grew up in his mind's eye. He saw the tragedy, at last, in its proper proportions, as a result of a whole series of events of which his own part was indeed only a part. Although he knew he must still bear his own guilt, a great burden was lifted from his heart.

He looked up at last across the supper table, into the slaty blue eyes which were still surprisingly young beneath the greying hair.

'How can I begin to thank you?' he asked. 'This sort of thing can distort your perception of life, you know. It twists and creeps into everything you do.'

'It isn't right that you should bear all the load.' Kate poured herself some more wine. 'Others, including Felicity herself, must take their part.'

Later, as David stood before his open bedroom window, he felt a great sense of peace. Kate's parting words were still in his ears.

'She had the opportunity to bring out all the very best of herself, the essence, and then, even better, she was able to give it away. To give it to you. That's real happiness.'

David let a prayer of gratitude float out into the night and then he climbed into bed and fell instantly asleep.

Across the landing Tim and Miranda were preparing for bed.

'I thought old David seemed a bit more like his old self tonight.' Tim wandered in and out of his adjoining dressing room as he undressed. 'I wonder who the old friend was that he visited?'

'I didn't know that he knew anyone down here,' said Miranda as she climbed into bed. 'But he looked . . . well, I don't quite know, really. I just didn't want to question him somehow.'

'He had a peaceful look, didn't he? But sort of exalted.' Tim joined her. 'Maybe it's the baby. I feel a bit like that myself.'

'Oh, Tim.' Miranda slipped into his arms and burrowed against him. 'I wasn't going to tell you but I've been trying for years. I haven't been on the pill at all. But nothing ever happened. I thought I'd never have a baby.'

'My poor darling.' A wave of tenderness washed over Tim and he held her close, caressing the feathery hair.

'I thought it might be a punishment for something I did. Something I said to . . . to Felicity. I was very cruel. And then she died. And then I couldn't get pregnant and I was afraid I might lose you. As a punishment.'

Such an outburst from the unemotional, reticent Miranda shocked Tim and his arms tightened about her. 'I don't think it works quite like that,' he said gently. 'It's more that our unworthy deeds eat into our own minds and corrode our lives. We punish ourselves. You've probably been tense and uptight and all you had to do was relax a bit.'

Miranda nodded against his chest. 'It was such a relief. I thought I'd explode while I was waiting. And then to see Daddy looking like he did when he came in. It was as if his face had been sort of smoothed out and I realised how unhappy he's been. Oh, Tim. If only Felicity hadn't died.'

'We must forget all that now.' Tim's voice was strong. 'We can't keep going back. If we let it, it will destroy our lives. You must put it out of your mind and think of the baby. We shall never know the ins and outs of Felicity's life. It's simply not for us to judge.'

'I know you're right.' Miranda clung to him, pushing away her private, closely hugged guilt.

Tim held her and let his mind range quietly over the events of the past few days. He thought of Polly and how easily he had been let off the hook. He remembered David's face as he had come into the library that evening. He thought of his grandparents and how he had held Hermione when she died. Thoughts mingled with dreams and presently he slept.

Thirty-six

THAT YEAR, CHRISTMAS AT the Old Station House moved on to a whole new plane, and was remembered for years afterwards by all those who took part in it. Polly and Maggie between them had worked hard, cleaning, polishing, cooking, preparing, and, when Thea and George arrived with three-year-old Amelia and the baby, Julia, the whole place was *en fête*.

Thea walked from room to room, her hands clasped, her eyes shining. How wonderful to be home, amongst her old friends and beloved belongings. She hugged Jessie and shed a few tears when Percy talked to her in Hermione's voice. Everyone was speaking at once and it wasn't until Maggie had finally gone home clutching exciting foreign presents for her and Wayne, and the children were tucked up for the night, that Thea and George could listen properly to everything that Polly had to tell them. There was so much to tell. Polly had made some recordings and been interviewed for television and Percy the Parrot soft toys were in the shops for Christmas. Much of this Thea knew already. Marcus had kept her well informed but it was exciting to mull it over and shake her head in wonder at these miracles.

'If only G.A. could have known,' she said to Polly later as they sat on the sofa before the fire whilst George gave Jessie a last stroll along the track. 'I hate it that she died whilst all that grief was going on with Felicity. She would have been so thrilled about Percy.'

'But if she'd been alive,' Polly pointed out, 'none of it would have happened. He'd have still been sitting at Broadhayes with her. I know that you used to like to do sketches of him but I doubt you'd have done all those drawings and stories.'

'I suppose you're right. I really got going as a sort of fight against Felicity. To help me not to give in. How odd life is.'

'You're so right,' agreed Polly fervently. 'Who'd have thought when I spoke to Marcus about you and Percy that one day he'd be launching me in a new career?'

'How is he?' asked Thea, drawing her knees up and facing Polly. 'We communicate mostly by letter. It will be lovely to see him again.'

'He's fine.' Polly gazed reminiscently into the fire and Thea watched the colour creep into her cheeks. 'He came down again a few weeks ago. He stayed at the Bedford and we went out to dinner. I felt a bit sorry for him, actually. He's all on his own this Christmas. His mother's going to friends and his son is abroad. He was quite philosophical about it but I felt a bit of a twinge. He's been so good to me.'

'And to me!' cried Thea. 'He mustn't be on his own. He must come here. Why not?' she asked as Polly gazed at her in amazement. 'That's what Christmas is all about, isn't it? I'll phone him up.'

'But what about George?' asked Polly as Thea leaped up from the sofa and hurried over to her little desk to find the address book.

'Oh, George won't mind. The more the merrier, he'd say. His mother's coming for Christmas lunch, so it will be a real old-fashioned gathering. I wish my father could come but Christmas is such a busy time for him. I'm going to telephone.'

She whisked out of the door and Polly remained staring at the flames, excitement building in her breast. She was getting used to how very pleased she always felt when she saw Marcus and the thought of spending a few days with him under the same roof filled her with a special kind of joy. In a moment Thea was back.

'He was thrilled to bits,' she announced, sinking down again beside Polly. 'Isn't that nice? He says that he's going to dash round and do some Christmas shopping in the morning and then drive down. He'll probably be quite late but he'll be in time for Christmas Eve. He can help decorate the tree. I can't wait to see the children's faces! Oh, Polly! It's going to be such fun!'

The next day there was more excitement. Tim telephoned to say that Miranda had gone into labour and he had taken her into the nursing home. He and David were waiting it out together. Thea immediately suggested that Tim and David should come to Christmas lunch.

'Do come,' she begged. 'If Miranda doesn't mind. Just come to eat. You can visit her before and afterwards. Anyway, by then she'll probably have had the baby and you can relax. Stay in touch.'

The telephone rang again later when they were sitting round the fire having tea. Tim was almost incoherent with joy and relief. Miranda had been delivered of a big healthy boy and they were both doing well.

Thea, who had gone into the kitchen to take the call, burst into tears. 'Now the girls have got a second cousin,' she cried. 'Oh, Tim. They'll all be friends just as we were. If only G.A. were here. If only she could have seen them all. Now you will come to lunch, won't you? Promise. It'll be so special. And we'll have lots of things for you to take back to Miranda. You will? Oh, bless you. Love to David. How does he like being a grandfather? Tell him we're looking forward to seeing him. Love to Miranda.'

She replaced the receiver and wept in earnest and Polly, who had slipped out behind her, put her arms round her.

'I'm happy really,' Thea sobbed whilst Percy eyed her from his cage. 'It's just I keep thinking about G.A. and all that she's missing.'

'Jesus wept!' exclaimed Polly. 'And after all the things you used to say to me! I'm ashamed of you!' She hugged Thea tightly. 'You know very well that she can see all that's going on and that she's with you all the time.'

Thea raised her head and stared into Polly's eyes. 'But you don't believe that,' she said, swallowing hard.

'How do you know?' countered Polly. 'Anyway, you do! You were always telling me things like that and reciting the collect for the ninety-seventh Sunday after Lent or something.'

'Oh, Polly. What a prig you make me sound.'

'Not a bit. It was all good stuff. I've tried it a bit myself. Jolly comforting and uplifting it is, too. But I wasn't brought up to it like you were. Stop crying, you daft old besom, and get the booze out.'

'Now I feel like I'm home,' said a voice from the doorway. 'Women weeping and talking about booze. Story of my life.'

'What signifies the life o' man,' began Percy, perking up a little, 'an' 'twere not for the lasses O.'

'My dear old bird, you never spoke a truer word,' said Marcus and held out his arms to the girls.

CHRISTMAS DAY DAWNED BRIGHT and clear. Amelia, who was just old enough to remember Father Christmas, woke early although Julia slumbered peacefully on and woke at the usual time to open surprised eyes upon a world of presents, wrapping paper, chattering adults and decorations. Thea and George went to church with Esme and Amelia, leaving Polly and Marcus in charge of Julia and the turkey, and arrived back as Tim and David turned up.

George was in his natural element as host: filling glasses, settling his mother by the fire with Julia on her lap, showing his pride in Thea's achievements and his adoration of his pretty daughters. Jessie sashayed to and fro getting in everyone's way and Percy worked through nearly his whole repertoire. Tim hugged Polly and they beamed at each other with the relief of those who know that they have been rescued from making a terrible mistake. And Marcus kissed Polly under the mistletoe in a way that made her come over all hot and trembly and mutter something about helping Thea. Thea, used now to entertaining, took it all in her stride and presided over the day with a confidence and joy that would have gladdened Hermione's heart.

Only David was a little restless and after lunch he took Tim aside and told him that he would like to pop out for an hour or so to see a friend. Tim, made expansive with fatherhood, had no objection so long as he was back in time for evening visiting at the hospital and

David let himself out into the quiet frosty stillness of the winter afternoon. He remembered the journey quite well and turned into
Kate's gateway moments after she had returned from Christmas
lunch with Cass and Tom. She was still on the doorstep and her eyes
widened with surprise and then pleasure as she recognised him.

'How nice,' she said as she opened the door and a large golden retriever came out to meet them. 'This is Felix. He's quite harmless.
Are you staying with your daughter for Christmas?'

'She was delivered of a baby boy two days ago.' David followed
her into the house. 'Tim and I have come over to have our Christmas
lunch with Thea and George but we've got to be back for evening visiting. I wanted to see you. To say Happy Christmas to you.'

'How nice,' repeated Kate, hanging up her coat. 'And thank you
for that quite beautiful card. I shall have it framed so that I have two
famous Porteous watercolours. I wonder that you have such a feeling
for the moor and you a townie.'

'Even townies are capable of experiencing beauty. Are you all
alone? Where are your boys?'

Kate let Felix out of the kitchen door into the garden and leaned
back against the Rayburn. She wore a long soft dress in an unusual
blue colour that made her eyes look dark.

'Giles is with his girlfriend upcountry and Guy is in Canada.'

'Canada.' David raised his eyebrows, undeceived by the light, brittle tone. 'That's a long way to go for Christmas. I thought you said
that he runs a yacht brokerage in Dartmouth.'

'He does.' Kate was silent for a moment. 'His father lives in
Canada,' she said at last. 'I think I told you that when we talked about
Felicity. He invited them out. Just suddenly out of the blue. None of
us had heard from him for eight or nine years. Giles wouldn't go but
Guy decided that he would like to make friends with him again.'

'That must have hurt. To leave you alone at Christmas to be with a
man who deserted him as a child.'

Kate looked at him. 'I knew that I was telling you too much that
evening,' she said. 'And you guessed at far more than I told you. Yes,

it hurts. It hurts that Guy was prepared to leave me alone for Mark. And Mark will know it and I hate the thought of the pleasure that it will give him.' She stared at David, daring him to sympathise. 'My brother is abroad and even Giles chose to be with his girlfriend's family rather than come home. Although they did invite me to go, too. Felicity warned me that I had given Alex up for nothing, that the twins would grow up and leave me, and she was right. But it was too late.'

'Have you been on your own all day?'

'No, no. I had lunch with Cass and Tom. I told you about Cass. I don't know what I would have done without her. But you can't live your whole life through other people and their lives, however close you are to them. Let's not talk about it. How nice of you to come. I wish I'd known. I've nothing special to give you.'

'I came to thank you and to tell you that you changed my life that day,' said David, moved by her loneliness and the dignified attempt to hide it. 'I wanted to ask if you ever come to London and if I could take you to a theatre or the ballet? Or a concert? I should like it so much.'

Kate laughed and shook her head. 'London!' she said and made big eyes at him. 'Heavens! I haven't been to London for years and years. And I couldn't leave Felix. But thank you.'

'Oh, please!' David was taken aback by the depth of his disappointment. 'I do so want us to be friends, d'you see? Please won't you think about it? Surely someone could look after your dog? What about Cass? Or bring him with you. I'm sure we'd manage.'

Kate looked surprised at his insistence. 'I'm not really a London person, you see,' she explained. 'I find cities so claustrophobic. And I don't have the clothes for it.'

'Then buy some. I really will not take no for an answer.'

'Goodness.' Kate chuckled a little. 'That sounds terribly fierce.'

'Please.' David held out both his hands and his face was quite serious. 'You have made life worthwhile again for me. Let me feel that there is something that I can do in return. You've just said that you don't want to live your life vicariously through others. Perhaps it's time for you to take your shoes off again.'

The laughter died out of Kate's eyes and, after a moment, she placed her hands in his.

'I can still feel the scars from the glass.' Her face was sombre. 'This Christmas seems to have opened them up again.'

'Oh, my dear.' David drew her gently towards him.

For a moment she resisted him and then gave in and allowed herself to be encircled in his arms. She rested her forehead against his shoulder and they stood thus for some moments in silence. Presently he put his fingers beneath her chin and tipped her face to his. Her eyes were big with fright but when he kissed her her lips opened beneath his and he held her more closely. When they drew apart she was trembling and he smiled at her reassuringly.

'I've thought of you constantly,' he said. 'Did you ever think of me?'

She nodded and he bent to kiss her again.

'I wanted the time to be right, d'you see? It was very important that this is you and me and nothing to do with anyone else. I didn't mean it to be quite so soon. I wanted to give you time to get used to the idea.' He moved his lips against her hair and strained her against him suddenly. 'Is it what you want, Kate? Or have I got it all wrong?'

He felt her shake her head against his shoulder and was filled with a wild unreasoning joy. He kissed her again then and felt her trembling joining with his own. Suddenly she broke away and went before him, leading him up the stairs and into her bedroom. She shut the door and stood looking at him. He guessed what it must have cost her to bring him here and, catching her to him, he took her to the bed and began to undress her. She stood shivering violently and he rolled her into the quilt, hesitating only to drag off his own clothes. Slowly, sweetly, he began to make love to her, gentling her into relaxation and stroking and kissing her into passion. She cried out when he entered her and her cries grew louder as they moved together until, after one great cry of triumph, release and pleasure, she subsided in a storm of weeping and he continued to hold her in his arms whilst the short winter afternoon faded into evening.

Thirty-seven

THEA AND THE CHILDREN remained at the Old Station House when George returned to Brussels for the last six weeks of his appointment. She saw no reason to expose Amelia and Julia to more upheaval and George agreed with her. So it was that Thea took up the reins of her own household once more and Polly was free to go to London. Now that it had come to it she was smitten with terror. It was one thing to plan a career from the safety of the Old Station House with Percy and Jessie at hand and Maggie to be impressed by it and quite another to step out, leaving its protection behind her, to wrestle with the world.

'But you'll have Marcus,' Thea pointed out when she realised that Polly was panicking.

'Mmm,' said Polly, to whom Marcus presented as much of a challenge as her new career.

She spent a few days packing or pretending to, played with the two little girls and wandered up and down the track with Jessie, and still she postponed the actual day of going. At last Thea took things into her own hands and telephoned Marcus when Polly was out shopping.

'She's got cold feet,' she explained. 'I know that she doesn't need to be there full-time yet and she could always come if you wanted her for something but the longer she stays the harder it will be for her to leave us. Her divorce has come through and I think she's desperately clinging to the shreds of her old life. We're all the family she's got now. Poor Polly. I don't want her to go either but now that I'm back she's at a loose end and it's not good for her.'

'Say no more,' said Marcus. 'Everything's ready for her up here. I'll come and get her. Don't warn her, though. She may find some good reason for hanging on.'

So it was that Polly returned one morning from a shopping trip to Tavistock to see Marcus's car parked on the tarmac. Her heart began to bump and hop and she hurried in to find him sitting with Thea in the kitchen, chatting comfortably.

'We had some business to discuss,' he said, rising to greet her and kissing her lightly on the cheek. 'So I thought that I'd kill two birds with one stone and fetch you at the same time.'

'Oh.' Polly was nonplussed. 'But I'm not ready. I didn't realise . . .' She looked piteously at Thea who, feeling an utter traitor, hardened her heart.

'I'm sure it won't take you long to finish off,' she said encouragingly. 'Doesn't matter if you can't get it all in or you forget something. After all, you'll have to come back to pick up your car, won't you? We'll load Marcus's car up this time and yours next time.' She glanced at Marcus.

'That's an excellent idea,' he agreed promptly. 'Just chuck it all in. You won't need your car to begin with. You start recording in a few weeks, you know, so there's lots to go through. Might as well make a start. I expect Thea will have you back for the weekend now and then.'

He winked at Polly and smiled and she felt a great surging mixture of love, excitement and terror. Thea got up from the table. 'If you've finished with me, I'll just go and check on the girls,' she said. 'It all sounds too quiet for my liking.'

She slipped out and Polly was left with Marcus, who continued to lean against the dresser, ankles crossed, his hands in his pockets.

'Best get it over with,' he said gently. 'Partings and new beginnings are always painful and frightening. No point in dragging it out. I know how much you'll miss them all but you'll be very busy and I shan't be far away, if you need me. If that's any comfort.'

He watched her for a moment and presently she smiled and nodded. 'You're right, of course,' she said but still she stood, rooted to the spot.

'Naturally,' said Marcus, trying for a lighter note and wishing that he could take her in his arms, 'I know that I'm no substitute for Percy. Or Jessie, come to that.' He sighed heavily. 'It's the devil of a job, competing with a parrot.'

'The Devil, having nothing else to do,' said Percy, who had hitherto remained silent, 'went off to tempt my Lady Poltagrue. My Lady, tempted by a private whim, to his extreme annoyance, tempted him.'

'If that damned bird wasn't making all our fortunes,' observed Marcus, while Polly went into fits of laughter, 'I'd wring his bloody neck. Off with you, wench! Go and get that packing done.'

As they raced up the motorway towards London, Polly watched Marcus out of the sides of her eyes. She looked at the long-fingered hands on the wheel, observed his long legs, the right knee casually relaxed towards his door, and experienced all the sensations that had been missing in her relationships with Freddie and Paul. As she lifted her eyes to his profile, he glanced at her. Their eyes met and instantly she felt as though she had been plunged in scalding water. She felt the scarlet blood suffuse her skin and stared blindly at the road ahead. Marcus was silent but imperceptibly the quality of the silence changed and became charged with emotion.

'When we get home,' he said at last, 'you will go upstairs into your flat and you will stay there. We will meet to discuss your contract and work and we'll go to the pub round the corner to eat in the evening, if you feel like it. But for one week you will reflect on the fact that I am eighteen years older than you are, that I have a grown-up son and a failed marriage behind me. I'm a workaholic and a slave-driver and I know that business and pleasure don't mix. If, having thought about all those things, you open that interconnecting door and come downstairs for any other reason than the above stated, you might get more than you bargain for.'

Polly slipped a glance sideways at him but he was staring ahead. Aware of her look, a smile touched his lips. 'Well?' he said.

Polly tucked her hand in under his arm and he involuntarily pressed it against his side.

'Promise?' she asked.

DAVID, RACING DOWN THE motorway to Broadhayes, passed Polly and Marcus somewhere near Reading. He was thinking about Kate. Ever since their coming together on Christmas Day, communication with her had been difficult. He had been obliged to hurry away, so as to be back to visit Miranda, knowing that Tim would be waiting impatiently, and Kate had been insistent that he should go, horrified lest he be late. When he telephoned her the next day she had been—well, what had she been? David swerved into the middle lane as a BMW hovered menacingly on his tail, lights flashing. It was so difficult to deduce how people were feeling by listening to their voices on the telephone. It was so easy to hide so much. Kate's voice had been, yes, shy. That was it, David decided. Shy and a little nervous, but friendly. He had wanted so badly for her to know how he felt, to put love, gratitude, comfort into his voice, but it was very difficult to do it when the other person was responding in monosyllables.

'May I see you again?' he'd asked at last. 'Please? Today? Tomorrow?'

She had hesitated for so long that he thought they'd been cut off and had cried out, 'Are you still there?' much too anxiously.

'Yes. Yes, I'm still here.' Kate's voice sounded as if she were smiling. 'And no. I think perhaps not.'

The relief he had felt at hearing the smile in her voice was swamped by disappointment at her reply.

'Oh, but why not, Kate?' The disappointment was patent in his voice. 'Just for a moment.' He suddenly wondered if she thought that he wanted to go simply to make love to her again and horror swept over him. 'Perhaps we could meet somewhere and I could buy you lunch?' he improvised hastily, trying to show that no such idea had been in his mind.

'I just feel,' said Kate, after another long pause, 'that it might be wise to stop now.'

'But why?' cried David. 'Didn't you feel that we have so much we could share? It wasn't just . . . well, it wasn't only . . . what we did together. Was it? That was wonderful. And terribly important. But there's so much more than that.'

'It was wonderful.' Kate's voice was firm. At least there was to be no doubt about that. 'I suppose that's why, in a way, I feel that we should stop. We don't have a future together. And it would be impossible to simply be friends after that. For me, anyway. I'm sorry, David.'

'But why can't we have a future?' demanded David. 'Why not, Kate? Surely not because of Felicity? Honestly, Kate . . .'

'No, no.' She interrupted him quickly. 'This has nothing to do with Felicity. You must see that we're simply poles apart. We're like two different species. It would be impossible.'

'I don't accept that,' said David at once. 'Listen . . .'

'David, I must go.' Kate cut in rapidly and decisively. 'I really should be somewhere else. Thank you for phoning. And for yesterday. It was . . . well, you know what it was. Thank you.'

There was a click and a buzzing and David flung the receiver back on the rest with a muttered imprecation.

At regular intervals during the following weeks he had telephoned her but with no success. She clung to her point and kept the conversations short. He wrote to her but received no reply and finally, in desperation, David decided to take matters into his own hands and go to see her. Ostensibly, the visit to Broadhayes was to see his new grandson but his real object was to talk to Kate. He had spent a great deal of time trying to design a plan that would appeal to her, that would give their friendship time and space to grow. It was difficult. Their ways of living were diametrically opposed and he racked his brain to see how they might be brought together. If she would not come to London then he must go to Devon. He was perfectly happy to weekend, many people did. George and Thea had done it and would, no doubt, do it again. It was not an ideal way to live but it was a way, a start.

He decided to go direct to Kate at Whitchurch knowing that he would be distracted until he had seen her. When he finally turned in at the gate, the winter afternoon was already darkening and a gentle rain fell persistently. He was relieved to see her car in the drive and hastened to the door and rang the bell.

Kate opened the door and stared at him for a few moments in silence, shock and dismay, battling with pleasure, in her face.

'Hello,' he said, wondering if she might shut the door on him. 'May I come in? It's rather cold and wet out here.'

'I'm sorry.' Kate held the door wider. 'It was such a surprise. Come in.'

She turned to lead the way down the hall to the kitchen and David followed her filled with terrible misgivings. Now that he saw her face to face again he knew quite surely that she would not be easy to influence. He also knew that he loved her. During that Christmas afternoon he had discovered all the sensations that had been missing in his relationships with his wife and with Felicity. But what were her feelings for him? Had he completely misjudged her and was their coming together to be an isolated event? His whole being rejected the thought and he bent to stroke Felix, who came to greet him. He murmured to the dog, fondling his ears, but with his eyes on Kate, who had automatically gone to put the kettle on.

'What a very determined man you are,' she said lightly.

'You've given up,' he said, straightening up. 'You've forgotten how important it is to fight for things.' His eyes fell on Felicity's painting. 'You've forgotten how the sand feels.'

'No.' She had looked taken aback at his opening statement but now she smiled a little. 'No. You reminded me of that on Christmas Day.'

'Oh, Kate.' Her reference to the very subject he thought she would avoid disarmed him. He sat down and looked at her. 'I love you, d'you see? That makes it easy.'

'No.' She shook her head. 'That just makes it *seem* easy. It disguises the pitfalls and deludes you into thinking that they don't matter. But they do.'

'Does that mean that you won't even try?'

'You see I've done it twice now. Love is not enough, David. It simply isn't. It doesn't overcome all the obstacles and make up for everything. Twice I thought it would. It's taken me years to learn to live alone. To risk it—me—all again is a luxury I simply can't afford.'

'You're so certain it won't work? Do you love me at all?' David saw that her eyes pleaded with him to let her off the hook but he gazed back, inexorably waiting for his answer.

'I don't see how it can.' She avoided the second question. 'You in London, me here. I hate cities. You'd be bored rigid in the country. I can imagine a sort of friendship . . .'

'No, no. That won't do,' David interrupted ruthlessly. 'I agree with you that for us it's all or nothing but not necessarily straight off. Many people I know weekend very happily. Why not us?'

'It's a half life. I've done it. I don't want that.'

David sighed. 'I'm only suggesting it as a compromise to begin with. I'm thinking of taking things easier. A sort of semi-retirement . . .'

'And do you see it taking place in London amongst your friends, with your club round the corner and theatres and concerts? Or down here? On Dartmoor, amongst the sheep and ponies with the rain pouring down?'

He was silent. He felt her fear and it was infectious. He could imagine how absolutely devastating another failure would be for her and had a vision of Felicity lying dead. His own confidence was shaken and he pushed his chair back and stood up.

'Will you telephone me if you change your mind? Or if you should need . . . anything? I do love you, Kate. I won't keep hounding you but please think about it. Don't just close your mind to the possibilities. No, don't get up. Please. Goodbye, Kate.'

He went out and she heard the front door slam and the car engine start up. After a while the kettle began to boil and she stood up and pushed it off the hotplate. She sat down again at the table and listened to the dog snoring in his sleep. Rain pattered suddenly against the window and a door upstairs slammed as the wind got up but Kate sat on, her arms folded across her breast, her head bent, fighting a private battle of loneliness and fear.

Thirty-eight

POLLY LAY IN THE bath, luxuriating in the hot scented water, and reflected happily on her life. The flat in Marcus's large Victorian house was small, cosy and just right for her. She liked to feel herself cradled high up under the roof, looking out over the chimneys, with Marcus a staircase away. They were, after all, taking things very slowly and carefully. He was giving her plenty of space to adapt and to make new friends whilst continuing with his own busy life and, as yet, the intercommunicating door had only been opened for the reasons that Marcus had laid down in the car. In public he was strictly her agent, it was a business relationship only—although they'd had some jolly evenings at the local pub—and Polly guessed he was as nervous as she was at plunging into anything that might commit him. She knew that, while she was his client and lived in his house, for him it would be all or nothing.

Polly watched a harvestman with its long ungainly legs negotiating the rim of the bath. *'Leiobunum,'* she said. Old habits die hard. 'Or *Philangium.'*

She thought of Paul and Fiona and the house in Exeter. It all seemed a lifetime away. How odd that ten years of her life seemed to have gone for nothing. There seemed so little to show except the scientific name of the harvestman who was now scaling the tap. Polly watched the eight wavering, cotton-thin legs with the two joints to each, and wondered idly what it must be like to go through life with sixteen knees. Or perhaps half of them were ankles. Paul, no doubt, would have been able to tell her.

She stood up and reached for her towel. Would she ever have the courage to pass through that internal door? Supposing Marcus were to reject her? Or laugh at her? She knew that he considered the years between them to be a far greater barrier than she did and suspected that he might need a little push to get him over it. But how to administer it? The door itself had become a barrier. To go through it now— apart from for those reasons that Marcus had stated—would make such a statement that they would both be terrified. They needed an intermediate, gentler step to start them off.

Polly wrapped herself in the towel and wandered along to her bedroom. In the small hallway she paused. Some instinct made her cross the carpet and open the door a crack. She gave a violent start. 'Jesus!' she whispered.

Marcus stood at the bottom of the steep flight of stairs, his head bent as though in thought. In his hand he held a bottle. Even as she watched him, he made to turn away.

'Marcus.' Her throat was dry and she spoke again. 'Hello,' she said.

He smiled up at her and she clutched her towel more tightly.

'I was coming to tell you that the studio phoned and we've got the contract.' He held up the bottle. 'Celebration?'

'Terrific,' she said. 'Great idea.'

They stared at one another.

'Coming down then?' he asked lightly, after a moment. 'Strictly in the nature of business, of course.'

'I've got a better idea,' said Polly. She held the door open wide, still clutching her towel with the other hand, and smiled at him bravely. 'Why don't you come up?'

WHEN KATE SAW FREDDIE at Tavistock market just before Easter she sensed some important change in him. There was a confidence in his bearing and a glow in his eyes which had not been there previously, and she looked at him curiously as he packed some cheese and a carton of free-range eggs into his capacious shopping basket and then beamed at her.

'Long time no see.' He looked her over carefully. 'You look tired.'

'That's because I am tired. You, however, look great. What's happened? Has Polly decided to change her mind and take up dog-breeding instead of being a television star?'

'No, no.' Freddie shook his head, laughing. 'Oh, no. That was all . . . well, it's all over. Never got started really.'

Kate raised her eyebrows. 'Well, you look very happy about it.'

'I am happy. Terribly happy.' And indeed happiness seemed to spurt out from all over him, fizzing and sparkling and showering her with its drops. 'The thing is . . .' He glanced round at the people thronging and pressing against them. 'I'd love to talk to you, Kate. Can you come back for a cup of coffee?'

'Why not? I've nearly finished. OK. Thanks, Freddie. That'd be nice.'

'Great.' He patted her shoulder. 'I'll go on and get the kettle going.'

He disappeared into the crowd and Kate finished her shopping, puzzling over the change in him. She struggled out of the great covered hall, went to fetch the car which she'd left in Chapel Street and drove slowly out towards Mary Tavy, parking where Felix couldn't see Charlie Custard. 'We'll have a walk on the way home,' she promised him.

The back door had been left open and she called out as she went inside. Charlie Custard came strolling to meet her, sniffing at her cords suspiciously.

'That's Felix, old chap,' she said to him as Freddie waved to her and the smell of coffee assailed her nostrils. 'He's a proper dog, not a lazy old hearthrug.'

Freddie chuckled. 'It's no good. You can't wind us up. We're impervious to insults, aren't we, Custard?'

'You're no fun any more.' Kate sat down at the kitchen table, glanced round and raised her eyebrows. 'Heavens, Freddie! What's been going on here? I can see bare surfaces and the cooker's turned white. Was that with fright when it saw you approaching it with a Brillo pad after all these years?'

Freddie burst out laughing and put down the coffee. 'Looks nice, doesn't it?' he said, looking round with satisfaction.

'Come clean, Freddie,' said Kate, putting in sugar. 'Who is she? Can she cook as well? '

'It's not a she,' said Freddie, after a considerable pause. 'It's a he.'

Kate stared at him, frowning. 'A he?' she repeated. 'How do you mean? Oh!'

She stopped short and Freddie met her eyes bravely. 'It's another man. I've realised that I'm . . . it seems that I'm gay.' He said the word defiantly if proudly but his eyes were anxious.

For some reason, Kate felt profoundly moved. After a moment, she put out a hand to him and he seized it eagerly, his face lighting up with all the joy that she'd seen in the market.

'I'm so happy,' he cried. 'It's so wonderful after all these years of feeling wrong. Never getting it right with girls. All the strain and things. Oh, the relief! You can't imagine. Nobody could if they weren't like it themselves.'

'Oh, Freddie. I'm so pleased for you. I never guessed. Is he . . . ? Will you . . . ? Sorry.' Kate shook her head. 'I really don't mean to pry. I hope he's nice.'

'He's wonderful,' said Freddie promptly. 'If I tell you who it is will you swear not to breathe a word? You're the only person I know that I can trust absolutely and it would be such heaven to talk about it all—about him—with someone.'

'I wouldn't dream of telling anyone.' Kate squeezed his hand and let it go. 'Do I know him?'

'It's Jon. Michael's cousin Jon.'

'Jon?' Kate's brow wrinkled. 'Oh.' Her face cleared. 'Of course. I met him during all that ghastly business with Polly. Heavens! But isn't he Foreign Office? Won't you have to be fearfully careful?'

'Terribly.' Freddie nodded and grimaced. 'Lucky that I'm so out of the way here. He can come for weekends and nobody's any the wiser and I can go up to London now and then. Just for twenty-four hours. The girl from the surgery comes and stays overnight to look after the dogs. It's tremendous fun. I'd forgotten what the big city was like. Never known it at all, actually. Jon calls us the Town Mouse and the Country Mouse. We're learning each other's worlds.'

'And it works?' Kate stared at him.

'Works?' Freddie's face blazed with enthusiasm. 'It's brilliant!'

'But what will happen when he retires. You know? Where will you live then? It's a bit different when it's full-time, isn't it?'

'Probably.' Freddie shrugged. 'We'll probably live here and spend a few days here and there in London. Why not? Best of both worlds. No good thinking of that yet. It's now that counts, isn't it? After all, it's all we can count on. Now. This minute. We may not be here next year, next week even. No time to waste. Even if it all finished tomorrow we'd have had this.'

'Yes, that's true,' said Kate slowly. 'I was saying that to someone not so long ago. It's the difference between living and existing. Sometimes, though, existing seems a wiser choice.'

'Not for us.' Freddie shook his head. 'Safer perhaps. Maybe less painful. But there may be years and years for me to exist in. I've had plenty already. I'm going to live for a change.'

Kate drove home deep in thought. She took the road out past Mount House School and remembered happier days when the twins had been there. She thought of the long empty years with Mark, the brief spell of passion with Alex and the lonely span of time since they had parted. She remembered, too, the joy and release of David's lovemaking and how hard it had been, after years of strictly self-imposed celibacy, to drop the barriers of protection and stand naked before a man she hardly knew and surrender herself to him. It had cost all her pride and he had given it all back to her, had given her those hours of freedom and cathartic pleasure and made her feel that it was she who had been the giver.

She walked Felix at Sampford Spiney and, as she walked, the moor seemed to enfold her in its great quiet spaces.

It's been like a mother to me, she thought. Or like God. Always there when I need it. Comforting, soothing, encouraging. It absorbs my worries and my fears and gives me courage to go on. But to what? That's the thing.

When she got in there was a postcard from David on the doormat. She read it as she walked slowly through to the kitchen. He would be down at Broadhayes next weekend for Easter and would love to see her. Love, David. She turned the card. It was a reproduction of one of his own paintings. He had sent her several now, begging her not to think that he was showing off but that he wanted to share them with her. Share. She had noticed that David used that word a lot. The picture was of an old dresser with blue china on the shelves. There were other things, too. David's love of minutiae showed in the myriad tiny objects that had been lovingly put there. As usual he had printed his telephone number carefully in the top left-hand corner just above 'My Dear Kate'. Kate stared at the card for some time and presently she went to the telephone and dialled.

The receiver was lifted at once. 'Porteous.'

The cool clipped word confused Kate and she hesitated and almost slammed the receiver down.

'Hello?' His voice was still impersonal. Not quite impatient.

'David.' Kate could hardly bring the name out.

'Yes?' The voice was different now. Questioning, hardly daring to believe. 'Kate? Is that you, Kate?'

'Yes. Yes, it is.' Kate felt that she might be crying. Or was it laughing? It seemed to be both. There was a complete silence from the other end and she swallowed, wondering how to go on.

'Just in case,' David's voice spoke suddenly in her ear. 'In case it helps you to say whatever it is you want to say, I love you. I love you, Kate. Just in case, d'you see?'

Kate nodded. Yes. It helped. But she still seemed tongue-tied. Her gaze strayed round the kitchen and came to rest on Felicity's painting. She gulped and swallowed and suddenly it was easy and she could find the words.

'David!' she cried and, at the other end, David clutched the receiver, his whole being concentrated on what she might say. 'Oh, David. Could you come?' She was trembling violently. 'Could you come at once? I've taken my shoes off. Oh, David. I'm going to need so much help to walk barefoot!'

'I MUST SAY,' SAID George, dealing with a cork with an experienced hand, 'that it's nice being just the two of us.'

'You mean with the children in bed and everything quiet and peaceful?' Thea was fiddling with saucepans at the Rayburn. 'Yes, it is nice.'

'Well, I didn't mean the girls.' George stood the wine on the kitchen table and sat down next to it. 'They're us really, aren't they? I meant that it was nice not to have other people around. You know. Polly or Tim or Maggie. Just us.' He poured the wine and sipped contentedly. 'Nice wine.'

'Look not upon the wine when it is red,' advised Percy in Hermione's voice and George laughed.

'Sounds like your G.A. was keeping old Edward under strict control,' he said.

'Percy's been in a biblical mood today,' said Thea, stirring things. 'We've had various collects and one or two verses from the Psalms, interspersed with some of Polly's blasphemies. Sounds very odd.'

'Here.' George filled a glass and took it to her. 'Something for the cook.' He put it into her hand and kissed her. 'Bless you.'

'Oh, George.' She took it and slipped her arm around him. 'I'm so happy, it's terrifying. We're so lucky.'

'We are indeed, my darling. Drink your wine. We'll have a toast to us.'

'Wine is a mocker, strong drink is raging.' Percy stuck to his guns.

'He must know the Bible by heart.' Thea smiled a little. 'I've got some news actually. I'm pleased you said that about the girls, George. I'm so glad that's how you feel. Because we're going to have another baby. Isn't it wonderful? Maybe it'll be a boy, this time.'

'Oh, Thea!'

'I know. Oh, careful, George! Mind! Let me go. The dinner will burn.'

'Better is a dinner of herbs where love is than a stalled ox and hatred therewith,' observed Percy, continuing to work his way through the Book of Proverbs.

'Blow the dinner. Put that glass down and come here. Oh, darling, what wonderful news.'

'Isn't it? Oh, George, I think I'm going to cry. Isn't that silly? I'm so happy really.'

George took her into his arms and began to kiss her whilst Percy eyed them contemptuously. Remembering Polly's habit of quoting from St John's Gospel in moments of duress, he abandoned the Old Testament.

'Jesus wept!' said the parrot.

1. In what ways is the importance of honesty a major theme in this novel?

2. What is the significance of the quote ç Joy cometh in the morningé on page 115?

3. Why does Felicityês attempted blackmail scheme fail?

4. Why is Percy so important to Thea and her story?

5. In what other Marcia Willett novels are Cass and Kate prominently featured? And how are they different or the same in other novels?

6. In what ways does Marcia Willett capture the problems many lovers have in establishing trust?

7. Why is Thea such a good mate for George?

8. Marcia Willett is particularly skilled at representing relationships in which one character is much older than the other. How is that skill illustrated in this novel?

9. At what moment of the novel did you most fear that Thea and Georgeês relationship would fail?

10. What does the novel say to you about friendship and family?

For more reading group suggestions, visit
www.readinggroupgold.com

A
Reading
Group
Guide

St. Martinê
Griffin